triscelle publishing

presents

Curse of Venus
Morrigan's Brood Book IV

By

heather poinsett dunbar

and

christopher dunbar

map of story locations

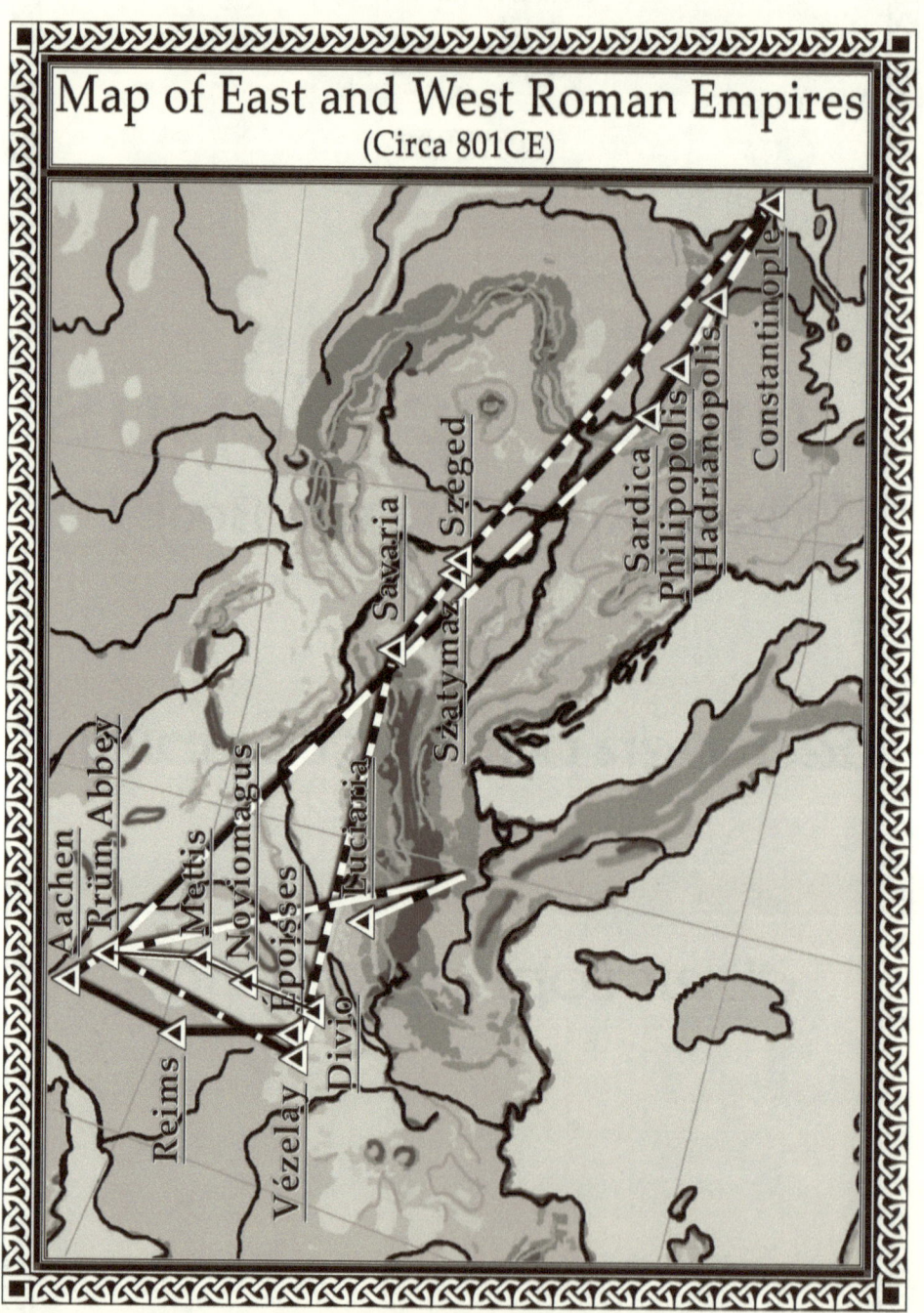

Map of East and West Roman Empires
(Circa 801CE)

Constantinople

Hadrianopolis

Philipopolis

Sardica

Szeged

Savaria

Szatymaz

Luciaria

Noviomagus

Époisses

Mettis

Aachen

Prüm Abbey

Reims

Vézelay

Divio

Map details are on the next page.

map guide

East and West Roman Empires, Circa 801 CE		
Period Name	**Modern Name**	**Modern Country**
West Roman Empire / Frankish Empire / Carolingian Empire		
Aachen	Aachen or Aix-la-Chapelle	North Rhine-Westphalia, Germany
Divio	Dijon	Burgundy, France
Époisses	Époisses	Burgundy, France
Luciaria	Lucerne	Lucerne, Switzerland
Mettis	Metz	Lorraine, France
Noviomagus	Neufchâteau	Lorraine, France
Prüm Abbey	Prüm/Lorraine	Rhineland-Palatinate, Germany
Reims	Reims	Champagne-Ardenne, France
Vézelay	Vézelay	Burgundy, France
East Roman Empire		
Constantinople	Istanbul	Marmara, Turkey
Hadrianopolis	Edirne	Marmara, Turkey
Philipopolis	Plovdiv	Bulgaria
Sardica	Sofia	Bulgaria
Savaria	Szombathely	Vas, Hungary
Szatymaz	Szatymaz	Csongrád, Hungary
Szeged	Szeged	Csongrád, Hungary

Legend

The return home to Vézelay

Pope Leo's retreat and return

Race to find Venus' mirror

Irene's pursuit and the journey to Vézelay

Land grab in Aachen

acknowledgments

Heather's Acknowledgments

Oh nuts, where was I going with this? I'd like to thank so many people out there for their assistance on getting the fourth book to print; especially, the hubby and our family.

Special thanks go to Ruth Davis Hayes, Sarah 'Sally' Aalderink, Khanada Taylor, Heidi Bowles Ellis, Tracy Angelina Evans, Kara Hash, the rest of the Writers Cabal, and you, the readers who poked at us with sticks at every event we went to and asked 'Dammit, where's book four???? I gotta know what happens next!' Also thank you, kitties for inspiring us. Ophelia, I miss you every day, and I know you'll be waiting for us. Thank you for the unconditional love.

It's been an interesting few weeks, but we're ready for the adventure. Let's face it, adventure is why we're all here. I hope our readers enjoy.

Christopher's Acknowledgments

This has been a difficult book to get through due to having a full-time job and procrastinating. My wife and co-author, Heather, and some of our friends encouraged me to kick the final rewrite into high-gear, and I stepped up to the plate, as it were (I hate combining multiple metaphors in a sentence).

Thanks to Ruth Davis Hayes, especially, for supplying some of the motivation that got me serious about finishing this book. When she expressed interest in completing the final edit of the manuscript, I saw the situation as an opportunity to keep my rewrite at pace with her editing and proofreading. I think we both encouraged each other on.

I would also like to thank Khanada Taylor for the brilliant cover art she drew for Curse of Venus;, Sarah Aalderink for completing the initial edits of the manuscripts;, Dayna Hartley for her work, way back when, helping me clean up the Triscelle Publishing logo we collaborated on;, and thanks to our family, friends, and fellow creative types... you know who you are... who have been there with us through thick and thin. Lastly, thanks to all of you readers who have joined the journey, as it were, through the Morrigan's Brood Series.

There are many stories to tell, so keep looking forward to the next stretch of road on your journey.

Dedication and Copyright Page

For Ophelia

December, 2013

Curse of Venus

Morrigan's Brood Book IV
Print ISBN-10: 1-937341-30-5
Print ISBN-13: 978-1-937341-30-5
by Heather Poinsett Dunbar
and Christopher Dunbar
Published by Triscelle Publishing
Edited by Ruth Davis Hays and Sarah E. Aalderink
Cover art, map, and website by Khanada Taylor
Triscelle Publishing Logo by Dayna Hartley
Copyright © 2013 by Triscelle Publishing. All rights reserved.

Visit our website and find us on WordPress, Goodreads, Shelfari, Facebook, the Library Thing, LinkedIn, Twitter, and many other places on the Net.

www.triscellepublishing.com
triscellepublishing.wordpress.com

Also available in several eBook formats

Lines of Blood-Drinkers

Algul – A line of Arabic blood-drinkers created by their God of War, Verethragna. Their known abilities include the power to create visual hallucinations in both mortals and in other immortals. However, their vulnerability lies in strong smells. Their numbers are small, due to a genocidal war between themselves and the remnants of the Ekimmu.

Deargh Du – An ancient line of blood-drinkers from Éire (Ireland) that trace their ancestry to the Goddess Morrigan. Their true talents lie in their magical skills and their fae-like beauty, known as glamoury. They can fly, create glowing light, heal mortals as well as other immortals, and draw down darkness and shadow. Their major weakness is the metal gold. After the creation of the Ekimmu Cruitne, the Deargh Du withdrew back to their native land and ceased interacting with other blood-drinking races.

Ekimmu – A group of blood-drinkers originating in Assyria from Zaltu, God of Strife. They grew in strength and power, eventually dominating the Middle East. However, other races, such as their enemies the Algul and the Lamia, began to hunt them down, decimating their population.

Ekimmu Cruitne – The Ekimmu, fleeing a genocidal war, removed themselves to the northern regions of Alba (Scotland). After meeting some of the Deargh Du, who traveled with the Scoti tribe, an Ekimmu and a Deargh Du conspired to tip the balance by creating a new being. Morrigan, in her rage, sought to confine them to their lands. Ekimmu Cruitne are struck by illness whenever they try to cross the ocean. Their greatest talent is their olfactory sense, making them excellent trackers. They can also heal others, fly, read minds, and enjoy manipulating games of chance. In addition, they can create the sensation of pleasure as well as pain in themselves and in their victims.

Lamia – According to legend, Lamia was a Queen of Libya who seduced Zeus. In retribution, Hera killed all of her children. Heartbroken, Lamia began feeding on the people of Greece, and before long, she had many new immortal children. The Lamia infiltrated Roman society, and soon Rome became their seat of power. The Lamia's skills lie in mind-bending, or manipulation. They even have an ability to enter dreams and influence the dreamer.

Ouphe – An ancient Saxon line of blood-drinkers that moved into Britannia during the Saxon conquest. Their strength is in their monstrous lycanthropic nature; many blood-drinking races can die from the wounds given by an Ouphe. Yet, the Ouphe are severely affected by silver. Their origin is a mystery.

Strigoi – A line of blood-drinkers that began from a cursed Greek beauty named Iris. Aphrodite's curse did not grant Iris and her victim's immortality; instead, they only survive fifty years after their transformation. The Strigoi are telepathic and unleash uncontrollable madness upon mortals and immortals alike. Affected mortals tear at their eyes and puncture their eardrums to escape the onslaught of sights and sounds. Despite their talents, Strigoi are physically weak, stunted, and are the ugliest of the blood-drinkers.

Sugnwr Gwaed – A British group of blood-drinkers created by Cernunnos, the Horned God of animals, wilderness, and the wild hunt. Their strengths include enhanced communication with animals and their talent for vocal persuasion. They can convince their victims of almost anything. They also fly, like the other Celtic lines, and have an aptitude for healing others.

Chiang-shih – A Chinese line of blood-drinkers that originated from Shenlong, a dragon God. Shenlong created the Chiang-shih to protect His earthly treasures from greedy mortals. While the Chiang-shih can control storms like Shenlong, they can only fly, in the form of a dragon, when the moon is full and have difficulty crossing water. Little else is known about them, as they choose not to interact with most of the western lines. Their true talents lie in their medical knowledge and their gifts.

Pacu Pati – Blood-drinkers from India that originated from Kali. The Pacu Pati tend to cloister themselves with their new families of other Pacu Pati and do not meet with the other lines. When other lines have witnessed the celebrations of the cycles of life and death, they tend to misunderstand the celebrations, and a lack of a common language generally adds to the confusion.

Other lines will be revealed in future works.

character guide

Marcus Galerius Primus Helvetticus	Marcus

Marcus cannot figure out what is bothering him. He doesn't sleep well, he finds his mind wandering when in the midst of a conversation. While thinking of the Strigoi fills him with fear, they aren't keeping him agitated. But who or what is?

Mandubratius	Awvarwy (*a-war-wee*)

Not since he recovered from his malaise at losing the Phallus Maximus has Mandubratius felt more purpose in his life. He feels it is time to mend broken bonds, to forgive past offenses, and to move forward as one. And then there is Máire...

Máire Ní Conghal	Máire (*moya*)

While Máire feels conflicted over her feelings concerning Mandubratius, what bothers her more is Marcus' apparent suffering. She wonders whether her curse, her inability to feel, has somehow affected him. Only Morrigan knows what haunts him.

Claudius Metrius Sertorius	Claudius

Unlike the other Celtic lines, and most blood-drinker lines in general, Sugnwr Gwaed do not create other Sugnwr Gwaed. That is Cernunnos' prerogative. Claudius has had no bond with a child, like Marcus has with Máire... that is until Horatio arrived.

Arwin Mac Alpin	Mac Alpin

Arwin misses home... Bath. He yearns for the full wine and mead he loved to imbibe. What do the Franks offer? Watered down wine, mixed with spices, and no mead! Arwin hopes this business with the Strigoi will end so he can drink proper spirits.

Tertia Amata Antonia	Amata

Amata never expected to actually fall in love with Edward. Mandubratius had asked her to get close to the alchemist to learn his secrets for explosives, but Amata found something more in the Ekimmu Cruitne. He makes her hot with passion.

Téa Uí Cennedi Uí Máine	Talia de Burgundy / Talia de Époisses

Soon, Talia de Burgundy will control all of the lands those bloody Franks took from her family. Soon, Godomer's legacy will be hers. If only she could find a way to get Divio and Vézelay, she would possess all of Burgundy! Afterwards... Francia!

Patroclus Statilius Messalinus	The Legate

Patroclus is gladdened to see his Co-Consuls, Mandubratius and Amata, so happy, after both dealt with Mandubratius' fight with madness. Mandubratius seems fulfilled with new purpose and Amata with new love... but what about Patroclus?

Edward	Edward, Edwina, Edgar, Edna

Creating devices that smoke, burst in to flame, or make the very ground shake are Edward's speciality... not tending to the needs of women. When Amata came into his life, however, smoke, flames, and explosions were not confined to his creations.

Sáerlaith Ní Adhamdh	Sáerlaith (*saer-la*)

After losing her home in Ard Mhacha to separatists, Sáerlaith finds herself unable to lead her people. If only she could find inspiration from somewhere, from someone, to shrug off her doldrums, but her guilt prevents her heart from healing.

Caoimhín of Ard Mhacha	Caoimhín (*kev-een*)

With Sáerlaith lost to her own self-pity, Caoimhín must lead the Deargh Du, a role he feels best suited to Marcus, but since Marcus is not here... who else would lead? If only someone could re-ignite the spark in Sáerlaith's heart. But who?

Irene the Athenian / Basileus	Empress Irene / Ειρήνη Σαρανταπήχαινα

Every time Irene looks into a mirror, she sees an old hag gazing back at her. Time has ravaged her once beautiful body. When a man comes along who offers her eternal youth for a special mirror she owns, forged by the Gods, of course she agrees!

Karl der Große, Carolus Magnus	Emperor Charles / Charlemagne

Despite being on the verge of war with the Pope over a disagreement of authority, Charles cannot help but find fault with his family. Not one of his legitimate children or his bastards would make a suitable heir. On second thought, there might be one...

Pope Leo III	His Holiness

With battle lines drawn between papal and imperial forces, Pope Leo waits for battle to ensue. He knows that he is on God's mission to drive out the demon scourge. However, if the man he crowned last year won't do God's bidding, God help him.

Julien de Divio	Julien

Julien has a secret that he must tell no one, or else his family might tear itself apart. He must grieve the loss of loved ones in silence. Still, he is comforted by his new Deargh Du family. Because of their love, he can hide his grief, but it hurts to lie.

Heloise de Divio	Heloise

Heloise is worried about a lot of things... Vézelay, her vassals, and of course her son Reginald, who lost his wife and most of his children to strife. Still, she will be damned if she lets the wrong kind of woman seek out his affections. He is vulnerable.

Reginald de Divio	Reginald

His wife and two of his children are dead. Many of his vassals are dead. After being on the run for weeks, Reginald and his vassals will soon return home, but he knows he will find the dead they left behind. If only he could find someone to console him.

Horatio di Reate	Horatio

Horatio never wanted to be a Lamia, but he knows he cannot go back to being mortal. Still, he is thankful Claudius, a Sugnwr Gwaed, has taken him in. If only Horatio could be like him. If Horatio ever finds the bastard who made him Lamia... death.

gods and goddesses of the series

Irish Pantheon – Tuatha dé Danann (People of Dana)	
Aine (*An-ya*)	*Goddess of love and fertility*
Aongas Og (*An-gus Og*)	*God of love and youth*
Brigid (*Bri-jid*)	*Goddess of healing, writing, water, and cats*
Dagda (*Dah-dah*)	*The 'good' God of many skills*
Dana (*Day-na*)	*The Mother Goddess*
Lugh (*Loo*)	*Multi-skilled God of battle, light, writing, and the harvest*
Medb (*May-v*)	*Goddess of sovereignty*
Manannán Mac Lir (*Mannan-awan Mac Lir*)	*Guide to the Otherworld and God of the wind, travels, sea, and sailing*
Morrigan (*Mor-ee-gan*)	*Goddess of death, battle, blood, and rebirth*
Nuada (*Nu-a-da*)	*God of healing and weaponry*
British Pantheon	
Cernunnos	*God of animals, wilderness, fertility, and the Wild Hunt*
Greek / Roman Pantheon	
Aphrodite (*af-rə-dy-tee*) / Venus (*ˈwɛnʊs*)	*Goddess of love, beauty, and sexuality / Goddess of love, beauty, and fertility*
Ares (*áreːs*) / Mars (*Mārs*)	*God of War and Manly Virtues / God of War; part of the Archaic Triad*
Hera (*Hēra*) / Juno (*ˈjuːnoː*)	*Queen of the Gods and Goddess of marriage, women and birth / Patron Goddess of Rome and Goddess of women; part of the Capitoline Triad*
Zeus (*Zews*) / Jupiter (*Joo-pi-ter*)	*King of the Gods and God of the sky, thunder, lightning, law, order, and justice / King of the Gods and God of the sky and thunder; part of the Capitoline Triad; Patron Deity of Rome*
Arabic (Zoroastrian) Pantheon	
Verethragna	*God of war and sexual potency*
Assyrian Pantheon	
Zaltu (*Zal-too*)	*God of strife*
Hindu Pantheon	
Kali (*Kālī*)	*Goddess of time and change; "She who destroys"; "Redeemer of the Universe"*
Chinese Pantheon	
Shenlong (*shén lóng*)	*A dragon god in Chinese mythology known as the "Master of Storms"*

pROLogue

The Journal of Máire Ní Conghal

ight after night, I find it more difficult not to cleave Mandubratius' head from his shoulders. Every time I see his face, I bombard myself with my own accusations. He killed my betrothed! No, he killed two betrothed and two uncles. He invaded Éire, and he and his Lamia feasted upon my clan.

The man is evil incarnate.

What truly upsets me is that I have had an opportunity to kill him. I crushed his chest and even broke his spine, but the Goddess held me back. To this night, I do not understand why She did this. Surely, whatever reason Morrigan had for this is not in place now. I should be able to walk up to him and sever his head.

Tonight, however, it is not the Goddess who stays my hand... it is this alliance. We need him and the Lamia against the Strigoi. The enemy of my enemy is my friend, after all, and as amazing as this seems, the Mandubratius I see before me tonight is, in many respects, not the same man that committed those atrocities.

Something has changed with him that I cannot explain. He does not seem menacing, nor do the rest of the Lamia. He is even being helpful.

Even so, Mandubratius is still very annoying, but I do not sense that he is using me and will soon kill me. In fact, that conniving, self-centered Briton pinched my backside before dawn. I felt like stabbing him somewhere non-vital.

It feels strange that my predilection is not to kill him. Should I not wish him dead for what he has done? Should I not desire to kill him myself?

After nearly three centuries, is that Mandubratius already dead? Is this the same man?

Yes, I hate Mandubratius, and I believe I always will, on some level, but I do not know if I could kill him. Maim, yes, but I do not think I can kill him...

At least, not the man I see before me.

chapter one

Prüm Abbey, 801 CE

andubratius awoke to the rather irritating sensation of a mortal shaking him. He could sense that the dying sun still warmed the earth above. Mandubratius uttered an annoyed snarl and opened his left eye to offer a withering stare at the mortal who dared to wake him in this rude fashion.

"Who dares to wake me?!" Mandubratius shouted, no longer able to contain his rage, focusing his vision on the plain-robed monk in front of him.

The man dropped to his knees and groveled, "Please forgive me. The abbot sent me," while lowering his eyes to the ground.

"Arrrr," Mandubratius grumbled, wondering why the abbot would wish words with him, but soon the matter grew clear, as he realized the monk must have been searching for Marcus.

"I have no business with your abbot! The man you wish to converse with sleeps over there!" As he spoke, Mandubratius gestured in the general direction of the other blood-drinkers.

The monk looked up, turned his tonsured head, and studied the sea of bodies. "Where? Who?" he asked.

"Marcus!" Mandubratius growled, although nobody rose. "Marcus!" he yelled again, though with far more force.

"WHAT!" a distant blurry figure shouted. A strong and longing desire within Mandubratius hoped that he interrupted what may have been a pleasant dream for Marcus.

"Some minion of the abbot thinks it's important to speak to the person in charge, which I assume is you!" Mandubratius then leaned back on his bedding. Hearing footfalls, he looked up to see Marcus approach the monk.

"Brother Ebbo, what troubles you?" Marcus asked with that honey-laced tongue of his, dripping with sweetness.

Mandubratius squinted as he considered why anyone would really bother learning the underlings' names... well centurions, perhaps, as was Caesar's practice, but not the common plebs.

As the conversation grew, Mandubratius' curiosity forced his eyes open.

"Soldiers have surrounded us," the monk whispered loudly to Marcus.

"Which soldiers?"

"Both, sir!"

Mandubratius could see Marcus tilt his head to the side.

"Both the armies of the Emperor and His Holiness," the monk restated.

"I see," Marcus stated in that reserved manner of his. "What is Abbot Sigibert's situation?"

"He's closed and locked the inner and outer gates," Ebbo replied.

"Is either army attempting to breech the gates?"

"No," the monk said before pausing. "When the papal army arrived, they demanded that we turn over those who killed their soldiers. The abbot responded with a message denying their request, and that's when the imperial army arrived. Now, there is a standoff with the abbey in the middle."

"Their numbers?" Marcus prodded him.

"I don't know," Brother Ebbo admitted. "I'm sure Abbot Sigibert knows though."

What a whining, sniveling, useless man. When next I feed, it will be from him, and I won't be gentle.

"Could you fetch him?" asked Marcus.

"He is deeply involved in the negotiations. He wishes for you to join him," the brother replied.

Marcus drew himself closer to the abbot, and then his glamoury surrounded him. "If he and I converse out there, where the armies may see us, it would give away the fact that he's hiding us. The Papal Army may just attack. However, if he meets us here, we can talk privately."

Mandubratius had to catch himself from being drawn in by Marcus' glamoury.

When Marcus pulled away from the abbot and withdrew his glamoury, his beauty faded a little.

The brother smiled and yelled, "Oh, I see! I'll go get the abbot, sir!" before leaping to his feet.

"Shhhh," Marcus hushed the monk. "Do this quietly."

"Of course," the monk replied in a quiet tone. "Thank you, sir. You are most wise!"

Why do the lower orders always refer to Marcus as 'sir'?

Mandubratius closed his eyes, hoping that he could sleep now, but then Marcus shouted, "Everyone gear up! Pass the word that we need to be ready!"

Mandubratius opened his eyes and witnessed Marcus kicking various people. The din of blood-drinkers grumbling would not allow him to enjoy sleep again, so he sat up. "Do you mind?" he asked Marcus and everyone else in the catacombs. "The sun has yet to set!"

"I'm not prone to explaining my orders," Marcus replied in a quieter tone than him, "but since you're here, I shall answer. I wish to depart for battle as soon as possible. That means gearing up now. Does that meet with your approval... Tolomei." An amused smile lit Marcus' face.

Does he seriously feel he is poking fun at me, as if my false name to the Pope can be used as some kind of jab? I think not.

"'Mandubratius' will do," he answered. He then rose, stretched, and began to dress.

Within a few moments, fully dressed officers gathered around a small table examining maps, but their impatient eyes kept glancing towards him.

A feminine voice half-growl, "Stop taking so long!"

Mandubratius looked up from his boots and stared at Máire. Her green eyes blazed with ire, and he found himself a little shocked and angry at her statement.

"Woman, I'll take as long as I damn well please!" he growled back at her.

"We are all waiting! Get your arse over here now," Mac Alpin bellowed at him.

By the Gods, that Ekimmu Cruitne can be loud.

He felt too tired to argue further and so he joined them, hoping he could soon chase down that monk for his morning meal.

Soon all of the officers, including Mandubratius, focused on the map.

"Based on Mac Alpin and Edward's reckoning, this appears to be how the Papal and Imperial forces are arrayed. Our mission is to inflict enough, sudden causalities upon the Papal forces that the rest will flee," Marcus stated.

A bloodbath sounds like an excellent suggestion.

"Our first step, when the sun sets, is to have one hundred Deargh Du draw down the darkness to cover our ascent. We'll fly over the Papal Army and descend amongst them," Marcus continued.

"No... no... no," a small voice called out, growing louder with each word.

Mandubratius noticed the Inspector General begin to pace. Everyone stared.

"Julien, let's speak about this in private," Marcus advised, revealing more of that reserved calm that Mandubratius disliked. The two men then strolled over to a dark corner.

Julien and Marcus probably wished for a silent conversation, yet their words traveled.

"Didn't we discuss this matter two nights ago?" Marcus asked.

Mandubratius noticed Máire biting her lower lip, as if she worried. Perhaps Julien was her child instead of Marcus'. Perhaps she felt torn between supporting her father-in-darkness and defending her child-in-darkness.

Such information will be very helpful.

Mandubratius then returned his concentration to the whispered conversation between Marcus and Julien.

"I'm sorry, but I think this is not the best approach," Julien whispered. "I think it will compromise our values. I mean, how is it balanced to attack unsuspecting mortals?"

"What do you recommend?" Marcus asked in a calm voice, although Mandubratius could detect overtones of impatience, annoyance, and…

Is that rage? Well, that would be my reaction. Why not just beat the puppy and be done with it?

Mandubratius raised a brow at Marcus, trying to fathom how a former Roman general and elder Deargh Du would deign to take a suggestion from a youngling.

"I think the objective is to prevent so many deaths," Julien replied.

Marcus shrugged a little. "Perhaps I allowed my hunger to have too much control. How should we complete this objective?"

That sounded like an apology! Perhaps he is senile and unmanned in his old age.

"Somebody needs to go to each camp and persuade the Emperor and the Pope not to fight. The Papal Army needs to return to the Papal States, and the Imperial forces can move back into their usual groupings, with King Louis and the rest of the Emperor's sons leading their soldiers to their home territories."

Marcus compromises too much.

Mandubratius returned to study the others around the map again and noticed Máire's eyes shift to her immediate family. Worry remained in her eyes.

Yes, Julien must be hers.

He heard a compliment from Marcus, and then the two Deargh Du returned.

"We have a change in plans, as I'm certain you have all heard," Marcus explained.

Mandubratius sighed. He would have really enjoyed a good slaughter.

Julien could hear Marcus following him through the maze of tunnels that led from the catacombs of Prüm Abbey to beyond the gates. The two men kept silent. Julien could sense Mac Alpin and Mandubratius behind Marcus.

A trap door, revealing a glint of starlight around the edges, cast an odd beam against the floor and opposite wall of the passageway.

Julien levitated to open the door. The smell of rain and mortals overwhelmed the scents of the other blood-drinkers. Once on the ground, he trudged in one direction and soon quickened his footsteps. His grandfather-

---

in-darkness had said nothing about their direction and allowed Julien to lead them away from the hidden door and Arwin and Mandubratius.

A few miles away they began to slow down. They soon came to a stop outside of the imperial forces' perimeter.

Marcus dropped the darkness, which allowed Julien to pick up an unlit torch and light it, thus keeping his actions covert. The two Deargh Du then crept several paces back into the forest. Afterwards, Marcus released the darkness, allowing the fire to be visible to the mortal soldiers. Marcus and Julien walked at a casual pace towards the closest guards.

"Halt who…" one of the guards began to call out, followed by, "Oh, it's you, Inspector General. Greetings to you and to your associate." The soldier motioned them forward.

Remembering the soldier's name, Julien called out, "Greetings to you, Hlodver," in a hushed voice just above a whisper as Julien and Marcus approached the soldier. Once they stopped outside of the perimeter, Julien asked, "Could you tell Ercanbald that I wish to see Emperor Charles?"

Hlodver motioned for a runner to relay the message and then regarded them again.

"I see you received a promotion," Julien said, embarrassed that he just now noticed the new rank insignia.

The soldier beamed, revealing his pride at the recognition of his new duties. "Thank you, Inspector General. I received this promotion to pueri a few weeks ago."

After a minute or two, a party of resplendent antrustiones and a well-dressed noble arrived, effectively ending the rather pleasant conversation. The stiff movements of the mortal noble caught Julien's eye. An etched frown lined the man's face.

The dullest man in the empire stepped in front of them and studied Julien and Marcus.

"Julien de Divio," King Louis drawled, "what are you doing here at this hour?" The Emperor's eldest son continued staring at him and Marcus in a fashion that revealed his thoughts about the both of them. Louis had not softened with his new responsibilities, which charged him with caring for his country and vassals. When Emperor Charles took his Imperial title from Pope Leo III, he left the Kingdom of Aquitaine to Louis. However, Louis continued to be a most joyless man with a very solemn court. Even his own father found him and his attitudes somewhat tiresome and pious.

"King Louis," Julien greeted, forcing himself to speak with calm fortitude. "We're here to speak with the Emperor about this situation between the imperial forces and the papal army."

"What would a mere gendarme know about such things?" Louis asked.

"I believe the Imperial forces may be outnumbered, but we may have allies that will assist," Julien replied.

Louis waved his answer away. "The Emperor is too busy to see you. Why don't you leave and return to wherever you, and your mercenary friend, came from."

Julien noticed Marcus smile a little.

"Why would you, the Emperor's son, walk all the way here to tell us to leave?" Marcus asked.

Louis did not even turn to face Marcus. "Did I hear a mere ant addressing me?"

Julien glanced at Marcus and watched his eyes become dark. "I am addressing you," Marcus answered. "I'm not your subject, nor am I an ant!"

Julien wondered whether dealing with himself and Mandubratius earlier had set Marcus on edge, as the other Deargh Du's eyes gleamed.

"Such insolence from rabble," Louis spat, "I shall–"

Julien pushed himself between the Emperor's son and the other Deargh Du. "I apologize for my friend," he said to Louis, although Julien knew his tone revealed little apology, but perhaps his words would be enough.

"He is expecting you," Louis muttered in answer.

"I thought you said the Emperor was too busy to see us," Marcus countered, but Louis ignored him.

"Follow me," the King of the Franks ordered, before turning his back on Julien and Marcus and began to walk towards the center of camp.

As the two Deargh Du followed the king and his escort, Julien glanced at Marcus and saw that his mask of tranquility had returned to his face.

Marcus said nothing to him.

Julien gave up trying to strike up a conversation and shifted his eyes forward, gazing at the array of tents and the soldiers on night patrol marching hither and yon.

As soon as the group arrived at what Julien presumed to be the Emperor's tent, owing to the elaborate embroidery and colorful banners that emblazoned the tent, two trustes, who stood guard around the tent, held up a flap.

Louis walked in, followed closely by Julien and Marcus. Julien sensed the tent flap lower behind Marcus.

"They have arrived," Louis informed his father in a resigned tone, before trudging over to a dark corner of the tent and skulking.

"Inspector General, I had a feeling you were about," the Emperor greeted Julien as he turned to face him. "And Marcus as well. That is not a surprise, since I have heard about the successful attack against the papal forces holding your family and vassals hostage. Well done." The Emperor smiled at them both.

"It was indeed a difficult task, Imperial Majesty," Marcus began to explain, "However, the Inspector General was most helpful with tactics and safeguarding the people of Vézelay and Divio."

Julien felt some shame.

"Perhaps you shall receive a dukedom for your valor, Julien." Emperor Charles' eyes returned to regard Julien.

"Thank you, Imperial Majesty." He felt himself turn red, as if he had just fed.

"So, Marcus, you are not here just to praise my gendarme, are you?" the Emperor addressed the other Deargh Du.

"You are most perceptive, Imperial Majesty," Marcus replied.

"Are you and your friends intending on annihilating the Holy Father's forces?" Emperor Charles smiled, while rubbing his hands together.

Marcus sighed and met Julien's eyes. He smiled for a moment and then said, "I'm afraid that such an attack would not be balanced." Marcus then looked at the Emperor.

Emperor Charles stared at Marcus. "What do you mean by 'balanced'?"

"What I mean is that our intent is to force the Pope to lay down his arms and return to Rome with as little bloodshed as possible," Marcus answered.

Julien could see the Emperor's face begin to redden.

"You have the power to destroy enemies of the empire, and yet you won't do it because it's not balanced?" the Emperor articulated through clenched teeth. Emperor Charles began to pace across the carpet.

"That's treason," Louis enunciated as he emerged from the dark corner of the tent.

"Do not interrupt me!" Charles ordered his son. "It is I who shall determine whether there is treason or not!"

Rebuked, Louis returned to the corner of the tent to brood.

Emperor Charles inhaled and seemed to allow himself to calm down. "I take it your men are positioned," he stated while looking pointedly at Marcus.

"And women, yes. We are prepared in case there is no other course," Marcus answered.

The Emperor smiled.

Julien could sense King Louis stepping forward to say something, but when the Emperor looked at his son, Louis retreated back to his dark corner, muttering under his breath.

"And if necessary, you will fight on the side of the empire?" the Emperor asked after taking a few steps closer to Marcus, entering his personal space.

"If it comes to a full-blown conflict yes, but Julien and I believe that the Pope will surrender without too much bloodshed. Rest assured, if they don't surrender, they will die." Marcus' eyes shifted towards Julien. "All of them." Marcus then returned his stare back to Emperor Charles.

Julien tried to ignore his fear.

The Emperor nodded. "Then I wish you success with this plan. In case it fails, I will prepare my troops for the battle."

Once Julien and Marcus had left the tent, Charles ordered everyone outside, save his son Louis, who seemed to have something to say.

Louis walked out of the shadows and approached the Emperor.

Before his son could utter a word, Charles said, "I needed to speak with them. I wish you would not play your games when time is important." Charles walked over to the central table and unrolled a map, placing bags of sand on the four corners to keep it open. He decided that ignoring whatever Louis blurted out for the moment would be best for his health and sanity.

"Why did you speak to that mercenary and that gendarme with such respect?" Louis asked in a heated tone.

Charles ignored his impulse to ignore his son. Instead, he looked up from the map and answered him. "Respect is what gained me the throne, Louis. If I give respect to others, they will assist me in keeping my empire. You may be emperor one day, but you will not keep it if you continue treating others with such contempt. The empire will disintegrate if you are not careful."

Louis groaned and then left the tent, not bothering to wait for guards to open the flap. On his way out, the King of the Franks berated his guards for not lifting the flap.

"I fear this is a lesson you will never learn," Charles murmured to the tent walls. He then called for his secretary. "Ercanbald?"

Mac Alpin did not try to hide his disgust as he glanced at that conniving, backstabbing, son of a harlot Mandubratius, as both men trudged through the forest.

What did I do to deserve this torture? This should have been Marcus' job.

A throat cleared, and Arwin turned his head to regard Mandubratius.

"If I'm not mistaken," the irritating Briton said in that I-am-superior-to-you tone of his, "we do have a mission to complete."

You have a mission with my sword's edge…

Arwin grumbled aloud, "I thought you were leading us to the Papal Army camp. You then pushed past me, and so I assumed you knew where to go."

"It's about one mile through the trees," Mandubratius answered haughtily. "So, have you been probing our surroundings?"

Mac Alpin studied the wooded path and nodded, even though that was not the full truth.

"Are there any hostiles?" Mandubratius quipped while staring at him over his left shoulder.

"There are always hostiles at an enemy camp," he admitted to the Lamia in an attempt to be evasive. If Arwin couldn't kill this particular Lamia, he would at least take great joy in annoying him as much as possible. Still, Arwin felt Mandubratius annoyed him more than he annoyed the Lamia.

Mandubratius shrugged. "That is very true. Now, I'll lead and you follow. Oh, and Mac Alpin, let me do the talking."

The last patronizing sentence grated on Arwin's nerves. A desire to stab Mandubratius in the back increased. After all, it would keep the other blood-drinker quiet.

As the two blood-drinkers approached the camp, Mac Alpin noticed that flickering torchlights lit the pathways. If they continued approaching the sentries posted at the perimeter, they would scare them, and then Mandubratius and Mac Alpin could end up at the pointy end of a spear or sword. While it would be a mere annoyance at most, it would cost the blood-drinkers valuable time.

Arwin looked over at Mandubratius to see what he planned to do, only to witness a wicked twinkle in the Lamia's eyes. The Lamia's face and posture revealed that he intended to frighten the mortals.

Arwin grimaced and grumbled to himself. Unwilling to engage the papal guards in this Lamia game, he shouted out, "Greetings!" to make their presence known.

Mandubratius turned red eyes toward him, revealing his disappointment.

"Identify yourself," one of the guards yelled back to them in Latin.

"I am Ar–"

Mandubratius elbowed him, cutting him off. "I'm Michael Tolomei, emissary of His Holiness!" the Lamia responded.

No one answered his identification, but soon the shuffling of mortal feet and the closer proximity of their scent announced their movements toward them. Torches revealed a sentry's face.

"You didn't say that there were two of you," he stated.

"Oh, him? He's just my servant… no one of importance," Mandubratius answered.

Arwin tried to keep his rising rage at bay.

"What is your business here?" the soldier asked.

"My business is with the Holy Father," Mandubratius purred.

Arwin felt a spark of energy and watched the other blood-drinker manipulate his prey, as the guard attempted to steady himself.

"I'll send for his secretary," the sentry murmured.

"No, I will not speak to his secretary. I will speak directly to the Pope."

The energy in the air increased, and then the guard nodded his head. He turned towards the center of camp and began walking, leaving his post unmanned.

"Shouldn't you have someone relieve you?" Mac Alpin asked, shocked at his question. Only Marcus or Claudius would think over this situation.

"Arwin," Mandubratius muttered while looking over his shoulder.

"Oh, yes," the guard said after shifting out of his reverie. He then whistled for another sentry. When the relief sentry arrived, the first sentry pointed towards his post.

Arwin watched Mandubratius glare at him, and he just smiled back at him. Perhaps now, Mandubratius felt more annoyed with him than he felt of the Lamia.

Good.

Pope Leo III paced the tent, while rubbing his hands together. Chilled air seemed to drift in from under the tent flap, so Leo strolled towards the carpet in hopes of finding some warmth.

His concern over heat faded, as Leo considered the difficult decision he had to make. Striking against the enemy would tear the empire apart. In contemplation of what action he should take, Leo studied the simple brown-colored walls of his tent. If he backed down, the church would appear weak. Everyone would believe God did not favor him, and they would see him as a coward.

He stared at the crucifix in the northern corner of the tent. "I'm just not sure," he whispered, hoping God would say something, anything, through a sign.

"Not sure of what, Your Holiness?"

Pope Leo turned toward the familiar voice and saw his emissary standing on the other side of the map table, flanked by some hairy barbarian.

Why did no one alert me to their presence? Where is my personal guard? How long have they been listening to me?

After a brief moment of silent prayer, his belief in God's infinite knowledge overwhelmed his concerns over his guards and their indecorous behavior.

"Forgive me, I spoke out of turn," Michael murmured, lowering himself to his knees. "I meant no disrespect."

The barbarian glared at Michael and then at Leo, before imparting some incoherent wisdom in his own tongue.

Leo extended his ring to Michael, who kissed it. "Arise, my son. All is forgiven," he informed Michael. "Now, what can I do for my emissary?" Leo eyed the barbarian, but then he realized Michael remained on the ground.

"I'm afraid that it's not a service for me," Michael said.

"Please speak openly, my child," he said before beginning to pace.

"In the course of performing my duties to you, I was captured by the Emperor's forces."

"And you escaped with the help of this person?" Leo asked while gesturing to the barbarian.

Michael lowered his eyes to the ground. "No, Your Holiness. I'm still a prisoner of Emperor Charles."

He studied Michael and realized his emissary wore no weaponry, while the barbarian's swords and knives gleamed in the candlelight.

"Then, who is this person?"

The stranger smiled a little.

"This man is one of the reasons I'm here." Michael held up his hands. "Before I explain this, the reason I've been permitted to enter your camp is to relay a message to you." His emissary's eyes turned dark again.

"What is it?" Leo bade as he crossed the room to place his hands on Michael's shoulders.

"Emperor Charles demands for you to surrender, unconditionally."

"What?!"

"I apologize for this grievous news," Michael whimpered after lowering his eyes again.

"How can the Emperor feel that his forces have a greater advantage?" Leo hissed. "Who does he think he is?"

Michael gestured to the barbarian and said, "My friend is from a land to the north of the Anglo-Saxon kingdoms, by the name of... oh, I've forgotten."

The barbarian kicked Michael and growled.

"He is a member of a group of warriors that the Emperor has allied himself with. There is a rather large force of them behind the abbey's gates," Michael continued. "If you don't surrender, they'll kill us all."

"How can that be?"

At that moment, Leo's clerk ran into the tent. "Holy Father! We are surrounded!" the clerk informed him, before cowering away from the huge stranger in the tent.

Mandubratius ignored the earlier din of soldiers outside of the tent. Soon, the shouts of alarm grew as an officer rushed into the papal quarters and waited for leave to speak.

"Yes, what is it?" Pope Leo's voice revealed the panic within.

Mandubratius reminded himself that this mortal never fought in battles, not like the Popes of the past.

"Holy Father, an army of barbarians advances on us from the gates of the abbey."

"I warned you," Mandubratius muttered in what he hoped sounded like a pious tone, enjoying the growing chaos around him.

"Show me this force of barbarians!" Pope Leo clutched the officer's arm, but then he stopped and looked back to Mandubratius. "Michael, arise and join us."

Mandubratius turned his gaze towards Mac Alpin, who tossed his dark mass of hair over his shoulder and shrugged. Mandubratius leapt to his feet and followed Pope Leo into the exterior wing of the camp. Three thousand warriors watched them from a distance. Meanwhile, the papal forces ran around, half-dressed, looking for weapons and armor. Mandubratius attempted to keep his laughter at bay, but he did hear Arwin sniggering behind them.

The three thousand carried torches and wore woad on their faces. Soon, a song echoed through the fields.

"They're singing that song about the innkeeper's daughter?" he whispered to Mac Alpin in Gaelic.

"That is the only song Marcus sings, and you don't want to encourage him to do anything musical," Arwin chuckled. "At least I wouldn't."

The flickering torchlight seemed to make the warriors' numbers appear even greater.

While glancing at the gathered officers, he noticed one begin to stammer mutely. Eventually, he managed to squeak out, "Are those... women?"

Mandubratius feigned squinting, since with his Lamia vision, he could see everyone with great clarity, and pointed to the painted women in the distance. "Yes, there are women."

Soldiers began muttering amongst themselves and made the sign of the cross, seemingly fearful of their God's punishment for seeing women in trousers. Even the Pope, who had been accused of adulterous affairs earlier last year, appeared to be frightened.

"They're undressed," Pope Leo muttered.

"Has this priest never seen a woman's bare arms?" Arwin asked in Irish.

"It's the result of a Christian upbringing," Mandubratius replied.

"What's going on? What are you two talking about?" the Pope screeched as he grabbed Mandubratius' arm, panic in his eyes.

"My friend informed me that now would be a good time for you to surrender," Mandubratius replied.

"Holy Pope, a wise man knows when he can't win," Mac Alpin said in Latin. "Are you a wise man?"

Pope Leo hesitated.

Mandubratius closed his eyes at the sound of wood and metal singing through the air, as a wall of spears flew at them. "Hesitation may kill us."

Most of the spears hit the ground a few feet away, several of which stuck in a neat circle around Pope Leo. However, one of those deadly projectiles stabbed the ground between the Pope's legs, piercing through his vestments.

Mandubratius could see Pope Leo stare at the vibrating shaft for a moment before gaping at the gathered forces of the Celtic blood-drinkers. Across the distance, Mandubratius could see a smirking Marcus being congratulated for his throw at the Pope. Mandubratius grudgingly had to admire the Roman's accuracy. An inch too close and Marcus would have castrated the Pope.

"Your Holiness, if you don't surrender, the next spears may not miss us," Mandubratius warned while walking around the spears, trying to sound frightened, but failing at it.

"Tell the Emperor and those barbarians that we yield," the Pope growled.

"I'll go to my side with the rest of the barbarians and tell them myself," Arwin stated. He then turned towards Mandubratius. "You're still my prisoner. If you run, I'll behead you and eat your heart." Arwin laughed before walking towards the blood-drinkers.

"Thank you, Your Holiness, for following my advice," Mandubratius said.

"I hope they don't decide to slaughter us all," the Pope whispered as he struggled to extricate his robes from the spear.

Mandubratius pulled Marcus' spear out of the ground, careful not to damage the Pope's vestments further.

Pope Leo thanked him with a nod, too embarrassed to speak, perhaps, and then the mortal began walking towards the tents.

"I'm sure that's a possibility," Mandubratius called over to the departing pope, "but I think they'll be civil. Then again, I may be wrong." He lowered his face and tried not to smile.

Marcus looked on as a papal soldier dropped his sword, shield, and spears onto the growing pile of arms. As the soldier pulled out a hunting knife, Marcus saw Emperor Charles shake his head. "You may keep that and your

Heather Poinsett Dunbar & Christopher Dunbar

bow and arrows," Marcus informed the soldier, who nodded meekly in reply before sheathing his hunting knife.

So far, the enemy had offered no trouble. However, one thousand of the three thousand "barbarians" remained to make sure that the papal troops behaved. A snarl or two appeared to be keeping them in line.

"I didn't realize you had so many forces under your command within the empire," Charles stated.

Marcus realized where this conversation might lead. He paused a moment, thinking over an appropriate way to avoid a direct answer. "They serve you and your empire," he replied, before flicking off a bit of woad from his fingers.

"How is it that I didn't know about a mercenary band of thousands in my lands? I have spies, gendarmes, and scouts everywhere. I know when a baby cries," the Emperor complained.

Marcus could see the Emperor's eyes darken. In answer, he said, "We travel in small bands. We stick to open country and travel only at night."

"I see. What will this cost me?" the Emperor asked before nodding to another papal soldier, as another batch of armaments landed on the pile.

Marcus considered what to tell him. As a mercenary, he needed to begin thinking like one, yet the promise to maintain the balance echoed in his mind. Morrigan made her wishes known again.

"My friends and I have an interest in Divio and Vézelay," he began to explain. "Those villages were both sacked. It would be a personal favor to me and my friends if our interests in those villages were taken care of in an expedient manner."

He realized he was asking the Emperor to aid his own people, but he hoped that the emphasis on this being a favor remained.

"Is there any party in particular that has your interest?" the Emperor asked.

"The Inspector General's family comes to mind. As I understand it, his brother lost his wife and two of his children. Most of the vassals were displaced, and several died. I realize it doesn't seem like payment for our services, but we wish to see them recover."

"So, you don't want gold, land, or title?" the Emperor asked, a resplendent grin of disbelief lighting his face. "I could find some to give you."

"Imperial Majesty, my associates and I travel light, and we don't intend on staying in Francia or the empire for long."

"Exactly what kind of mercenary are you?" a confused Charles asked.

"We seek compensation in the form of... alliances and information," Marcus replied. "We feel that the favor of an important figure is worth more than his or her weight in gold."

At that moment, another papal soldier dropped his weapons on the pile.

The Emperor began pacing, and then he started rubbing his hands together. After ten steps, the Emperor turned back to face Marcus. "I agree to your terms," the Emperor responded. "Now tell me, what is that blue paint on your face?"

"It's woad. We use it to give the appearance of ferocity," Marcus answered, although he deliberately avoided mentioning the other affects of wearing woad. Marcus then attempted to excuse himself, wishing to wash, but before he could take his first step, the Emperor asked another question.

"This compensation is for services rendered thus far, correct?"

Marcus turned back towards the mortal. "Yes."

"So, should you continue to be in my employ from this point forward, you will require additional compensation?"

Marcus shrugged.

"Would it be under the same terms?" The Emperor's eyes grew cautious.

"That depends," he replied.

"On?"

"Well, it depends on whether something is worth more than an alliance or information." Marcus then noticed his dirty, ragged nails. He felt a moment of shame, yet he needed to speak with the other blood-drinkers soon, and he would probably get them dirty again should he clean them now. While contemplating his nails, Marcus heard a soft chuckle.

"Well, I certainly hope that I can afford your services," the Emperor added.

"I'm certain that will not be a problem, Imperial Majesty," Marcus acknowledged with a smile. "Now, I must speak to my associates."

The Emperor nodded and returned to watching the long line of papal soldiers dropping their weapons and shields on the cold dirt.

"This is our worst defeat since the founding of our army," Mandubratius heard Pope Leo III grumbled under his breath. A prominent pout grew as his forehead wrinkled in consternation. His mood seemed to reflect the grey clouds, as a storm threatened to wash the papal encampment away.

Mandubratius found himself fighting his laughter again. Part of him wished for the Pope to offer some resistance. He then calmed himself with the sobering thought that this army could be considered the descendants of the once mighty army of Rome.

"At least there were no causalities, Your Holiness," Mandubratius said.

You and all of your mortals would be dead now, had you decided to be stubborn.

The Pope shook his head and sat down on his chair. "My head is on my shoulders, Michael, but I feel that they have broken my spine. Perhaps I should have ignored your warning and attacked the enemies on both sides."

Mandubratius managed not to roll his eyes at the ludicrousness of the Pope's suggestion. Of course, Leo did not know his enemy. "Holy Father, you and your men would likely be dead now, if you had decided to battle the mercenaries and Emperor Charles." He then crouched down to look into the mortal's eyes. "I simply can't allow the Church to suffer such a blow."

The Pope gazed at him with wide eyes. "You think that they would have killed me?" His voice revealed his shock.

"I think that is why the barbarian joined me to speak with you."

"But... he was honor-bound, and I'm his pope," Leo whispered, as his eyes swam with confusion. "I serve as liaison between man and the Almighty."

"Holy Father," Mandubratius responded as he stood. "He is a Godless heathen. He and his associates would have killed you and I, had you not surrendered."

The Pope's mouth opened in shock. "You are saying that the man who beat back the Pagan Saxons has allied himself with Godless barbarians?" the Pope whispered.

"I suppose they have their own Gods," Mandubratius answered, "but they have no reverence for the One True God. That is why I could not allow you on the battlefield." He then slammed his fist against a table to accentuate his false point. "You must survive to convert them!"

"That doesn't excuse Emperor Charles for allying with infidels. Perhaps I should excommunicate him... or have him punished as a heretic. Yes," the Pope exclaimed in a quiet, conspiratorial voice, before he began drumming his fingers on the wooden arm of his folding chair.

Tired of this conversation and this fool's presence, Mandubratius cleared his throat. "I need to leave soon, Your Holiness. I humbly beg your forgiveness for being their prisoner."

"No, Michael. You stay with us. After all, the barbarians have no honor."

"But I do," he said, hoping that Pope Leo didn't hear the catch in his voice. Mandubratius could not take much more of this torture, always having to keep his concentration focused on reining in his laughter. Deciding more influence was needed to get his way, Mandubratius exhaled and then looked the Pope in the eyes, willing him into his control.

"I must teach these people about the One True God," he told the Pope.

After a scant second, Pope Leo stood up and made the sign of the cross. "May God bless and keep you from harm, my son."

Triumphant that his torture was at an end, Mandubratius bade, "Thank you, Holy Father," before kneeling and kissing the Pope's ring. He rose again, took a few backwards steps from the Pope, and then departed to rejoin the rest of the blood-drinkers.

chapter two

As the blood-drinkers filed back into the catacombs, Talia grew ever more fearful. Each of the woad-wearing blood-drinkers stared at her as they ambled into the inner depths of the necropolis. They seemed to judge her for not joining them in the fight. Some appeared to stare at her with apparent disgust in their eyes, while other gazes promised a slow and cold death, but Mandubratius would arrive soon and keep her safe from harm.

Soon, Amata and the Legate appeared, wearing blue woad on their faces, but even their faces revealed growing hatred.

Despite the harsh looks, Talia knew Mandubratius would come around and assist her with regaining control of Burgundy. He had promised to do so. Mandubratius could manipulate Charles. After all, the vassals needed protection, and the various Frankish rulers would not step in to assist their underlings. The vassals needed her, and Mandubratius would make Charles see that. Talia allowed herself a small smile, knowing she and Mandubratius would soon leave these weak lines behind.

When Máire and Marcus passed by, Talia looked up and noticed Marcus placing his right arm around his child-in-darkness, before glaring at Talia. Máire merely clenched her jaw and said nothing, while staring into the darkness within the catacombs.

Talia met his stare and allowed her rage to grow.

How dare a mere Deargh Du judge me?

At that moment, Mandubratius and the burly Ekimmu Cruitne arrived, gracing the end of the line of blood-drinkers taking shelter in the catacombs. A long, thin ribbon of pale purple lit the horizon, promising sunrise.

"I'm glad you decided to come out of hiding," Mandubratius said in greeting. "It's a beautiful morning, and you missed one of the greatest battles never fought. I'll have to write about it, one of these nights."

"I'm sorry I missed it," Talia commented, before placing her right hand on his left arm.

"You're not sorry at all," Mandubratius deadpanned.

"You know me too well. I generally try to avoid battles… you know that." She then took a step closer to him and inhaled his scent. Something about the smell of woad from the other blood-drinkers, or the hours of confinement facing her, made her desire him. Desirous of an intimate morning with her sponsor, Talia slid her left hand down his back, but he pulled away.

"I'd love to stay and play with you, but the sun rises soon, and everyone else is inside now." As he pulled away, Mandubratius gave her a mischievous smile.

"I don't like it in there. Let's stay in the abbot's quarters. I'm sure he won't mind, once you're finished with him," Talia answered. She then wrapped her right arm around back. "I'll do whatever you wish," she swore in a voice husky with desire.

"But my love," he whispered in her ear. "It's too late for that, and if you stay out here, you'll die." However, his smile remained devious.

"But they all hate me down there." Talia hated hearing herself whine, but that was all she could do.

"Hate? You? Nobody hates you."

"Oh no?" she asked. "What about Amata? What about Marcus and Máire? All three would try to kill me. You know that!"

"Honestly, Talia, I know of no such thing. Whatever gave you that idea?" he asked as he pulled away once more.

Unwilling to give in to his rebuke, Talia persisted, drawing closer to him, trying to lock Mandubratius into an embrace. "I can see it in their eyes. They are so eager to strike me down," she whispered.

"My, you have a most vivid imagination," Mandubratius purred.

Talia growled and then slapped him. "I know they hate me. Don't you dare treat me like I'm some simple fool!"

"I would never do such a thing," Mandubratius drawled, while smirking at her. "Now, let's go inside or you'll turn to dust."

Talia looked up and noticed the sky continuing to brighten with the rays of dawn. She then pushed past Mandubratius and scrambled for the cool catacombs. Behind her, she heard the creaks and groans as Mandubratius closed the doors. Silence welcomed her. She knew they all still watched her.

Soon, Mandubratius crept up behind her, pushed her into a dark corridor, and began pressing his groin against her backside. His gyrations against her sensitive parts brought a warm flush to her face.

"Where did we leave off?" he whispered, while rubbing his cold hands down her arms. "Oh yes, you wanted me."

He began fondling her rump, but then she pushed him away, a feat requiring nearly all of her strength.

"I like it when you pretend to be unwilling," he purred, before spinning her around and backhanding her.

Talia fell onto her hands and knees, enjoying the pain of scraped and rasped skin and the anticipation of far greater pleasures, when she felt cold air as Mandubratius lifted her dress. As she felt him penetrate her, she uttered an annoyed grunt, concerned that the other blood-drinkers would all see their coupling, but she desired attention from him, any attention. Soon, her pleasure crested, and Talia began to utter soft noises.

Mandubratius grunted as he released inside of her. After sliding himself from her, he spanked her backside. He then knelt next to her, extended himself close enough to kiss her ear, and whispered, "I know of no better way to end such a victorious night."

She tried to control her stilted breathing.

"I'm not done yet, but I can tell you're exhausted, Talia. I'll go find someone else," Mandubratius informed her, before standing up and pulling away. "Why don't you go to our bedding? I'll join you in a moment." He then pulled on his trousers.

She uttered an enraged grunt as she punched Mandubratius in the thigh.

He laughed and walked away, leaving her alone and feeling dirty.

Talia rose and began to creep towards a bowl of cloudy water set out for hygienic needs. She dipped in her hand and began washing her face. Of course, her face needed less cleansing than other areas of her body. Before washing her lower areas, she looked around, hoping no one would see her cleanse herself. Since no eyes greeted her, Talia began washing her loins.

Once finished, Talia headed deeper into the catacombs, meandering around prone bodies, and found their bedding.

Why does he always play these games? I know he cares for me.

Talia lay down on the bedding and closed her eyes.

After a few minutes, she felt someone lift her blankets, lie down next to her, and then pull the blankets up around them.

"Never leave me again," she murmured, assuming the person behind her was Mandubratius. "I'm so lonely when you aren't with me. Promise me you won't leave."

"But Talia, wherever I go, you are with me," Mandubratius replied.

She felt him scoot closer, press his groin against her rump again, and reach under her head to cup her left breast. She warmed herself in the feeling of love. After a few moments, she began to drift into sleep.

Claudius stood patiently and surveyed the people gathered around him.

The council meeting began, as usual, with the various leaders of the blood-drinker lines standing around a table covered by a map. Emperor Charles stood with them, and he seemed to shiver a little in the cold recesses of the catacombs. The Emperor then started pacing in an apparent attempt to warm himself.

Claudius closed his eyes for a moment, pretending he was the person in charge of this meeting. His former superior officer, and oldest friend, had earned his spot in the torchlight, but Claudius found himself missing the responsibilities of leadership a little. Then again, after the battle with the Lamia, the politics involved in leading the Sugnwr Gwaed had become painful.

Claudius pondered when the God of the Hunt might decide to bring them back into His realm. Their contests in the Otherworld led to roles of leadership in this reality. Distractions had kept him occupied during the last competition, and so his leadership waned, while others, most of them younger hunters, took his place. Perhaps he should have expected that. After all, his ascension to leadership did not occur during the contests. It simply came when the Ouphe attempted to invade Britannia.

Claudius pushed away those thoughts and began concentrating on the current conversation, which progressed from the movements of the Papal Army towards Rome to the Strigoi.

"I think it's time to pursue the mirror," Marcus stated, drawing grumbles from some of the gathered blood-drinkers. "The papal army has left. We can bring the mirror back to the empire, in case there is a resurgence of the so-called demons."

The Emperor stopped in the midst of his pacing. "Mirror?" He turned to face Marcus. "What mirror?"

Claudius witnessed a small flash of surprise flit over the Deargh Du's features. Marcus seemed somewhat distracted these nights. Perhaps he would keep an eye on him. Claudius experienced some curiosity at what story would come from this.

Marcus cleared his throat. "Imperial Majesty, we have reason to believe that there is a holy relic in Constantinople that will cleanse the minds of these murderers."

"How can a mirror be a relic?" the Emperor asked.

"They say it belonged to Saint Peter," Marcus seemed to improvise. "He showed it to a woman cursed with leprosy. When she looked into the mirror, it cured her. It cures many illnesses."

"Impressive," the Emperor commented before smiling. "So, where in Constantinople is it?"

"I'm not sure precisely, but we'll find its location."

Claudius could sense glamoury surround Marcus, who had said nothing about the Basileus Irene.

"Are all of you going to Constantinople?" The Emperor's tone suggested that he would approve of such a movement of troops.

"Not all, only a small contingent. Wouldn't you all agree?" Marcus asked, looking over the gathered contingent.

Most of the blood-drinkers nodded and shrugged.

"And where will the rest go?" Emperor Charles asked.

"I've invited the mercenaries to help rebuild Divio, Imperial Majesty," Julien replied. "They will go to our home in Vézelay and gather supplies to take to Divio."

"That's wonderful," the Emperor replied with too much enthusiasm. He did not hide the worry in his eyes. "Well, you have my blessing on your endeavors. Ercanbald will give you my seal to enable swift passage through the empire." The Emperor then gestured for his secretary to join them. "We'll return to Aachen in the morning," he added. "Some of my scouts are following the papal army."

"If you are willing, we'll meet once again before our party departs for Constantinople."

The Emperor nodded his assent to Marcus and left with his staff, leaving Ercanbald, who handed over a sealed document. With his mission complete, the mortal returned to the world outside.

"Now, who shall go where?" Marcus asked.

While everyone prepared to leave, Talia spied the Emperor and his soldiers leaving through the front gates of the abbey. She frowned for a moment before continuing to prepare for the journey with Mandubratius to Aachen, where he would inform that insufferable Frank that she would now be in charge of Burgundy.

That makes little sense, for we will arrive before the Emperor. Perhaps I could find entertainment along the way.

After a few moments, Talia felt the eyes of the others weigh on her, so she decided to leave the catacombs for fresh air. Once she exited the catacombs through the front wooden doors, Talia meandered towards the church. Along her roundabout route, she observed mortals sitting down to their evening meals, and she could smell the scents of meat drifting with the winds.

She soon found an empty, wooden bench, away from the mortals, sat down, and closed her eyes, dreaming about Constantinople.

Several blood-drinkers filed out of the catacombs and began to gather near where she sat. They seemed to continue a conversation they had begun while in the catacombs.

Talia tried to ignore the conversation, but soon she heard someone speak of Constantinople, and then she sensed him. She looked up and gazed upon Mandubratius, who strolled towards her, beaming with supreme confidence and serenity. She grew warm as he drew closer to her. His very presence made her feel at peace. Everything would be well. They'd dance in the palace.

Instead of walking up to Talia, Mandubratius stepped past her, but then she felt one of his fingers sliding across her back in a gentle caress. The finger tickled up her neck, over her earlobe, and into her hair. He then sat down next to Talia, wrapped his right arm around her, and looked into her eyes.

Talia felt a little light-headed, so she tucked her head onto his shoulder and sighed, feeling such contentment. She could sense other blood-drinkers walking by, but she ignored their presence.

"You are so ravishing," Mandubratius murmured in her ear. "It's a shame you won't be able to accompany me to Constantinople."

Talia blinked, unsure of what she heard. She jerked her head up and gazed upon Mandubratius' face, which sported a large smile, and she felt her own smile begin to fade. Her throat started to choke with sobs, but then she realized that he was joking.

She smiled at him and asked, "So, when are we leaving?"

"Within the hour," Mandubratius replied before playing with a curl of her hair.

"Oh, good. I have heard the others saying how magnificent Constantinople is during the spring," Talia answered, basking in the beauty of how she pictured the magnificent city of Constantinople.

"Yes, it is," he purred. "I remember it vividly. The palace there took my breath away, and the smell of the ocean made me feel so... invigorated. The people were kind, and yet so wildly decadent. They ate the best food... I could taste it in their vitae. I bought some beautiful clothing there, too. I remember watching the moonrise, and the weather there seemed perfect. I never felt cold in Constantinople."

Mandubratius paused and then closed his eyes, but his smile remained.

"It sounds like a dream," Talia said. "I can't wait to go there."

"Perhaps one night, after the war with the Strigoi is over," Mandubratius drawled.

Talia felt her face tighten up to the point of causing pain, and she could feel her cheeks warm.

"'Perhaps one night'? Are you telling me that I'm not going with you to Constantinople?" Her rage began to grow.

Mandubratius' serenity faded, but the smile remained in his eyes. "You are not. I told you that you were not going."

Feelings of abandonment warred with her ire. "What about what you said before we slept," she spat at Mandubratius. "You said that I'd always be with you!"

Mandubratius placed his right hand over his chest. "In my heart, Talia, you'll always be with me."

"That is not what you said!" she shouted before standing up.

"Yes, it is," he muttered in a dark tone, but he still continued to smile.

"You said you would go to Aachen with me," Talia argued. "Then, we can go to my home and rule Burgundy. No, we shall rule the empire!"

Mandubratius started laughing. When his chuckles grew louder, he lowered his head as if to gain control of his laughter. "Oh, that is precious! I almost believed you there for a moment!" His face then took on a serious mien, which usually prefaced his lecturing to her as if she were a child.

"The road to Constantinople is full of thieves. It's dangerous, Talia, and we must negotiate with Empress Irene, and she doesn't like Franks or foreigners."

Talia's sensed her vision redden as her rage grew within.

"Then, why is Marcus going?" she growled. "Why are Mac Alpin, my idiot niece, and the others all going?"

Mandubratius stood, before taking a few steps away from Talia. He seemed to consider his words before speaking. "Well, they are warriors and can defend themselves," Mandubratius answered. "Besides, most of them can fly, but you can't, my treasure," he cooed.

"What kind of reasoning is that?" Talia sputtered. "Neither can you!"

"Yes, but I have contacts in the Imperial Court. They will help me, so I am necessary, but you are not... at least not for this mission."

He extended his left foot close to her right foot and shifted his weight, leaning in closer to her. His eyes revealed a hunger. "You do have so many other talents," he murmured, before reaching for her right arm with his left hand, but she batted his hand away.

"You cannot tell me that I can't accompany you," Talia hissed.

At that moment, an unseen blow to the head knocked her backwards, and she collapsed on the ground.

Mandubratius stood over her for a moment and then knelt, but instead of straddling Talia, he pinned his left knee against her chest with an unimaginable force. He then clenched her throat with his hand and began to squeeze.

Talia gasped in pain, fearing for her life.

"I am your consul and your sponsor," Mandubratius growled at her, revealing his nature. His ember-red eyes bore into her soul. "You do as I say, or I will kill you. You will go to Époisses and not complain about this anymore!"

She closed her eyes as the pain became all-consuming. She could feel her voice box collapse under the force of his grip, and she soon became woozy from the pressure he exerted on the veins in her neck. As she felt her bones begin to crack, she wondered when he would squeeze hard enough to pulverize her neck and yank off her dislocated head, rending flesh and sinew.

Will he display my head as a prized possession? If my end comes, so be it. At least his hands, and not some Strigoi monster, will deliver my death.

By some miracle, Talia soon felt his grip on her throat decrease, but only by an infinitesimal fraction.

"Have I made myself clear?" he murmured.

She tried to gasp an affirmative, but her crushed throat would not allow her to form words.

Apparently understanding her intent to agree with him, Mandubratius purred, "Good," before releasing his grip on her devastated throat and removing his knee from her chest.

She could tell that he had broken her sternum and a few ribs. Talia hoped he would allow her to feed so she could speed up her healing, now that she had learned her lesson.

"Now, present yourself," he murmured in her ear. "I wish to make sure the point is driven home in the presence of everyone here."

Her fear rose again as he picked her up and forced her onto her knees. He then pulled up her dress.

Máire returned to packing after watching the scene with cool detachment, believing that Talia deserved far worse than what she received. She soon sensed Julien join her, so she looked up at him. His face revealed worry and disgust.

"Why is that Lamia... the supposed representative of Pope Leo, raping that other one?" Fury reddened and tightened his features. "I've never seen such horrible behavior. My niece could have seen it!"

Máire shrugged. "He's demonstrating that he's Co-Consul of the Lamia, I think. It shows that he's willing to defile one of his own to prove that his line must obey him. Besides, my aunt deserves no pity. She's a monster, Julien."

"How can you feel that way about your own family?" he asked.

"She's not my blood. Besides, my family is Marcus, Arwin, Claudius, Edward, and you. She destroyed much of my mortal family, and I will not speak of her any further." She hissed the last sentence, feeling a desire to rant and lose control.

Before she could criticize Julien for butting in again a hand clamped on her shoulder. She moved her gaze from the hand, to the arm, to the body, and then realized it belonged to Mandubratius, who she saw clasping Julien's shoulder with his right hand.

"Did you two enjoy the show?" Mandubratius asked as he leaned closer to Julien.

"How could you rape a woman in front of everyone? My family could have seen that display, not to mention our imperial allies, or the monks! They are our hosts, and now if we need their assistance again, they may decide to turn us away."

Máire held her tongue. None of her family could proclaim innocence. She could not protect Julien all the time, and arguing with Mandubratius would be nothing short of pointless.

"Would it trouble you to know that I see no problem with anyone witnessing me mete out justice as I see fit? Even if my victim was a mortal woman and her children begged me to stop, I'd still do it."

She watched Mandubratius smile, apparently enjoying the torment.

"Do you believe me to be barbaric, Inspector General?" Mandubratius queried after leaning even closer to Julien.

Julien scooted back from the Lamia's advance. "Yes."

Mandubratius withdrew his hands from both of their shoulders and then stood in front of Julien. The Lamia's smile soon faded, and his eyes began to reveal something resembling sadness, but much darker.

"It appears to me, boy, that you've lived a sheltered life, if you believe forced penetration of a woman to be barbaric. I could tell you such stories, puppy, of atrocities far greater than mere rape extracted against the helpless."

She witnessed the Lamia look inward. Part of her wondered whether he now felt some guilt for his actions. Máire even speculated that something might have been done to him, yet any pity within washed away when she remembered what he had done to her family... to the Deargh Du... to Éire, over two hundred years ago.

"I have no knowledge of what circumstances befell you, but I have seen horrors," Julien informed him.

Máire thought Julien looked a little shaken. She considered whether she should comfort him, but Mandubratius would likely mock him for running to mammy. She then noticed Mandubratius emerge from what she assumed to be his assessment of the past.

"The puppy blathers about a few little terrors he witnessed," he spat. A smirk graced his face.

"Do not mock me, and do not call me puppy!" Julien growled.

"Oh, I've seen far too many horrors. I shall go into the sun, for all of the dreadful acts I've seen! Oh, woe is my life for seeing such awful sights," Mandubratius bleated with much derision and scorn. He tucked his face into the sleeve of his tunic and made sounds of mourning.

Julien raised his hand to strike the Lamia, but Mandubratius dodged and grabbed Julien's right arm. Julien then brought his left hand to bear.

Máire could tell Mandubratius prepared to break Julien's arm, so she rushed forward, raced around behind Mandubratius, slammed her right fist into Mandubratius' arm just behind his elbow, and then grabbed his left wrist.

After grabbing his right wrist and pulling it away, she witnessed a strange lust in the Lamia's eyes. She realized that her close proximity... this partial embrace... might be taken out of context.

"So, this is how I can get you to come closer and be intimate with me," he whispered. "I'll have to do this more often."

Máire must have loosened her grip without realizing it, for Mandubratius extricated his right wrist from her grasp. She felt one of his hands caress her backside. Her right hand became talon-like, and this time she clasped his right arm, driving her nails into his flesh. She prepared to knee him in the groin from behind.

"Until then," Mandubratius teased before wrenching away his limbs from her, though at considerable cost. Of course, those wounds would heal without leaving a trace.

After watching the Lamia Co-Consul leave, Máire regarded Julien and pushed her son-in-darkness to a nearby wall. "Never let him draw you in!"

"But Máire—"

"No! He drew you in so he could show his dominance." Máire released Julien but locked her gaze on him. "Another thing. If you're going to strike, do so as a Deargh Du, not as a mortal. You must fight like a blood-drinker."

"I can fight," Julien replied.

"Against mortals, you are an excellent warrior," Máire informed him. "However, you have much to learn, in terms of fighting blood-drinkers." She wrapped an arm around Julien and smiled. "I'm sorry we both had to deal with that bastard." She tried to calm down.

"What atrocities do you think he was speaking about," Julien asked.

"I have no idea," Máire admitted. "Oh, yes, there was a time when he nearly died at my hands." She smiled as she watched Julien's eyes widen. His face lit up, and she patted his back.

"I think we have some packing to complete," Máire said. "Let's be grateful Mandubratius will have to travel apart from us."

Caoimhín could sense Marcus trying to gain his attention, yet the last scene between the Lamia still made Caoimhín feel weak and ill. Couldn't Marcus just leave him for now? Perhaps such brutal matters didn't disturb soldiers.

"What's the matter? Why are you looking so... agitated?"

"What just happened between Mandubratius and that female Lamia," Caoimhín said with a shudder.

"Oh, come now." Marcus' eyes widened. "You haven't seen brutality like that before? You may have not been a warrior, but I'm sure you have seen severed heads before. Druids did not participate in battle, but I know you have seen much." Marcus grew quiet for a moment. "Caoimhín, I need your assistance. I have a mission for you."

Caoimhín remained silent, wondering how Marcus could ignore the Lamia's disregard of common decency.

"Please," Marcus bade, meeting his eyes again. "Sáerlaith is not herself right now. Our line needs you to act in her stead."

Caoimhín nodded his head. "What is the mission?"

"I would like either you, or another Deargh Du of your choosing, to spy on Talia," he nodded towards the blonde Lamia, who remained on her knees even though Mandubratius had left her, "without being noticed."

Caoimhín furrowed his brow. "I'm curious why she's worthy of being watched."

"Mmmm." Marcus gave a bit of a shrug. "Something..." His eyes conveyed a feeling of grave foreboding. "It just does not feel right to allow her to run loose without supervision. She is chaotic... she even tried to manipulate the Emperor. She's not to be trusted alone."

Caoimhín recalled that he had seen that woman before...

Isn't she Máire's mother? No... aunt. Can it be her?

"She is the one that allowed for much of the trouble to occur in Béal Átha an Fheadha, right?"

Marcus nodded his head.

"I understand." Caoimhín wondered how Máire was handling her traitorous aunt as an ally... an effort that must weigh heavily on the young Deargh Du's mind. "How should I report her activities?"

Marcus closed his eyes in apparent consideration and then opened them. "It would be impractical to report to me. Perhaps you could report to Sáerlaith when the time is right, when she's feeling as if she can be in charge once again. Just keep an eye on Talia. I doubt she'll retire to her home and stay quiet."

"Very well," Caoimhín acknowledged with a smile, grateful he now had a way to get Sáerlaith involved. He knew it would be some time before Sáerlaith would want to accept responsibility again, but this small task, receiving his reports, might just help her. "I will do this."

"Thank you," Marcus replied. Also, please keep an eye on Sáerlaith. I am certain that she will move past Ard Mhacha soon. After all, we need to consider what to do after we have dealt with the Strigoi threat."

Caoimhín embraced Marcus and said, "Walk with Morrigan. I hope Sáerlaith will return to our council soon."

"Thank you," Marcus replied, while patting Caoimhín's back. "May She guide you and the rest of our line."

Amata watched the two groups, one comprised of herself, the other Lamia, and about twenty-five of the various Celtic lines, and the other large gathering. The two groups faced each other and began their farewells. They shed tears, embraced, and kissed each other with a strange almost-formality. Amata embraced them when someone would approach her, but she did not seek out the hugs of others, for this was not her way. After a few moments observing the two groups exchanging farewells, she sensed Mandubratius approach her.

"I'm a little surprised Talia didn't remain for this," Mandubratius stated. "She just ran off."

Amata could see the satisfaction in his green eyes. He looked so much like a pleased cat that enjoyed a game with a hapless mouse.

"You know quite well why she left. How could you have done that to her?" Amata demanded, not that she truly cared. The entire affair reminded her too much of Felician's death, not that Felician didn't deserve his end.

"She needed it," Mandubratius replied, "and so did the others. They needed to see that I'm consul of the Lamia."

Amata elbowed Mandubratius. "Co-Consul!" she hissed.

"My mistake, of course," Mandubratius cooed. "I wouldn't dream of it being any other way."

Damn him for smiling.

"We will speak of this later."

"Of what?" Mandubratius batted his eyelashes at her, playing the innocent.

Amata stared at him with clenched teeth. "We will speak of this... later!" She then grabbed his testicles and squeezed. A soft gasp caught her attention, and Amata studied him closely.

"I'm certain I'll enjoy that," Mandubratius whispered.

Amata squeezed harder until she heard a small 'eep'. His eyes revealed pain. Not wishing to cause his testes to burst like ripened grapes, she released him, but Amata felt pleasure causing him pain. She tried to keep from smiling.

"I can't wait," he deadpanned.

Sáerlaith stood aside from the two groups and watched the entire process with detachment. She would miss Marcus, and part of her wished to stop him and return to Ard Mhacha. However, the balance called to her, informing her that she needed to allow Marcus to obtain the mirror.

Marcus, she noted, began to walk towards her. As he approached, Sáerlaith experienced some doubt as to her ability to speak. She wanted to tell him everything in her head, but she knew that to be her own conflict.

Once Marcus reached Sáerlaith, he stood toe to toe with her, looked into her eyes, and said, "We will be leaving soon."

"I know," she informed him.

He continued to study her face and eyes with his beautiful orbs. Sáerlaith could not help letting herself become lost in their diamond-blue depths. "We will reclaim Ard Mhacha. We will reclaim the home of the Deargh Du, but now is not the time."

For the first time since that ill-fated night in Ard Mhacha, Sáerlaith could feel herself smile. He felt the same way she did, it seemed to her, and his resolve and vow bolstered her mood.

When Marcus embraced her, she kissed him and whispered, "Thank you for confirming our purpose."

"The honor is to serve the balance, Sáerlaith," he replied before kissing her brow. He then backed away from her and began striding for the group going to Constantinople.

"Go with Morrigan's blessing," she told him as the distance between them increased. "Know that your mission is Her will."

Horatio spent most of the time since rising avoiding the four Lamia mingling amongst the thirty blood-drinkers bound for Constantinople. He sniffed the air again, wondering how Claudius could tell each line from the others by smell.

He darted glances at the Lamia again. The dark-haired female spent her time talking to the one called Edward. The Legate spent his time helping the others pack their supplies.

Horatio looked around for Mandubratius, hoping that one wouldn't notice his stare, and then noticed the final remaining Lamia rolling up his bedding. As Horatio looked on, he could see Marcus ambling towards Mandubratius.

"So, are we to carry you the entire way to Constantinople," Horatio heard Marcus say to Mandubratius.

The Lamia chuckled and seemed to allow a mischievous smile to light his face. "No. We'll have our own means of transport, thank you. In fact, we should engage in a wager."

"Oh?" asked the Deargh Du, who sported a raised brow. "On what?"

"I wager that a Lamia sets foot in Constantinople before a Deargh Du, Sugnwr Gwaed, or Ekimmu Cruitne does," Mandubratius challenged.

"What are we betting on?" Marcus asked as he looked over his nails.

"The winner gets to cut off the loser's left arm," Mandubratius answered.

"Tempting... tempting." The Deargh Du began to pace. He then chuckled and said, "We could call you 'Awvarwy of the Short Arm', after I win."

"So, do you accept the wager?" Mandubratius seemed to be attempting to intimidate Marcus by leaning closer to him.

Horatio swallowed, uncomfortable with the interaction he was witnessing, so he walked over to Claudius in order to gain the elder's perspective.

"How can either man offer up a limb for a wager?" he asked in a whisper.

"Limbs will grow back, and it won't hurt that badly after the first hour," Claudius commented with a shrug. "Besides, feeding and healing from one of us will restore the arm by the next night."

Marcus and Mandubratius' conversation drew Horatio's attention again.

"I would agree with this wager with a slight change," Marcus said.

"Do I detect cowardice in your voice, general?" Mandubratius quipped.

Horatio could see a smirk tighten Marcus' face. "I just wish to be clear that we're speaking of people in this party, and the Lamia already living in Constantinople are not acceptable consideration. Is that agreeable?"

Horatio watched as disappointment slipped over the Lamia's face for a brief moment, but soon Mandubratius smiled.

"I assure you, no Lamia live there," Mandubratius informed Marcus.

Horatio heard someone behind him chuckle quietly, but he kept his focus on the two men.

"Mandubratius frequently lies, and we all know it," Claudius whispered. "And he knows we know it. He just enjoys the game. After all, he succeeded in annoying Marcus."

Confirming Claudius' words, Horatio saw impatience color Marcus' face.

"On second thought, I'm not in the mood to cut off your arm," Mandubratius replied. "It would be entertaining, but honestly, dealing with the mess, it's not really worth it. I don't want your blood on my new tunics."

The Lamia began pacing again, studying the walls of the catacombs.

"Then how about a wager for pride?" Marcus asked.

"I accept then."

Mandubratius and Marcus clasped arms, each judging the other.

After releasing Marcus' hand, Mandubratius added, "Just to be sure we have an advantage... Lamia, move out!" Three blurs raced out of the catacombs.

Marcus chuckled again. "Let's get into position. Claudius?" the Deargh Du asked while looking over his shoulder.

"Wait," Horatio called as he followed Claudius and Marcus. "Why didn't you tell them that I'm Lamia?"

"Mandubratius thinks all the younglings created from the papal army are dead. If he knew one of them survived, he might decide to kill you," Claudius answered. "Don't worry, I won't let him, but I'd rather not put him in a position where he thinks he needs to kill you. So, we'll just let him think you're one of the Celtic lines."

"So, can you sense where your brethren are?" Marcus asked while continuing to look at him over his shoulder.

"Yes, I can sense them," Horatio could feel his mouth turn down in a frown, "but they are not my brethren."

The Deargh Du muttered to himself. "There are two ways to hide the fact that you're Lamia."

Horatio inhaled, willing himself to keep from feeling any rage at being referred to as Lamia.

Marcus continued. "You can run behind them, or we can carry you. Before you decide if you wish to be carried, know that your benefactors will have to fly higher than the rest of us so the Lamia won't see you. They... your kind I mean, do have excellent eyesight." Marcus shrugged. "If you decide to fly, I warn you that it will be bitter cold up there."

Horatio didn't want to run after the Lamia, because it would imply that he considered himself one of their party. "I'd rather fly," he said.

Marcus turned away and yelled out something in some strange language. A few moments later, a stunning blonde woman arrived.

"Fianait, you and Claudius will keep an eye on Horatio, and the rest of us," Marcus informed her.

"Two will carry me?" Horatio asked.

"We'll be traveling fast. I hope this will keep Fianait and Claudius from becoming too tired. I'll send relief in a few hours." Marcus closed his eyes. "Get in the air, now. I've lost the Lamia, and I want to keep my pride."

Horatio inhaled as Claudius and Fianait wrapped their arms around him and left the ground. He closed his eyes, feeling ill as the wind hit them. Soon, however, Horatio gave in and opened his eyes. The land receded as they flew higher. Once they passed through the clouds, he began to shiver. Ice even started to collect in his hair and his beard.

"Are you alright?" Claudius asked.

"Aside from the ice, I'm fine," Horatio answered.

"Don't worry. An hour before sunrise, we can descend," Fianait added.

"I'm just happy to be here instead of trailing after the Lamia," Horatio admitted. He tried to stop wishing he were anything other than a Lamia, because that was something he couldn't change.

Reginald, who stood alongside Emperor Charles in what had been the center of the papal army's encampment, studied the many carts, abandoned by Pope Leo's forces, which once carried swords, shields, spare armor, bows, arrows, and other armaments… all of which the imperial soldiers had confiscated. The Emperor had graciously given Reginald leave to utilize these carts, and their beasts of burden, to transport his vassals and family back home.

As his family boarded one of the carts, Reginald gazed at the vassals and soldiers of the garrison, who loaded the other weapons carts with tents, wine, food, firewood, and other supplies from the Emperor.

"On my way to Aachen, Reginald, I shall send riders to gather additional supplies and building materials and then send them to Divio and Vézelay."

"Thank you, Imperial Majesty," Reginald said. He also felt thankful for the mercenaries' help rebuilding Vézelay and Divio. They had already left to scout the way back home.

The two men returned to surveying the former papal encampment. Very little remained from their occupation, aside from the weapons carts. They had taken all of their tents, provisions, and the rest of their baggage train.

"This was my least bloody victory, Reginald, and yet the enemy has not been vanquished… just disarmed… for now," the Emperor muttered.

Reginald could sense concern in the older man's voice, but Reginald felt confident the Emperor would be prepared to deal with any retribution the Pope may send their way.

"Forgive me," Emperor Charles added, glancing at Reginald, "but I must speak with your mother before you leave. May you have a safe journey home." The Emperor patted his shoulder and walked over to Reginald's family.

After a minute or two, Reginald noticed the Emperor wave at him in farewell before returning to his personal guard. Meanwhile, he could see Dreu waving to him in the distance, signaling that their party could leave now.

Reginald took the reins of his horse, placed his right foot in the stirrup, and then in one fluid motion, he flung himself over to sit in the saddle. He felt confident that any lurking bandits might try to avoid the garrison, if the mercenaries haven't gotten to them first.

Before catching up with the others, Reginald trotted back to the abbey to take one last look around to see whether any others remained. Soon, sounds of sobbing snared his attention, and so he turned in the saddle, half-expecting to find a misplaced child. Instead of a child, he saw a beautiful woman who stared at him from behind a stone wall. As Reginald drew closer, he noticed that she sat in a puddle of mud. Dirt and blood smeared her bruised yet noble face, and mud caked her once beautiful clothing, concealing its fine material and needlework. Although sobs wracked her body, every once in a while she would glance up at him, but she refrained from making full eye contact.

Reginald stopped his horse next to the woman so he could lean to his right and look more closely at her. This time, when she looked up, she made eye contact with Reginald. Her tear-filled, yet piercing, blue eyes stared into his, and he felt as though he might join in her sorrow. Reginald felt his mouth open in horror. He then dismounted his horse and stood before her. "What horror has befallen you?" he asked the woman.

"I was wronged by a lower born, and I am left here to beg for assistance. To... to..." The stranger swiped her right hand across her eyes to wipe aside her tears. "To... grovel for any kindness."

Reginald crouched down to her and extended his hand. "Let me render that kindness."

The woman stared up at him with happy, hopeful eyes. "Who is this man who desires to be my benefactor?"

"I'm Reginald de Divio, and I assure you that I won't wrong you."

She accepted his hand, and he helped the woman to her feet.

"My family and vassals are traveling back to Vézelay and Divio," Reginald explained. "Would you like to accompany us?"

She nodded. "I'm Lady Talia of Époisses, and I accept your invitation with gratitude. You will be rewarded in kind for this generosity."

Reginald smiled. "Come. My mother and sister will see to your needs." He helped her onto his horse, grabbed the reins, and then led the horse out of the abbey grounds and down the road to where the papal army had camped the previous night. Soon, Reginald spotted the caravan, which still waited for him. He led his horse to his family's wagon. Once at the cart, he helped Talia down from his horse.

"You are most generous," Talia whispered.

After opening the door to the cart, Reginald found his mother, sister, and daughter preparing to sleep. He hoped the road would not be too bumpy for them to sleep comfortably.

"Mother," he greeted.

His mother looked at him, at Lady Talia, and then back at him, though this time, her eyes widened in surprise.

"This is one of our neighbors, Lady Talia of Époisses. We will take her home." He met his mother's eyes, assuming she would disagree with him.

"Of course," his mother stammered while nodding at Lady Talia. "I believe we have enough blankets."

Reginald helped Talia into the cart and closed the door. He then grabbed the reins of his mount, launched himself onto his saddle, and trotted to the front of the caravan. After he nodded to Dreu, the captain of the garrison turned, whistled, and began motioning for the caravan to begin its trek home.

chapter three

"**W**here does your line draw your strengths?" Máire heard Horatio ask, although she did not know whom he addressed.

Máire glanced over at Claudius, wondering whether she should answer first. She had replaced Fianait a few moments earlier. The Celtic lines had decreased the speed of their flight because the Lamia could not apparently keep up. However, she suspected that Mandubratius had planned this. A conversation with him might be entertaining, even if she already knew the tale.

She could see Horatio staring directly at Claudius, so she decided to ignore the question.

Claudius seemed to study the stars. "I was called to the hunt by Cernunnos, the Horned God of Nature."

"How did you answer the call?" Horatio asked.

"Well, it began during Caesar's first invasion of Britannia," Claudius began to explain. "My men, my commanding officers, and I all needed sustenance. We… that is Caesar sent us to Britannia during the fall, and we were low on supplies, so we all went hunting. One day, I'd been tracking a large magnificent stag that had eluded me for hours. Once the sun set, I thought I had cornered the beast. I dropped to my knees behind the trees, reached for my bow, nocked an arrow from my quiver, gauged the distance, accounted for the wind, and drew my bow. I aimed for its heart, hoping for a quick kill."

Claudius paused and closed his eyes. His face seemed to grow serious and still.

"The stag locked eyes with me as I aimed… only it wasn't a stag anymore. I beheld a horned man, who possessed bright, golden eyes, which reflected back at me. The horned man then took a few cautious steps towards me.

"I lowered my bow and relaxed the string. I felt compelled to approach this golden-eyed, horned man, despite my misgivings about moving closer. As I neared, his mouth moved, and all I could hear were the sounds of the forest and its animals. Then, I heard a voice in my head, my own voice."

Claudius shifted his eyes back towards Horatio. All the signs of his earlier laughter and playfulness had faded into a disconcerting seriousness. Máire decided to resume studying the landscape beneath them.

"The voice said, 'you have stalked your quarry well, huntsman of the southern lands'. I asked Him who He was, and I heard Him say that He was Cernunnos of the land.

"Then, I said something about His name being unfamiliar to me, and in response, I heard laughter in my head. He said that His name was not well known in the south.

"Cernunnos then said, 'tell me, Claudius of the southern realms, why are you stalking the stag?' I told Him that my people were starving and that I had volunteered for the hunt."

Máire could see Claudius start to smile again.

"He said no others were with me. After more small talk, I discovered I was in His realm, and He told me the stag would have been pleased to lay down its life to feed us." Claudius motioned that he planned to skip most of that conversation. "Then, Cernunnos asked whether I would like to join His hunt. He challenged me to present my skills to Him. If He deemed me worthy, I would receive many gifts, that is, if I did choose to enlist in His hunt.

"I explained that time was of the essence, but He said that time did not exist in His realm. Cernunnos asked me whether I needed to think on His offer. He then added that the stag would wait for me in my world if I wished to leave.

"I could not think to do anything else than to just agree to His terms. I still don't know why I said yes, other than my desire to prove myself." Claudius grew silent for a moment.

"If you wish, I will tell you the tests later... some other night. The last involved fighting a Briton with spears. After I bested the other warrior, Cernunnos asked me again if I wished to join the hunt."

Claudius inhaled. "I informed myself that I needed to go back to my own hunt, and that games with a strange deity from another land should be avoided, yet I couldn't ignore my desire to join this group." He smiled again. "I said 'yes', and then... then He transformed again, and I found myself on the ground.

"A giant bear held me down and began to feed from me. I almost lost consciousness. I could smell the vitae as it dropped to the ground, and its potent aroma became overwhelming. Then, the bear transformed back into Cernunnos, and He held me up and told me to drink. As I began to imbibe, all I could hear were the songs of the animals and their rapid heartbeats. I wished to remain there forever, drinking that pure essence, but then Cernunnos pulled His arm away from my mouth. I felt like begging for more, but refrained from embarrassing myself.

"He told me that He would call for me after the next sunset, and then we would hunt. This was my day to say goodbye to my friends, because the hunters never saw the light of day again. He patted my shoulder and walked into the shadows."

Claudius gave a little shrug. "I fell over and felt my hands land on my bow and arrow, which was still nocked in the bow. As Cernunnos had promised, the stag waited for my return. He met my gaze, lowered his head, and then in my mind, I heard his permission to take his life. After killing my prey, I carried his carcass back to camp.

"I remembered what Cernunnos had said about my last day in the light, and I went to Caesar to ask after the fates of Marcus and Mandubratius. The scouts had not seen them, so I asked permission to look for them myself. After all, I should have traveled with my commanding officer.

"Caesar gave me permission to leave, and so that night, I went into the woods and began to change. I fell down and felt nothing but tremendous pain in my legs. The animals of the wild began crying with me that night." Claudius then fell silent.

Knowing Claudius had finished his tale, Máire said, "I always enjoy the story of your transformation."

"Yes," replied Claudius. "It's a very different experience from the Deargh Du, though I know Morrigan challenges Her initiates as well."

"It sounds as though you have a special bond with your creator," Horatio muttered.

"I think all Sugnwr Gwaed have the same relationship with Cernunnos," Claudius replied. "I'm not special in that regard."

"With me, there was no acceptance, there was no test, and there was no assent. I was, for lack of a better word, raped. My humanity was yanked from me. I was created to be tossed aside at my creator's whim, and I almost was." She watched Horatio's eyes cloud over. "If you had not shown pity–"

"It was not pity that stayed my hand," Claudius interrupted him.

"I know, but I envy your transformation."

"If we ever find out who did this, I'll help you hunt him or her down and kill them," Claudius promised.

"Thank you," Horatio replied, sporting a large grin.

"Can I help?" Máire asked.

"I'd be honored. I heard about what happened... when the Lamia attacked your home. We should have revenge together," Horatio replied.

She mused that perhaps such action might be unbalanced, but Máire decided Horatio deserved a chance for vengeance. She soon sensed her son-in-darkness rejoining them.

"Have you come up to relieve one of us?" she asked, as she attempted to shake the ice from her plaits.

"Perhaps in a bit," Julien answered. "Primarily, I'm here to speak to you about my lack of abilities in fighting like a blood-drinker."

"I feel that I have little to offer fighting against other blood-drinkers as well," Horatio added. "I move quickly, but not quickly enough."

"Alright," Máire said. "I know of a way for you both to help each other practice while we're flying."

"How is that?" Julien asked.

"It's quite simple," she said with a smile. "Claudius, change your grip so Horatio's arms are loose. Now Julien, fly under Horatio so you're facing him."

She watched, as the other Deargh Du followed her instructions. "Closer," she said. "Move so you two are at an arm's length apart. Now, you two will play a game. The objective is simple. Hit each other in the face as quickly and as frequently as you can. Also, you should hit each other as hard as you can. Otherwise, it's a pointless test."

"You can't be serious," Julien replied while staring up at her.

"I can't hit someone who outranks me, let alone someone who is nobility," Horatio added.

"I'm serious," she said to Julien. Máire then returned her attention to Horatio. "You're both younglings. Neither of you have rank or status in my eyes. Oh, and one more thing," she added while smiling at Julien. "You have an advantage because you can fly, so you can't go beyond arm's reach of Horatio."

"How can I possibly avoid being hit?" Horatio asked.

"You can't," Claudius answered, "but neither can he. That is the point of this game."

"What if I don't want to play this game?" Horatio's mouth turned in a most amusing frown.

"I could let you fall until you develop an interest in the game," Claudius teased.

"I'm your initiate… you wouldn't," Horatio whispered.

"Every hatchling has to fall or fly from the nest," Claudius replied. "You said yourself that you needed assistance and training."

"Alright, but only if I can count this as a test of my worthiness," Horatio grumbled. He then returned his attention to Julien. "Are you ready?"

"It seems I have little choice," Julien answered. "I can't exactly say 'yes' or 'no', can I?"

"Alright, prepare yourselves," Claudius said, while smiling at Máire.

Julien's entire face ached. While the test did assist them both in learning how to move faster, Máire and Claudius spent most of the practice speaking to each other in Gaelic, and Julien believed them to be betting on who would score the most hits. After a moment, he could sense Edward flying up to meet them from beneath the clouds.

"What happened to them?" Edward asked.

"They're just being boys," Máire answered. "Are you here to relieve one of us?"

"No," Edward answered, before studying Julien for a moment. "Marcus sent me up here to tell you three that we're going to make camp."

"Tents," Máire grumbled, while scrunching up her nose a little. "I suppose it's better than sleeping in the dirt."

"Then, there are no villages nearby?" Julien asked after righting himself to make it easier for him to speak with Edward.

"The closest town has no inn, and our party is too large to sleep at a local farm," Edward answered. The Briton then turned to Máire and asked something in a foreign tongue.

She answered Edward in that same guttural language.

In response to whatever Máire said, Edward's face erupted in surprise. He said something else, before disappearing through the clouds below.

"What did he say?" Julien asked Máire, who began to descend, along with Claudius and Horatio. Julien followed, hopeful to get a clear answer from Máire.

"Hmmm?" she asked with a smile prominently displayed upon her face. "Oh, nothing of importance."

Julien felt a burning rage at the prospect that she and Claudius probably set this game up earlier for their own amusement. Perhaps she even planned the entire cataclysmic event with that despicable Lamia.

As they passed beyond the thick clouds, heading towards the ground, a small camp in a clearing of the forest came into view, and he could see the others pitching tents. After touching down on the ground, he felt a great deal of gratitude for being able to stand on his feet again.

Without the ice-cold wind numbing his body, Julien slowly sensed a throbbing pain well within his head and jaw. After rubbing his head and mouth, he looked at his hand, only to see flakes of dried blood. He decided to head towards a bowl of water, but at that moment, Máire approached him with a smile firmly set on that beautiful face of hers.

"Poor man," she cooed. "It lasted longer than I thought it would, but you did learn, and I'm proud of you." She reached for him, but Julien slapped her hand away.

"Why did you make me do that?" he growled at her.

"It was either Horatio or me, and I assure you that you would have been carried back if I had challenged you. I deserve some gratitude." As Máire reached for him again, her otherworldly eyes revealed a growing hurt.

Julien reached out, caught her hands in his, and sighed. Out of the corner of his eyes, he could see Claudius healing Horatio, and it finally dawned on him that Máire just wanted to heal him. Julien decided to drop his defenses, and he raised Máire's arms so her hands touched either side of his face. He soon felt her healing warmth, which made Julien close his eyes.

After a few moments of bliss, a masculine voice intruded upon Julien's relation.

"Banbh Ceanúil, Edward told me that Julien and Horatio participated in a fight that you and Claudius orchestrated. Why didn't you tell me? I could have placed a wager."

Julien opened his eyes and witnessed Marcus smirking at Máire.

"Don't even think of speaking to Arwin," Marcus continued. "He's furious and says you're not his Banbh Ceanúil anymore."

Máire chuckled. "Claudius and I were holding Horatio. Fine, you can have a share of my winnings."

"Oh no, I'm not so easily bought," Marcus purred. "You… owe me now."

Julien rolled his eyes.

"Is that the only reason you're here?" Máire asked Marcus.

"Actually, I was hoping there was some way you could help conceal our tents. A Druid's mist would be most appreciated."

"A mist?" Máire asked while patting Julien's shoulder, the healing session apparently at an end. "I will do so. It will conceal us during the day."

"Mist?" Julien, who still felt some achiness, whispered.

"Not now, Julien. I have workings to do… and I must feed." Máire smiled and then stepped away.

"Lieutenant," Marcus called to Claudius. "Can you help us set up the rest of the tents?"

Claudius nodded, turned on his left heel and right toes, and began walking towards the tents.

Marcus' eyes settled on Julien and then Horatio. He grinned and said, "Well fought." After winking at Julien, Marcus rushed to catch up with Claudius, leaving Julien and Horatio alone.

Horatio stepped over to Julien. His red-flushed face bespoke of embarrassment. "I didn't… hurt you, sir, I mean, my Lord?"

Julien shook his head. "I can't believe we were told to fight each other." He sighed. "I hope there will be no animosity between us. Are you well?"

Horatio shrugged. "Nothing sleep will not fix. I suppose this is something…" He paused. "I mean, they are from a strange time, sir. I'm certain such games were common, back then."

Julien nodded his head. "I'm sure. Just stop calling me 'sir' or any other title or honorarium." He smirked. "Besides, you heard what Máire said… we are both younglings, in their eyes. Equals."

Horatio nodded at him.

Julien then took a step to stand next to Horatio, reached out his right hand, and patted the other man's left shoulder. "I think I'll go to sleep now."

"I think I will, too," Horatio replied. "I think for the entertainment we offered, we deserve a good rest."

Marcus yawned and shook his head in an attempt to help himself clear out his thoughts about their rush to reach Constantinople. He then knelt down and began rolling up one of the tents. After rolling up only about half of the tent, Marcus could smell Lamia approach him. When he looked up, Mandubratius caught his eyes. Amata and Patroclus, who trailed after him, both seemed somewhat annoyed. Of course, Amata managed to hide it better. Mandubratius, as usual, just looked like a pleased cat.

Marcus returned his attention to rolling up the rest of the tent, when he heard a throat clear. He looked up again, only to see that Mandubratius now looked serious and concerned. The sudden change made Marcus grumble inwardly.

What could possibly be the problem now?

"So, you're packed and are prepared to leave?" he asked Mandubratius.

"Yes, but there is a slight problem," the Lamia replied.

Marcus returned his focus to rolling up the tent in an attempt to express his disinterest in whatever the traitorous Briton had to say. However, Marcus doubted his ploy would deter the persistent Lamia.

In a whiny voice, Mandubratius complained. "Amata is footsore, and frankly, Patroclus is complaining about having to run."

Marcus heard a strange, annoyed grunt from Patroclus.

"I see," Marcus responded, while making brief eye contact with Mandubratius. "So, now you wish to be carried?" He lowered his eyes back to the tent to carry on the illusion of packing the tent, even though he had just finished rolling it up and had wrapped some rope around it so he, or someone else, could sling it over his or her shoulder.

"It's not for my benefit that I am asking. It's for them." Mandubratius' voice dripped with false concern. "They're my responsibility. You fly so quickly that we cannot keep up. If you only take Amata and Patroclus, I would be alone on the ground, at risk. It's best if you carry me as well as Patroclus and Amata."

Marcus felt Mandubratius' eyes examine him.

"Didn't you finish tying up that tent a few minutes ago?" the Briton complained.

Marcus made a show of setting the tent on the ground and stood up, furious with the game. He closed his eyes and willed himself to become calm. He then opened them and said, "We are in a hurry. We can go faster if you run and we fly. The Strigoi can come out at any moment. They are slow. However, you are slowing us down... deliberately." He managed to keep all the emotion out of his voice.

"Marcus, you and I both know that you passed us last night, very early. You and the rest of the party had to slow down so we could catch up. I don't accept that argument. Lamia are just slower than the Celtic lines," Mandubratius argued.

Marcus closed his mouth to keep himself from stating that he didn't care what any of the Lamia thought. He proceeded to attempt to calm himself again, when Mandubratius interrupted his thoughts.

"I'm willing to challenge you for the honor to have us carried."

The opportunity to beat Mandubratius senseless made Marcus smile... considering their history, Marcus yearned for a time to put the Briton in his place. Now would be that time. Still, Marcus' mind whispered a warning that he could not trust Mandubratius to fight fairly, but soon the clamor from the gathering bolstered his desire for blood, and so he dismissed his misgivings. Yes, Mandubratius would not fight fairly, but neither would Marcus.

"Accept the whelp's challenge," he heard Mac Alpin bellow.

"He'll limp the rest of the way tonight," Máire added.

While the others continued shouting, Marcus considered that he'd never hear the end of it if he didn't consent to the contest soon. With his decision made, Marcus began to draw one of his gladii. "I accept the challenge."

"Wait," Mandubratius bade as he stepped back. "My challenge is not combat."

"What is the challenge then?" Marcus asked as he sheathed his blade, though he half expected this was a ploy so Mandubratius could launch a surprise attack.

"I noticed that you have a Fidchell board in your pack," Mandubratius stated. "I challenge you to a game of Fidchell. If I win, your people have to carry us."

"And if I win?" Marcus asked, while preparing himself for the worst.

"Then we walk," Mandubratius stated with a shrug.

"That doesn't seem like much of a consequence for losing to me," Marcus commented.

"Oh, fine," Mandubratius answered, "then choose a consequence for my loss."

Others began yelling out suggestions. Marcus heard someone recommend making the Lamia run naked, which he felt sounded like a great idea. After all, the Lamia hated the cold. Marcus smiled a little before announcing his counter-challenge. "If I win, you three will run naked to our destination."

Mandubratius appeared to consider the offer.

"Oh, as if anyone would get a good look at you three," Claudius laughed.

Mandubratius shrugged. "No matter... I'll win. Now, run along and get your Fidchell set so we can get started on this game."

Marcus closed his eyes, tiring of Mandubratius' patronizing tone and wishing the game could be over quicker. Fidchell games could go on for hours. "I realize I've accepted your challenge, but we are in a hurry."

"Marcus, Marcus, just play with expediency, then. You must think too much when you play!" Mandubratius answered. "There," said the Briton while pointing to his right. "I've found a short and sturdy stump for the board. We can sit down on either side of it."

Marcus grumbled and then went to his pack. He opened it and began digging about for the Fidchell set, as well as a cup and die. Once he located and extracted those items, Marcus strode over to the stump, set the game pieces upon it, and sat down on the ground. Marcus then held up the cup and said, "Highest roll chooses their side. We'll use my set, because I don't trust your dice."

Mandubratius chuckled. "And while I trust you, I don't entirely trust the Ekimmu Cruitne, here. No offense," he said while smirking at the gathered blood-drinkers.

Marcus sighed. "Now, you're just trying to extend the game time," he muttered, of course Mandubratius did have a point. Even though Arwin or any of the other Ekimmu Cruitne were not playing, they could still have an influence over the outcomes of dice rolls. "Very well, Arwin, take your line out of sight. We'll signal you when the game begins."

Mac Alpin whistled and motioned for the other Ekimmu Cruitne to follow him.

Marcus could hear Edward muttering about inconsideration. Once the Ekimmu Cruitne had left, Marcus began shaking the cup. After three seconds, he let the die fall on the board.

The crowd murmured approval at the five showing at the top.

Mandubratius leaned over and smirked. "That will be hard to beat." He then picked up the die, took the cup, and began to shake it. A moment later, he dumped the cup over and revealed a six.

"I choose the chieftain," Mandubratius announced, before handing the cup and die back to Marcus.

Marcus soon noticed Claudius waving a torch overhead, apparently signaling the Ekimmu Cruitne to return. As Fidchell itself was not a game of chance, Ekimmu Cruitne could have no influence over the game.

"Oh, the weaker position," Marcus noted aloud.

"The sweeter my victory, then," Mandubratius answered. "I'm almost sorry that I didn't include a stipulation that all of you would have to fly naked. Ah well."

Marcus cleared his throat, hoping to get Mandubratius to concentrate and start the game. "Your move, chieftain."

"Oh yes," the Lamia acknowledged, before looking over the board and then back up at Marcus. Soon, all the joviality faded from Mandubratius' expression, and his eyes turned cold. "I will enjoy this."

Fianait stood in close proximity to the combatants at the Fidchell board and watched the match with much fevered amusement. She missed this... the contest, the light-hearted conversation, and the wagers. The other Deargh Du laughed and joked amongst themselves, seeming to forget all the problems they had faced in Ard Mhacha. Fianait marveled at Marcus' brilliance for turning this game into entertainment for all.

She then noticed that Máire, the only Druid in their party, stood next to her. She had barely seen Máire during the past two decades. Soon, Fianait's curiosity overwhelmed her, and she felt compelled to talk to Máire. "So, do you play Fidchell?" she asked.

"I hate that game," Máire muttered. Although Máire didn't look up at her, Fianait thought the Druid seemed rather cross.

"But... it's the game of our ancestors and chiefs," Fianait replied, feeling a little hurt. "It's our game."

Máire's face revealed confusion. She then took a side-long glance up at her and said, "Fianait? Did you just say something? I'm sorry, but I am a little distracted."

"I just asked if you played Fidchell."

"Oh," Máire said, finally meeting her eyes directly. "I'm sorry... I misheard you. Yes, I do sometimes play Fidchell, although I play at more appropriate times!" Máire shouted the last phrase. She glowered at Marcus and Mandubratius both, though neither of them even turned their heads to acknowledge her. Máire, in turn, grimaced and then uttered a half-growl.

"Perhaps we can play when it's a more appropriate time," Fianait suggested.

"Yes, very nice," Máire said. "I will look forward to it." Máire seemed to scan the crowd for a minute, and then she lowered her head. "I apologize," she stated. "I realize now how very selfish I'm being. Here I am, trying to stop it, when you and those here who fled Ard Mhacha are finally finding some joy and are laughing."

"No need to apologize," Fianait replied. "It's quite entertaining. They almost look like old friends."

Máire rested her left hand on Fianait's right shoulder, leaned closer to her, and whispered hot words in her ear. "Have you forgotten what Mandubratius did? He invaded Éire, killed many Deargh Du, and my family. If we didn't have a common enemy, Marcus and Mandubratius would be trying to kill each other. They are not... friends." Máire's words ended in a terse hiss.

Fianait had not expected such vehemence. The Ekimmu Cruitne, Sugnwr Gwaed, and Deargh Du all fought each other, long before the discord between the Lamia. Things changed after a passage of time. However, mentioning this point about how enemies changed and evolved to Máire, in her current emotional state, would only serve to increase her rage. So, instead of arguing, Fianait decided to compromise.

"I'm sorry," Fianait began to explain. "You are right, of course. It's..." She paused. "I think it's because, after all we've been through, we're looking for any friendship, even in our former enemies."

Máire drew back a little, nodded, and smiled. "Again, this is probably a result of undue impatience on my part," she said. "I just know Mandubratius wishes to amuse himself, and he will annoy anyone to do so."

At that moment, the gathered forces around them erupted in triumphant cheers... figures danced and embraced each other. Fianait looked around to see what had happened, but the revelers blocked her view. Máire begin to tug at her son-in-darkness' shoulder.

"What happened?" Máire asked Julien.

"Marcus won, I think."

"You think?" Máire smirked.

"Well, he made the last move, and then everyone started cheering and standing. I take that to mean he won," the Frank replied, just as the blood-drinkers behind them surged forward.

Through a break in the crowd, she could now see Marcus packing away the board and pieces. He didn't even appear to be gloating or pleased with the victory.

Mandubratius, on the other hand, stood aside and watched Marcus pack, smirking the entire time, but he did not help.

Once Marcus finished packing, he pulled the pack onto his back.

Mandubratius then extended his right hand to the Roman.

Marcus stared at the offered hand and then at the Lamia. After a second or two, Marcus stepped in and took his arm.

Fianait could see them both lean in and whisper to each other. Soon, she saw Mandubratius' smile fade, and then both men withdrew from one another.

Marcus seemed to study the blood-drinkers, before settling his gaze on his vanquished foe. "Now would be a good time, Mandubratius."

"Of course… of course," the Lamia purred. Mandubratius motioned to the other Lamia, who nodded and began to back away. He then proceeded to walk through the crowd and approached Máire, effectively blocking Fianait.

After pulling off his cloak and smiling, Mandubratius said, "I have a favor to ask you, Maél Muire."

Fianait could feel the temperature soar, so close to the quick-tempered Druid.

"That is no longer my name, and referring to me in that way won't get your favor done," Máire replied. As the crowd began to clear, Fianait witnessed the hatred in Máire's eyes.

"Forgive me, Máire," drawled Mandubratius as he made a grand bow.

Máire's eyes darted towards Fianait, but then she shifted her view back to the Lamia.

"What is the favor?" Máire asked.

"Well, Marcus doesn't trust us to carry our own clothing, so he wants us each to convince someone to carry our clothes. Would you be so kind as to carry mine?"

"Why me?" Máire asked. Her eyes revealed suspicion and wariness.

"Because you're friendly to me," Mandubratius answered.

"I despise you," Máire replied. Fianait could hear the hatred in Máire's voice, even though she spoke in a soft, even tone.

The Lamia sputtered in feigned shock. "So, what of this kindness we've shared and our camaraderie? Surely, you wouldn't be friendly with someone you despised."

Fianait almost started laughing at this scene. She felt herself shake a little.

"We've wasted enough time, here," Marcus interjected. "Find someone to carry your clothes." The other Deargh Du then pushed past the other blood-drinkers. What Fianait assumed to be impatience and building rage darkened his eyes.

Fianait noticed the other Lamia had removed their clothing and were in the process of gearing up. Patroclus looked a little cold, while the lovely Amata appeared to be holding up well, thus far. Fianait watched Amata pass her cloak and traveling gear to a smiling Edward.

Mandubratius resumed pleading with Máire, who seemed uncomfortable.

"I'll carry them," Fianait offered while extending her right hand. She grew tired of this game and just wanted to put an end to it. Besides, she couldn't help her curiosity.

Mandubratius turned to look at her. "And who are you?" he asked. He seemed to size her up.

"I'm Fianait," she replied in an even tone. "We met on the battlefield in Mhuine Conlon."

"Just hurry up," Marcus grumbled.

Máire walked away and started to gather her gear.

"Very well," Mandubratius answered. He then dropped his gear and weapons and began to undress.

She gathered his clothes as he tossed them towards her. In short order, she caught his tunic, trousers, and shoes. Fianait then noticed the Lamia picking up his gear and weapons.

Mandubratius turned to face Marcus and asked, "Are you satisfied?"

"I'll be satisfied when I see the three of you, running and naked, moving quickly in that direction." Marcus pointed towards the east.

"Hmmmm." Mandubratius turned his eyes back to Máire. "So, that's why Máire is always in such a foul mood. You've turned from Roman to Greek."

Everyone, including Fianait, fell silent and looked over at Marcus to see what he'd do. She could see Máire's face pale.

"Mandubratius," Fianait uttered a strained whisper. "If you don't behave, your clothes may wind up in a lake. You'd be stuck without warmth, and I doubt anyone would donate their spare clothes or blankets for you."

As Mandubratius turned back to her, his mischievous grin faded. "You wouldn't."

Fianait levitated off the ground and asked, "Mac Alpin, where is the nearest lake?"

She heard laughter, and then the Ekimmu Cruitne replied, "Two miles due east, Fianait."

Mandubratius grumbled, "Marcus, my apologies for the crude comments."

"Greek or Roman, I'll kick my boot up your arse if you don't start running," Marcus said before turning away to help another blood-drinker with his gear.

"Oh, very well," Mandubratius sighed. He then gestured to the other Lamia to start without him. As they rushed away, Mandubratius turned back to Fianait. "Perhaps we can meet later. I can thank you properly for carrying my clothes." A twinkle warmed his eyes.

"You just lost your trousers," Fianait stated as she hovered around him towards Máire.

"That was the idea," she heard him answer, and then a blur shot past her, heading towards the east.

"Are you really going through with that?" Máire asked.

Fianait smirked. "No. I'll drag them through the mud, though. However, I may take his offer for company later. It's cold, and he appeared to be in excellent condition. He's quite attractive for a Lamia."

Máire's eyes widened. "You wouldn't."

"Let's take to the sky," Marcus ordered in a gruff manner, effectively ending their conversation.

Fianait chuckled as she took to the sky. Below her, Máire still appeared confused and somewhat disgusted.

Mandubratius looked over at Amata and smiled.

She seemed to concentrate on running and said nothing.

Mandubratius decided to get her attention by clearing his throat.

"What?" Amata groaned, while clenching her teeth. She managed to look displeased and cold at the same time.

"This trip has yielded more information about Deargh Du than I thought possible," Mandubratius admitted. "Have you gotten any information from 'Edward the Exploder'?" He thought he had made a wonderful play on words, but he felt slight disappointment that she hadn't laughed. In order to fill the silent void following his hilarious joke, Mandubratius emitted a loud chuckle.

Amata said nothing for a moment, but after a few seconds of silence, she answered. "He continues to evade my questions."

"Perhaps you should try sterner measures with him," he replied, although he had his doubts she would try any manipulation with Edward.

"We will see," Amata muttered.

After running a few more miles, Mandubratius began to smell mortals in the distance, and so he stopped. Without the wind from his fast journey blasting him in the face, he could feel the soft breeze wafting the aroma of animal dung and other smells that indicated a farm stood nearby.

After running out of sight, both Amata and Patroclus ran back into view and stopped to look at him.

"Took you long enough to realize I had stopped," Mandubratius teased. "Are either of you hungry?"

"I could use some vitae," Amata replied, while rubbing her hands together. "What about you, Patroclus?"

Patroclus shivered. "If the two of you feed, I will as well. However, I urge caution. We do not want to get far behind."

"This won't take long," Mandubratius replied. "I think I smell a farm not too far away. That way," he added, while pointing to the east.

Mandubratius ducked into the woods and began to run at a slow pace through the thick underbrush, as the dense forest prevented faster travel... at least if one wished to prevent bare skin from being scratched by every branch and twig in the dark wood.

Amata and Patroclus followed close behind.

Mandubratius began to consider who would take the farmer, hoping also that there would be a wife and children upon which to feed, so they wouldn't be stuck drinking the blood from livestock.

As soon as he pushed past some trees, impatient with the distance between himself and the farm, he prepared to run, but then a strange buzzing noise distracted his thoughts from the hunt, and a debilitating pain began to grow and fester in his head.

"Strigoi!" someone shouted.

Was it me?

Mandubratius could hear his own disjointed noises of pain. He then struggled to look at Amata and Patroclus. He managed to spot Amata falling to her knees and sobbing into her hands. While he couldn't see Patroclus, Mandubratius could hear the Legate's piercing screams, which made him shut his eyes.

Soon, Mandubratius could hear strange chanting in his head, and he longed for a stick or rock to bash his skull. "Nagirrom." Voices demanded compliance and became shrill. Visions became reality, and reality became torture. "Nagirrom," the shrieks continued, over and over. The screaming melded, and Mandubratius could no longer discern his own screaming from Amata's and Patroclus'. In an effort to drive the voices out of his brain, Mandubratius started banging his head against the ground.

Blood. I can taste my own blood.

As Marcus flew with Arwin and Horatio, he suddenly felt something wrong... something he could not distinguish, so he beckoned to Arwin, who shared the burden of carrying the yawning, young Horatio, and the three blood-drinkers stopped mid-flight.

"What is it?" Mac Alpin asked.

Through patches in the cloud cover, Marcus scanned the heavily wooded landscape below, which yielded no shapes, beyond greening and blooming trees.

"Arwin," Marcus asked, "do you smell the Lamia?"

Mac Alpin uttered a grunt, revealing boredom with the conversation. "I can smell him, but barely."

Horatio studied them both before addressing Arwin. "You can smell them, but Marcus cannot?"

"Aye, I can... barely," Mac Alpin acknowledged with a slight shrug, owing to the burden of carrying Horatio. "My kind has very good noses." Then to Marcus, Mac Alpin said, "Let's fly down to the rest of the group."

Marcus nodded, and so they began to descend.

"What do you think they're up to?" Horatio asked.

"Nothing good," Marcus answered, just before they reached the rest of the party. He freed his left hand and pointed it at Claudius.

The Sugnwr Gwaed took his position carrying Horatio.

Marcus then hovered closer to Máire. "I cannot see the Lamia, and Arwin cannot smell them... rather, he said he can barely smell Mandubratius," he informed her in a loud voice, allowing their conversation to carry to the others.

His daughter-in-darkness frowned and shook a plait of hair away from her eyes. "Does this mean we need to do something?" Máire asked. "This is probably little more than an amusement for Mandubratius."

"I would think Mandubratius would call more attention to a way to waste time," he replied. He then mulled it over for a few moments. Soon, a strange sensation, the same one that had hit him earlier, convinced him that these were no Lamia games. "Form aerial attack formation," he ordered.

Mac Alpin rejoined them. "Strigoi?" asked the Ekimmu Cruitne, whose countenance became one of concern and dread.

"I'm not certain, but something is warning me that the Strigoi may be joining our friends," Marcus replied. "If we fly at them, and strike them fast, they will not be able to hit us with their madness as easily."

At least I hope that will be the case.

Julien decided to cover the eastern boundaries of the forest, while the remaining twenty-five blood-drinkers headed in other directions. After flying at tree-top level for a few minutes, a strange scent caught his attention. He began heading in that direction, when he witnessed a strange, hunched figure dart away. The sight of orange eyes revealed what he feared.

He considered calling the others, but he decided it would take too long. He must attack the Strigoi before it could escape.

Julien drew his sword, held it extended over his head, and flew towards the Strigoi, concentrating on the loping figure in the distance, willing his mind to focus on the task at hand. No madness seemed to creep towards him as his blade connected with the Strigoi's head, rupturing it, drowning Julien in a spray of gore. He flew through the space that had occupied its head, but Julien had overestimated his angle of descendent and his speed. He crashed into the ground, leaving a trough in the dirt, and tumbled for a few yards.

Heather Poinsett Dunbar & Christopher Dunbar

Once his body settled, Julien refocused on his surroundings. His head swooned, and he felt some pain in his left shoulder and arm. He closed his eyes in an effort to sense other friendly blood-drinkers who might be nearby.

Suddenly, the crackling from the rustling of leaves drew his attention behind him to the trees to his north, and he could see orange-glowing eyes studying him. Within seconds, strange visions and sensations began to overwhelm him. In an effort to drive out these horrible sensations, Julien inhaled to focus himself and began whispering a mantra. "This is not reality. This is not reality. This is not reality." He focused on his whispered words, repeating them over and over again, trying to shut out everything else, but the noises and the increasingly voluminous and numerous voices, like some insane chorus, grew louder in his mind.

Despite the cacophony of terrific voices yearning for him to perform horrible acts upon his own body, Julien closed his eyes again and willed his body to begin healing, and soon the pain in his arm and shoulder began to subside, somewhat. Even the voices in his head started to drift away.

No longer did he feel under maddening scrutiny. The sensation of something watching him faded, as he began to control his fears. Wondering whether the threat had indeed left, Julien opened his eyes. Where they had been before, no glowing eyes remained. A further look at his surroundings also yielded no threats.

Was there really a threat, or was I just imagining everything?

Julien concentrated on the sounds in the forests, wondering whether he was truly safe, when noises in the distance made his suspicions swell again.

I'm dreaming... aren't I? I have a desperate feeling I am not.

The noxious scent of Strigoi prickled his senses, bringing full awareness to his predicament, confirming that he did not slumber. He could sense six approaching him... close... too close. He knew that he could not call to the others without the Strigoi finding him, so Julien positioned himself into a defensive crouch and waited. He did not dare reach out for his blade.

After Claudius caught wind of Strigoi, Lamia, and fresh blood, he drew his sword and went to the ground. He then spotted the bodies, some moving and some not, in the middle of the forest and began creeping towards them.

Claudius watched as a Strigoi pushed others aside to begin feeding from Patroclus.

The other Strigoi gathered, watching as this one fed. They seemed oblivious to his approach from their back.

Claudius crept closer to the one feeding from Patroclus and rushed in. He struck the Strigoi through its shoulder, while pivoting the heel of his blade against the Strigoi's neck, severing its head, left arm, and shoulder.

The other Strigoi shrieked and began to scurry away.

Soon, Claudius could sense his traveling companions arrive, and he watched as many of them swooped in to collide with a Strigoi. He looked around to see where he could be of assistance, only to witness Edward killing one that fed greedily from Amata. To his right, Claudius also caught sight of Máire killing the Strigoi that stood over Mandubratius.

A sucking sound drew Claudius' attention to his left in time to see Marcus cleaving the heads off the remaining pack of Strigoi. All that remained now were headless, bloody corpses and the unconscious Lamia.

"Form a perimeter," he heard Marcus whisper, as the Deargh Du returned to the other blood-drinkers.

Blodwyn glided towards him from the opposite direction and inclined her head to the path behind her.

"How many?" he whispered.

"A few," Blodwyn whispered back to him. "About forty yards."

Claudius nodded before turning back and waving his right hand to get Marcus' attention.

Marcus looked up, and in response, Claudius held up three fingers and then pointed towards the direction Blodwyn had indicated.

Claudius saw Marcus gesturing for a few warriors to stay and protect the Lamia. As the Deargh Du began walking towards him, Claudius could see Edward kneeling over Amata and then feeding her.

Claudius took a defensive position to Marcus' left, Máire took the other side, and Mac Alpin and Horatio joined them from behind.

Three Strigoi appeared in the distance and were soon joined by others.

"Pick a target and attack," Marcus whispered.

Julien drew down the darkness, but he heard the Strigoi continue to stagger towards him, so he levitated and prepared to leave. He then realized that if he attacked, he would catch the Strigoi unaware. While still cloaked in darkness, Julien hovered over his sword, reached down for the hilt, and grabbed it, but then a disquieting voice, similar to the insane cacophony he had heard in his head earlier, began to call out "Nagirrom, Nagirrom, Nagirrom" in a chant.

Julien second-guessed his wisdom in facing the Strigoi alone, but before he could disappear, an explosion wracked his head, and he uttered a cry as the pain began to increase. He soon lost his concentration, and he felt the darkness fade away.

With his eyes and mind blind to the world around him, Julien could only sense pressure and then pain as arms clutched him. The pain soon increased, as he felt the Strigoi batter his head and shoulder against a tree trunk. His mind continued to lose itself under the maddening onslaught, but a cracking noise brought Julien back to reality.

He felt aching pain radiate in his left arm. He tested his arm by trying to move it, but then he came to the realization that the Strigoi had broken his left arm, yet the hilt of his sword remained firmly grasped in his right hand. As Julien marshaled up the strength to make use of his sword against the Strigoi who confronted him, it became distracted by something and moved away. At the same time, the voices in his head began to diminish a little. They became weaker... more unfocused.

Julien stood up, hoping he had the strength to flee, when he witnessed five more Strigoi shuffling towards him.

Suddenly, the heat and flash from an explosion surprised him. He could see that the Strigoi had stopped advancing, but then their chants for Nagirrom began anew.

Julien decided to attack the one in the middle, while they seemed distracted, but now that the other Strigoi had closed the distance with his original target, Julien thought he could dispatch all of them in a short, fast flight.

Julien exhaled and then launched himself at the Strigoi in the center, forcing it to the ground, but something began twisting his still wounded, left arm, causing excruciating pain, as if the Strigoi wanted to rip his arm off.

Despite the agony he felt, Julien managed to remain focused on his other arm, and he willed himself to swing his sword. His first cut sliced into the Strigoi's left shoulder. Julien yanked out the blade and began to swing wildly at one Strigoi, then another and another, flailing his sword about, like the Saxon berserkers that were whispered about in the halls of the palace. In short order, he had beheaded and dismembered all six of the Strigoi.

With the eminent threat averted and the voices in his head now subsiding, Julien collapsed on top of one of the Strigoi, folding his mangled left arm at an odd angle under his body. Julien felt his mind drift and allowed his body to relax... to heal, but he soon realized that he wasn't alone.

Julien raised his aching head, wanting to affirm his other senses that informed him that Deargh Du, Ekimmu Cruitne, and Sugnwr Gwaed neared him, but the strain consumed him, and he felt his head come to rest upon the bloodied ground.

Someone knelt down next to him and began stroking back his hair.

Julien looked up and saw it was Máire. Feeling relief at the sight of his mother-in-darkness, Julien closed his eyes.

"Make sure there are no others here," he heard Marcus say nearby.

"Six Strigoi," he heard Arwin mutter. "That is quite an impressive feat."

"Can you stand?" Máire asked.

Julien considered his injuries. While his left arm still throbbed, along with the occasional shooting pain from his fractured bones, the rest of his body felt better. Even his head seemed well enough, considering what he had just gone through while facing the Strigoi. Feeling recovered enough to get up, Julien whispered, "Yes, but I need help."

Máire reached under his right arm with both hands and helped him rise.

As she helped him stand, Julien heard other voices mutter things about finding no more Strigoi in the area. No news could have relieved Julien more.

"Let's get Julien to the tent with the others victims," Máire said.

Julien then felt another set of hands under his left arm, and together, Máire and someone else, helped Julien walk through the woods to the tent.

"I have a feeling we are not going to continue tonight," Julien heard Marcus say. "Claudius, please tell the others to set up camp with the tents. Some extra rest may do us all some good."

Unsure of how far the two blood-drinkers had dragged him or when they had pulled him into the tent, Julien became aware of the soft bedding beneath his back and head and of the figures moving around him. Soon, he felt bathed in warm, healing energy, and then he could feel the sweet, potent taste of vitae, as someone's lacerated arm came into contact with his blood-caked lips. Julien latched onto the arm and feasted, closing his eyes as he became overwhelmed by the life force flowing into him, mending him.

A pat on his left cheek indicated to Julien that he needed to stop feeding, so he released his grip on the arm and opened his eyes, only to see Marcus staring down at him.

After pulling his arm away from Julien, Marcus said, "Well done."

"Thank you," Julien whispered. He then closed his eyes and slept.

As soon as the sun set, Marcus crawled out of his tent and surveyed the area. He could see that several others had also wandered out of their tents.

Marcus grew introspective, for a moment, contemplating the strange nightmares that had chased him most of the night, but then a hand began to rub his back, drawing him away from his contemplation.

"Did you sleep at all?" Máire asked.

Marcus shrugged, not wanting to admit the truth. "I'll be well after I feed."

Máire nodded her head. "I'm going to check on Julien and the others. I have a feeling the rest of our party are hungry as well." She then departed for the tent with the recovering Lamia and Julien.

Marcus strolled over to the common tent, where Claudius waited for him. Together they spread out a map of the region on a large table. As Marcus and Claudius began to study the map, several of the blood-drinkers joined them.

"We are approximately here," Claudius said while pointing to a position on the map. "We can be at Sardica in a few hours. It will be a strange journey because we may have to carry a few others besides Horatio, so it would be best if we make haste and then feed after we get there."

"We can find little game here," added Fianait. "Perhaps the Strigoi fed from and killed most of it."

"And, if we linger in the woods hunting for game, we may be attacked by Strigoi," Mac Alpin added.

"Yes. We must make haste. How fare our wounded Lamia friends?" Marcus asked as he scanned the faces present for someone who he knew had stayed with the Lamia in their tent.

"The Legate is somewhat coherent, but Amata and Mandubratius are still unresponsive, sir," Horatio replied.

"I think this means we'll have to carry them." Marcus shrugged, considering how much of a drain it will be for everyone. "Let's start packing."

The gathered blood-drinkers each filed out to prepare for departure, but before Máire could leave, Marcus stopped her.

"Máire, I know no one will volunteer for this duty, but..." He could see realization dawn on his daughter-in-darkness... she knew what he was about to ask. "Help me carry that Briton."

Máire sighed. "I planned on either helping Horatio or Julien, if necessary."

"Julien appears to be in good shape, for a man who suffered a dislocated shoulder the night before," Marcus replied. "Do this as a favor to me... please."

She uttered a noise of annoyance. "Alright then, but you will owe me."

Sardica

Fianait landed with the group about a mile away from an inn. As the others began to feed upon the livestock in a barn and game from nearby fields, Fianait left for the inn. Though tired from the long flight and a lack of fresh blood, she managed to tap into enough energy to fly there.

When she got close, Fianait landed behind a darkened corner of the building and began to extend her senses. Several mortals came to her attention... one of whom seemed to be milling about near where she stood. Fianait set her best nonchalant smile on her face and strolled around the corner.

The mortal appeared to be a stable boy in his late teens. He seemed much more palatable than cattle or horse, but business took precedence over feeding.

So, instead of feeding from the pretty stable boy, Fianait sauntered by, giving him a wink when he met her eyes.

Perhaps later, pretty boy.

After walking around the building, she came to the door, opened it, and walked in. The inside of the inn seemed much like any in which she had set foot. A large, burley man sporting a thick gray beard and fat nose stood behind a bar. She assumed she beheld the innkeeper. When she looked at him, he presented her with a smile bereft of several teeth.

"What can I do for you, my lovely," asked the man in Greek.

Fianait set her coin purse on the table and spilled out several silver coins. "I need all of your rooms for the next few nights," she requested, while allowing her glamoury to increase.

The innkeeper stared at her and then nodded his head.

"And undiluted wine," she added.

Now, where is that stable boy?

"Are you certain you can feed on your own?" Máire asked Patroclus as she half-carried him into one of the windowless chambers.

"Honestly, I just want to sleep. I know I did nothing, but I just need rest." The Legate stumbled for a moment. "How are the Co-Consuls?"

"Edward is feeding Amata," she answered. "We're taking shifts with Mandubratius." Máire helped Patroclus onto one of the beds and began to pull off his boots.

He soon started to snore, but the sudden sounds of hammers striking wood woke up the Legate. "Mmmmm?" Patroclus muttered.

"They're covering the windows in the other rooms, I think. Go back to sleep," Máire whispered.

"Promise to protect me." Patroclus' hand latched on her arm. "I've seen you fight. Bellona guides you," he replied in a sleep-filled voice. "Only a deity can protect us from those monsters."

"Of course I will," she promised, before patting his golden hair for a moment. She then nodded to Edward, who placed Amata into the other bed.

"Please keep an eye on him," she whispered to Edward, who simply nodded. Máire then entered the hallway and walked into the chamber where Claudius and Arwin worked on securing the room from the deadly sun.

Once in the room, the echoing of hammers resumed, but this time without distance and solid material to muffle the sound.

Máire sat down on one of the beds and began to rub her forehead, while watching the activity as Claudius and Arwin finished covering a window.

"It seems that Edward has formed a strong attachment to Amata," Claudius said, while looking at Arwin. A few rare lines on Claudius' face revealed worry.

"It's just an act," Arwin chuckled.

"No," Claudius countered. "This seems to be beyond an act, Arwin. You need to talk to him."

"I will," Mac Alpin said while staring at them both. "Once she recovers, he and I will speak about it. It's nothing more than a mere fling."

While contemplating the implications of Edward coupling with Amata, Máire noticed Julien and Marcus appear in the doorway.

"Did you notice the change in tactics that the Strigoi employed against us?" Julien asked, before sitting down next to her.

She noticed that he now appeared fully healed.

"Was there a change in their tactics?" a seemingly confused Marcus asked.

"Surely, you noticed," Julien replied.

"I think that we were upon them before they could use their mental strikes against us," Claudius replied. As his gaze drifted from Marcus to her, his face revealed great concern.

Julien nodded. "It was strange. Instead of a haphazard attack, they spoke to me. I just remember grunts from them before. The mental attack seemed more focused. They also worked together," he stated. "I have never seen them act in unison in such a way." Julien then paused for a moment. "Perhaps my judgment on these things is clouded."

Máire saw Marcus shake his head a little before he answered, "If you believe their attack has changed, you are probably right. If the Strigoi are able to focus their energies, they will be more devastating. Perhaps there is someone assisting them hone these skills. Maybe their initial attack did not meet with success, so they returned home to regroup." She heard a strange tremor in his voice.

Máire bit her lip. She could not remember a time when Marcus ever exhibited fear. The Strigoi could still be affecting him. "Perhaps we should make haste getting to Constantinople," she suggested.

"So, what should we do about the Lamia?" Claudius asked.

The others looked at her. Perhaps they deemed her their 'healer'.

"Patroclus should be able to travel. Amata and Mandubratius are still unresponsive. I do not know what is wrong with them," she informed the rest.

"Should we leave them behind?" Julien asked.

"That would be hard to do, since Mandubratius knows the mirror and the Empress," Arwin replied.

"We will continue carrying them," Marcus added, before sitting down on one of the beds. "I feel a bit too agitated to sleep." He then opened his pack.

"How about we play a good game of Fidchell?" Mac Alpin suggested. "You almost lost to that Briton. Perhaps we could all use the practice."

Marcus chuckled a little. "All right then," he answered before pulling out the board and game pieces.

chapter four

The Wilderness between Prüm and Mettis

Talia awoke as the cart went over a bump. Angered that some mortal's sloppy driving had awoken her, Talia sat up and looked over at the front. Instead of a person of lower order she could easily intimidate, and feed from if necessary, she saw Reginald de Divio slapping the reins against the horses' backs, causing them to flick their tails in what appeared to be annoyance.

Reginald continued driving them on their path, following the torchlight ahead.

The drivers must have switched shifts.

Talia scanned the skies, knowing that the stars and moon would fade into blue, soon, making way for the killing sun. The special heavy tents would grant her peace during the day, assuming she could somehow convince him to make camp before sunrise, so she wouldn't have to sleep in the ground. Besides, after a serene bath a few hours ago, she didn't want to get dirty all over again.

She considered manipulating Reginald, but Talia knew the disadvantages, as well as the benefits, to such a practice. The sting of Charles' rejection of her for a Deargh Du still ached. While her gifts enhanced and increased as she grew older, the other elder Lamia could do so much more.

Why can I not have the same gifts as they?

Talia grimaced, while thinking of her sponsor. There had to be another way to get Reginald to stop and set up camp. Perhaps if she could get closer to him… employ her other gifts, she may get him to see reason. Otherwise, she will have to excuse herself to do her business… for the next nine hours. With her decision made, Talia began to crawl closer to him.

"Is that you, Lady Talia?" asked Reginald, before straining his neck to view her.

Talia frowned, having believed that he could not hear her. Perhaps her growing hunger made her sloppy.

"Yes, it's me," Talia answered. "I apologize for startling you."

"I wasn't startled," Reginald said while smiling at her, but then he quickly fixed his gaze back on the torches in front. "Are you having trouble sleeping?"

Talia chuckled. "No, my Lord, I'm a being of the night."

As Reginald glanced back again, his demeanor seemed subdued.

"For the last several nights," he added, "I have been as well. I'll be glad to greet the sun again soon."

Talia attempted to think of an appropriate reply.

"Lady Talia?"

"Yes?"

"If you wish to converse, please feel free to join me on the bench." Reginald slowed the horses and then reached back towards her with his right hand.

Talia looked over the bench. While it was wooden and offered little in comfort, it would still be better than the hard wood of the bottom of the cart... and it would be easier for her to be convincing.

"Thank you," she said, before taking Reginald's hand and climbing to the front.

Once he had helped her over the seat, Reginald released her hand, nodded to her, and resumed driving. "You appear to be feeling better," he commented.

"Yes. I had time to take care of some matters," Talia said, as she stared at the light in front of the train of carts. "Are you in better spirits as well?"

He turned his head and looked at her with pain-filled eyes.

She noted his vulnerability and how useful that would be later.

"Sadly no," Reginald answered, before staring at the road again. "My spirits are as low as they have ever been. I'm certain a lady of your prominence would not care to hear tales of sorrow from a low soldier and landowner."

Talia smiled for a moment. "You do not have the manners of a low soldier."

Reginald smiled. "Once we arrive in Divio, I will have someone take you to Époisses."

"That would be very kind," Talia answered, before falling silent for a moment, waiting for him to ask the obvious. She knew he wished to know how she ended up like this, but she also comprehended that he would not ask such a forward question, so Talia decided to introduce the issue. "I'm certain that you must be wondering how a lady ended up in my position," she murmured, hoping she displayed something that resembled shame.

Reginald's eyes moved back to her, revealing pity. "I had not intended on broaching that subject. I deemed it a private matter," he stated. "However, if you wish to tell me, I would be most happy to listen."

Talia nodded her head. "I was accosted by the papal army on my way home from Aachen. They assailed me." She paused for a moment, allowing Reginald to assume the worst. "I later escaped when the imperial army arrived at Prüm Abbey."

"I assume that the soldiers were not punished for the injustice done to you?"

"No," Talia answered, slipping some vehemence into her voice.

Reginald leaned in closer to her and murmured, "I am truly sorry that the guilty did not suffer for what they did. I offer any aid that you may need in addition to the assistance in returning to Époisses."

Talia let a tear glide down her left cheek, knowing he would witness it.

"That is so very kind of you, my Lord. Thank you."

"Call me, Reginald," he told her.

Talia nodded and swiped at her eyes. "Then you must call me Talia." She inhaled a shaky breath. "I don't know what I would have done had you not seen me."

"I can appreciate your trauma," Reginald said, while meeting her eyes for a brief moment, once more.

"Have you suffered as well?" She allowed her voice to reveal compassion.

"Yes, at the hands of the papal army," he said. Anger and sadness laced his voice.

"How horrible, Reginald," Talia whispered. "What happened, if you wish to speak about this?"

"My wife and two of my children were killed by the so-called 'Soldiers of God'," Reginald hissed. "My eldest daughter and I will have to return to where my family lives and rebuild."

She watched Reginald lower his head.

"I grieve for your loss, Reginald. I hope those who perpetrated these barbarous acts will suffer for their crimes."

Reginald's eyes moved to her again, and this time, tears covered them. "You are most kind," he said. "Thank you."

During their conversation, Talia continued to sense the warning of the sun's arrival... now nearly eminent. She needed to get to a tent soon... but how? Deciding upon an approach, Talia nodded and then fluttered her eyes closed for a moment, feigning sleepiness.

"Are you feeling fatigued?" Reginald asked.

"Hmmmm?" She allowed a little hint of a yawn to escape her mouth. "Oh yes, I am a little..." Talia yawned again, "tired."

"You can sleep in the cart. We are planning to drive in shifts until the horses are foaming. We have several hours of driving time before we can set up camp."

"But Reginald, it is most uncomfortable to sleep in a jostling cart," Talia purred.

"There must be some padding back there," Reginald stated while maintaining his focus on the road.

"It's not so much the padding as the constant movement and bumps."

"I'm truly sorry, but we should continue so we can reach Burgundy as soon as possible," Reginald answered.

Talia could see he would not change his mind on that matter, so she decided to try another tactic. She moved her arms overhead in a graceful stretch and began dusting herself off, allowing her hands to caress her breasts, which caused her nipples to grow erect. She then allowed her eyes to drift to Reginald as she reached for a blanket to cover herself. She caught him watching her with some intensity for a few moments. His features even reddened due to embarrassment, she surmised.

"I apologize," he said. "I didn't mean to stare."

Talia lowered her hands and let the blanket settle on the bench, permitting a clear view of her erect nipples, which stood out through her thin dress. "I'm not offended," she cooed, while staring back at Reginald, hoping she would not have to manipulate him just yet. "Do you find me attractive?" She paused. "Forgive me for asking such a thing. It's been so long since a man of your bearing has looked at me in that way." She allowed her voice to grow husky. "Even longer still since I have been touched by a man of standing." She then rubbed her legs together, concentrating on increasing her desire. Perhaps a mortal could smell her in this close proximity.

Talia lifted her right leg and placed her foot on the edge of the riding platform. She then used her right hand to raise her dress, allowing the torchlight to reveal a slice of her leg.

When Reginald grabbed her left knee, she knew he yearned for her.

"If we set up camp, you can have me," she purred.

Reginald did not respond right away… he seemed to focus on driving, so Talia took his right hand from her left knee and guided it between her thighs. She then faced him and revealed the hunger in her eyes.

"Stop the horses! We're making camp!" he shouted.

Desperate widowers could be so easy to control.

Sardica

Outside the inn, Julien grunted as he grabbed Mandubratius' legs. "I grow very tired of carrying these Lamia," he hissed, as they scrambled through an open door and into the greasy air of the inn's interior.

Sounds of argument drew Julien's eyes to the common room, revealing Claudius and Marcus, who appeared to be in a very intensive bargaining session with the innkeeper.

"Let's just go to the end of the hallway," Máire said, before readjusting her grip under the Lamia's armpits. The unconscious Mandubratius' head lolled from side to side.

Once at the end of the hall, Julien kicked in a door, revealing a small, dark room.

"Will this do?" he asked.

"I hope this is the worst of their accommodations," Máire answered. "Yes, it's fine. It's doubtful he'll get to see it that much. Thanks for the help," Máire said as they placed the Lamia on the small bed in the tiny room. All of their accommodations would be tight this day.

Julien made a face and said nothing at first, but after a few moments, he blurted, "I think this is a waste of time."

"Don't let Edward hear you say that. He's very worried about Amata. I think he's in love with her." Máire wiped her forehead before rolling Mandubratius onto his back. She began to pull off his belt, boots, and other traveling clothes, leaving Mandubratius in his tunic and trousers.

Julien chuckled. "You're bothering with getting him comfortable? You swear up and down that you, Marcus, and many others of our kind, as well as most of the Celtic lines, hate this Lamia, and yet you take care of him. As for Edward, I'm not planning on visiting Amata, so I doubt he'll hear me say that I think we should leave these two here. I'm glad Patroclus is awake, though. How many more nights will we have to carry these two?" he complained.

"What do you mean?" Máire asked.

"This has slowed us down considerably. We only covered half the distance we normally do."

Máire pulled over a stool to Mandubratius' side, sat down, and then asked, "You had mentioned that you wanted to leave them behind, but I thought you were joking. Are you truly proposing we abandon them here?"

Julien shrugged and scratched at his chin, trying to think of an idea that made sense. "Yes. We could leave two or three of our escorts to care for them. Later, we could return on the way back."

I hope she responds to logic, even though emotion seems to be her guide.

Máire sighed, before biting into her wrist. She then forced the Lamia's mouth open and held her wrist to his mouth. As her wound spurted blood into his mouth, Máire massaged Mandubratius' throat with her other hand.

Julien remained silent for a moment, waiting for her to respond, but no answer came his way. Finally, his growing impatience peaked, so he decided to force the issue. "Well, what do you think?" he demanded. In frustration at the continued silence from Máire, Julien began to pace. "My idea is not without wisdom and logic."

After a few moments feeding Mandubratius, Máire placed a hand on the Briton's shoulder and closed her eyes.

"Well?" Julien demanded once again, this time while leaning over her... practically shouting the question in her ear. She seemed to acknowledge him with a slight twitch on her cheek, but she reacted in no other way to his query.

What do I have to do to get her attention? Slap the top of her head? She'd kill me... or at least pulverize my organs.

"I'm healing him," she murmured in a trance-like voice. "He's our ally... we have to try something. Anyway, Marcus insisted."

Too flustered to take any further action or make any other demands, Julien sat down cross-legged on the floor and grumbled to himself in Frankish, hoping she would be unable to understand his words.

At some point during his angry introspection, Julien noticed Máire move her head, and he then realized that she had finished healing. He looked on as she wrapped a cloth around her wrist to keep it from staining her already filthy clothes, which seemed like a pointless effort.

"Besides," she continued, as if there had been no pause from when Julien had first asked the question, "while there is logic in your idea, the success of this mission relies on Mandubratius' involvement. Therefore, we need to take Mandubratius, and Amata, with us. We are journeying on this mission together."

"What if they do not wake up?"

Máire stretched her neck from side to side. "Then we will make offerings and hope for the assistance of the Gods and Goddesses."

As Máire stared down at him, Julien glared back at her with what he felt was a tight lipped grimace. He then stood up and sulked out of the room, but he could still hear her say, "You'd better appreciate this."

Julien turned around, curious whom she addressed, and then peaked through a crack between the door and the door frame. Máire seemed focused on the Briton's still form on the bed. He then saw her lean in a little closer to Mandubratius, as if she might kiss him, but then Julien heard the bed shaking, as well as muffled sounds coming from the Briton.

As Awvarwy raced towards the goal, he kicked Braith, the goalkeeper. Awvarwy could hear Gaelen and Wybryn cheering him on as he ran with the ball balanced on the hurling stick. He laughed as he pushed his way past Dai, sending the younger boy to the ground.

With his path to the goal now clear, Awvarwy ran, barely feeling the earth and the green grass under his feet. He turned as he passed the goal, triumphant, and tossed the leather-skinned ball up in the air. It landed back on his hurling stick.

His team of foster brothers cheered and raced towards him, knocking him down in their joy, but he continued laughing, even as they helped him back to his feet.

Awvarwy heard the rare laughter of elder men and women, who watched the game between the boys, before they returned to their work.

"You've only seen seven seasons, and yet you play like the warriors," Wybryn stated. His foster brother had witnessed several more seasons than Awvarwy.

Awvarwy felt pride shine at such a compliment, but he didn't want to embarrass himself, so he merely shrugged. He then tossed up the ball again. "Did you see Eifion try to catch us?" he asked. "I tripped him, and while we were wrestling for the ball, his ring fell." Awvarwy held up his left hand, revealing the silver ring on his thumb.

"You pinched it?" Gaelen asked. "You shouldn't have."

"I'll give it back," Awvarwy promised. "He'll just have to apologize for splitting my lip, first!"

At that moment, he heard a throat clear. He turned to face the source of the sound and found himself looking up at Habren. Awvarwy blushed for a moment. He believed Habren to be the most beautiful girl in all of Trinovantum. Too bad she was twice his age and getting married in a few months to another one of the house servants. He rather hoped for a kiss from her for his skillful moves, but he had a feeling she'd never comply.

"I'm sorry for interrupting you, Awvarwy," she said, while giving him a pretty smile. Her golden hair lifted in the breeze. "Your mother wishes to see you in the drying house."

Awvarwy felt a moment of impatience. His mam always interrupted his fun with what she touted as being important lessons. Then again, he excelled at these secrets of the Druids. Awvarwy allowed some of his impatience to turn into excitement, but it still interrupted his fun. Mam had mentioned something about a vital skill necessary for Druids a few days ago.

"Thanks, Habren." He felt himself glow red. He then turned to his foster brothers. "Can you take this back to the dun?" he asked while raising his instruments of battle.

The other boys nodded.

Awvarwy tossed the ball towards Gaelen and handed his hurly stick to Wybryn.

After saying brief farewells to his foster brothers and the girl of his dreams, Awvarwy wandered towards the house where his mother dried her herbs and concocted her potions. Most of the time, he'd meet her in the distant grove to the west for his lessons, which is where he would gather plants and speak to the variety of beings living within the confines of the shaded woods.

As he neared the small hut, Awvarwy heard shouting inside. All the clan avoided the drying house whenever raised voices echoed from it, but Awvarwy decided to investigate, so he carefully ducked under a small window to hear the conversation.

"I don't want you to teach him about the ways of the Druids," Awvarwy heard his father command. "He's a warrior, Nerys. That's my choice."

"It was not your choice, Manaywdan. It was never your choice," his mother scolded. "The Druids selected Awvarwy. He should be in Éire now. He should have left a year ago, after they visited!"

"I didn't marry you so that the Druids could have sway over me!" his father

Heather Poinsett Dunbar & Christopher Dunbar

exclaimed. "Rather, I married you so I could have sway over them!"

Awvarwy heard a snort and then a short burst of loud laughter from his mother. He smiled for a moment, but then he jumped as he heard a loud thump, along with the sounds of pottery shattering.

A soft, little moan made him blink back a sudden onset of tears. He bit his bloody lip to keep from crying out.

"Are you blind to the ways of our people?" his mam asked. "Did you really think your union to me would give you power over the council? How small you are, Manaywdan." She delivered the last sentence in a loud and angry hiss.

Upon hearing a building masculine grunt of anger, Awvarwy crouched and prepared to run in and save mam, but then the grunt ceased.

"Why is it that you never respect my wishes regarding my son, Nerys?" his tad asked in a heated tone.

"But he's not your son!"

Awvarwy closed his hands over his mouth to stifle himself.

My father isn't my father?

"I know that! You were pregnant when we were married," his tad scoffed.

"But I wasn't showing."

"I knew the signs. I'm not a fool," his father answered, practically spitting his words. "Besides, if I hadn't seen it before we were wed, your son's eyes give him away. It's obvious he was fathered by another man. I married you because I believed you would give me more children of my own."

"So, you admit Awvarwy is not your son." His mother's voice rang of satisfaction.

"At least not in the ways of blood, no."

"Then, let me send him to Éire," mam pleaded. "Manaywdan, it's not too late."

"That is not my wish!" His father... the chieftain sounded like he growled through clenched teeth.

Awvarwy shuddered, remembering his punishment the last time the chieftain sounded like that.

"But he—"

"He may not be my son by blood, but he's the only man to carry my name. If the clan knew the truth, that I have never fathered children, I'd lose my place as chieftain. Besides, in the eyes of the law that your precious council created, which I uphold, Awvarwy is still my son."

Awvarwy heard a series of pained grunts. He could almost see his mother standing up, ignoring her aches.

"Do you know what your pride has cost you this last year?" Mam asked.

Awvarwy leaned in closer to the window to hear her words.

"My pride?" his father roared.

Mam's words grew gentle. "Why do you think crops have failed, Manaywdan? Why do the herds wither and die? Why do the shoals yield little fish for our clan?"

"It's just a bloody run of bad luck, Nerys!"

In a harsh tone, his mother yelled back, "You insulted the Druidic council! You insulted our sacred Gods, the Twylyth Teg, and the Tuatha dé Danann, the Gods of the Druidic order in Éire, when you forbade Awvarwy to go to Éire. They will all punish you for this pride!"

"How dare you," his father growled, before exhaling another deep masculine grunt.

Then, the strange sound of a falling body echoed towards Awvarwy's ears, accompanied by the crash of more pottery, and then a series of masculine groans resonated through the hut. Moments later, Awvarwy heard the door to the hut open, and out walked his mam.

His mother walked tenderly over to him and fixed Awvarwy with a forlorn look. She shook out her hair, causing the dust from the clay pots to cascade from her black hair. Her brown eyes gleamed with a beautiful but sad calm. "Come, Awvarwy. We must go," she murmured before stretching her long, pale right hand towards him.

When Awvarwy took her hand, she pulled him up.

How did mam know I listened in? Then again, mam always knows when people watch her.

"Where are we going, mam?"

As Mam led him away, he looked over his shoulder, only to see his father through the door. Blood splattered his father's face. He lay still, moaning and twitching a bit as if in pain.

"We're going to Éire," his mother announced. "Don't worry, Awvarwy, he's alive… he just won't stop us."

Mam kept the horses at a fast pace, which made Awvarwy's hair whip about his face.

Awvarwy clung to the front of the chariot, as the horses continued to gallop, wishing he could drive the horses himself. After all, Tad… the chieftain had allowed him to guide the chariot the last time he went hunting. With his mind made up, Awvarwy turned to his left to ask Mam about that, but then the worried expression on her face silenced him, and the thrill of the fast ride faded to a distant memory, opening the way for more startling recollections to come forth.

My tad is not my tad…

Awvarwy felt crushed by that realization.

"You'll love Éire," mam told him. "Éire is paradise, and you and I can learn in peace. I will seek the council there."

"Mam, who's my father?" Awvarwy asked.

"Manaywdan, your father," she answered.

"Please don't lie," he begged her. "I heard you and him talking."

Mam fell silent.

Awvarwy felt a stinging impatience surround him. "Why won't you tell me? I want to know who my father is!"

"I can't tell you, sweetheart. Your father will come to you when you are ready to know who he is."

"What if he dies before I'm ready?" he asked before looking over at Mam.

Mam smiled for a moment. "I doubt anything could kill him."

He wondered what she meant by that. Before Awvarwy could open his mouth to ask about her meaning, he began to hear the rumbling sounds of another chariot approaching at a fast pace.

"Mam," Awvarwy blurted out, "my, err... your husband approaches us quickly."

Mam turned and looked behind the chariot, but then her face grew more worried. "Hang on," she called before whipping the horses.

Awvarwy turned back to look at the other chariot, and he saw the chieftain raise a spear and prepare to throw it at them. After turning his face into the wind, he shouted, "Mam, he has a spear!"

Mam yanked back on one rein, which caused the horses to turn sharply to the left. Awvarwy held on for dear life and closed his eyes, until a loud thud behind him brought attention to his imminent danger. Awvarwy opened his eyes, looked to the rear of the chariot, and stared in fearful silence at a lodged spear, which still vibrated from its forceful impact. He could also hear the chieftain curse at his missed throw.

"That means just two left, Awvarwy. We'll be fine, sweetheart," she announced.

Awvarwy closed his eyes again and wondered whether the chieftain aimed for him.

"Kneel down, Awvarwy," his mother ordered.

He did what his mam told him to do.

"Look back carefully and tell me when he's about to throw the next spear," mam said.

Awvarwy opened his eyes, trying to focus at the task at hand... trying not to dwell upon the fact that the man whom he had called 'tad' wanted Awvarwy and his mam dead. One hard glance at the trailing chariot revealed the chieftain hefting another spear and preparing to throw it at them.

"Now," Awvarwy yelled before steeling his grip on the chariot's hand holds.

Mam pulled back hard on the reins, crouched next to him, and then wrapped her arm around him.

He heard one of their horses scream in pain, but their chariot continued to move. Awvarwy dared to stare back at the chieftain, as Mam stood up and reined in the horses to run towards the forest.

After the quick turn, she began coaxing them to run faster again.

Within seconds, Awvarwy felt a large hand grab him, yanking him into the air. At the same time, he heard a grunt of pain, and then it sounded like the chariot came to a stop. Fearing the worst, Awvarwy began to kick at the arm, drawing a loud series of curses, but the hand dropped him. Awvarwy fell to the hard ground, knocking the wind out of him. He struggled for air, but his chest hurt too much.

"Mam?!" he squeaked. Awvarwy tried to sit up and managed to roll onto his side, but then saw his mam lying next to him. He first noticed her bruised face, but he cried out in fear upon seeing the spear lodged in her back.

Awvarwy heard the chieftain's armsman, Glyndwr, ask, "What do you want to do with them?"

"She has an altar at a grove that is less than a mile from here," the chieftain answered.

Awvarwy stumbled to his hands and knees to try to run, but he collapsed, when a heavy, blunt object connected with his head, causing what felt like lightning to shoot through his body. His head throbbed in pain, as blood began to run into his eyes. He then felt someone lift him and roll him back into the chariot.

Through blood-covered eyes, Awvarwy managed to catch a glimpse of the chieftain dropping Mam next to him in the chariot, before climbing in and standing next to Glyndwr. He felt a jolt as the chariot resumed driving.

Awvarwy wiped as much blood from his face as he could and stared at his mother. As he looked at her, his mam stared back at him. He then saw her reach for his hand, so he offered her his trembling hand while trying not to cry.

After what seemed like an eternity staring into his mam's pain-wracked eyes, Awvarwy sensed the chariot stop, and then he felt Glyndwr grab him by the scruff of his tunic, lifting him out. His hand fell out of Mam's weak grasp.

"Bring my carving knife," the chieftain ordered.

Glyndwr slung Awvarwy over his left shoulder… apparently so the armsman could free up his right hand to reach for the blade.

Within seconds, Awvarwy could hear the blade sing as Glyndwr released it from its sheath.

"I have it. Where do you want the boy?"

"He will watch," the chieftain answered, drawing forth a wave of anguish. "He will witness what happens to those who try to betray me."

Awvarwy felt Glyndwr begin to walk into the grove.

"Your blade, chieftain."

Once Awvarwy heard the chieftain walk past them, he began to struggle to get away again, but to no avail.

The breezes cooled the blood on his face, and the grove whispered sweet magic. He could remember Mam calling to those forces and the beings that wielded them. He held fond memories of stirring her cauldrons and speaking to the animals of the grove.

In the midst of his tranquil reflection, Awvarwy felt Glyndwr place him on his feet on the ground.

As Awvarwy struggled to keep standing, he tried to blink the blood out of his eyes. He then tried to find strength to run, but he felt woozy… as though he might fall down, and he could barely keep his eyes open. However, through his failing vision, he managed to see the false Tad drop Mam onto the altar, causing her to cry out in pain.

"Rub his eyes clean, Glyndwr. He's going to see this. Force his eyes open if you have to!" the chieftain yelled, before raising the hunting knife over Mam's chest.

"No, don't kill Mam," Awvarwy begged, while trying to keep Glyndwr from touching his eyes, but the armsman's vice-like grip held Awvarwy's head immobile while rubbing a dirty rag in Awvarwy's eyes with the other hand.

The chieftain turned back to him and said, "Ah, the bastard has a tongue. Keep it well hid, or it shall be removed on this altar and placed next to your mother's. I considered killing you as well, since you are not my son, but I have no others. I cannot have the clan know that I can't father children. It would mean that I lose the chieftainship. No one but Glyndwr and your mother know that someone else fathered you. So, I still need you, Awvarwy. I will still train you to be a warrior, and you will be the heir to my property. After all, it's not your fault that your whore of a mother sought the comfort of another man. I forgave her for that transgression, but Nerys insisted on disobeying me when it came to raising you."

Awvarwy felt too stunned and too frightened to respond. He would not die this day… the chieftain had made that perfectly clear… but his mam… how could he live with this man, calling him 'Tad', after witnessing the brutal act about to be performed before his eyes?

What surprised Awvarwy most about this surreal situation was that his mam did not plead for her life. Instead, Awvarwy could hear her whispering words of love for Awvarwy and prayer to her beloved Gods and Goddesses, as the beauty and magical energy of the grove intertwined with the horror and ugliness of the impending bloody murder of his mam. Yet, the chieftain seemed unaffected by her words.

The man Awvarwy once thought of as his tad smiled at him for a moment before continuing. "She insisted on you becoming a Druid, when clearly you were destined to be a warrior and Chieftain of the Trinovantes. You see that, don't you, Glyndwr?"

"Yes, chieftain," Glyndwr answered.

"Your mother betrayed me, Awvarwy. She wished to kidnap my son and drag him to Éire against my wishes. My honor demands satisfaction. So, I must punish your mother in the most brutal fashion I can think of. Awvarwy, I truly love your mother, but I must do this. I only wish the cowards on the Druid council were here to be butchered for their conspiracy in these matters as well. No matter."

The chieftain raised the blade. "One of their ilk will find their sister soon enough. They will know never to trifle with my family again."

The blade dropped, drawing forth a piercing scream from his mam. The crescendo scattered birds and other flying beings and drove an ice-cold chill down Awvarwy's spine.

His fath… the chieftain began flaying Mam's skin from her body, drawing out further screams.

Awvarwy attempted to run again, this time towards the altar, not away… he had to save his mam, but Awvarwy couldn't free himself from Glyndwr's strong grip. His body still wished to give into the blackness, but the screaming of his mother echoed in his head. She called for him and for the Gods and Goddesses, begging for death. After a few moments, nothing but the whimpers of someone near death remained. The rest of the grove and the forest beyond stood silent, as if listening for his mam's last gasp.

Awvarwy could hear the clink of metal against stone as the chieftain set down his knife on the altar. He then looked on as the chieftain, whose arms and front were drenched in his mam's blood, walked over to Glyndwr and Awvarwy.

The chieftain grunted and said, "The deed is nearly done. Come, Awvarwy, have a taste of your mother's heart while it's still warm." The chieftain grabbed a hold of Awvarwy's shoulders and dragged him towards the altar.

Máire pulled the cloth from her wrist, folded it so the clean portion faced outward, and began to wipe the sweat from Mandubratius' face. He continued to twitch, fidgeting every few seconds for the last half hour, regardless of her ministrations. Despite her revulsion of the man, she found herself concerned.

While Máire stared at the prostrate Lamia, she contemplated how they reacted to the mental attacks by the Strigoi, considering, perhaps, that their recovery differed from the Deargh Du and the other Celtic lines.

Máire debated leaving the room, because she had a feeling that she could do nothing more to help Mandubratius. After all, Marcus had only asked her to feed and heal Mandubratius, not tend to him as if he were a helpless child.

Weary from her feeding, Máire leaned back on the stool and sighed. "Why do I ever bother?" she muttered to herself. She despised Mandubratius. He had killed her loved ones! Perhaps it would be best to pull her blade and finish him… here and now.

What good has that Lamia done anyway?

She stared down at him, trying to picture her killing him, slicing through his neck with one swift stroke… all of his transgressions against her paid… but he looked so… helpless. Máire knew she wouldn't wish the pain of the Strigoi's attacks on anyone… not even him. Besides, they needed the leech.

Without warning, the Lamia sat up ramrod straight and screamed, "Mam! Mam!" Mandubratius then opened red eyes and began looking around himself. "Mam!" he sobbed.

Máire rose quickly from the stool, feeling it collapse to the ground behind her, and rushed to his side at a speed only a Deargh Du could muster. She then grabbed Mandubratius' shoulder and held him steady, worried that he might hurt himself. "Shhhh," she said, while meeting his clouded eyes. "The nightmare is gone, Awvarwy. Whoever was hurting you isn't here. It was just a bad dream."

"Mam?!" he called again. Soon, Mandubratius seemed to see her and began to babble in the old Briton tongue, breathing heavily during his ravings. "My father. My father killed my mother, but he's not my father, not my father! Mam's dead. Mam's dead." Once he managed to blink his eyes clear, he shouted, "You're not Mam! Where's my tad?"

"Your father and mother aren't here, Awvarwy. I'm Máire. I used to go by Maél Muire, remember? You're here with me at an inn. We're on our way to Constantinople. Remember? I'm Máire, Awvarwy." She wondered whether using his real name would assist him in remembering.

"M... Máire?" he mumbled as he scanned the room. "Where am I? What happened?" He still seemed unable to catch his breath, despite the fact he didn't really need to breathe.

"We're at an inn in Sardica. You and the other Lamia were attacked by the Strigoi," Máire explained.

"The rest are alive?"

"Yes. Amata is unconscious, but alive. However, the Legate is awake."

"So... we're all safe?" Mandubratius asked.

Máire released him and grabbed the cloth. She dabbed at his forehead again. "Yes, Awvarwy, we're all fine."

He inhaled deeply, apparently calming himself. "Well then," he murmured. "Please forgive me for my emotional outburst. It seems that I'm now in control of my mind, no doubt due to your skills at healing." He caught her hand and stopped her from further mopping his brow. "I can take care of myself now," he said.

Once she pulled away, Mandubratius dropped her hand.

He stretched. "I appreciate your tending to my needs, but I wish to rest."

"Don't you need to talk about your dream?" she asked.

"Dream? No- my dream was rather dull. Nothing worthwhile to remember or discuss, Máire."

Máire righted the stool and sat down, unwilling to dismiss what she had witnessed. While part of her could care less about his suffering, some remote part of her wanted to offer comfort.

"Are you certain you're well? You seemed to be delirious, moments ago."

"Delirious?" Mandubratius smiled. "How very amusing. Did I speak during this alleged delirium?"

"Yes," Máire replied. "You cried out that your father killed your mother and that he wasn't your father at all."

Mandubratius burst out laughing. "How preposterous! My father was the chieftain of the Trinovantes, and my mam…" He paused for a moment.

Máire noticed that his laughter died away and sadness returned to his eyes. "She wanted me to become a Druid, like the council wanted, but I became a warrior."

"You were chosen to be a Druid?" Máire nearly fell off her stool in shock and disbelief.

"They were mistaken," Mandubratius answered.

"What really happened to your mother?" Máire asked, meeting his eyes.

"She was killed by brigands, if you must know. Don't you have other things to do besides bother me for my family history? If my body weren't so weak now, I'd go downstairs and lift a cup with Mac Alpin, Marcus, and Claudius. I'd guzzle that swill they seem so fond of…" He paused again. "Yet, I'm weak and I'm tired," Mandubratius said. "It would please me to rest in this dark room."

Máire felt her anger rise. He didn't appreciate her for tending to him, but then again, that was typical for most men.

Why would he be any different?

"Very well," she said, before rising from the stool. "I will leave you to your void." Máire then turned for the door. As soon as she placed her hand on the latch, she heard him call her name.

"Máire?" Mandubratius called in a soft, pleading voice.

Once Máire faced Mandubratius, she could see him staring up at her without guile or even a trace of manipulation in his eyes.

"I truly wish to thank you for restoring me," he said. "I owe you my sanity. If there is anything that I can do for you when I'm recovered, please ask it of me."

"Very well," she said. Thinking that in this rare, apologetic state he may be willing to confirm what she remembered of his dream and to put it into context, Máire asked, "Was there anything that you told me that was true? That your mother was killed by brigands, your father was chieftain, that you appreciated the fact that without my help you'd be insensate still?"

"My, my, Máire," Mandubratius purred. "It was all just a dream."

Máire realized that any further prodding would be useless. Mandubratius' wits had returned. However, she knew that despite his bluff, he appreciated her efforts, and for some reason she could not fathom, Máire felt some gratification in that. She then gave him a genuine smile. "Perhaps I'll know the truth someday." Máire opened the door, but as she stepped across the threshold, his voice gave her pause.

"Perhaps you already know the truth," Mandubratius answered. "In dreams, everything is truth."

Máire heard his laughter diminish as she let the door close shut behind her. She stood in front of the door and stared at her feet, unsure about what she had just witnessed. She scanned her memory, trying to ascertain whether Mandubratius had ever looked that terrified. What horrors did he witness that would make him cry out? He had never spoken of an immediate family, even in the days of her mortality.

Just then, someone shoved her shoulder, breaking her contemplation, so she looked up... only to see Marcus and several others.

Her inward focus had blinded her from sensing their approach. "I didn't hear you," she admitted.

"We've been here trying to get your attention, Banbh Ceanúil," Arwin said.

Upon noticing the drawn blades, she felt a mix of fear and confusion.

Marcus placed a hand on her shoulder and stared at her, engaging Máire to lock her eyes on his. "We heard screaming. Are we in danger?" he asked.

"It was Awvarwy," she answered. "He is..." She didn't want to reveal too much. "He was delirious and started screaming. Then, he woke up and asked me to leave him."

"We woke up for Mandubratius' nightmare?" Arwin grumbled in irritation.

"At least it's not the Strigoi, again," Claudius replied.

The sounds of grumbles and sheathing blades preceded the shuffling of tired feed, as the majority of their party meandered back into the rooms. However, Máire saw that not everyone returned to their beds.

Patroclus approached her and asked, "Is there something I can do? Perhaps I can speak to him."

"I have a feeling that it wasn't just me that he didn't wish to see," she answered, a little curious as to why Patroclus would want to see him. "I'm not sure if I would advise it."

Patroclus' eyes revealed candor. "I've been through this before with him."

"Before?"

Without preamble, Patroclus wrapped Máire up in an awkward embrace and whispered in her ear. "I'm not supposed to tell you this, but after our trip to Éire, he began suffering from delusions and outright madness. He would have nightmares, and even visions while awake. He would babble incoherently. For nearly a full year, Amata and I had to keep him in seclusion, while she and I ran the government."

Máire tried to keep her mouth shut, astonished as she was not only by hearing this admission by Patroclus, but also because she could not imagine the suffering Mandubratius must have gone through… mad for nearly a year. She also contemplated the amount of dedication it required to take care of Mandubratius' needs for so long.

"How did you help him recover?" she asked Patroclus.

"He did it himself," the Legate explained. "We visited him one evening, and he was the old Mandubratius, without an explanation of what had happened. We are not sure what stopped his deterioration."

Máire could tell that Patroclus did not speak the entire truth. Something about how Mandubratius was cured, or how they found him, seemed contrived.

The Lamia can keep their secrets, but what really cured him?

At that moment, an unexpected voice chimed in. "So, is he well enough to travel?" Julien asked, interrupting Máire's thoughts.

Máire released her embrace with Patroclus and replied, "I'm not certain." She still felt strange… uncomfortable… about the entire situation with Mandubratius. "He's coherent, at least coherent enough to ask me to leave."

"I'll ask him," Patroclus suggested, before turning back to look at her.

Máire realized that she blocked his path, so she stepped away.

Patroclus opened the door, walked into the room, and closed it.

Máire then grabbed Julien's elbow and ushered him down the hall towards the corner, around which she sensed the others waited. Sure enough, once she turned the corner to the adjoining hall, Edward and Marcus came into view.

"What will we do if he can't travel tonight?" Julien asked.

Máire, Julien, and Edward looked at Marcus, who then set his gaze on her.

"Why are you looking at me?" she asked, while trying to keep impatience from her voice.

"Because you know more about illness than the rest of us," Marcus answered. "What does your judgment tell you?"

"We can carry him again if necessary," she answered. "In fact, we should probably carry them all, if we need to move without delay. However, it may be best to give them some time to recover."

"I wish we could leave them behind," Julien stated. His words carried.

Máire tried not to laugh at his closed-mindedness, so instead she smiled and nodded. "Julien, that's a horrible thing to say," she managed to utter. She then lowered her voice. "I'm sorry to say this, but we need him. If Mandubratius can't travel, we won't travel." She turned her eyes back to Marcus and added, "That's my judgment."

Marcus nodded and then turned towards Edward. "How is Amata?"

At the mention of Amata's name, Máire wondered whether Mandubratius and Amata would share similar experiences.

"She's still unconscious," Edward answered. "She seems to be peaceful... no twitching, at least. She almost looks like she is asleep."

"Have you tried to wake her?" Marcus asked, at the risk of stating an obvious question.

However, Edward looked surprised. "No," he admitted. "It seems best to allow her to come out of this naturally."

"Very well, we shall wait until they're awake," Marcus said with a shrug. "If I'm up when Patroclus leaves Mandubratius' room, let me know what he has to say." Marcus, followed by Edward, headed toward the room to the left.

Julien loitered in the middle of the hallway, apparently waiting for their door to close. He then asked, "Is Amata as pivotal to this mission as Mandubratius is?"

"No, but–"

"So, if he's well enough to travel and she isn't, shouldn't we move on? We can leave someone to watch over her," Julien argued, interrupting her.

"After hearing Marcus' argument for waiting on Mandubratius, you want to leave someone else behind?" Máire asked. "It's because she's a woman, isn't it?" She felt her throaty whisper grow heated. "If I were unable to travel, would you leave me behind, or any of the other women here?"

Julien's ears turned pink. He then raised his hands and began uttering excuses, which Máire ignored.

Unwilling to hear his blathering any longer, Máire slapped him hard across his left cheek with her right hand and then stared into his eyes. The look of stunned shock brought a momentary sense of satisfaction. "I admit that if Mandubratius were not important to our success, I'd leave him behind, but not because of his gender or his line. It's because he's an utter bastard. That's why I'd leave him behind. We won't leave Amata behind because she's unconscious and female! How would you feel if we left you? You think on that before going to sleep. If you find yourself alone tonight, don't come crying to me about it!" she snapped.

Julien lowered his head and began to walk away, shuffling his booted feet.

Gods, Mandubratius is right. He acts like a puppy, sometimes.

While Máire felt a pang of guilt, she resisted taking him into her arms. One had to be stern with children, sometimes. She then went around the corner and stared at the door to the room where Mandubratius rested. After creeping closer to the door, she rested her left ear against the wood and listened. She heard no sound, other than breathing and an occasional snore.

Patroclus must have fallen asleep.

Máire turned away and began heading to another room they had prepared, hoping to avoid family. She yawned as she opened the door to the room.

chapter five

The Wilderness between Prüm and Mettis

fter Heloise exited the tent, she examined the dark skies above in contemplation of how sleeping through the entire day had worked wonders for her. She then drew her gaze back to earth to see the preparations being made for breaking camp and leaving this place.

A few soldiers stood at watch, while the others started the process of packing up the tents.

With the soldiers toiling in their duties, the vassals sat down to dine. To her, they appeared to be at ease.

Heloise stretched her arms overhead and listened to the chirps of the insects… nature's music… until laughter intruded upon her serene repose. She faced the source of the laughter, only to see her eldest son help that Lady Talia out of a tent. Heloise cringed at the apparent excess intimacy in their glances and touching. She felt her face turn down in a steady frown… her earlier tranquility now a distant memory.

How could he sleep with a stranger?

At that moment, a voice calling her name drew her attention away from her son and his lusty guest. "Lady Heloise?"

Heloise turned to face Alais. "Yes?" she asked as she smiled at the serving girl.

"I hope you do not mind, but I stopped the guards from taking down your tent. I placed water for washing in there for you."

"That is so very kind. Thank you. I haven't had a decent wash in some time."

Alais smiled, but instead of leaving, the servant remained standing. Heloise looked on as her ready grin became a frown and her eyes lowered.

Concerned, Heloise asked, "What is it?"

Alais raised her eyes and stared at a fixed point above Heloise's left shoulder.

Heloise turned around to look in the direction of Alais' stare and saw Reginald and Talia kissing in a most indiscreet manner. Heloise swore under her breath, concerned that the vassals would start gossiping about Reginald and his… woman.

"Mmmm, nothing my Lady," Alais stated before ducking away, but then Heloise's daughter arrived.

"Is it true?" Lirienne asked in a demanding voice.

Heloise turned to face Lirienne and asked, "Is what true?"

"What the vassals are saying," Lirienne began to explain. Her blue eyes revealed some annoyance. "They are saying Reginald is... enjoying some stranger... that woman we picked up outside of Prüm."

Heloise sighed. "Perhaps," she admitted.

"Mother, someone needs to investigate." Lirienne began to pace. "She's probably some common prostitute that stole someone's clothing and is passing herself off as the Lady of Époisses."

"I shall speak with Lady Talia," Heloise answered.

"Good," Lirienne mumbled. "If she's a liar, we will chase her out."

"And if she's a noble, we'll speak to her all the same," Heloise promised. She then noticed Dreu waving at her... or them. She could not tell, although she assumed Dreu signaled to advise her that she needed to complete her packing so they could leave, but she admitted that she could be mistaken.

Her daughter, however, seemed to know full well the audience of Dreu's gesture. "How exciting this is!" Lirienne's eyes seemed to flash as she watched the handsome captain of the garrison. "I'm going to go sit in the cart that Dreu will drive." Her daughter then practically skipped away.

Heloise rolled her eyes. "Youth," she muttered, before walking back into the tent to wash up so she could join the others and resume their journey home.

Sardica

Once Mandubratius awoke from his disturbing slumber, he began to feel the memories of a confusing dream fade, thankful that no nightmares haunted him. Soon, however, hunger tugged at him, but he felt too weak to feed himself.

He began to look around the room, in hope that someone stood by to attend him, and sure enough, his eyes settled upon a snoring Patroclus. "Patroclus," he whispered, not wanting to disturb the others.

The Legate moved a little, but he did not wake.

"Patroclus!" he said, louder, but the man still didn't budge. Mandubratius then leaned over, picked up a boot, and threw it at the other Lamia.

Immediately after the boot impacted with the Legate's chest, he sat up and stared at Mandubratius. "What?" the Legate blurted out before rubbing his eyes.

"Wake up."

Patroclus rose up to stand at attention. "Co-Consul, I'm sorry, I didn't realize I had fallen asleep and that it was you who had woken me."

Mandubratius waved away the excuse. "I forgive you this once. Now, I need some refreshment. Bring me some of that swill the innkeeper calls wine and a meal."

"Immediately, Co-Consul," Patroclus responded before walking to the door and stopping.

"Do you wish for me to get someone to watch over you while I'm gone?" Patroclus asked while staring back at him.

Mandubratius grumbled, "Don't be silly. I'm quite recovered from my encounter with the Strigoi. I have no need of a nursemaid."

"Very well, sir." Patroclus inclined his head in a nod and then left the room.

Mandubratius sighed as he leaned back in the bed, remembering the dream involving a harem of beautiful mortal women serving him wine. He could still sense the aroma of rose, jasmine, spiced wine, and almond oil. How he yearned to return to his blissful slumber... perhaps if he just closed his eyes...

At that moment, the door to the room opened and closed.

Thinking Patroclus had returned with wine and sustenance, Mandubratius started to push the dream away, yet the scent of wine remained. Once he managed to open his eyes, he saw the glint of metal as a dagger plunged into his chest. Pain shot through his body, causing him to convulse, jerking his legs around, and forcing his eyes closed. He could even feel blood flooding his lungs. Mandubratius almost wondered whether he might die, but it seemed whomever stabbed him did not want his head.

He knew who would do such a thing and tried to open his eyes to confirm his suspicions. "Máire, it's about time," he hissed.

"It's not Máire who stabbed that dagger into your chest, Sponsor," a youthful but still masculine voice informed him.

Mandubratius forced his eyes open and focused on the face... soon recognizing it as Horatio's. He could see hatred and some satisfaction in the boy's eyes. Still, Horatio did not hold the dagger.

What kind of nincompoop could he be?

Mandubratius uttered a breathy chuckle, before coughing out blood. "So, I'm your sponsor, Lamia." He could feel a grin light his face. "I must compliment Claudius for maintaining this ruse. Come now, child, do you really believe this pesky little dagger will kill me?" He started laughing as Horatio's eyes revealed confusion.

The youngling still thinks like a mortal.

Before Mandubratius could offer any further pithy observations, he heard the door open. He looked up, only to see Patroclus flinging his tray aside and drawing his spatha. Mandubratius then saw Claudius, Marcus, Mac Alpin, and Máire rush in after him.

"Stop!" Claudius shouted. "Put down your sword."

Mandubratius looked on as the Legate turned towards the other blood-drinkers before glancing at him. He then motioned for Patroclus to lower his sword.

As Arwin wrestled Horatio away from Mandubratius, he could hear Claudius shout, "Get him out of here."

"By Morrigan's Strength, we just finished healing you," Máire grumbled. He watched her turn towards the hallway and shout, "Fianait, get more bandages!" She then glanced around the room, before asking, "Who's fed?"

"I have," Patroclus answered, seemingly more calm than before. "I left him so I could feed."

"That's what I'll need you to do," Máire groaned, before sitting down across from him.

The loss of blood soon began to draw Mandubratius from the realm of consciousness. He felt his eyes droop as fatigue beckoned for him to plunge into near-death.

"First, I'll have to remove the dagger, and then I shall begin healing the wound," he heard Máire grouse.

Mandubratius felt the urge to reply that such a process would be obvious to anyone, but that dark pool of near-death pulled harder at his consciousness. Refusing to give in to the darkness, Mandubratius forced his eyes open and saw Máire staring down at him while holding a handful of bandages... what appeared to have been someone's spare tunic.

"Awvarwy," she whispered as she leaned closer. "This will hurt. Please don't struggle."

'Awvarwy' she called me. Ah...

"This will be a pain I'll enjoy, then, as you are inflicting it," he slurred. He then felt a shot of pain, as Máire pressed on his chest with one hand and ripped apart his tunic. Mandubratius uttered another raspy laugh. "You didn't plan this, did you? It's a most interesting way for us to become more intimate," he whispered, enjoying the anticipation of the excruciating pain to come.

She sighed. "You may feel as you wish... I do not care. We just need you to stay alive for the duration of this quest." A lovely and cruel smile lit her face. "Afterwards, I may decide to kill you with a dagger of my own." Without further preamble, Máire gripped the dagger with her left hand and then wrenched the blade out.

At that moment, blissful agony rushed through his body. Ever since Mandubratius had become a Lamia, experiencing a wound that would have killed a mortal always seemed to bring unmatched gratification. He would live, when others would have died. While he assumed his friends and enemies thought of his odd fascination with pain as a sign of madness, he derived pleasure from the knowledge that he would live.

From somewhere in his semiconscious mind, Mandubratius heard the blade land on the stone floor and skip across its hard surface. With the blade now removed, he could feel even more blood surge from his gaping wound, and the call of near-death resumed its siren call.

Despite his darkening awareness, he could feel Máire's hands upon his chest as she forced the wound together, and soon after, he began to feel her healing energy flow through him. He could almost see that energy coursing through him, mending his torn flesh.

Through his stupor, he heard voices on the verge of sounding coherent, but he could not distinguish words or speaker. Still, he managed to make out a feminine voice saying, "Patroclus, it's time." Mandubratius then felt Máire's hands move away, only to be replaced by another pair, and soon healing energy coursed through his body once more, causing what remained of his pain to drift away.

Mandubratius felt an arm slide under his neck and prop him, while another arm... this one bearing a bloodied wound... pressed against his mouth. The taste of blood caught his attention, and he began to feed. Each swallow of the pleasurable sweetness brought him closer to brightness. Mandubratius would not die this night.

Soon, he felt the arm pull away. While Mandubratius still felt weak, he began to feel more like himself. He blinked open his eyes and saw Patroclus cradling his arm.

So, you fed me, my friend. I thought I recognized the taste. I must remember to reward you in some obscure way.

"Thank you," Mandubratius whispered. He truly felt thankful for the offering, as well as for Máire's ministration.

"If you had not been weakened by the Strigoi attack, you would have been able to pluck the dagger yourself," he heard Máire grumble.

"Thank you again for your assistance," he said. Mandubratius then stared down at himself, at the freshly dried blood, which began to itch, and complained in the most authoritative tone he could drum up in his weakened state. "Isn't someone going to wash me?"

"At once, Co-Consul," Patroclus sounded off as he snapped to attention and swung his right arm across his chest and then into the air in salute. The Legate then marched out of the small room.

Always the soldier, that one.

Mandubratius felt his strength slowly return, though he still suffered from exhaustion. He considered propping himself up in bed, but he needed help. He scanned the room again, looking for someone else he could manipulate into helping him, when he noticed Claudius.

You! I shall have words with you.

He studied the others for a moment before addressing everyone in the room. "May I speak to Claudius... alone, please?" he heard himself squeak.

The ladies shared a glance before walking towards the door. On her way out, Máire offered him a strange half-grimace as she walked past Claudius.

Once the door closed behind them, Mandubratius stared at Claudius, who stared back. No one spoke for what seemed like a quarter-hour.

Finally, unable to take any more silence, Mandubratius blurted out, "Why didn't you tell me he was Lamia?"

Claudius took a seat on the stool and studied him for a moment, apparently judging him in silence. Finally, after some apparent deliberation, the Roman Sugnwr Gwaed answered him. "Marcus thought it best to continue to convince you that Horatio was of my line."

"For the success of the mission?"

"Yes. We believed that if you knew of Horatio's origins, you might decide to kill him, seeing as how he was the last survivor of the Lamia army you sent to Britannia."

"So, this is no ordinary child of mine," Mandubratius uttered in a dry chuckle. "How ironic that he attempted to kill me. Did you not suspect that he was going to attack me?"

"Horatio did express a desire to harm you, but he seemed too fearful to carry out the threats."

As Mandubratius ran a hand over his forehead, he considered how trustworthy his so-called 'allies' might really be, as well as what treatment he might expect once he retrieved the mirror. "Did you even think to warn me?"

"To warn you would have required us to tell you who he was. Marcus and the rest of us agreed that we should wait awhile," Claudius answered, before rubbing his hands together in apparent apprehension. "We all thought that after Marcus spoke with him, he would be fine and leave you be."

"I understand Marcus' desire for caution, but his judgment might have left his precious quest without a key asset... me!" Mandubratius leveled his stare at Claudius and waited for his reply, but none came swiftly. After waiting for a grueling few seconds, fatigue set in from his previous outburst, so Mandubratius sighed and relented. In a calmer voice, he asked, "So, what of the youngling? What punishment will he suffer?"

Claudius pursed his lips. "I'm certain Marcus and I will think of something equitable."

Mandubratius propped himself up on his elbows and looked at the dagger on the ground. "'Equitable' would be allowing me to drive that dagger into his chest," he hissed. "Do you think Marcus would allow that?" Based on what Mandubratius saw in the Roman Sugnwr Gwaed's eyes, he considered that Marcus and Claudius must have decided to make a pet of Horatio.

Claudius shifted his gaze to the dagger for a moment and then met Mandubratius' stare once again. "No."

"No matter," Mandubratius stated, with as little concern as he could muster, as he eased himself back down. "Whatever punishment Marcus selects, I'll accept, as long as I have a chance to talk to the boy."

Claudius' eyes glowed gold as he leaned forward. "Why?" he half-growled.

"I intend to teach him about what it means to be Lamia."

The Sugnwr Gwaed leaned back on the stool and said, "I don't think that's a good idea. Horatio may kill you next time."

Mandubratius smirked. "Now, give me some credit, Claudius. I'm as old as you, and much more used to assassination attempts." He witnessed Claudius masking his feelings.

Perhaps they are all sleeping together. Interesting.

Soon, however, Mandubratius began to feel exhaustion settle around him again. He could hear the harem girls begin to call and make sweet promises, as the room began to turn gray.

"I'm finished with you," he whispered to Claudius. "I wish to be alone, now. Please tell Patroclus to hurry with that water."

After closing his eyes, Mandubratius heard the warrior stand up.

"Good lad," he whispered, though unsure of whether he addressed Claudius or the eunuch that brought wine to the harem.

Horatio worried about his future, as Mac Alpin guided him towards a bench in the corner of the sparsely populated common room on the first story of the inn. The Ekimmu Cruitne then pushed Horatio onto the bench and sat down across from him.

Horatio looked into the elder's eyes for a moment, but he could not discern what Mac Alpin was thinking. He inhaled and lowered his eyes, wondering whether this blood-drinker would be his executioner. Horatio then glanced up to face Mac Alpin once again and met his eyes.

Perhaps he plans how to do the deed?

At that moment, loud noises echoed through the inn. Horatio noticed Claudius and Marcus walking down the small staircase from the upper level. While Marcus' eyes seemed unreadable, Claudius did not even meet Horatio's eyes, although the Roman's visage revealed guilt.

Mac Alpin scooted closer to the wall and then grabbed Horatio's shoulder, although Horatio felt he needed no prompting to move.

Claudius sat down next to Horatio, while Marcus sat next to Mac Alpin.

Horatio wondered whether they were to be the judges while Mac Alpin carried out the sentence.

During the silence that followed, one of the innkeeper's daughters began passing out mugs of wine.

Horatio felt his attention drift as he watched Marcus accept a mug and then take a long draw from it. However, an elbow in the side refocused his attention on Claudius, who motioned towards the wine. As Horatio reached for his mug, he noticed that all three blood-drinkers remained silent. He then took a sip, puckering his lips at the sour taste of undiluted wine, and wondered whether he needed to beg for his life.

No. These men are battle-hardened warriors who would not have pity on the likes of me.

When Marcus put down his mug, Horatio thought he would begin to speak, but instead, Marcus exchanged glances with Arwin and Claudius. Something seemed to pass between the three men. Then, Marcus' eyes turned hard as he looked at Horatio, who lowered his eyes in dread.

"What you did," Marcus began to say, but his words hung in mid-air, perhaps to frighten Horatio, who expected to hear a grave sentence, "we would have all loved to do what you did."

Horatio looked up in shock into Marcus' eyes.

"You know his character, even though you've barely known him." Marcus then motioned to his associates. "We've known him much longer. He led an invasion against the Deargh Du and he's done much to harm our lines and... our Banbh Ceanúil."

"Who?" Horatio blurted.

"Máire," Marcus answered. "She's our piglet."

Such an odd nickname for such a strange woman.

Claudius started chuckling into his hand and began to snort, although Horatio thought the display rather contrived.

"Our impressions of her giggling and snorting aren't the best," Arwin admitted.

Horatio began to realize that they didn't plan on executing him for his crimes.

Marcus interrupted Horatio's musing by making a show of peering into Horatio's full mug. "If you don't like the way we order wine, we can ask the innkeeper to warm and spice it for you."

While Horatio desired to agree, he decided it would be better to join them in drinking undiluted wine. "No, I want to keep drinking this," he said. He then tried to remember what Marcus had said about Mandubratius. "What did he do?" he asked while pointing to the ceiling.

"Various misdeeds," Marcus began to explain. "There is much he's done, yet surely now you know how important he is to our finding this mirror. You realize the lives of blood-drinkers, as well as mortals, depend on finding this mirror."

Horatio felt a growing guilt gnaw at him. "I've been selfish," he admitted. "My desire for revenge overtook my reason."

Arwin barked a loud laugh. "That's the story of my life, Horatio, revenge before reason."

Marcus leaned forward. "We're talking about Horatio, not you. I must admit to some curiosity, though, about this tale of vengeance."

"Ask me again when I'm drunk," Mac Alpin replied dismissively, before taking another draught of wine.

Marcus then turned his attention back to Horatio. "Were you a soldier in my legion, I would have had you crucified."

"Mark his words," Mac Alpin deadpanned, before laughing into his hand. "He's done it before."

"Yes, he did it to Mandubratius," Claudius chimed in before joining in the laughter.

Horatio watched them laugh but felt too frightened to say anything or join in. He lowered his eyes, unable to understand the source of their mirth.

"No, I didn't crucify him. We merely nailed him to a tree," Marcus said with a smirk. "I thought he had betrayed our cohort." The Deargh Du's eyes began to gleam.

"How long ago was that?" Horatio half-whispered.

"About," Marcus said, before closing his eyes, "eight hundred and fifty years, I think. I... and he... were still mortal, then." He then opened his eyes and stared at Mac Alpin.

"Younglings still, the two of you," Mac Alpin grumbled.

"We digress," Marcus drawled before propping up his bare feet onto the opposite bench. "There still needs to be some punishment meted against you, Horatio." The Deargh Du then looked over at Claudius and said, "You've been quiet, lieutenant. How should we punish him?"

Horatio chugged down the rest of his wine and placed his empty mug on the bench next to him.

"Well, it's not like we can put him on kitchen or latrine duty. However, boot polishing comes to mind, everyone's boots except for you, of course, since Julien is still polishing them," Claudius answered. A smirk showed prominently on his face.

"I'm not sure whether Mandubratius would approve of such a punishment.

After all, it's not much of one," Marcus suggested, before chuckling.

"Since when have you cared about his approval?" Arwin asked.

"In the interests of smoothing over this difficulty, I'm willing to take his approval into consideration." Marcus then wiggled his feet about and stared at them. "If he disagrees, we'll reconsider."

"Next time you try to kill him, take off his head," Arwin whispered as he leaned in. "Anything else is just a wound that will heal."

"Also, you should make sure we don't need him," Claudius added. Horatio looked on as the Sugnwr Gwaed prepared to pull off his left boot, but he stopped when Máire raced towards them.

"What's wrong?" Marcus asked as he stood up.

"Amata's awake," Máire answered with a half-smile.

Máire spun around and headed up the stairs, while Marcus, Mac Alpin, and Claudius followed.

As Horatio watched the others race away, he wondered whether they would change their minds and decide to crucify him.

Running and loud talking, in what Julien assumed to be Gaelic, echoed through the hallway, distracting him from his work. Julien stared down at the boots for a moment, trying to remember where he had left off, and then returned to his duties.

Soon after, a knock at the door drew his attention. Julien sensed a Lamia behind the wood, whom he assumed to be Horatio, and decided to grant his entry. "Come in."

The door opened, and Horatio peeked inside the room. "May I join you?"

Julien nodded. "Please do so."

Horatio crept into the room and then closed the door with great care. He leaned against the near wall and began to slide down into a sitting position. Horatio appeared to be ill at ease, as if a great deal of weight rested on his shoulders.

"What's wrong?" Julien asked.

Horatio said nothing at first... he just stared at his hands.

Julien considered pushing Horatio for answers, but he decided to wait.

After a few moments, Horatio finally spoke. "I tried to kill Mandubratius, but I failed."

In astonishment, Julien dropped Marcus' boot.

How much I would love to punish that man for calling me 'puppy' all of the time! But try to kill him?

"You look surprised," Horatio said.

Julien considered Horatio's comment. "You tried to kill Mandubratius," he repeated, unsure he heard Horatio correctly.

"I now know that he's the one who... sponsored me. So, I went into his room when Patroclus was gone and stabbed him in the heart with a dagger." Horatio rubbed his brow.

"You stabbed him?!"

"Yes." Horatio stared down at the dirty floor beneath them. "I thought it would kill him. I was very surprised when he just kept talking and laughing at me."

Julien nodded his head. "Apparently, we can only meet death in the sunlight or when someone takes our head."

"Arwin Mac Alpin told me that... after I had done the deed." Horatio smirked.

"I suppose you didn't consider our quest," Julien observed, as he scanned the boot, only to find another smudge.

"I've been dressed down by Marcus, Mac Alpin, and Claudius, although mostly by Marcus! I don't need you to tell me what I did was wrong." After a few moments of apparent introspection, Horatio added, "They are most confusing, are they not?" He lowered his head. "I don't understand their jokes. Half of me feels amused, while the other half thinks they're going to kill me. I feel like I was traveling between an acting troupe performing comedy on stage and an executioner performing an execution at the gallows. In both situations, everyone is laughing but me!"

"We've spoken of this before," Julien said, "and I agree, it is most confusing. However, they are old and strange. We must learn to understand them, because they aren't going to change for us."

"But the mortals we've encountered here see them as barbaric, and the women in our party are seen as little more than whores," Horatio whispered, before looking around, seemingly fearful for voicing his opinions. "You have seen the innkeeper and his family avoid us all as much as possible. Julien, we are monsters." Horatio shuddered. "Then, there is that undiluted wine."

Julien set down the boot and smiled. "Yes, it is most vile, isn't it, but have you tried their mead?" He felt himself shudder.

"No," Horatio said, while shaking his head. "What is it?"

"It–"

At that moment, the door flung open, interrupting what he was about to say, and Julien found himself agreeing with the idea that the elder blood-drinkers were most uncivilized.

"Julien and Horatio," Máire announced as she walked into the small room. She then leaned up against the wall near Horatio and sank into a sitting position, nearly mirroring Horatio's earlier movements. After pulling her knees up, Máire wrapped her arms around them and clasped her legs.

Julien thought that she appeared to be a little pale. Perhaps she fed or healed Amata.

She stared at Horatio and smirked. "Thanks to you, I had to heal the leech again," she drawled.

"Is he well?" Horatio's voice revealed some possible confusion about who the leech could be.

"Mandubratius will be fine to travel tomorrow evening," Máire stated, "and Amata is also healing nicely."

Julien inhaled, in shock at the news. "She's awake?" He felt a little guilt for wanting to leave Amata behind.

Máire's eyes settled on his and became bright green, revealing her nature. "Yes, she is," she said. "Amata was angry that you wished to leave her behind."

"You told her?" Julien could hear his voice waver, and he felt his face fall.

Máire's grave face suddenly erupted into a smile, and she began to chuckle, which seemed quite inappropriate to Julien. "No, Julien. I just wanted to see that look on your face. I didn't tell Amata anything." Her chuckling continued for a few moments.

Horatio grumbled to himself before facing Máire. "This is what Julien and I were speaking of earlier!" he bellowed. "Why would you do that?"

Máire's smile faded. "It was just a joke, Horatio. In this life, we must all find some amusement. Life is far too long to spend it as a monk." The smile soon returned to her face.

Julien resumed studying the floor and contemplated the lesson at hand. "I hope someday I will understand what you are saying," he informed her.

"I hope so, too," she answered. She then turned her eyes towards Horatio, and her gaze became soft and gentle. "Horatio, I need to speak to Julien. I know there is not much privacy here, but I desire it. May I impose upon you?"

Horatio nodded and then arose. "Perhaps they do adapt," he said to Julien. He looked over at Máire again before leaving the room.

Once the door closed behind Horatio, Máire repositioned herself by scooting in closer to him. She rolled onto her knees and placed her hands on her thighs and her rear end between her feet. She studied him for a moment in a disconcerting manner.

Julien wondered whether she planned to hit him again.

Then, in a sudden movement, her hands sought his face, and she raised herself on her knees, pulling him in for an aggressive and passionate kiss. She must have felt his shock, for she drew her hands away and eased her lower body to the floor.

"I am so sorry for my treatment of you this morning and for the past few nights," she whispered. Máire blinked, as if she were trying not to cry, and she seemed to bite her lip. "I am too judgmental, and you and Horatio are right. We know little about Frankish customs or behavior. Please forgive me." Máire then ducked her eyes.

Julien watched as her curls and plaits of hair shielded Máire's face from his sight. He extended his right hand and stroked back her hair, revealing her beautiful, full face. "I forgive you." He smiled and watched her eyes light up.

"Thank you," she murmured, before embracing and kissing him again.

Molten pleasure grew as he felt her mouth trace over his throat. They began tossing aside clothing. Warmth pooled within as she surrounded him. Julien inhaled, wanting to taste her. He then pushed aside the thick curls of her hair and began to feed from her. All thought and sensation faded into budding bliss as vitae trickled down his throat.

After counting everyone who had assembled downstairs to depart, Marcus realized that Máire was not among them, but he could still sense her in the building… upstairs. He clomped up the stairs, jogged to her room, and peaked through the open door. Before him sat Máire… packing. Marcus crept up to her, leaned over her shoulder, and teased, "You are one of the worst packers I've ever commanded." He fixed a smirk on his face upon seeing how she rolled everything into tight balls.

In response, she looked up at him and raised her right brow. "I don't tend to fold when there is a time limit," she admitted.

He nodded. In contrast to the rest of the group, Máire smelled wonderful, like a gathering of lavender and other flowers, but then he detected trace scents of something familiar.

Ah… the aroma of coitus.

"You overslept too," he said, after deciding not to tease her too much about her encounter with Julien, whose subtle scents he detected, despite Máire's efforts to mask her bodily odors with oils.

She shrugged. "The strain from healing these last few nights has not been easy to bear, for any of us. Not to mention that there is a lack of suitable food."

Marcus placed his hands on her shoulders and rubbed for a moment. "I know. Thank you for doing all you did. When you're ready, come meet us downstairs." After turning to leave, he noticed Arwin standing in the hallway, so Marcus joined him, and then the two men started walking down the hall.

"The innkeeper demands more money," the Ekimmu Cruitne groaned as he scratched his beard.

"Did you and Claudius speak to him?" Marcus asked before reflecting to himself that Claudius usually handled this sort of thing through his own gifts.

"Yes, but the innkeeper is quite stubborn. Our attempts did not succeed."

"So, Claudius was insistent?" he inquired.

"Not in that way," Mac Alpin replied. "He doesn't want to waste his strength. The food, and healing–"

Marcus held up his right hand. "I know, Arwin. I agree… it's a strain. I can understand any reluctance. I shall deal with the innkeeper." Before going down the stairs, Marcus pulled out a purse and tested the weight in his hand. Once he reached the ground floor, he could see the innkeeper standing by some barrels, looking quite perturbed.

"My friend says we owe you more money," Marcus challenged.

"Yes," the innkeeper uttered in a snarl. "First, you and your friends drank all my stock because of your insistence on undiluted wine–"

"And we paid extra," Marcus commented, cutting off the innkeeper.

"Second, one of your friends bled all over the bedding and floor! It smells wretched in there. It dripped into our quarters below, which now need repair."

Marcus closed his eyes, conceding that the man made a point. "How much for the cleaning?" he uttered through clenched teeth.

"Twenty sou," the innkeeper barked.

Marcus began emptying his purse and counting out the money, but he paused when the innkeeper opened his mouth to speak.

"One more thing," the innkeeper uttered.

"What?" Marcus attempted to curb his growing annoyance.

"One of your companions has been at my daughter. She tells me that she has morning pains."

Marcus looked up and stared at the innkeeper before pulling the money back into his purse.

"You just lied to me. If your daughter has pains now, someone else had coitus with her before we arrived. For your dishonesty, I'm keeping this money." He turned away, intending to leave, but out of the corner of his eye, he witnessed the innkeeper grab a large knife. Before he could do anything stupid, Marcus fixed him with a glare and allowed his glamoury to increase.

"You're pleased with the compensation we've given you," he snarled. "You won't cheat anyone else." Marcus inhaled, closed his eyes, and tried to push back desires that the Strigoi must have inserted into his brain somehow. His inclinations and thoughts wavered from strange dreams to unfamiliar opinions. After managing to suppress these dark musing, Marcus opened his eyes and saw his reflection through the eyes of the innkeeper.

The innkeeper appeared confused and frightened. "Yes, I am satisfied, and I won't cheat," he groveled, before backing away.

Marcus departed the presence of the beguiled mortal and headed outside.

He then approached the contingent of Lamia. "Are you all well?" he asked the two Lamia Co-Consuls.

"We're quite well," Mandubratius answered, with what seemed to be a genuine smile. "Thank you for asking."

Marcus closed his eyes again, concluding that dealing with Mandubratius would be a bit much tonight. After opening them again, he fixed his gaze on the gathered Lamia. "To avoid the Strigoi, we'll have to travel high off the ground, above the clouds. It will be very cold, so I suggest you all wear cloaks, if you don't enjoy the bitter, freezing cold."

He heard a grumble from Amata, who began unpacking extra clothing.

Mandubratius smiled, radiating joy. "I'm certain we'll manage just fine. Now, who will carry us?"

I certainly will not!

"We'll take turns carrying the four of you," Marcus answered before walking over to where the Celtic lines had gathered. "Get in two lines and count off to four. The one's are responsible for Horatio, two's will shift carrying Patroclus, three's, you are in charge of Amata, and four's will convey Mandubratius. We'll change shifts halfway. I'll assist when needed. Let's go."

Marcus hoped this leg of the journey would offer little, in terms of surprises.

The Wilderness between Mettis and Noviomagus

Reginald shook Talia for a moment, trying to rouse her, but instead of waking, she uttered a few garbled words, pulled the blankets over herself, and resumed snoring. He then stepped out of the tent and began looking around the camp. He observed that many people packed, while many others cooked over fires. His daughter soon came into view, racing around with some of the other children and a few soldiers from the garrison, including the new captain. His mother, however, did not seem to be present… nor was his sister.

As usual, his mother ignored him, and he found himself once again confused by her actions.

After watching the children and soldiers at play, Reginald noticed one of his mother's servants watching over the packing of provisions. He walked up to her and, hoping he remembered her name, he asked, "Alais? Have you seen my mother?"

"Yes, my Lord," she said after lowering her head. "She and your sister went to pray at the shrine."

Reginald felt immediate doubts about his mother praying for anything… at least in an appropriate manner. However, he felt it best, at this point, to pretend that this would not be out of the ordinary.

"I see," he answered. "Where is the shrine?"

"The Shrine of the Sacred Heart," Alais answered while gesturing to the east. "Actually, they seemed to head that way," she added, while pointing to the north. "I think they said something about picking berries for the children."

"I see," Reginald answered while trying to keep overtones of disappointment from coloring his tone. He then headed north.

A mile later, he stopped, upon seeing two figures a short distance away beginning to bow to the setting sun.

"Mother," Reginald called out before waving his right hand, catching her and Lirienne's attention. Instead of shouting his displeasure to the forest, he walked over to the two women. "You know I'm not comfortable with this delving into the dark arts! Do you want someone to see you?" He looked around, hoping no one witnessed this atrocity.

His mother rose up and said, "Reginald, what you do is most disrespectful." Her frown, combined with her old visage, became most frightening. Even Lirienne's annoyance seemed to color her appearance.

Nevertheless, the time for this foolishness will end here and now.

"It's my right to interrupt when I witness my mother and sister prostrating themselves to the setting sun, as if it were a God!" Reginald called out.

"Is there a purpose to this interruption, elder son?" his mother asked as she dusted off her hands.

"Yes, there is. I wanted to make sure you weren't making a fool of your family by practicing witchcraft, yet I now see my concerns were well-founded."

Resignation colored her face. "Why is this always such an issue with you?" she asked.

"We have guests and strangers in our party," he answered in a heated tone. "I don't want the vassals to gossip about the Lady of Vézelay's dark deeds!"

His mother turned to Lirienne and said, "Go back to the camp and make sure all is prepared for our journey."

Lirienne nodded and then left.

With his sister gone, Reginald prepared for one of his mother's tirades.

"Guests?" His mother's face soured, graced with a slight smile. She appeared as though she had finished eating a lemon. "There is only one guest you refer to, is that not correct?"

"Yes, we are speaking of one guest," Reginald sputtered. "I don't want her to feel that my family and I are tainted. She is our neighbor."

"You're trying to impress a woman who you picked up off the road. You have no idea who she is," his mother replied. Her face reddened as she spoke.

"She is Lady Talia of Époisses!"

"We've never met Lady Talia," his mother answered with a sneer. "That woman," she accused as she pointed towards the south, "could be an imposter!"

Reginald felt his outwardly calm demeanor melt away with his anger. "I believe her to be honest," he argued.

His mother wrung her hands. "Even if that were so, why would she be abandoned at an abbey in such a state? She smelled of rank coitus."

Reginald felt his mouth open in shock that his mother would utter such language in front of him. "Soldiers accosted her."

"At least... according to her tale," his mother retorted in a calmer tone.

"Are you suggesting Lady Talia lies?"

Heloise uttered an annoyed grunt. "Must we speak in circles, Reginald?"

Reginald threw up his hands in angry frustration. "I'm not the one speaking in circles! I'm here to tell you to cease this dark magic. I don't wish to debate about our guest."

Heloise lowered her voice, and in an even tone, she uttered, "My concern is not so much whether she's Lady Talia as she claims. My worry is that your wife and sons have yet to be buried, and you're already fornicating with a woman you just met. Not to mention that you've been seen. I do not wish our family more misfortune as a result of your dalliances."

Reginald felt redness overwhelm him. "You speak of dalliances as if this family has never engaged in covert sexual relations."

He felt satisfaction upon witnessing the shock in her eyes after voicing his accusation. Reginald knew he had touched on a secret of hers. "As a young boy, I saw you come home late many nights, after father died. When you would come in to kiss me and Aldabert, I pretended to sleep, and most of the time, I would hear a man's voice... a voice I had never heard before."

His mother's eyes turned cold blue. "I believe you were dreaming, Reginald." Her words revealed her own rekindling rage.

Reginald could not help the humorless snort that uttered from his throat. "Then, mother, I believe that what you witnessed earlier was also nothing more than a dream."

She glanced at the starlit sky and back at him. In a calm, officious voice, she said, "Everyone should be assembled by now. You must not keep the vassals and garrison waiting."

Reginald turned away, tired of this fight, but happy he was able to draw the last wound. "Yes, I mustn't keep them waiting." Reginald started walking away, basking in his victory, but soon his nerves tingled ice-cold upon hearing footfalls approaching. His mother followed. Reginald stopped, letting her catch up, and prepared for another volley, though he did not look at her.

"Mark me, Reginald. This woman will bring misery to our family, if you continue your dalliance with her."

"That's your opinion, mother," Reginald spat before walking faster.

chapter six

Outside Philipopolis

áire sighed. Once again, Marcus had stuck her with carting Mandubratius about. Julien had left after a few hours of dealing with that bastard Briton, so now she remained to carry him.

Damn Marcus for assigning me to this spot!

Suddenly, she felt unbalanced, which broke her concentration. She and her ballast began to fall, but Máire managed to reassert her focus on her flying. She then turned her head to her left and demanded, "Why are you wiggling?" Out of the corner of her eye, she could see him turn his head a little to stare into her face. "Do you wish us to fall to the ground?" she prodded, before chiding herself for asking such an idiotic question. She should simply drop him.

"I just wished to talk to you."

"Can it wait until we land?" she asked him, daring to peek into his large, green eyes. She hated to admit it, but sometimes she could not ignore his arresting eyes. His long eyelashes seemed rather odd to see on a man, but they made his eyes appear larger.

"No, it cannot," Mandubratius purred in a manner befitting a cat.

"Alright then, what is it?" Máire sighed, preparing for the worst. Would he grab her breasts, drone on about his disappointment in their quest so far, or pine after the beauty of the night sky? Who could possibly know?

"Why do you dislike me?"

She wondered whether she misheard that question. After all, he whined, managing to resemble a pouting child.

Men and their pouting could be so annoying.

"What was that?" she asked. Maybe she had not heard him correctly.

She could feel him stretch his hairless chin closer to her right ear. "You and I would be perfect together," he whispered. "We would be the very best of lovers, Máire. You know it, and so do I."

Máire felt as if a dagger of ice penetrated her abdomen. "Perhaps I need to restate the many reasons why I do not like you, Mandubratius," she replied. "You killed Seanán and my uncle Cennedi, you were responsible for the death of my uncle Fergus, and you have tried to kill me."

"Those were merely misunderstandings," he answered. "I am truly enamored with you. Please do not be so cruel with my heart, Maél Muire."

"Ha!" she cried out, with as much derision as she could muster. "The only reason why you might possibly feel that way, Mandubratius, is because you have not had me. If you had approached me in a manly fashion, you probably would have found me to be most dull." After a brief pause, she added, "And my name is 'Máire' now... has been for over two-hundred-and-seventy years!"

She felt him tilt his head a bit to rest on her right shoulder. He then cooed in her ear. "Since you have not had me, you do not know how well I can make you forget our past oversights and transgressions."

Máire shook her shoulder in distaste, hopefully communicating to him that one more slight would leave him plummeting. "Believe me when I tell you that any physical contact from you is not pleasurable. If you try anything, the only pleasure you will receive is... the wind as it plays with your hair before you hit the ground."

"Mmmm," he murmured. "I will take that risk. We both know you would not hurt me. You just cannot admit that you want me, because it is just so naughty... something the honorable Máire would never do."

Surprise and shock gripped her all of a sudden, when she felt a hand cup her, then several hands.

How many hands did Mandubratius have?

A burning rage grew within, so she rolled over, forcing him away. Her ears heard sweet music, as the masculine calls of her name diminished with the increasing distance between her and that man. Suddenly, Máire felt a strange force against her body grow, and then the foreign reality disappeared.

Máire awoke, upon realizing that someone lay on top of her. Before she could think over her actions, she drew a small dagger and rested its point against Mandubratius' jugular. "You are not invited to my dreams," she hissed. Of course, the thought of plunging her dagger into his throat would give her some satisfaction, but the act would also leave her messy... and then who but Máire would have to heal that bastard... again.

It is not worth it.

Instead of thrusting the point home, she pulled the knife away from his throat and shoved him off with her free hand. Máire chided herself for forgetting warnings about how the Lamia could slip into the dreams of those in close proximity to them.

"I was not up to mischief," he hissed back, before rising. "I just wanted to thank you for taking care of me again and to offer you my unending love and affection." A twist of a smile played upon his face as he slinked towards his empty bedding.

"Love and affection are the furthest things from your mind and body," Máire replied. "Behave yourself. Besides, I don't want any cause to injure you further, because Marcus would be sure to make me heal you... yet again."

"I will attempt to behave myself and not earn further injury, even though you wound me with such accusations."

What were once snores of contented sleep coming from the gathered blood-drinkers sharing the tent became snorts of laughter and ridicule. Máire could hear the others in the next tent toss and turn at the noise, at a time when the heat of the midday sun still warmed the tent.

Mandubratius rose slightly and then faced her, fixing his eyes on hers and drawing her in. "You and your sponsor should try the redemptive powers of forgiveness. Then again, this behavior of yours makes it very difficult to ignore you. Sleep well, my love." He grinned before curling up in his blankets.

Máire sighed and turned away, hoping her dreams would lapse into the same boring tales and soft warnings about the Strigoi as they did most nights. She closed her eyes, willing her confusion to dissipate like morning mist.

Vézelay

As Caoimhín flew in the layered formation high in the sky, he scanned the grounds below for the Strigoi. After what seemed like an hour, he heard Cathair Mac Domhnaill whistle to him, and so Caoimhín turned in order to join the outlying Ekimmu Cruitne.

"I think we're closing in on Vézelay," Cathair informed him as soon as Caoimhín drew close enough. "I smell livestock and wild animals, but no people other than…" he inhaled, "… a few corpses. There," he added, while pointing. "That looks like a village and what remains of a garrison."

"I'm taking half of the party to scout the grounds," Caoimhín said. "Please keep the rest above on watch." The Ekimmu Cruitne nodded, before calling out orders to the rest of the party.

Caoimhín landed outside of the ruinous garrison and scanned the burnt building, revealing few bodies of mortal soldiers, which lay at rest, clad in the colors of the Pope.

"I see Edward still plays with incendiary devices," he commented to Maon.

The other Deargh Du shook his head and offered a mirthless chuckle. "We should be happy he did not burn down the rest of the village, then," Maon replied.

Cathair landed close by. "We have found no Strigoi about, Caoimhín."

"Very well. Have the de-facto leader of the Sugnwr Gwaed and the rest of the personal teams meet us in that large dwelling in the distance. It must be the home of Lady Heloise. We'll devise teams to scan the buildings for materials to take to Divio."

As he walked towards the house, a number of warriors followed him. After trekking along the stone-laid path to the home of Lady Heloise, Caoimhín stepped through the doors and began a cursory search through the building.

"Sir," Maon called, upon exiting one of the rooms to the west. "I found a basement downstairs with beds."

"You mean cots, correct?"

"No. Two or three proper beds, and yes, there are many cots."

"I'll have to see this for myself," Caoimhín said before marching to the basement. "We'll draw lots for who stays here while we're in town, provided the Ekimmu Cruitne do not manipulate the results," he chuckled.

Cathair joined him downstairs. "I can make no promises on that," he replied before laughing. "Come back upstairs. We've gathered reports."

As Caoimhín followed him upstairs, he heard Maon follow behind him.

"How many bodies?" he asked Cathair.

"Eleven vassals and twenty-four papal soldiers," Cathair answered.

"It seems we first must bury the dead." He turned to one of the Sugnwr Gwaed. "Please take a party of fifty for a burial detail. Place a personal item at each site so we can mark who is there. If possible, bury them in the cemetery near the church." He then faced the rest of the party that joined him. "Now, what manners of building supplies are here that we can deliver to Divio?"

"We have lumber, rope, tar, nails, carpenter's tools, hay, thatching, and livestock, as well as several wagons and carts in supply," Cathair replied.

"How about food and water?" Sáerlaith asked.

Caoimhín felt some shock upon hearing her speak.

"I found the village storehouse," an Ekimmu Cruitne spoke, upon joining Caoimhín and the others. "There are grains, salted meat, and fruit within, as well as stored drinking water and wine."

"Excellent. While the burial detail is engaged, the rest of us will fan out and bring together the livestock and the carts," Caoimhín said before pausing, considering the next task. "We'll haul the supplies tomorrow night."

The gathered blood-drinkers parted and began attending to their assigned duties, leaving Sáerlaith and him behind.

Caoimhín then turned to Sáerlaith and said, "Thank you for joining us. Does this mean you are taking back the position of leadership?" He met Sáerlaith's dark eyes.

"No," she answered. "I just didn't want to shirk my duties."

"I understand," Caoimhín replied, although he wished she would snap out of her malaise and resume leadership of the Deargh Du.

"I wish to be alone, Caoimhín. Why don't you join the burial detail? You can aid them in sending the souls home."

"Where will you go?" he asked, concerned about her wellbeing.

"I'll be in the gardens and the grove of this house. They look very pleasant,"

Sáerlaith answered.

"There is a grove?" He felt some surprise at that, given how Christians erected churches on top of groves or just destroyed those sacred places entirely.

"Yes. You should see it before sunrise." Sáerlaith offered him a sad smile and then walked out of the house.

The Wilderness between Noviomagus and Divio

Talia closed her eyes for a moment in an effort to continue feigning sleep, which seemed unnatural at night, yet everyone in the cart slept, except for herself and Reginald's child. After a second of contemplation, she corrected herself, remembering that Reginald drove the cart.

Talia resumed her musing concerning her present circumstances. While Reginald's mother seemed more polite to her, Talia often found his mother's piercing gaze settle upon her, as if she suspected something but held her tongue. Not long after attempting to discern Heloise's motives, the child interrupted her thoughts again, while playing with a cloth doll. Talia frowned, finding the entire game a little annoying. She couldn't think, for all of the chatter.

The cart jostled again, and Reginald's mother, sister, and their serving girl shifted in sleep, but they continued snoring.

Reginald's daughter seemed to notice that Talia watched her and smiled. Her entire face blossomed in that smile. The little girl then held the doll towards Talia. "Do you want to play with me?" the little runt asked.

Talia stared down at the young cretin and mused about how delicious the young could be. However, she managed to ignore her instincts to feast from the urchin and instead studied her. Talia began to notice how this child didn't seem to resemble Reginald. In fact, the little runt appeared to favor her uncle.

Could this be Julien's spawn?

As Talia scrutinized the girl, the brightness in the child's eyes began to fade. Talia realized she needed to act if she wanted to confirm her suspicions.

"Yes, I would like to play. Is she for me?" she asked the mortal child, while tracing her right index finger over the doll.

"She's mine," the child uttered in soft reply, "but you can play with her."

Talia smiled. "Oh, I understand. You wish to lend her to me for now. Don't worry. I shall return her."

An idea came to her mind about how to discover more about Reginald's family. She could even use this child to deflect the suspicions of his family.

Talia held up the doll and said, "Hello," speaking for it in what she hoped sounded like a funny, childish voice. "I'm Lady Talia. What is your name?"

"I'm Clotilda of Divio," the girl answered, "but everyone calls me Tildy."

"Mmmm, what should I call you?" she asked, beaming at the girl. Talia had not even used manipulation yet.

"I don't like 'Tildy'," the mortal muttered, before pushing back her hair. "I want to be called 'Clotilda'."

Talia leaned forward. "'Clotilda' is a beautiful name," she purred. "Did you know that Clotilda was a Burgundian princess? She is the ancestor of Emperor Charles. It's a very special name," she added, smiling at the girl.

Wonder sparkled in Clotilda's eyes. "My mother never told me that! Mother is with the angels now." Sadness seemed to darken Clotilda's face. Her smile faded, and the mortal child bit her lower lip.

Talia saw a tiny tear escape the corner of Clotilda's right eye. The older woman leaned in and brushed away the tear. "My mother died, too," she whispered. "I'm truly sorry."

Clotilda swallowed and nodded her head. "I still have my papa, though," she said with a sad smile. "Do you?"

Talia closed her eyes, thinking over her last memory of her father. He had kissed Talia, put her in the cart with her cousins, and rejoined her grandfather in defending their keep against those vile Franks. The memory of seeing him die caused tears to well up in her eyes, despite the centuries, and a bitter taste rose in her throat. As Talia swallowed her bile, she stared at Clotilda and wished to smash her teeth for bringing back that recollection.

"No," Talia answered in a soft tone, after regaining her control. "My papa walks with the angels, too."

Clotilda leapt into her arms and hugged her. "I'm sorry that you lost them both," the mortal whispered.

Talia patted Clotilda's back and then held up the doll, hoping this would distract the child. "So, do you want to play?" she asked the child.

"Yes," Clotilda chirped, before moving to her knees, revealing a gleaming smile again. "But, we must be quiet."

Talia made the doll bow to Clotilda. "I know your name," she squeaked in a voice for the doll. "What is mine?"

Clotilda giggled. "Your name is Máire, like the Fire Queen."

Talia felt her face tighten in a grimace. This would be a very long night.

Outside Philipopolis

As Edward watched Amata dress herself, he felt his longing for intimacy increase. He sighed, wishing for more time to spend with her, but the sunlight faded, harkening their departure from this place... and they still had to pack.

After pulling her trousers over her feet, Amata turned towards Edward and said, "I do believe it's time for you to rise from our bed and get dressed." She chuckled, and then a wistful smile played about her face. "I don't think you want Marcus yelling at you for slowing down our party."

Edward sat up in his bedding and leaned towards her in as seductive a manner as he could muster. "We have plenty of time," he murmured, before caressing the fingers of his right hand down her bare spine, towards her lower cleft. "Why are you in such a rush to leave me?"

"Oh, Mandubratius told me that he wanted my assistance to speak with Horatio. He thinks a gentle voice will keep the boy's ears."

Amata faced away from him and pulled up her trousers.

Before Amata could reach for her tunic, Edward scooted behind her, with his legs to either side of her, cupped her breasts from behind, and then nudged his erection against her backside, hoping she would moisten herself and slide backwards. "Are you certain that you are needed so soon?" he asked. He then leaned in and kissed her throat and right cheek.

Amata contorted her body around to her right and placed her left hand on the side of his right cheek. "Edward, I'd love to, but I cannot. Mandubratius can be as demanding as Marcus... or your sponsor."

Realizing he would not experience coitus before leaving his bedding, Edward felt his erection fade. He then stood up, stepped back from his lover, and tried to smile. "Perhaps, when it's my turn to carry you, we can send off my partner and spend some time together." He then kissed Amata again.

"In the sky?" Amata gasped in disbelief "That sounds dangerous."

Edward grinned. "But it would be exciting and add to the experience."

"We shall see," Amata answered, though her voice seemed to express doubt. She then kissed him a final time before leaving the tent.

Edward resumed packing, but after a few moments, he heard the tent flap rise again. He hoped Amata had returned to him, but when he turned to face the tent's opening, he saw Mac Alpin and Claudius enter. Both men, he saw, knelt down and began packing their own supplies. Neither blood-drinker spoke to Edward.

Soon, a muffled conversation outside of the tent drew his attention away from his father-in-darkness and Claudius. Edward strained his hearing, but managed to recognize Marcus and Máire talking loudly in the distance.

"I don't care! I'm not going to carry the leech," Máire stated.

"Everyone has to participate, Máire. If fate selects you, then you must. Fate chooses tonight... not I."

Not again.

Edward tried to focus on anything other than this conversation, but something within him just had to listen to another argument between Máire and Marcus.

"You can assign another group to that duty," Máire replied. Edward could sense the venom in her tone, even from this distance.

"I can't make an exception," Marcus stated.

"But–"

"That is how it must be," Marcus uttered in apparent frustration. "Perhaps you should finish packing."

A grunt from his father-in-darkness drew Edward's attention back to his own duties. He knelt beside his supplies and once again resumed packing.

"Mmmm, did your woman leave already?" Mac Alpin asked as he patted Edward's shoulder from behind.

Edward felt lonely and bitter at the reminder. "Yes," he answered in a heated tone. "She went to speak to Horatio with Mandubratius." He attempted to cover his feelings of jealousy, since the Celtic lines believed such emotions to be a waste of energy.

At that moment, the tent flap opened again, and in walked a disgruntled Máire, followed closely by Marcus.

"Is that such a good idea?" Máire asked.

"If anyone can placate Mandubratius, it's Amata," Marcus replied.

"I was referring to Horatio," Máire said.

Edward felt Máire had directed the question at him, but before he could respond, Marcus chimed in.

"I'm certain that Horatio will find Amata more sympathetic than his sponsor." Marcus then began helping Claudius pack.

"Should one of us eavesdrop?" Claudius asked, while rolling up his bedding into a neat roll.

"Mmmm..." Marcus muttered. Edward saw the Roman Deargh Du look up to study the blood-drinkers in the tent. "Surely Mandubratius would think it an insult if he sensed one of us listening to him." Marcus then seemed to consider his words for a moment. "That is... if he catches us," he specified. "If he doesn't catch us, then there's nothing to be upset over. Besides, if Horatio and Mandubratius come to blows, it would be in our best interests if someone intervenes and breaks up the fight."

Since he was apparently not part of this conversation, Edward focused his attention on packing the incendiaries he usually carried in pockets sewn into the strap he wore across his chest.

"I wager that Horatio will win, should they fight," Mac Alpin boasted.

Claudius uttered a grunt and began to disappear in the shadows of the tent, as if attempting to avoid notice.

"Well, I'm not going," Máire whined. "If I have to carry Mandubratius, I'm not going to help him now."

After filling all of the pockets with his incendiaries, Edward hoisted the explosives-laden strap over his head to his left shoulder and then shoved his right arm through the opening. As he finished donning his incendiaries, he heard Marcus laugh.

"I wasn't going to send you or Claudius," Marcus stated.

Edward paused in his efforts to finish packing to glance at Claudius, who shrugged before asking, "Why not me?"

"You are trying to avoid the duty, lieutenant, not that I can blame you. This duty is best suited for an Ekimmu Cruitne. Arwin, can you suggest one?"

A swat between Edward's shoulders awoke him from his reverie, and a chill ran down his spine as the realization dawned on him that he would be chosen for this repugnant task.

"Edward can do it," Arwin informed Marcus, confirming Edward's suspicions. "Can't you, lad?"

Edward glanced up at his father-in-darkness's face and saw a smile brighten up his features.

"Very well," Edward acknowledged with a sigh. He then rose up and began to pull on the rest of his supplies.

Marcus walked over to Edward, wrapped a strong hand around his neck, and pulled him into a conspiratorial embrace. "Remember," Marcus whispered into his ear. "Don't let them sense you, and don't tell us what you hear until we have privacy. Besides, it will give you ample opportunity to see your woman again."

Edward witnessed a spark in the Deargh Du's eyes, and soon the other blood-drinkers greeted him with mocking smiles. With everything now packed, Edward sighed and then exited the tent.

Amata pondered over the entire process of any activity mid-air and decided that it must be some sort of joke. After pushing her hair behind her ears, she found Horatio sitting in a corner of the camp, frowning, while staring at the sky. She then saw Horatio turn towards her, and she pondered how to approach him. She also knew that Mandubratius waited about five hundred yards in the distance. Her sponsor did not want to stray too far from camp and risk another attack, but he had explained that he wanted to be far enough away to avoid casual eavesdropping.

"Hello Amata," Horatio muttered as he looked up at her. "So, you've come here to do your duty?"

Amata swallowed, surprised by his directness.

"I heard you and him speaking this morning," Horatio stated.

She wondered whether everyone could hear their conversations.

"So, where is he?" Horatio asked. "Where is my sponsor?"

Amata met his gaze. "I'm to take you to him."

"And how were you planning to persuade me?" he prodded while digging at some dirt with a toe.

"I debated about several methods," Amata admitted, "such as lying, manipulating, seduction, or simply threatening you." She shrugged.

"All good choices," Horatio replied, before he began staring at the ground. "So, what is your decision?"

"I shall attempt telling the truth. Awvarwy requests the opportunity to talk with you about what you are and who you may wish to be," she answered. Amata considered sitting down next to him, but she instead decided such intimacy would give the wrong message.

"Claudius and I already had that discussion," Horatio grumbled.

Amata crouched and then knelt on the grass. "I respect Claudius, and I'm certain that he presented what he believed to be a non-biased perspective of our line, but he's not Lamia, nor did he have to suffer a life he did not choose."

Horatio looked over at her and blinked. "Are you saying that you didn't choose your life?"

Amata smirked for a moment, considering the question. "My circumstances were to accept this life or die. However, that is a choice. No, I was referring to Awvarwy. He did not choose to be Lamia. His mortal life was ripped from him."

"So, that is why he took my mortal life from me, because his was taken as well?" Fire and vehemence enshrouded his voice.

"Horatio, you know well he didn't specifically target you. Usually, we transform large groups for our own preservation." Amata paused before continuing. "If we are faced with our own demise, and there are mortals about who can aid us in our defense, we sponsor them, as we did during your transformation. We tell them that they now have the option to be the warriors of God. Then, we give them enough information to follow our leadership and defeat our enemies. In both of these cases, the expectation is low that the new Lamia will survive. Those that do survive join the ranks of Lamia with us."

Horatio seemed to study the mud and newly sprouted grass again. His gaze then settled on her, and he seemed to become lost in thought. "Your words make some sense," he admitted after a long pause.

Amata rose up and offered him her right hand. "We can talk about this more as we walk."

Horatio nodded before taking her hand. "So tell me, how was Mandubratius sponsored?"

"He was transformed by my sponsor, Felician," Amata replied. "We found

Awvarwy nailed to a tree," Amata added. "I didn't want to see him die. It seemed such a waste to see a brave warrior dying. I could see so much in his eyes, so I asked Felician to sponsor him. I had never done the act before, and there were stringent rules about our numbers, back then."

"Did he have a choice?" Horatio asked. "Did you ask him?"

"No," she replied.

"I think I'm beginning to understand," Horatio stated.

"I'm glad to hear that."

After walking several paces, Amata stopped upon hearing Mandubratius' voice. She then traversed around a series of rocks and found him, sitting on a rock and smiling.

Mandubratius motioned for Horatio to sit down across from him. "Amata," he said as he turned towards her. "Thank you for escorting Horatio. I think it best that you return to the camp and tell Marcus that we'll be along soon."

Amata raised a brow, surprised that he had just dismissed her. "Very well," she acknowledged, while nodding her head. She then released Horatio's hand, before turning to face the youngling. "Be honest, and he'll be honest with you." She met Mandubratius' eyes after saying those words, hoping she had not lied. Amata then started back towards camp.

Mandubratius' voice echoed behind her. "Now, let me tell you about the Lamia."

Divio

Reginald urged the horses to quicken their pace, since the cart seemed to slow once again. Even he felt himself drifting off as midnight loomed, and at this late hour, he could hear the start of another guessing game between Clotilda and a seemingly weary Lady Talia. Giggling highlighted their game.

After listening to their game for a few minutes, Reginald noticed that the garrison detachment in the lead stopped, and he looked on as Dreu dismounted and walked beyond the torchlight from the carts and other riders.

As Reginald stopped his cart, he heard the others behind him stop.

Dreu stared down at the road for a moment, but then he seemed to look up into the stars. At that moment, another soldier joined the garrison captain, and Reginald could tell that an exchange of whispered words occurred. Dreu then turned towards the carts and walked over to Reginald.

"Why have we stopped?" he asked Dreu, skipping the pleasantries.

"My Lord, I must show you something," Dreu answered.

Reginald nodded his head before hopping off the cart. He then followed Dreu towards where the garrison captain had stood a moment before.

"What is it?" he queried, hoping Dreu would not be so evasive. He then followed Dreu's finger, which pointed down at a mile marker. After glancing back at the garrison commander, Reginald said, "So, we're almost in Divio. Is there some other reason you brought me here?"

"Next time there is a strong wind, inhale deeply," Dreu said.

Reginald waited for a moment, until a gust of wind blew, carrying the stench of rotting putrescence. The horrible smell caused him to gag. Reginald lowered his head, unwilling to contemplate the source of the reek.

"I think that I should send a few men forward to survey the town, my Lord. The rest will set up camp here," Dreu suggested.

"I agree, but I'm going with those men," Reginald stated.

Dreu nodded. "I thought you would, my Lord. I have already called for a horse for you." The garrison captain then turned about and began issuing orders to the rest of the garrison to set up camp.

"Don't let my mother go near Divio," Reginald added. He didn't want her to see what could possibly be waiting for them.

"You heard him," Dreu added after turning back to the other soldiers.

Soon, a soldier escorted a saddled horse to Reginald, who climbed aboard. He then nudged the horse towards Divio, hoping it would not bolt at the vile stench. As the horse plodded towards the village, Reginald saw that Dreu and two other soldiers had joined him.

Within a mile, farms came into view, and Reginald could see fallen bodies in the distance. For every foot they traveled, the rotting smells grew, causing him to control his impulse to vomit. The smell of rot and dry blood grew so strong that he began to taste it.

After riding past the farms, the road headed into the town.

Reginald remembered where Flor and his sons had stood at the church, and soon that very building came into view. He rode up to the church and dismounted a few feet from the steps.

There, at his feet, he could see a small body, and he could discern the gold and red of Flor's dress.

Reginald dropped to his knees and began sobbing uncontrollably. Somewhere in some disconnected part of his mind, he could hear his sobbing overwhelm the sounds of the night. After exhausting himself, Reginald heard the scuff of a boot against stone and looked up, only to see Dreu standing in apparent supplication a few feet away from him.

Reginald inhaled, gained control of his emotions, and met Dreu's eyes.

"We cannot stay here... at least not now," Reginald stated while wiping his face. "We will bury the dead. When we get back to camp, I will rally the men, and then we'll lead them back here."

Dreu nodded. "I'm sorry for your loss, my Lord."

Reginald climbed back onto the horse. It took all of his strength to refrain from embarrassing himself further in front of his underlings. "Thank you."

Heloise tried to ignore the smells drifting from Divio as she continued setting up camp. She didn't know how long they might be here. After all, Reginald might need extra assistance from her vassals to clean his village.

She pondered for a moment whether he would ask for help. She would offer it, if he asked, but this was his home.

At that moment, Remi stopped in front of Heloise and addressed her. "My Lady, we were thinking about digging the latrines in the north. Does this meet with your approval?" Remi leaned against a shovel he carried.

"An excellent suggestion, Remi," she praised. Heloise then glanced about, looking for Tildy. "Have you seen my granddaughter?" she asked the servant.

Remi nodded. "I believe I saw her playing with Lady Talia."

Heloise scanned the torch-lit areas around the camp and soon found her granddaughter and Lady Talia at the edge of camp. Tildy sat across from Lady Talia, who held a doll. Apparently noticing Heloise's scrutiny, Lady Talia waved at her.

Heloise found herself waving back. "Please continue your work," she said to Remi before walking towards Lady Talia, who beckoned for her to join them.

"Lady Heloise," Lady Talia greeted. Her impeccable grin seemed to mask her complete disdain for the older woman, but Heloise, with her experience attending the Frankish court, recognized such deceptions.

Tildy stood up and ran over to embrace Heloise's legs. "Grandmamma, look what Lady Talia made for me," Tildy squealed, as she held up her new doll and practically shoved it into her grandmother's hands.

Heloise accepted the doll with grace and began tracing her fingers over the fine fabrics. "What a lovely doll," Heloise said, before looking at Talia.

"Since Reginald offered me fresh clothes, I thought it best to use my torn clothing to make another doll for Clotilda, so she and I could play," Talia informed her.

Heloise resumed scrutinizing the doll's fabric and soon came to the conclusion that such fine material must be extravagantly expensive. To Heloise, the exquisite material demonstrated Lady Talia's priorities towards her vassals, if she even had vassals... if she were indeed a 'Lady'.

"Thank you," Heloise responded to Lady Talia, before returning the doll to Tildy. "It's a most generous gift." She then crouched to Tildy's height and asked, "Did you thank Lady Talia for the doll?"

"Yes, I did, grandmamma," Tildy giggled.

"Wonderful," Heloise said, before tickling Tildy for a moment, eliciting much laughter and squirming. "Perhaps you should share this grand gift with the other girls. Go play with them for a while."

Tildy nodded and then hugged her new friend. "You must tell me the rest of the story later," Tildy told Lady Talia.

"Of course," the blonde woman answered, before embracing Tildy for a moment and releasing her.

Tildy ran to the other children, leaving Heloise behind with her son's painted whore.

As Heloise sat down across from Talia, she noticed that a serene smile spread across the younger woman's face. Neither woman spoke for a few seconds. Finally, Heloise decided to break the silence between them. "I see Tildy has developed a friendship with you."

"Yes. Clotilda and I have become good friends," Talia replied.

Heloise looked around the camp to make sure Tildy didn't hear them. She then reasserted her gaze upon Talia. "You've also captivated my eldest son," she added.

Talia's eyes narrowed a bit, and her smile became strained. "Your son admires my qualities."

Heloise began to smile, trying to match Talia's expression, but with less smugness... at least she hoped it was a smile. "That is most interesting, because I know what traits he favors in women, and you are not his usual preference."

Talia tilted her head to one side. "Really? What does Reginald prefer?"

"He prefers mousy women that exist as background," Heloise answered.

"Truly?"

"Yes, especially those that do not talk back to him and obey his every whim."

"You are correct in that I have none of those qualities," Talia stated.

"Yet, you have him enthralled with you," Heloise argued, but she willed her smile to remain in place.

"Perhaps his tastes have changed, of late," Talia countered, before shrugging.

"Perhaps," Heloise said by means of deflection, but unwilling to concede to the trollop.

"Is there something wrong?" Talia asked before scooting in closer.

Heloise recognized the attack for what it was... a lead in with a sympathetic-sounding platitude, more intimate proximity to let down one's guard, both intended to convey the illusion of sisterly bonding... and soon after, the back-stabbing begins. Being among the Frankish Court had taught many lessons.

Unwilling to play this game, Heloise decided to be honest, somewhat.

"I'm dismayed that my son has become intimate with another woman so soon after seeing his wife killed. She hasn't even been buried, yet."

Talia's posture loosened, and her eyes focused on the ground. "I... I had no idea." She looked up at Heloise's face but did not meet her eyes. "He did not tell me of his wife's recent passing."

Heloise sensed her eyebrows rise in surprise. Surely, Reginald had said something to this harlot. Her doubts about this woman grew larger than before. She considered calling this woman 'usurper', 'whore', or some other, equally condemning, name loud enough for all to hear, but then Talia's eyes focused on hers. They seemed to glow red, but then the redness seemed to be just a trick of the torchlight.

"You must believe me... I didn't know," Talia stated.

Talia's words seemed significant. The younger woman knew nothing about Flor or her death. Heloise's past concerns over this new relationship between Talia and Reginald seemed silly.

"I believe you," Heloise said after a moment of contemplation. She then raised her right hand and offered it to Talia.

"Thank you," Talia greeted with a sweet smile, while her chilled fingers slid around Heloise's hand.

"I should return to my duties now," Heloise said.

"What a shame. We had a most pleasant conversation," Talia said, before helping Heloise to her feet.

"Indeed," Heloise said before smiling. After brushing herself off, she started walking towards the center of camp, but after only two paces, a nagging question arose. She turned to face Talia so she could ask it.

Talia's face revealed a little surprise, but the younger woman soon hid it well with a ready smile.

"Before I go tend to the vassals, I have one more question for you, if you don't mind."

"Go ahead, Lady Heloise," Talia said in a demure tone.

"Now that you know that Reginald's wife is not yet buried, what are your intentions towards him?"

"Friendship... his, Clotilda's, and yours as well," Talia answered.

"I'm sure we'll be good friends," Heloise said. She sauntered towards the other woman, embraced her, and received kisses from Talia on her cheeks.

After Talia pulled away from their embrace, Heloise resumed her walk towards the camp, but she soon felt her stomach clench, as if she couldn't remember something important, but what? Since nothing popped into her head as being particularly worrisome, Heloise decided that 'the something' would return on its own.

Hadrianopolis

As Marcus and the rest of the party approached the town from the sky, he noticed Mac Alpin wave over to him, so Marcus motioned for the others to join Mac Alpin and hover over the town.

"I can smell about thirty to forty Lamia in Hadrianopolis," Mac Alpin said as soon as Marcus and the others closed the distance.

Marcus felt a tinge of anger for not knowing that the Lamia had established such a strong presence this far east, although he was aware the Lamia's influence spanned to the far eastern reaches of China and beyond. Still, when he looked over at Mandubratius, he couldn't help but feel left out... surely Mandubratius should have told them, as part of this alliance, of a significant Lamia presence out here who could have been some help against the Strigoi. "There are Lamia in Hadrianopolis?" he asked, before drifting closer to the blood-drinkers carrying Mandubratius.

"Lamia you say?" Mandubratius queried in a manner of a shopkeeper caught trying to sell whelks as oysters.

"So, you didn't know there were Lamia here?" Claudius inquired as he too hovered closer, while sharing Amata's burden with Edward.

"In truth, they aren't Lamia, at least they are not part of the Lamia community," Mandubratius replied in a tone that sounded truthful, but Marcus decided to maintain his skepticism.

"So, they are separatists?" Edward asked.

Mandubratius uttered a strange half-laugh. "In a manner of speaking, yes, they're separatists. You see, when my sponsor died, a significant group of Lamia who did not agree with the successors to Felician decided to establish their own community. I'm sure they call themselves something different."

"Why haven't we encountered them before?" Marcus asked, still feeling upset about not being informed... and for not being aware of them himself despite his many forays through this part of the world.

"They tend to hide well," Amata stated with a shrug. "In fact, most Lamia probably do not know of their existence."

"There's a rumor that those who left were hunted and killed," Mandubratius added, "but it's unsubstantiated, and I don't know who started it."

"Are you serious?" Claudius asked as he stared at Mandubratius.

"Well, the successors wanted to convince others not to abandon the Lamia. They hoped spreading the rumor would accomplish that goal," Mandubratius answered, though he still smiled as if pleased with some joke of his.

Marcus grumbled under his breath. "Your political machinations aside, Mandubratius, are they a threat?"

Patroclus' movement caught Marcus' attention, and he saw the Legate turn his eyes to the stars as if removing himself from the discussion.

After reverting his gaze to Mandubratius, Marcus watched the Briton study the ground beneath them for a moment, as if giving the matter a good deal of thought. "Well," the Lamia spoke after a long pause, "the traditional rivalries with other blood-drinkers still exist with these blood-drinkers. However, like others of Lamia blood, they wouldn't be able to tell a Lamia from any other blood-drinker."

"Then, let's just avoid Hadrianopolis and continue to Constantinople," Máire suggested, before adjusting her hold on Horatio. "We can set up camp after another hour of travel," she added.

Julien, who helped Máire bear Horatio, seemed uncomfortable just hovering with his share of the burden.

"You'd propose we go traipsing about Lamia territory without announcing ourselves to whoever considers themselves in charge of these lands?" Mandubratius asked. "You're liable to make more enemies for us, Máire."

"They would attack us for camping in the wilderness?" Claudius asked.

"Wouldn't you be concerned to find a group of well-armed soldiers outside of Bath? Wouldn't you attack first and then ask questions?" Mandubratius asked, with a great deal of incredulity coloring his tone.

"We'd sense them coming and defend ourselves," Mac Alpin answered with a good deal of bluster.

"Yes, and we'd manage to win the battle," Mandubratius added. "However, we'd rush the rest of the way to Constantinople and be attacked by a larger group there. This is familiar territory to them."

There is a larger group of Lamia in Constantinople?

"What do you propose?" Marcus asked, frustrated at the lack of reliable intelligence in this realm.

How could I not know?

"I would suggest that instead of walking into town as mere travelers, we should arrive as lords of the western realms and stay at the Lord's house," Mandubratius answered with a smile.

"Wouldn't that get us killed?" Máire asked.

Mandubratius chuckled. "You don't think like a Lamia, Máire."

"You're making it obvious," Julien stated, before getting what appeared to be a more comfortable hold on his burden. "You are confident enough to displace the local Lord. Therefore, you must have an army behind you."

Mandubratius grinned. "Inspector General, are you sure you're not a Lamia?"

"Won't we be in danger?" Edward asked.

"Not during the day."

Patroclus seemed to regain his tongue. "They will undoubtedly send a messenger to speak to us."

"I wouldn't be surprised if a few soldiers followed them," Amata admitted.

"So, we shouldn't keep ourselves in one place," Marcus stated. "We should split into groups."

"Marcus, you think very much like a Lamia. I'm impressed," Mandubratius stated with a smirk plastered upon his face.

Marcus shrugged. "I think like an old Roman general, that's all. Line up, and we'll divide into three groups."

A few minutes later, Edward and Julien lead the majority of the blood-drinkers in setting up camp outside of the city. Máire, Mac Alpin, and Patroclus led another group to the opposite side of the city, after dropping off Marcus, Mandubratius, and Amata on the outskirts of the city.

After being set down, Marcus, Mandubratius, and Amata began strolling through the streets at a slow pace.

"Are you sure about this?" Marcus asked Mandubratius, still wary of having to trust the backstabbing Briton.

"Of course," Mandubratius stated, before taking Amata's arm. "I want to be seen so everyone will know."

They then walked through the entrance to the lord's home.

"How do you know they will be willing to accommodate us?" Marcus asked, after stopping at the closed gate.

Amata's face radiated beauty. "You know we can be quite persuasive. Have no worries."

"I see." Marcus could hear doubt in his voice, so surely the Briton sensed it as well, he reasoned.

Mandubratius began banging his fist against the gate door.

Soon after, Marcus heard the shuffling of feet, and then he saw a bleary-eyed old guard open the gate and squint at them.

Speaking in Greek, the old guard muttered, "What business do you have at this hour? The sun isn't up yet."

Marcus watched Mandubratius stare at the soldier for a moment before smiling in a self-important manner. In Greek, the Briton announced, "I am Michael Tolomei, emissary of the Pope, and I demand that your lord provide us with accommodations until my party concludes its business in your town."

"The Pope?" The soldier appeared confused.

"Yes, His Holiness Pope Leo III," Amata confirmed, while smiling at the guard. "We work for him."

The guard's cheeks seemed to redden as he lowered his eyes. "My Lady, he has no dominion here," he said, daring to meet Amata's eyes.

"Didn't you hear?" Mandubratius stated, apparently interrupting Amata before she could respond. "Emperor Charles and the Basileus Irene have wed. The Pope is now the shepherd of the Eastern Empire as well as the Western."

The guard's face seemed to transition from confusion to clarity as the Lamia's manipulation took affect. "Oh yes, that is right."

"That is precisely why we are here," Mandubratius answered. "The Pope asked me personally to come to the east to spread the word of his arrival."

"The Pope is coming here?" the guard chirped in excitement.

Mandubratius leaned in as if to divulge a secret. "Actually, the Pope is here right now. Shhhh," he shushed the guard. "He's in disguise." The Briton then nodded towards Marcus.

The guard dropped to his knees and blustered, "Your Holiness," before leaning forward to grab and kiss Marcus' hand and ring.

Marcus caught a glimpse of Mandubratius smiling as he regarded, with much disdain, his now slobbery hand.

"That's enough… my son," he told the mortal.

The soldier stopped kissing his hand, but he remained on his knees.

Mandubratius leaned in to Marcus and whispered, "Give him a blessing."

"I don't know any Christian blessings!" Marcus uttered tersely in Gaelic.

"They're all in Latin, so he won't understand it. Most Christians don't."

Marcus returned his attention to the kneeling mortal and intoned in Latin, "May you have a long life and many large children." Then in Greek, once again, he said, "Now, please stand up."

"The Lord and Lady, and their family, are in Constantinople," the guard said, after getting to his feet.

"I'm sure they won't mind if we stayed in their home," Mandubratius purred. "It's an honor, after all. Would you please take us to our rooms? Also, please tell no one we are here, yet."

The old guard nodded and then ushered them through the gate.

Once inside, the blood-drinkers followed the guard into the house.

"Why did you tell him I was the Pope?" Marcus growled at Mandubratius in Gaelic.

"Please, your holiness, calm yourself," the Lamia stated in Greek with smile as they walked through the lavish house. Then in Gaelic, the Briton added, "It was necessary. This way we will receive the attention we need."

As Marcus ducked by the gilded décor, he hoped it wouldn't be the wrong attention.

chapter seven

Divio

eginald tried to stifle his yawns as the priest droned on about death and hellfire. Reginald closed his eyes and rubbed the back of his daughter, Tildy, who had fallen asleep about ten minutes ago, after whining about how hungry she felt.

Damn the priest for arriving so late and insisting on starting the funeral service immediately. We had only just finished the burial!

He could hear sobbing behind him, yet he felt nothing.

Has my empathy disappeared?

Foul smelling incense burned around them in a sad attempt to cover the smell of festering death.

His eyes wandered over to Talia, who appeared to be serene, despite all of this death around them, but then her face changed, revealing fear.

Talia touched his arm and whispered, "Reginald, please forgive me. I must go." She then rose from her seat and started for the door.

"Wait!" he called out to her, ignoring the solemnity of the event, before gently nudging Tildy towards his mother.

The priest turned away from the altar and stared at him in apparent protest, but Reginald ignored his reproving stare and ran after Talia.

He caught up to her outside the church door and reached out for her. "Why are you leaving so quickly?" When Talia turned to face him, he swore that he saw her eyes glow red.

"Do not follow me," she said in a commanding whisper before lowering her gaze. She then looked up at him with limpid, blue eyes. "I must go. I will return soon."

Reginald blinked, upon finding no trace of Talia. Thinking that he must have missed her, Reginald turned back towards the church, but the sound of horses and carts drew his attention to the road. Soon, he could see Dreu riding towards him. "Is there something wrong?" he asked the garrison captain.

"No, my Lord," Dreu answered with a smile. "The foreign soldiers that assisted us at Prüm Abbey have arrived. They brought us supplies."

Out of the corner of his eye, Reginald spied a man and a woman walking towards them. The woman's regal grace made him consider bowing in her presence, while her consort exuded a strange, princely beauty as they both glided away from the carts and livestock. Reginald attempted to remember the last time they had met, as the man walked up to him.

"You must be Reginald, Lord of Divio," greeted the man, whose words rang with a strange, yet lovely accent.

"I am," he replied. "Who do I have the pleasure of addressing?"

"I am Caoimhín of Ard Mhacha," the man said before gesturing to the woman. "This is Sáerlaith of Ard Mhacha."

Reginald bowed his head towards her and then looked at him. "Thank you, Caoimhín, for these supplies. I offer you and yours my hospitality."

"We are not just delivering supplies, my Lord. We'll stay as long as needed."

Reginald felt surprise at the generosity but also concern at the logistical requirements for hosting the foreigners. "I thank you. I truly appreciate the assistance, but I do not have the means to support an army."

Caoimhín seemed even princelier as he leaned a little closer to Reginald. "I can appreciate your concern, but our army is self-sustaining," the foreigner enunciated. "Allow us to pitch our tents, hunt, and work at night."

Reginald did not find the request odd at all. In fact, something in this man's eyes made Reginald feel a strange reassurance… a strong understanding that all would be well. "I thank you. Yes, that's fine." He then turned to address Dreu. "Work with them to gather whatever they need and allow them to set up their tents wherever we have space. We will assist them in unloading their carts after the funeral." As soon as he finished speaking, he felt one of Sáerlaith's hands touch his.

"My Lord," she spoke in her singsong voice. "Let us take care of this. You need to rest after the funeral."

Something about her beauty seemed to make his worries fade like a bad dream. "Alright. Thank you," he murmured before embracing her and then Caoimhín. "I need to return to the funeral mass." After reluctantly turning away from the two captivating people, Reginald walked back to the church.

Once inside, he could hear the priest continuing to babble in Latin. After walking down the aisle, Reginald sat next to his mother, who looked at him but said nothing.

His mother's face seemed unreadable, yet she placed a hand on his and squeezed gently.

Reginald, feeling gratitude for the touch, extended his chin so he could whisper in her ear. "Our help has arrived."

Hadrianopolis

Marcus awoke upon hearing Mandubratius or Amata snoring. Unwilling to rise, he rolled onto his back on the small bed they had dragged into the main bedroom from an adjoining room. He stared at the ceiling and allowed his senses to expand. While he could perceive the rising moon, he also detected intruders... Lamia. He had to admit that Mandubratius' plan seemed to work so far... it had drawn out the Lamia, but what next...

A knock on the door drew his attention away from his inward journey, and Marcus sat up. He also noticed that Mandubratius, who shared the lord's bed with Amata, sat up as well.

Mandubratius chuckled as he smoothed his left hand over his hair. In Latin, he said, "I hope you've washed, Marcus. Prepare to have your holy arse kissed."

"I can sense a dozen or so Lamia outside. I don't think they'll be interested in an antipope," he answered.

"I know," Mandubratius remarked. "I was rather hoping for some amusement."

At that moment, a voice on other side of the door called out to them. "I thought I recognized the audacity and now the voice confirms it."

Mandubratius smirked before rising from the bed and walking towards the door.

Amata sat up, stretched a bit, and said, "I recognize that voice." She appeared a little more concerned than her companion did.

After reaching the door, Mandubratius flung it open and shouted, "Nicodemus!" However, once he had opened the door, he began to back away.

Marcus caught a glimpse of six swords, protruding through the doorway, pointed at Mandubratius' chest.

"How rude," the Briton whined in what seemed to be a casual manner, "waking up a gentleman with swords? Nicodemus, you wound me."

The Lamia Marcus assumed to be Nicodemus... the best dressed of the group... seemed to ignore the baiting. "What are you doing here?"

"Nicodemus, I think it's obvious what I'm doing here."

"Can you be any less ambiguous? I suppose not," the other Lamia said.

"I was sleeping," Mandubratius stated in his melodramatic manner, before crossing his arms over his chest.

"Mandubratius, stop being obtuse and answer Nicodemus' question," Amata said, her voice tinged with ire.

"Yes, yes, yes, Amata." Amusement grew in Mandubratius' eyes. "I just wanted to pay our eastern brothers a visit."

"Just you three?"

Mandubratius laughed and began to pace the room while the sword points followed him. "Do you really think I'd arrive here with such a small band, Nicodemus?"

Nicodemus glared at Mandubratius. "Hmmm, do I think you're insane? Only an insane person would come here with such a small escort."

Mandubratius' smile grew. "Or perhaps I have a sizeable army of soldiers close at hand."

"And what would you intend on doing with this sizeable force, should it exist?" Nicodemus asked.

Mandubratius sat back down on the bed he shared with Amata, assumed a casual pose, and looked Nicodemus in the eye. "Why, we're out hunting Strigoi, of course."

Nicodemus lifted his sword blade so it rested against his shoulder and began pacing in the room, while his men raised their blades but stood motionless. "And you think the Strigoi are here?" he asked Mandubratius.

Marcus felt like he should say something. After all, he was the antipope! "We know they are here," he muttered.

Nicodemus set a dismissive glare upon Marcus and examined him as if he were a pile of dung on the Via Apia. "I don't recognize this one. Who is he?" The other blood-drinkers began studying Marcus as well.

Before Marcus could respond, he heard Mandubratius emit a rather forced sigh.

"Oh, that one is but a minor child," Mandubratius explained. "I will punish him later for his insolence. Pay him no mind."

"So, the Holy Father is a mere underling?" asked Nicodemus.

Mandubratius smirked and leaned back on his side as if reclining at an orgy. "Oh, come now, Nicodemus. That was just a ruse to get your attention."

"And you really did come here to chase the Strigoi?"

"My dear friend Nicodemus," Mandubratius purred, enunciating each word, "If we are to have a real discourse on these matters, we should have them in an appropriate environment... an environment that involves good wine and vitae."

"I am sure the lord won't mind relinquishing his hall to us. Will that suit your needs?" Nicodemus asked.

Mandubratius shrugged. "That sounds splendid. Will you give us a few moments of privacy so we may dress for this stimulating conversation?"

Nicodemus nodded his head. "Yet, I must insist on leaving behind some of my men to make sure you find your way to the great hall."

Marcus felt like arguing, but then the realization dawned on him that if he spoke out of line, Nicodemus would expect Mandubratius to punish him, and Marcus did not want to grant the Lamia bastard the pleasure.

"Very well. I accept that and look forward to their company."

Nicodemus and most of his men left, while those few who remained sheathed their swords.

Marcus fumed in silence, unwilling to suffer the consequences of a loose tongue.

"Well, let's not keep Nicodemus waiting. Get dressed," Mandubratius ordered.

Figuring Mandubratius would complain if Marcus took too long preparing, Marcus decided to refrain from washing himself with the basin of water nearby, but he still tended to his nails and anointed himself with scented oils, since his body stank.

"Marcus," Mandubratius called as soon as Marcus capped his oil, "give me your oil."

"Yes, dominus." Marcus refrained from groaning as he handed the bottle over to his false master. After all, the bastard Briton smelled awful and needed something to cover up his stench, too.

Once the three blood-drinkers finished dressing, the guards escorted them to the hall, where soldiers began to light candles and torches. Soon, the hall glowed with a warm radiance, and then the soldiers carried in cups of bloodwine.

After a minute or two waiting to be seated, Marcus began to feel weak, and he realized that some of the Lamia soldiers wore gold. He did his best to hide his weakness, but the sight of the metal still brought him apprehension.

One of the soldiers setting the table gestured to an empty stool, so Marcus strolled up to it and prepared to sit, but he caught Mandubratius staring at him with a strange half-smile.

Mandubratius' smile then faded, and his face became stern. "If I witness or am told of one more instance of insubordination from you, I will have you beaten. Is that understood?"

Marcus took a quick glance at Amata, who winked at him, but did not appear to be amused. He lowered his eyes, deciding to continue the ruse, and attempted to appear cowed. "My apologies... Dominus." He then stood behind Amata.

Mandubratius raised his cup and cried out, "May we Lamia all live long and glorious lives."

Amata passed Marcus a cup, which he raised in toast. However, he soon noticed that Nicodemus and others did not join in.

"Mandubratius, you know we no longer consider ourselves Lamia," Nicodemus stated.

"But your blood and mine come from the same source, does it not?" Mandubratius smiled before taking a sip of his drink.

"That may be, but we are the Children of Ares, not Lamia."

Marcus had not previously known of the Children of Ares, yet there seemed to be much distrust between these so-called Children of Ares and Mandubratius. Of course, Marcus assumed everyone distrusted that bastard Briton.

Nicodemus continued speaking. "Returning to our previous conversation, how did you come to be hunting Strigoi?"

"Some aspects of my ruse ring with truth. As far as His Holiness is concerned, I am Michael Tolomei, his emissary. He has tasked me with the hunting of the Strigoi. My underling," Mandubratius added, before nodding towards Marcus, "has similarly influenced the Emperor to charge him with hunting the Strigoi. Not bad… for a child."

"So, your chase of the Strigoi brought you here. How successful have you been?"

One of the other Lamia cleared his throat. "We've heard rumors of thousands of innocent townspeople and priests killed."

"Mostly due to the madness," Nicodemus stated.

"We've killed some," Mandubratius countered before glancing at Marcus. "Marcus, how many have we killed?"

"Sixty, Dominus," he replied, finding it easier not to darken his tone upon calling Mandubratius 'Dominus'.

Mandubratius regarded Nicodemus once more.

Nicodemus seemed rather pale. He then took a long draught of his wine. "That is… most impressive. We have found them difficult to fight."

"Yes. It is very difficult, especially if you have been lucky enough to be struck with their madness. Everyone in my company has been unfortunate at least once," Mandubratius admitted.

Nicodemus shrugged a little. "Many of our number have suffered from it."

"At least it's not fatal," Amata offered in a dry and listless tone.

"She speaks," Nicodemus uttered. "I was curious whether you would continue to let Mandubratius do all the talking, Amata." The Lamia seemed to study Amata.

"Well, we are of equal rank, but I understand how he loves listening to his own voice. I prefer to listen, sometimes. It gives me ample opportunity to strike from the shadows." Amata smirked and then stretched.

"Nicodemus, I'm curious about something," Mandubratius added as he began pacing. "Why are so many Children of Ares in such a small town on the fringe of the Eastern Empire?"

"As I mentioned before, we've encountered the Strigoi. Our leaders felt that we should mount an attack from Hadrianopolis, and so we did, but the

Strigoi seemed to have disappeared. We believe that they may return, so we remained here."

Mandubratius stopped pacing and stared at the leader... an aghast expression set upon his face. "Nicodemus, you're not amongst the leadership?"

"Mandubratius, you know full well I was not the highest ranking of those who left," Nicodemus answered.

"Yes, that was Titus Marius, I believe. The leadership included him, Gaius Crescentius, and Diomedes, as I recall. I remember being most disappointed to see Diomedes leave with you. Is he well?" Mandubratius began to pace again, and as before, he faced away from the Children of Ares.

Marcus could see Nicodemus grin.

"I'm certain you are aware that we caught him giving information to your spies. We executed him as a traitor."

Mandubratius sighed, seemingly disappointed, but he still kept pacing. "He could be such a stupid fool."

"Now," Nicodemus drawled as he leaned in towards Mandubratius and glowered in a stern manner. "Give me a good reason why you, and your cohorts, should not share the same fate."

"Nicodemus," Mandubratius sputtered. "I am hurt by your change of tone."

Marcus attempted not to laugh.

"I believed that we were in the middle of a civil conversation, but then you had to resort to threats," whined Mandubratius. "Come now, surely we can be friends in these dark nights. We both must deal with the Strigoi."

"Mandubratius, surely you can do better than that. The night you murdered Felician is the night you betrayed all of us. So please, betrayer, give us a real reason not to execute you," Nicodemus hissed.

Marcus cursed himself for only carrying a few small daggers. He felt certain that he could disarm the two Lamia closest to him, but such action might foil their mission.

Mandubratius casually sat down, reached out, and took his wine. He swirled it and sipped it, seemingly savoring the taste, before smiling at the other Lamia as if bemused by the entire event. "Hmmmm, what can I possibly offer... You have killed no Strigoi, yet we've killed sixty. I'm sure that knowledge must be of some... value," he drawled before extending his smile to an unbelievable width.

Nicodemus unsheathed his sword and slammed it into the table, drawing startled stares from his men. "That is indeed of value," Nicodemus admitted, practically spitting his words. "What is it that you want for this knowledge?"

"No, no, no," Mandubratius purred before stretching in a most relaxed fashion. "This is not a negotiation for you to conduct."

Nicodemus hit the table with his fist. "This is outrageous. How dare you belittle me? I'm not a child, like the plaything that stands behind you!" he shouted while motioning to Marcus with an outstretched right arm.

Mandubratius smiled and then appeared to study the table for a moment, before looking up at Nicodemus. "You may have more years in this world than I, Nicodemus, but I have always been, and will continue to be, superior to you. I… simply… cannot make such a negotiation with someone from a… lower station."

"Very well," Nicodemus hissed. "I will take you to see Efialtes myself."

"And my party must accompany me, for their entertainment value if nothing else," Mandubratius added.

"Oh, very well. They may accompany you. We will leave tomorrow night, an hour after dusk."

Mandubratius stood up. "Thank you for your generosity and hospitality. I hope you do not mind if my associates and I retire to the local tavern for some entertainment… and sustenance."

Nicodemus grimaced. "Of course. It is a pleasure being in your company again," he uttered through gritted teeth. "Yet, you choose to drink with the common folk?"

"Yes, they can be amusing, Nicodemus. That is why I feel this business about class is so pointless when they are so much fun," Mandubratius answered.

Says the exalted Co-Consul of the Lamia.

After taking a sip of his fifth goblet of wine, Mac Alpin spat out the watered-down beverage and grabbed the innkeeper's belt. "This time, do not dilute or heat it," Mac Alpin demanded to the innkeeper, who gave him a blank stare. Mac Alpin then repeated himself in Greek upon realizing he had asked the question in Latin.

The innkeeper nodded before walking to the counter where he prepared the drinks.

Soon, a cold cup of wine found its way into Arwin's hands.

At that moment, the door to the outside opened, and Marcus walked into the room. His eyes appeared downcast, fixed on the ground as if he were a cumal. A few more Deargh Du followed him in, trailed by Mandubratius and Amata, arrayed in resplendent clothing.

To Mac Alpin, Marcus seemed to be playing the part of a demure servant, while Mandubratius appeared more smug than usual. Other Lamia, garbed in fine clothing, entered the inn as well. Arwin looked on as Amata and

Mandubratius sat down at the table behind them, and then Marcus joined them, but instead of sitting with the group, he stood behind them.

Why would Marcus play along with this Briton buffoon?

"You look lovely this evening," Mandubratius commented to Amata. "Don't forget that we leave soon for Constantinople."

"I will not forget," he heard Amata answer. She paused and added, "Thank you, my love. You look very nice too."

Mandubratius turned towards Marcus. "Wine!" he ordered.

Marcus bowed before walking to the innkeeper and asking for wine. After receiving the requested bottle, Marcus then obtained two goblets for the Lamia, gripping all three items with care.

"I cannot believe Nicodemus has yet to rise in rank," Mandubratius stated as he snatched the offered goblet of wine from Marcus. "After four hundred years, he's still a pompous lackey, and that Efialtes is nothing like his namesake. He's a mere boy, not a nightmare."

"The 'pompous lackey' and that 'mere boy' have ears here," Amata murmured, although her words carried as if she allowed them to be heard.

Mandubratius grinned before sipping his drink, but then he made a face. "What is this?" he growled at Marcus. "Undiluted wine!" Mandubratius emptied his goblet of wine, followed by Amata's goblet, onto Marcus' boots. "Fix this immediately! If you dawdle the next time I desire drinks, I will have you flogged! Now, bring us proper wine!"

"The honor is to serve," replied Marcus.

Arwin could tell Marcus struggled to hide his growing anger. In fact, Mac Alpin could not even imagine himself being able to play the servant role to Mandubratius... or to anyone, for that matter.

Mandubratius raised his empty goblet as if to strike Marcus with it. "I did not ask you a direct question. You are not to speak unless I ask you a question. Is that understood?" Mandubratius paused while waiting for a response, but then he added in a cajoling tone as if speaking to a child, "I just asked a direct question! You can answer!"

"Yes, Dominus," Marcus murmured, though Mac Alpin could detect a strong tinge of anger coloring Marcus' tone.

"Good. For a moment, I was considering having you castrated, but I don't feel it's necessary, yet," Mandubratius hissed before feigning to toss his empty goblet at Marcus.

Mac Alpin watched Marcus bow his head and retreat to the innkeeper to fetch the proper wine. Upon returning with the diluted wine, Marcus poured some into both empty goblets. He then turned away from his 'master' and began studying the rest of the inn.

"It will be great to return to Constantinople. I miss the city and its wonders," Mandubratius stated before examining his nails for a moment.

"Yes, indeed," Amata answered. "It's hard to believe we'll be leaving tomorrow night. I hope our escorts won't slow our pace."

"Not with Nicodemus in the lead," Mandubratius said. "I remember when he lived in the temple. He was a centurion. If anyone knows how to keep a quick pace, it's a centurion."

Soon, Mandubratius and Amata finished their drinks.

"Marcus, we are leaving. Assist Amata out of her seat."

Marcus reached out his right hand and helped Amata to her feet.

"Thank you," she said, but then she seemed to realize that she had made a mistake.

"Amata, don't thank our slaves… it spoils them," Mandubratius said.

All of the other Lamia stood as well. One opened the door to the outside while another went through. Soon, Mandubratius and Amata departed with Marcus and the remaining Lamia in tow.

As Mac Alpin finished his wine, he sensed Claudius walk into the inn.

"So, what's the news?" his Sugnwr Gwaed friend asked in Gaelic.

"The bloody leech and Marcus put on a charade for the Lamia. I'm not sure what the intent was, but tomorrow night, they leave for Constantinople," Arwin answered in Gaelic. "I think they mean for us to follow them."

"Then, we shall find as many of our party as we can and meet at the church ruins outside of town. We will discuss our preparations there," Claudius answered. "What about Marcus?"

"He's pretending to be Mandubratius' servant. I have no idea why he agreed to such a thing. It will definitely cost that Briton dearly when this is over," Arwin said before chuckling.

"Do you think it will come to blows?" Claudius asked while grinning profusely.

"If not blades."

"Then, I wager twenty on Marcus," Claudius said.

Mac Alpin laughed again. "I am not taking that wager, Claudius. Find some fool for that. Hurry, lieutenant, let us find the others. Nighttime is waning."

"Why don't we fly in, grab the mirror and leave?" Julien asked Claudius, who carried Horatio between them, while Edward and Mac Alpin guarded the front and rear of their party. "I mean, why does Mandubratius need to meet up with these Lamia?"

Julien looked down at the indiscriminate figures of Marcus, Mandubratius, and Amata, who ran alongside some unknown Lamia.

Claudius uttered a half chuckle. "The best way to understand the motivations of a Lamia is to become one."

"Claudius, don't avoid the question," Julien said.

"Because of the Strigoi threat, all these eastern Lamia are on patrol and would likely detect the Lamia on the ground. It would not look good for the leader of the Lamia to be caught in the middle of the Eastern Empire by his old friends or enemies," Claudius answered.

"So, how does encountering them in the town improve the situation?" Horatio asked.

Máire flew in closer and said, "You heard the leech. He wanted to choose the ground for the confrontation. He somehow negotiated his way into being escorted to Constantinople. Why they agree to see him, I do not understand."

"Suffice it to say, his journey takes him past many ambush points where the Lamia may have been caught had they journeyed alone," Claudius added.

Soon, a light misting of rain began to fall.

Edward slowed down and joined the conversation. "Speaking of ambushes, I smell a large group of forty Lamia coming up behind us on the roads."

Arwin joined them. "Where are they heading?"

"It appears that they are following the first group of Lamia, Children of Ares, whatever. However, they are changing their formation as they go as if they expect to encounter forces between themselves and the first party," Edward answered.

Claudius looked over at the rest of their party and asked, "Do any of you feel that we need to change position?"

Arwin shrugged and met Edward's eyes.

"We will in a few minutes," Edward stated.

Curiosity drove Julien to his next question. "What do you think the Lamia are doing?"

"If I were a general and wished to draw out my enemy, I'd make a show of having a small force with high profile soldiers. I would try to make the enemy think that they can advance on my comrades and trap them," Claudius said.

"A good thought," Mac Alpin added. "Let's head towards the southeast again."

After a few more minutes of flying, Mac Alpin turned back towards them. "Where are they now, Edward?"

"They're staying on their original course and closing in on the first group," Edward answered.

When MacAlpin held up his hand, they all stopped. He then peered down at the merging groups.

"The group with our comrades has turned around. Now, they are joining the second group," MacAlpin said. "They appear to be staying true to course."

"I would imagine the second group is confused, now, as if they had expected some other group of blood-drinkers," Máire added.

MacAlpin nodded his head before motioning for them to get back into formation and resume flying again.

Marcus could smell the party of Lamia, or Children of Ares, as they approached, while keeping his senses aware of the party of Celtic lines flying above him.

"Halt!" Nicodemus called out while thrusting his left hand skyward and raising his makhaira in his right hand.

While Marcus attempted to appear surprised, he noticed that Mandubratius didn't look worried or surprised at all.

Soon, one of Nicodemus' men rejoined them.

"Did you find any soldiers, lieutenant?" Nicodemus asked.

"No sir, we did not."

Nicodemus then turned to the Co-Consuls. "Mandubratius, can you explain this?"

Mandubratius laughed. "What do you wish for me to explain, Nicodemus?"

"I expected that you would relay a message to your soldiers at the inn and that they would follow us to Constantinople. I cannot have an armed band of men running loose through the Eastern Empire, so I planned to greet your friends, disarm them, and order them to accompany us to the city," Nicodemus answered.

"And you found no one," Mandubratius stated before shrugging and offering an innocent smile.

"Yes… we found no one," Nicodemus responded as he stared at Mandubratius.

"Of course, there are two possible explanations. They could be using some magic to hide from you, or they're better at tracking and hiding than you believe them to be," the Co-Consul of the Lamia replied.

"There is a third possibility, of course."

"And what is that possibility?" Amata asked.

"That you never possessed an army," Nicodemus accused before crossing his arms over his chest and glowering at Mandubratius, who inhaled and feigned shock.

"Never had an army? You think I would walk into Hadrianopolis, insist on staying at the lord's home, and provoke you without an army to back me up?"

"It does seem rather odd for you to act as you have without some force to protect you. If there is an army back there, they better leave us be. Shall we continue?" Nicodemus asked. He then motioned to his men, and in a moment, everyone began to run again.

As they ran, Marcus watched Nicodemus adjust his spacing so he could run closer to Mandubratius. He could still hear their conversation despite the rapid impacts of many booted feet.

"I will find your little army, and when I do, they will join us unarmed or they will join the wind as dust."

Marcus could still sense the others, flying above them.

Divio

"If there are no other questions, let us get some sleep," Caoimhín stated, in hopes that this would be how he needed to handle things. After all, Sáerlaith still seemed lost in her own thoughts and doubts.

While watching the other leaders of their combined force leave the tent, Caoimhín caught sight of one of the Ekimmu Cruitne leaders pointing him out to an underling, who then approached him.

"Yes?" he asked in a pleasant manner while attempting to avoid sounding officious, as he studied the stranger. Caoimhín gave the underling his undivided attention.

"Sir, I have just returned from my patrol to the east, and I have a report. I found a female Lamia hiding in the woods."

Caoimhín closed his eyes for a moment, considering the possibilities of this intelligence.

This could be Talia.

He scratched his chin before asking, "What was she doing?"

"Digging a hole," the Ekimmu Cruitne scout replied.

Caoimhín nodded his head. "So, would you recognize the location? Would you be able to find her again tonight?"

The Ekimmu Cruitne's mouth widened into a pleased smile. "My nose never fails me, sir."

Caoimhín chuckled. "Excellent. As soon as the sun sets, take three warriors and bring this Lamia back to camp unharmed. Persuade her if you can, although I doubt she'll listen. Still, try to make her listen."

"Yes, sir," the Ekimmu Cruitne acknowledged before leaving the tent.

Caoimhín studied his nails for a moment and then cupped his chin with his right hand. "What are you doing out there, Talia?"

As soon as Talia awoke, she realized that she could not see or breathe, as cold, wet mud had drenched her face while she had slept, covering her eyes and infiltrating her mouth and nose. Fear of suffocation flooded her mind as she tried to cough and snort out the invasive mud. However, she soon remembered that she did not need air to live. That realization helped Talia calm herself, yet the cold, damp mud still caused her to shiver uncontrollably.

Talia prayed for the rain to stop and for the moon to banish the sun.

Why did I leave Divio? At the least I could have enjoyed sleeping in a comfortable cot. The Celtic lines would have acted as proper hosts and waited a night or two before killing me.

Soon, she could sense the sun's rays dwindle and fade.

Talia shoved her arms above her, pushing away much of the dirt and sod she had pulled onto her, and hauled herself up into a crouch. As a light sprinkle of rain began to rinse some of the caked-on gunk from her hair, Talia coughed up what remained of the silt that had entered her mouth. She then wiped at the mud on her face and wondered at her appearance.

Talia crawled the rest of the way out of her mud hole and then rolled onto her back, allowing the cascading rain to wash away the muck coating her body. Talia closed her eyes as she wiped herself off, helping the rain cleanse her. After a few moments basking in the rain, she extended her senses, hoping to detect nearby sustenance, but instead of a deer, she perceived the unmistakable sensation of four blood-drinkers.

She swiped at her eyes, opened them, and glared at the interlopers, who stood in front of her in a non-threatening manner. "What do you want?" she asked in Gaelic, assuming these people wouldn't understand a civil tongue.

One of the men smiled at her and replied, "Caoimhín would appreciate the honor of your presence, Lady Talia."

Talia sat up, flung off more mud, and snarled, "Who is this Caoimhín and why should I join you?"

"He's one of the leaders of our alliance," a female warrior answered.

Even though they all sounded so calm and rational, Talia assumed they would kill her as soon as possible. Unwilling to show weakness, she attempted to control her fear.

"I have nothing to say to any leaders of the alliance. Tell him I wish to be left alone."

"We're all concerned for your safety," another one of the rabble informed her.

"My safety?" Talia scoffed getting to her feet.

As she stood, three of the four blood-drinkers quick-walked around her to cover her from four directions, yet all of them still stood casually... even confidently.

Concerned that they might attack her, Talia reached for her dagger, only to discover its absence. "I do not need this Caoimhín, or your alliance, to protect me," she spat as she considered her options.

"But the Strigoi–" the female warrior began to say before Talia cut her off.

"I don't care about your struggle with the Strigoi. Now, why don't you and your warriors leave me in peace?" Talia prepared to leap and escape the trap, but eight meaty paws grabbed her. "Let me go this instant! You have no right to accost me!"

They ignored her as they took off in flight.

"I'll get you for this," she screamed. "You will all suffer."

Caoimhín did his best to listen to all of the parties yelling at each other and at him. Earlier, in the nights he spent in Ard Mhacha, he had believed that vassals worked quietly, but his recent experience contradicted that notion.

When Caoimhín awoke, the entire population of vassals seemed eager to shout out all of their status reports at him, and now he needed to prioritize these duties. He felt like a Roman clerk, at this point, left to handle the duties of an official who went to celebrate in some local festivities.

Marcus loves this sort of thing. Why isn't he here, handling these aspects about the sewage detail?

Caoimhín pondered why he had to care about water and food supplies while the mortals continued clamoring for attention.

Even Reginald de Divio seemed bored and most annoyed with the complaints about the placement of irrigation for the crops.

The mortals soon formed into two groups arguing for different spots.

With his patience at an end, Caoimhín rose from his chair and shouted, "That's enough!" He then pointed to one of the chief complainers. "You... We'll leave your dam intact. You," he added while pointing to the leader of the opposition. "We'll have a separate stream from the reservoir for you."

All the mortals stared at him.

"Now, is there any other business?" Caoimhín placed his hands on his hips. "No? Then, go back to your dwellings and tents! Dismissed!"

No one said anything at first, but then a din rose, followed by shouts of, "You can't tell us that!"

Reginald finally found his feet.

I wondered when the Lord of Divio would take command of his vassals.

Reginald raised his chin, and in Latin he yelled, "He said you're dismissed! Go back to the camp or your homes!"

The grumbling stopped as soon as their lord repeated his orders in their native tongue. Very soon after, the other mortals filed out of the tent, but the blood-drinkers, who appeared relieved, remained.

One walked over to Caoimhín and muttered in Gaelic, "Where would they be without us... and here they complain."

Caoimhín glanced at Reginald, who he knew hated exclusion from conversations and likely suspected foreign words. "Just get it done," he said to the waiting Sugnwr Gwaed. He didn't want to think about this anymore. While Caoimhín sat down to look pointedly at Reginald, the other blood-drinkers filed out of the tent. "Is there something you require?" Caoimhín asked while attempting to curb the growing annoyance in his voice.

Reginald shook his head. "I wish to thank you for doing such great work here." Despite the pleasant words, the Lord of Divio's voice dripped sarcasm and contempt. "I greatly appreciate you and your... warriors' assistance in rebuilding Divio. I only wish there was some way to repay you."

Caoimhín bit back the rather rude reply that threatened to escape his mouth. "The honor is to serve," he answered in an even tone, wishing again that Marcus could have been here to say that. Before he could think of anything else to say, he sensed more blood-drinkers, including one Lamia, approaching them from outside.

The sound of twigs snapping drew Reginald's attention towards the flap.

Caoimhín could hear a feminine voice utter many Gaelic and Latin expletives. As soon as the flap rose, he could see the exhausted warriors leading Talia. He studied her for a moment, taking in her disheveled appearance. Talia's formerly fine clothing seemed, now, little more than mud-soaked, tattered rags.

"You!" Talia accused in Gaelic while pointing her right index finger at Caoimhín. "What business is it of yours to send your ruffians after me? Am I to be your prisoner, then?"

After seeing Mandubratius debase Talia, his pity for her had grown, but now, it faded away. "You're not my prisoner," Caoimhín began. "All I–"

Reginald interrupted him. "I can't understand a single thing you're saying. Please speak in Latin." Despite his desire to be included in the conversation, the Lord of Divio seemed content to stare at the floor.

Caoimhín cleared his throat and restated himself in Latin. "I was just informing Lady Talia that–"

"Lady Talia?" queried Reginald in an incredulous tone before standing and rushing to her side. He took her muddy hands with his clean, manicured hands and asked, "What have they done to you?" He then regarded Caoimhín, and in a vehement tone, he yelled, "I want the men who did this brought before me so I can deal with them properly!" After revealing a burning glare, Reginald turned his attention back to the warriors holding Talia's arms.

Caoimhín felt his rage boil. "I shall speak in whatever language I choose! As for Lady Talia, no one did this to her. We found her this way. I requested this dialogue so I could assure her that we were not trying to hunt her down!"

"Your warriors are most unfriendly, Caoimhín," Talia informed him.

"Why would she think you were going to hunt her?" Reginald demanded.

Lady Talia smiled at Reginald, but then in a condescending tone she drawled, "My sweetheart, I'm fine. Wait for me, and I will join you soon."

"Alright, my dove," Reginald responded before exiting the tent.

"If what you say is true, then tell your ruffians to unhand me!" Talia growled at Caoimhín in Gaelic.

He nodded and said, "Release her."

Talia turned and slapped one of the men. "That was for grabbing my thigh, earlier." She then turned towards Caoimhín, straightened her back, and reflected a regal air.

"Now, then, if I'm not your prisoner, is it too much to ask for a bath and some clean clothes worthy of my station?"

Caoimhín considered his options. A benefit of command allowed him to deny any request. However, he decided that might be a mistake, in this situation.

"Have Reginald's house servants see to it," he informed the warriors. "You're all dismissed."

Talia nodded and left the tent, and the rest of the blood-drinkers followed.

Alone to his thoughts, Caoimhín sat down and pulled over another chair. He then propped up his feet and closed his eyes. Despite not needing to breathe, Caoimhín still felt comfort inhaling, holding his breath, and exhaling.

Tomorrow night will be an improvement, or so I hope.

Reginald debated whether to go back into the tent, and at the same time, he wondered why he had allowed Talia to order him out. While he mused about the events of the past few minutes, he noticed the tent flap rise, and then Talia and her escorts exited the tent. She looked calm and regal, despite the muddy rags she wore.

"Where are you taking her?" he demanded.

"We're taking her to the river so she can bathe," a woman answered.

"Forcing me to bathe in a cold river is not what I had in mind," Talia uttered. "What about my clothes?"

"I'm sorry, Lady Talia, but there are no other places we know of to bathe," another warrior stated.

"And the only clothes we're aware of are the homespun clothing that we found in Vézelay," another added.

Talia stopped and spun around to address her escorts. "I will not bathe in a river or wear clothing meant for vassals."

Sensing the time to intervene had arrived, Reginald cleared his throat, and in a calm voice, he said, "Perhaps I may be of some assistance."

Talia's face grew bright as she smiled. "How?"

"I have a proper bath at my home, and you are most welcome to use it."

Talia's demeanor darkened. "Most kind, but I have no decent clothing."

"I might have clothing that would suit you," Reginald added. He felt a momentary stab of guilt for offering Talia his wife's clothing, but Reginald didn't know what else he would do with it but give it away.

"I graciously accept your offer," Talia murmured before latching onto his left arm. "If you would excuse me," she said to the guards.

He then began to walk her towards his home. "How did you come to be in such a state?" he asked after several paces.

"I was accosted again," she said and then lowered her eyes.

He knew exactly what had happened. "You must be distraught for experiencing that situation twice," he said. "I can send soldiers to hunt down those brigands and bring them to justice."

Talia shook her head. "No, it's not necessary. I'm sure, like most thieves on the roads these nights, they've moved on for greener pastures."

"Still, I'll have Dreu send out patrols in all directions."

As they approached the front door, Vicelin opened the door, while Gudela peered out at him. Lamp light from inside his house bathed the front walkway in a warm glow.

"Please heat up enough water for a bath," Reginald asked them. He then turned to Gudela. "This is Lady Talia. Please assist her. She requires a bath."

Gudela dipped her head and offered Talia an arm. "Right away, my Lord."

Talia's face lit up in a smile.

"I'll find you some clothing," Reginald informed Talia before turning away to go into his wife's vacant quarters.

"Thank you," he heard Talia say, but Vicelin called, "Pardon me, my Lord."

Reginald stopped and turned to face his servant. "Yes, Vicelin?"

"Your wife's quarters are dark. Please take my lamp to light your way. Gudela has placed fresh candles in her room."

Reginald nodded his silent thanks as he accepted the lit lamp. He then resumed his melancholy jaunt to his wife's quarters. Once the door closed behind him, he took a few moments to take in his surroundings, to breathe the air in his deceased wife's room. Reginald swore he could still smell her. Everything around him reminded Reginald of Flor... her dressing gown draped on the chair in front of her dressing table, which also held her jewelry and her hairbrush and combs. Even the room still held wisps of her scent.

Part of him wanted to stay here a while, languishing and dining on the ashes of her memory, but that evening, he had said goodbye to her. Reginald knew he had to move on, and giving away some of his wife's clothes seemed to be a good first step.

He began to go through the trunks of clothing and footwear and found a few pieces that might suit Talia. After draping the clothing over his shoulder, grabbing appropriate footwear, and selecting a few choice articles of jewelry, Reginald walked back to the room near the kitchen, where his guest, covered with a woolen blanket, sat down in a large chair. No specks of mud remained attached to her skin or hair.

Talia stared up at him and smiled again. Her teeth gleamed. "This is quite an improvement," she purred.

"Your appearance has improved, though you were still beautiful, even with the mud," he replied.

"Thank you," Talia murmured, lowering her eyes. "I cannot wait to bathe."

At that moment, the servants came by with the first batch of steamy water.

Talia uttered a pleased sound and stood up from her chair. "That looks full enough to start. Would you help me please?" she asked before offering him her left hand, which looked small compared to his. Once Reginald took her soft hand, Talia tossed aside the blanket.

Reginald tried not to stare at her exquisite nakedness, but he knew he did it and felt guilty for his lust. Given her state, she didn't deserve this treatment.

As Talia settled into the tub, another servant rushed in and began to pour more water into the tub. Talia sighed a pleased coo.

He tried to argue with his erection and met her eyes again.

"Are those for me?" she asked him, catching Reginald by surprise.

He had forgotten about the clothing and felt flushed at the embarrassment. "Yes. They belonged to Flor, my wife." He held them up.

"Can I see the other?" Talia queried.

He shifted the darker dress to the front.

Talia tilted her face to study it. "She had excellent taste in clothing," she commented before stretching a finger to run over the material.

"Yes," he said, feeling flushed again. "She did. I'll leave you to bathe," he added before turning away.

"No… don't go," she called out. "I could use the company, after what I've been through."

Reginald sat down in her vacant chair.

Talia stared at him as another servant poured more water into the tub.

"What is it?" Reginald asked, feeling nervous at her direct eyes.

"I was just comparing your face to your brother's," Talia commented. "I remember meeting him before in Aachen. You and he bear very little resemblance to one another."

Reginald smiled at Talia. "Yes, my mother says that he takes after her side. I favor our father."

"Perhaps," Talia quipped as she stared into his eyes. "I can see some small traits common to her in Julien, but nothing between you two. Even if you favored your father's side, you would share some similarities, I should think."

Reginald felt stunned by her questions and wondered whether she doubted his parentage. "I knew my father," he said. "We appeared alike."

"Did you notice any likeness between your father and Julien?" she asked.

Reginald said nothing as he tried to find words.

"Oh, don't take my words to heart, Reginald. This bath is so wonderful. Please, tell Gudela to bring a hairbrush for me when they have filled the tub."

On impulse, Reginald decided to go speak to his mother. He felt like talking about this with her.

"Reginald," Talia's voice rang, and so he turned back towards her. "I also noticed that you and Clotilda bear no resemblance to each other."

"What?"

"Perhaps she favors her mother's family… like your brother," Talia added.

Reginald fell silent again. Now, he doubted his younger brother's parentage as well as Tildy's.

No, Talia has to be mistaken.

"Are you suggesting that both my mother and my wife have been unfaithful?" he asked.

"Hmmm?" Talia turned away from untangling her hair. "Oh no, no, no, no. I was not there, so I was… I cannot say who is faithful and who isn't. All I know is what I see with my eyes. Perhaps, if you would look closer at your daughter's face, you will see what I see. She doesn't resemble you at all."

Reginald stumbled out of his chair and backed out of the room in order to find his mother and Tildy. On the way out of the room, he nearly bumped into Vicelin. Rage burned within him as he yelled, "Watch your step! You almost spilled that on me!" He then stormed out of the house.

---

chapter eight

áerlaith sat down in the tent after spending the evening cleaning out a small grove of trees, which no one would appreciate, save herself. The effort had allowed her to escape the onslaught of noise between the Celtic blood-drinkers and the mortals.

She sensed Caoimhín walk into the tent, and he began talking to himself, or perhaps to her, about someone while he washed up before sleep. He then yammered something about Marcus before muttering about Julien's brother.

Sáerlaith let the words move past her and returned her thoughts to Ard Mhacha, but she soon sensed Caoimhín approach her.

"Did you hear anything I said?" he asked in an incredulous, yet concerned tone.

Sáerlaith blinked and tried to understand what he had asked. "No. I am sorry, Caoimhín, but I was not listening," she admitted.

Caoimhín studied her as if she were a fascinating variety of plant. "When was the last time you fed?"

Sáerlaith considered his words. "I don't recall," she answered after a brief pause. She then saw Caoimhín rip into his arm, causing her momentary shock at the violence of his sudden movement, and he shoved his bloody appendage into her mouth. Sáerlaith tried to resist it, but she felt Caoimhín wrap his other arm around her and hold her still. Soon, the fog surrounding her began to fade. After feeding for a few moments, she felt Caoimhín pull away.

He reached into his pack and fished out some bandages and herbs used to aid in healing when fellow blood-drinkers did not have enough energy to heal. Caoimhín began to bind his wound.

Sáerlaith swallowed the rest of the blood and wiped at her mouth and chin. "Why did you do that?" she demanded. "I didn't want any blood."

Caoimhín stared at her as if she were simple. "If you didn't feed, you'd fade away from us."

"That is precisely what I intended to do."

"Why would you wish to do such a thing to yourself?" he asked as he knelt in front of her.

"I have no purpose," Sáerlaith informed him. "Our home is gone, many have died, and I had no power to stop it. I'm useless."

Caoimhín grabbed her shoulders. "You have a purpose. You are our leader, our High Councilor. You are High Councilor because you have Morrigan's blessing. If Morrigan did not believe in your talents, you would never have had those duties thrust upon you."

"Our home is gone," Sáerlaith whispered. "Our beliefs are fading, as are we. Before long, we will be nothing but dust in this world."

Caoimhín slapped her.

The first contact only startled her, but the second blow made her face burn. She felt surprise, rather than anger.

"I need you to lead us," Caoimhín challenged. "I was not chosen by either Council. Morrigan encouraged the Council to put their faith in you. We need you, and the Celtic lines require you as well. If you don't resume your role, we will fail our mission. Is that what you want, Sáerlaith Ní Adhamdh?"

She felt dread at the thought of leading the Deargh Du again. She feared that she would make the wrong decisions, and yet she knew Caoimhín spoke the truth. Sáerlaith wiped the tears from her eyes and said, "I will think on your words. However, I need to sleep now."

She lied down on some bedding, and through her darkening vision, she saw Caoimhín crouch next to her and begin rolling out his blankets. "Thank you for feeding me," she murmured.

Caoimhín smiled at her. "It was my pleasure."

Once Sáerlaith awoke, she sensed the sun's rays begin to fade. Soon, the entire tent began to cool, and she felt the soothing comfort of night's embrace.

The sound of labored snoring drew her attention from night's reemergence, so she sat up and looked over at Caoimhín, the source of the snoring.

Sáerlaith shrugged off her bedding and knelt in front of his belongings. She went through his bag, hoping she wouldn't disturb him with the noise of her search. She hated going through his things, but she thought he wouldn't mind. She soon found and removed a pack of sponnc, a Druid's egg, some shells, a few stones, some other herbs, a few flasks of mead, and a few bowls.

Sáerlaith picked up the sponnc and a bowl and then drew down the darkness around the tent so no one would see her. She then crept into a field and headed to a familiar destination. The dewy grass wet her feet while walking to the long-forgotten grove, heavy with branches and forgotten celebrations.

Once she arrived at the grove, Sáerlaith knelt on the spot she had prepared the night before for workings and built a fire. She set the bowl and the sponnc over the fire and closed her eyes, which ran as smoke began to gather. She then leaned towards the fire, taking care to keep the flames from her clothing.

Sáerlaith wiped away the sweat beading on her forehead and began to deeply inhale and exhale the fumes. Sometimes, meeting the Phantom Queen seemed easier, but this time, she could not steady her concentration.

She placed her hands on the ground, hoping to find a connection, but a sudden headache and violent coughing kept her unfocused, cluttered, and dizzy with thought and worry. Sáerlaith rolled onto her side and then to her back. With the onslaught of the sponnc, she felt compelled to close her eyes.

At that moment, a bright light penetrated her eyelids, confusing her, so she opened them to identify its source, only to see the sun radiating warmth without burning her.

Sáerlaith sat up and stared at the sun as if she had never seen it before. Soon, the sound of a song on the wind drew her attention away from the sun. The accompanying strings of a harp made her heart knot in homesickness. She sat in the old grove, as if she hadn't moved from where she had begun her ritual, but Sáerlaith soon realized that the grove appeared clean, fresh, and young.

She then spied a group of cloaked Druids walking towards her.

They must be the source of the singing.

As the Druids approached, she expected to receive a greeting, but they said nothing to her as a circle enclosed around her. A fire began to roar from a stack of burning kindling and wood in the center of the grove, and then sponnc smoke began to permeate the air, as if last night's ritual began anew but with different people performing it.

After a minute or so, the music faded, only to be replaced by exuberant chanting. With the crescendo, Sáerlaith could discern the cacophonous squawking of ravens. Their discordant music grew as the chanting reached a fevered pitch.

Then, an unkindness of ravens swooped in and circled the grove, flying with increasing speed and energy, until they melded together in the center and became Her.

Morrigan stepped out of the amorphous gloom and walked towards her. Morrigan's hair and clothing seemed simple, yet She still radiated an understated glory. Her face revealed an innate strength, but a resigned sadness softened Her features.

The Druids seemed oblivious to Her arrival and continued to chant. Morrigan even walked through a Druid.

Sáerlaith dropped to her knees.

"Arise, my daughter."

Sáerlaith stood and watched as Morrigan walked the circumference of the grove. "What is this place?" Sáerlaith asked as the Goddess passed her again in a stately walk.

"This place?" Morrigan's dark eyes settled upon her for a brief moment. "Oh, this is the place from where you called me. Only, this is how it looked long ago, by your reckoning."

Sáerlaith felt surprise at having traveled in time, so to speak, and she wished to learn more. "Who are they calling?" she asked Morrigan.

"They're calling me," Morrigan replied. "But they knew me by a different name. They called me Cauth Bodva. They used this grove for centuries." The Goddess paused for a moment, and then Her words became a whisper. "They were happy, here… very happy. That is, until the Romans arrived."

Sáerlaith examined the skies, which darkened before her eyes. She then returned her attention to Morrigan. "Why have You brought me here?" she asked Her.

Morrigan drew closer before speaking. "This place was very important to me. It is still very important to me. These people were worthy of my love. They made great strides in my name, but then they were defeated. Their existence disappeared in the blink of an eye. No one since has offered me his or her devotion here in this place. As the years pass..." Morrigan fell silent again and seemed to study the grove before turning Her face to the Druids. "More and more of these places fade into dust."

The fresh wound in her heart for Ard Mhacha ripped anew, and Sáerlaith felt her eyes water, but this time, it was not from the sponnc. She gave in to her sorrow and began to weep. "I feel the loss as well." She sensed the Goddess turn towards her, and fear welled up in her heart. Sáerlaith made eye contact with the Goddess and, to her, Morrigan's eyes looked like icy pools of blackness that could swallow her soul.

"You may feel the loss, but you've done nothing about it," Morrigan accused, effortlessly gliding to stand in front of Sáerlaith. Disappointment colored Her features.

When Morrigan came within feet of her, Sáerlaith resisted the urge to lower her eyes and fall to her knees.

"I may have lost devout worshippers at this time," She said while gesturing to the grove and the assembled Druids, "but I've still adapted to the changes, and this grove will be used for worship again. Although they won't call my name, they will call me."

Sáerlaith tried to understand what She meant by that, but her fear and sadness still warred within. As she wiped away more tears, she felt Morrigan's eyes bore into her own, as if the Goddess laid her bare to the sun.

"So, what have you done to adapt to your new reality?"

The question startled Sáerlaith, and she found it difficult to find words with which to respond. "I–" she stammered when she felt Morrigan's forehead press against hers.

Sáerlaith experienced a sensation of dread, as if she could pass into the Goddess' eyes and disappear into the nothingness.

"You cower behind younglings. You eschew any responsibilities. You've let others make decisions that are rightfully yours to make!" Morrigan shouted at her. Each condemnation echoed around her, reverberating off the trees and the sky itself.

Sáerlaith pondered whether She planned to send her to the Field of the Judged.

In a commanding yet softer voice, Morrigan stated, "You are not facing this challenge as well as I had hoped. You mustn't dwell on what you cannot control."

Sáerlaith felt a mental nudge to kneel, and she obeyed the command without question. She witnessed Morrigan kneel as well, allowing for room between them.

In a motherly tone, Morrigan added, "I gave you these gifts for a purpose, my child. It saddens me that you aren't using them. I know there is strength within you. I've seen it before. Overcome your loss and fears. Move on, or you will fail."

Morrigan's mouth softened from a frown to a bittersweet half-smile.

Sáerlaith lowered her eyes, feeling humiliated, as she reflected on how she had *ignored her own talents. The Deargh Du needed her more than ever before. She needed to lead... not dwell on what could not be undone. Upon finding her resolve rekindled, she looked up at the Goddess. "I will not fail." Then a question occurred to her, but Sáerlaith felt fearful asking it. Still, she knew she had to ask that question. "My Queen, why–" she began to ask, until Morrigan rose to Her feet.*

"Yes, my child? You want to know why I allowed such a schism in the Deargh Du?" A mischievous smile lit the Morrigan's face.

Sáerlaith nodded.

"If you look down, your path may lead you to your answer."

Sáerlaith studied the ground in front of her knees. Upon finding no solid answers, she looked up towards Morrigan again, but where She had stood, nothing remained but mist and smoke. Even the Druids had faded into nothing but smoke, which smelled of sponnc and other heavy herbs.

Dizzy from her ordeal, Sáerlaith fell back against the grass again, as the sunlight darkened, harkening the re-emergence of night.

Soon, the mists cleared, and Sáerlaith stared at the ancient and weary grove, which basked in the moonlight.

The Goddess' last words lingered on the breeze.

Reginald tried to suppress a yawn while listening to Caoimhín, as the man continued droning on, listing administrative accomplishments and touting all of the projects they had finished.

After each of Caoimhín's talking points, delivered in a monotonous tone, the rest of the gathered party would nod and mutter amongst themselves. The merchants spoke in varied Frankish dialects, while the mercenaries conversed in their odd tongue and in Latin.

Reginald took a moment to look at his mother, studying her while thinking over Talia's comments about his family and daughter. After speaking with Talia, he had gone to play with Tildy and studied her. Although she did resemble her uncle, Reginald had also seen elements of her mother and her grandmother's family in Tildy. He reasoned that this explanation could be why she and Julien shared common features.

Why would Julien have any interest in Flor, anyway? They had been friends since childhood, but nothing more.

Reginald ceased his musing when Caoimhín cleared his throat. To Reginald, Caoimhín looked tired from his duties, from having to deal with the common people... something to which the Lord of Divio could relate.

At that moment, the tent flap raised, and a queen entered the tent. Lady Sáerlaith had appeared vacant-eyed earlier, but now she seemed focused, energetic, and enthusiastic. Something had changed her. Everyone turned his or her eyes towards her, which drew a smile from her fine features.

"Caoimhín, I shall take over from here," she said before touching his right shoulder with her right hand.

Something about this seemed appropriate to Reginald... a woman in charge. None of the mercenaries looked surprised. In fact, they appeared pleased. His worries about a woman taking control of the conversation faded, as the woman smiled at all present.

"I have heard from Caoimhín. I think it's time we returned to Vézelay to begin repairs," Lady Sáerlaith announced in a confident tone while looking at Reginald's mother.

"I would be most grateful for the help," his mother replied. "I cannot speak for my son, but I'm very impressed with the repairs here."

Sáerlaith then looked at him.

Reginald couldn't drum up a response right away, but he finally managed to utter, "Yes, thank you so much for your assistance and continued offers to aid us," once he found his tongue. "If my mother will permit me, I will accompany you to Vézelay." He needed an opportunity to talk to his mother and another chance, perhaps, to see Julien and Clotilda together.

His mother nodded her head. "You are always welcome in Vézelay."

Sáerlaith looked over the gathered persons. "It's settled, then. We will leave tomorrow night. Now, are there any other questions?"

No one spoke.

"Dismissed," Sáerlaith stated. "Let's begin to pack."

While the others left the tent, Reginald's mother hovered by Sáerlaith and Caoimhín. Reginald decided to remain in his seat, for now.

"I see your spirit has returned," Caoimhín said.

Sáerlaith placed her right hand on Caoimhín's left shoulder. "It was always there. I just needed some time to think things through."

Caoimhín held the tent flap for Sáerlaith and Reginald's mother.

"Mother," Reginald said, wishing for a moment of her time.

"Yes, Reginald?"

He rose from his chair and said, "I know you'll be excited to return home."

"Yes. I was not made for this constant traveling," she admitted. "I hope the meadow is in bloom. Tildy loves the flowers there." As she returned his smile, the candlelight made his mother look a decade younger.

"I'm certain she will have a lot of fun. I know it's been difficult for her," he added before sighing.

"It's been difficult for all," his mother said and then took his hand. "However, your home is restored now."

Reginald considered asking his mother about Julien's relationship with Flor, but instead, he decided upon another line of questioning. "Mother," he began. "I just noticed something interesting about Clotilda. She seems to bear a striking resemblance to Julien."

His mother chuckled. "Of course, she does. Most of my family, and my son and granddaughter, have the same cheekbones and mouth."

"Yes, of course," Reginald answered as he scrutinized his mother's face for her reaction. Her eyes revealed a strange suspicion, which quickly faded. He decided that forcing the question now would not work. Besides, he really needed to see Julien next to Clotilda. Only then would he know for sure. "I suppose we should pack for tomorrow." He then walked over to the tent flap and held up for her.

"When Vézelay is repaired, I'm going to hold a large feast for our friends, vassals, and family," his mother announced.

"And I will drink to your health," he informed her.

As soon as they entered his home, his mother ducked down the left corridor to her room, while he turned to the right. When Reginald arrived at his room, he found Talia and Tildy playing with her dolls again.

Talia looked up at him and smiled.

He could see the question in her eyes. When he shook his head, Talia's smile faded, and she returned her focus to Clotilda, who ran towards him. He picked her up and received a kiss.

Why did this question of parentage matter so much to Talia? How could she think such a thing? There has to be a reason why.

Constantinople

As Marcus and his escorts ran through Constantinople towards the ancient Hagia Sophia, or the Church of Holy Wisdom, he tried to remember the first time he saw the building, which seemed to be in the middle of reconstruction again. He saw beggars in front of the building's steps. Some slept, while others raised outstretched hands as they continued to wait for alms.

The group of Lamia and Children of Ares slowed down as they approached the back of the church. Soon, another group of gilded soldiers joined them. Marcus shuddered when he neared the Lamia wearing their golden finery.

The soldiers marched ahead and split in unison before the cathedral. The two closest to the doors opened them, as the rest of the party approached.

Marcus walked with the party to the back of the church, behind the icons and religious relics on display, towards a plain, wooden door. The soldiers in front held open the door, and the group walked down a long spiral staircase.

The group stopped at another ornate door, and Nicodemus used a knocker to alert others to his presence. A few arrow slits on the side of the door opened, catching Marcus' eye.

"Who goes there?" a voice called out through an arrow slit.

"It is Nicodemus." He seemed to pause a little before looking through one of the slits. Nicodemus then raised his voice. "I bring guests and information. I wish to speak to Efialtes."

"And the code?"

"You can see it's me, Nikolas! Why do I need to repeat the code?"

Quiet laughter echoed in the stillness. "Rules are rules, even though they don't always make sense," Nikolas answered.

"Very well," Nicodemus pouted. "The password is 'Dionysus'."

The laughter from the other side grew. "I'm sorry, but that was the code for last month."

"How am I supposed to know the new password?" Nicodemus yelled. "I was in Hadrianopolis for over a month!"

"It was sent by messenger."

"And when did the messenger leave?" Nicodemus seemed at the edge of his self-restraint.

"Several hours ago." An explosion of chuckles echoed through the hall.

Marcus saw Mandubratius grin. "Quite a show, isn't it?" the Briton whispered to him.

"And it takes a night to reach Hadrianopolis. How was I supposed to get this message?" Nicodemus answered, before turning grim eyes at Mandubratius.

"Oh, alright, enter," came Nikolas' voice.

Marcus heard scraping from the movement of metal against wood. Soon, he saw the door opening, followed by the rising of the portcullis and more sets of doors opening.

Once inside, another Lamia joined them. A deep frown warped his features. "Nicodemus, why are you home early?" he asked.

Nicodemus saluted him. "I bring news and visitors for Efialtes."

The other Lamia nodded, but his frown deepened. "Have you succeeded in your mission to eradicate the Strigoi?" He gestured for everyone to begin following him through the corridors.

"No," Nicodemus answered after falling in step with the him. "However, they have withdrawn, and they have not attacked us."

"Withdrawn?" The other Lamia looked shocked. "How many did you kill?"

"Sadly, not one."

"How many losses were there?" After the other Lamia turned down another hallway, the other Lamia looked pointedly at Nicodemus.

Nicodemus shrugged. "We lost ten," he answered.

The unnamed Lamia sputtered an angry chuckle. "It does not seem that your campaign has been successful, and yet, the Strigoi have left. I will relay this information to Efialtes."

Nicodemus touched the other Lamia's shoulder and stopped him. "Adriano, I must speak to him personally."

Adriano shook his head. "You've given me your report. What information do you have that you feel is worthy for Efialtes' ears only?"

"Because, there is a way to kill them," Nicodemus said.

Adriano crooked his neck to regard Nicodemus and raised a brow. "Intriguing. I believe that this will grant you an audience. I will report your request. If he agrees to see you, I will return. Otherwise, I will see you and your associates out."

Nicodemus nodded and bowed with much solemnity. "Thank you."

Adriano clapped his hands, summoning mortals. "Escort Nicodemus and his guests into the waiting room and provide them with sustenance."

The mortals bowed and motioned for Nicodemus and the rest of the group to follow.

The group then walked through more halls into a room with three lounges. Everyone in their party sat.

The servants left the room, but they soon returned with blood and wine.

Mandubratius smiled. "Nicodemus, when you were amongst us, you never had to beg for an appointment, now did you?"

Nicodemus scoffed. "I never once desired an audience with you."

"Really?" Mandubratius drawled. "Well, if you had desired one, you could've seen me straight away. I must say that I'm rather impressed with this décor."

Nicodemus shrugged. "This? This is as decorative as the servants' quarters. Even the mortals' latrine is more ornate."

Marcus felt burning against his arms, so he adjusted himself, but the gold-gilded trim of his chair still burned his skin. Finally, he jumped up and looked at the Co-Consuls. "May I stand, sir?"

Mandubratius' face revealed annoyed confusion. "I can't, for the life of me, imagine why you would be sitting amongst your social betters. So yes, stand up immediately. I will punish you later for this insolence."

Marcus shook out his arms and then backed into an unadorned, marbled corner of the room. He felt great relief being away from gilded surfaces.

Nicodemus chuckled again. "I would hate to be a servant of yours."

"What a servant likes and dislikes is not my concern. So, how long will we wait?" Mandubratius asked as he drummed his fingers against an armrest.

"Not long, I believe," Nicodemus replied. "I'm fairly well respected in the Council."

"You don't say? You are a council member, and yet they send you on this soldier's errand and force you to wait at the front door like some snot-nosed messenger." Mandubratius smiled at Amata, whose face turned up in a grin.

"That's not true," Nicodemus uttered in a half-growl.

Amata added, "In Rome, a council member would never be asked to perform such a menial task... dealing with the Strigoi. In fact, I believe, because of your low rank, we will be very lucky indeed if Efialtes bothers to take the time to hear your information."

Nicodemus' eyes glowed red.

At that moment, Adriano walked into the waiting room. "He will see you."

"It appears that today is your lucky day, Nicodemus," muttered Mandubratius before standing up and following Adriano.

Marcus filed in behind Mandubratius, while the rest of the party stood up and followed.

A pair of guards at the end of a long hallway, more ornate than the others, opened a set of gilded double doors. Marcus peered through the group of Lamia in front of him into a throne room fit for an emperor. Bright, flickering oil lamps lit the jeweled room. Mortal and Lamia servants walked past them to pay homage to their great master.

On a raised dais, a young Greek man sat. Efialtes wore a beard, but he only looked a few years older than Horatio. As Mandubratius had said earlier, one could not mistake this foppish boy for a nightmare. The boy stood and squeaked, "Nicodemus, why do I waste my time with your presence? I am disappointed by your failure."

"But, my Lord—"

"Silence!" Efialtes' face and eyes glowed red with fury. "I have not given you leave to speak." He then strutted down the dais. "I can see that the Strigoi have withdrawn, but whether that is because of your actions or not, I cannot say. In my estimation, it is possible, regardless of their cause for leaving, that they may yet return." Efialtes walked a few paces in apparent thought, and then spun back around to glare at Nicodemus. "Yet, you have killed none and lost ten. Explain yourself!"

"My Lord, you do not understand. They drive us to madness. Those who are incapacitated, they kill. We cannot get close enough to kill them."

"If they are so dangerous, how is it that you only lost ten?" Efialtes asked.

"I gave my reserves arrows to drive the Strigoi away from a distance, beyond the range of their madness," Nicodemus replied. "However, we could not hit them soon enough. In moments, they were upon us."

"Tell me, Nicodemus, what is this vital information you wish to present?"

"I bring someone I wish to introduce to you. He has the information I wish for you to know," Nicodemus explained.

Efialtes waved his left hand dismissively, as if impatient. "Then introduce your companions."

"This is—"

"I am Mandubratius of the Lamia, and I have never been treated so rudely in my life," Mandubratius challenged. He rushed his sentences together, giving no break for Efialtes to interject. "I would think someone of your supposed class would know how to treat guests, especially those of my sister's and my stature."

Marcus tried not to smile, whereas Efialtes looked as if he would explode.

"Guards!" the leader of the Children of Ares shouted. At his call, around one hundred armed soldiers rushed in, surrounded Mandubratius' party, and pointed their swords at the Co-Consuls and Marcus. "How dare you bring our arch nemeses into our midst?" he asked Nicodemus.

"Efialtes," Mandubratius stated in an even tone while raising both hands in a gesture of truce. "Do you really need all of these guards just to talk to us? Come now, I'm not uncivilized or a threat to you. Besides, what your cowardly errand boy did not tell you is that I know how to kill Strigoi, and I also know that they will indeed return."

"Efialtes," Nicodemus added, "This traitor will give us the information we need to survive these attacks."

Mandubratius huffed a bit. "I am most hurt. I could not have conceived that you would be any more rude and insulting to my associates and me. You will refer to me as Consul of the Lamia. Of course, Amata believes I should be referred to as Caesar, but that term is so archaic."

"Insolent bastard! I shall have you executed! Disarm Nicodemus and his party!" Efialtes demanded while looking rather like a petulant child.

Marcus grew tired of this game and, while looking at Mandubratius, wondered whether he needed to attack. However, before he could take action, Amata stepped forward.

"No, you may not," she said with great calm in her voice.

"Amata, I'm talking to the..." Mandubratius glanced at the so-called leader of the Children of Ares. "What is your title, Efialtes?" He then looked back and smiled at his Co-Consul.

Efialtes revealed fangs, apparently too furious to voice anything else.

"This... acolyte of the third order," Mandubratius added.

Efialtes made no move to attack. Nor did he order his men to do so either.

Amata patted Mandubratius on his back. "You are accomplishing nothing more than irritating him. Sometimes your lack of negotiating skills upsets me." She then looked directly into Efialtes' ember-red eyes. "Step aside, brother, and I'll show you how to negotiate."

Marcus watched Amata smile at Efialtes.

"I apologize, my Lord, for this awkward situation that has developed because of a misguided fool." She slowly started to step in Efialtes' direction, focusing on his eyes. Her walk exuded power and grace. Amata then began to pull off her clothing, starting with her belts and outer coverings, revealing extreme confidence with her every step.

When Marcus glanced at the others, Mandubratius appeared surprised. However, the Children of Ares looked horrified, and their swords wavered. Marcus reasoned that Mandubratius must have suggested this ploy, since the Lamia seemed to be losing the battle to suppress his smile.

"I offer knowledge in exchange for our safety, our freedom, and permission to obtain an object we seek," Amata cooed as she glided closer to Efialtes.

"Pu... pu... put your clothes on, wench," Efialtes stuttered, looking very much a young, virgin boy.

"If I respect you by calling you 'my Lord', you will address me as the Lady Consul of the Lamia. How dare you call me a wench? I am older and of the same social status as you!" Amata's eyes flashed as she took another graceful step closer to Efialtes. "In addition to my terms, I add your life and the lives of your associates to the bargaining table," Amata stated.

"Wha... what do you mean?" Efialtes stuttered once more.

Amata tugged at an inky lock of hair. "My escorts and I have killed sixty Strigoi. What is that compared to a mere hundred of the Children of Ares? You have allowed me to come into close proximity to you. I could kill you in a mere second, and within the next twenty seconds, all of the soldiers in this room would be dead." Amata smiled. "However," she purred, "this is not a threat. We are just two comrades negotiating."

Efialtes regained some measure of composure, but he still swallowed when he spoke. "You have killed sixty of them, and I shall not doubt your word."

"That is wise," Amata said before shaking her hair to one side.

"There is much value indeed, if you can give us the knowledge of how to defend ourselves against the Strigoi."

Marcus realized that he would be stuck in dispensing this knowledge.

Efialtes clapped his hands three times, and in response, the guards sheathed their swords and stepped back to their previous positions.

Marcus could see a measure of relief on their faces, and yet, Nicodemus still appeared to be frightened, as if he feared execution.

Efialtes seemed to study Amata for a moment again. His initial embarrassment over her lack of clothing had apparently faded. "I'm curious, Lady Consul... what object is it that you seek?"

"It is a mirror in the possession of Empress Irene that we seek," Amata explained. "It is a bronze mirror with beautiful etchings and carvings."

Efialtes nodded. "I have heard of this mirror. It will be difficult to obtain, but I will give you and your Co-Consul leave to acquire it. Please understand that our relations with Her Imperial Majesty are tenuous. We cannot be seen to aid you. If you accept this condition, I shall accept the bargain in its entirety."

"I accept the condition and know you will not aid us. However, you will also not hinder us," Amata stated.

Efialtes took two more steps dais to stand toe-to-toe with the taller Amata.

Marcus felt some amusement at the sight of this cub acquiescing to a queen lioness he had tried to out-roar.

"I accept this bargain," Efialtes stated. He and Amata then embraced and kissed in a very chaste manner. "Perhaps this bargain we've sealed can lead to more permanent relations between us."

Amata smiled again. Despite her nudity, she still radiated cold and regal beauty. "Perhaps, my Lord. Thank you."

Efialtes turned his attention away from Amata and began addressing his men. "Adriano, draw up papers of passage. Nicodemus, I'd like you and your men to stay with us." He turned back to regard Amata. "There is much we must discuss, Amata. Would you be so kind as to discuss, at your leisure, the finer points of Strigoi eradication with one of my generals?"

"I would be most delighted. However, if it pleases you, I would like your general to speak with my general," she said.

"Of course, if they are of equal class..."

Marcus raised a brow at Mandubratius, curious about the mention of class. Perhaps this had been another reason the Children of Ares left Rome. They seemed preoccupied with matters of status. Certainly, it could explain why a whelp like Efialtes could rule over the Children of Ares.

Mandubratius said nothing in reply to his glance, but Marcus could see a slight nod from the Lamia.

"That is a grand suggestion," Efialtes continued. "I meant no disrespect, requesting that you speak with a mere general," he added.

Amata chuckled. "No disrespect was taken, my Lord. Thank you. I assure you that they are of equal rank. I present General Marcus Galerius Primus Helvetticus of the Lamia." Marcus stepped forward and bowed to Efialtes, who waved him away.

Soon, another Lamia arrived from a different door and nodded to Marcus.

"This is General Gaius Naevius Tacitus Britannicus," Efialtes said. "You two are dismissed to discuss whatever must be discussed."

"I shall go as well, my Lord," Amata added. "My Co-Consul and I must discuss our renewed friendship with our old associates." Amata gathered her clothing, tucked them under her left arm, and took Mandubratius' outstretched hand with her right.

"Very well," Efialtes stated with a sigh. His face revealed disappointment. "I hope we will see each other again soon, Lady Consul."

"We shall see each other very soon," Amata cooed. She and Mandubratius then led Marcus and Efialtes' general out of the throne room.

After leaving the room, Amata and Mandubratius dropped hands. "Marcus, Gaius, and I will discuss the Strigoi. Mandubratius, you meet with our associates above and pursue our other objective."

"My plan exactly," Mandubratius stated. He met Gaius' stare for a moment. "It will be my pleasure." He then motioned for a guard.

One snapped to attention and stepped forth. "Sir, if you wish, I can lead you to the surface."

"Thank you."

Marcus noticed a spark in the Lamia's eyes, and he wondered for a moment whether the guard would survive.

Amata turned to the still-silent general of the Children of Ares. "Gaius, is there someplace we can sit and talk?"

Gaius bowed. "Yes, Lady Consul. If you will permit me, I will escort you myself to a comfortable sitting room."

"Yes, that would please me. Marcus, be a dear and carry these," Amata suggested before handing him the rest of her clothing.

"Yes, Lady Consul."

Amata uttered a musical laugh. "Do not derive too much pleasure from carrying my clothing. Please lead on, Gaius."

"Just follow me," Gaius drawled.

When Amata pointed to a tabletop, Marcus placed her clothing on the table. He then looked on as she began dressing, but General Gaius' voice drew Marcus' attention to him.

"Lady Consul. It's been a very long time, hasn't it?" Gaius tilted his head to the side and watched her dress for a moment, before shifting his eyes to Marcus. "May I call you Marcus, Galerius, or do you prefer Marcus Galerius? We are not as formal here as we were once." Gaius then stretched out his right arm, which Marcus clasped firmly.

Marcus chuckled. "It's been a good many years since anyone called me anything but my praenomen. You may refer to me in the familiar, and I hope I may do the same."

Marcus redirected his attention to Amata, whom he realized had just finished dressing.

"Neither of you need to stand on my account," Amata said. "Please sit down, both of you."

"Thank you, Lady Consul," Marcus and Gaius both said in unison.

Gaius gestured for Marcus to take his choice of chair. "Please refer to me in the familiar as well. I'm not sure whether I'd even respond to Naevius, now."

Marcus sat in the chair least gilded, hoping he could continue hiding his weakness to gold.

"By the by," added Gaius as he sat next to Marcus, "Your name is familiar."

Unsure how to respond, given the clandestine situation within which he was introduced to Gaius, Marcus smirked and said, "Well, yes, there was Galerius, the Emperor," hoping Gaius hadn't known of Marcus' name as a Deargh Du, which could undermine Mandubratius' plan.

"Oh yes, of course, but it is not just your nomina," Gaius said.

"So, where have you heard my name before?" Marcus felt a moment of fear as Gaius continued to study him.

"While keeping the peace in Britannia, under the command of Trajan, I happened across a statue commemorating the lives of the dead, those who went beyond the call of duty, from Julius Caesar's first mission. The statue held your name in great prominence, and it even bore your likeness. Is it a coincidence that both you and Mandubratius met with your respective fates during the same campaign? I do not recall seeing his name on the statue."

Marcus thought about answering, about lying, but Amata thankfully cleared her throat, drawing Gaius' scrutiny towards her.

"It was certainly no coincidence, Gaius. I am certain you remember my sponsor." Amata met his stare. "Felician and I were scouting Éire when we happened across these destitute survivors of a shipwreck, and lo and behold, we discovered Mandubratius and Marcus. Felician couldn't resist the propensity for maliciousness that Mandubratius exuded, and Marcus was my personal plaything... my pet, if you will. Isn't that right, my pet?" Amata asked while patting Marcus' leg.

Marcus cleared his throat a little, remembering the status of the sponsored parties among Lamia. "Yes, Lady Consul."

Amata smiled before moving her hand away.

Marcus thought about mentioning how Mandubratius had returned to

Caesar, supported his cause during the civil war, and even fought on his side against Pompey at Pharsalus, where he 'died', but if Amata wanted Gaius to know Mandubratius' life history, she would have mentioned it.

With nothing else forthcoming from Amata, Marcus' thoughts drifted back to the statue. "Gaius, I did not realize that such a statue existed. Where is it? I'd enjoy seeing it, the next time I'm in Britannia," he said.

"It was once in the middle of the plaza on the southern coast," Gaius replied. "However, one night, it was stolen. No one knew who took it, but there were rumors that the barbaric Picts had absconded with it."

Marcus noticed Amata growing impatient with their conversation. "Perhaps, one day, I shall gaze upon it." He decided to change the subject before Amata made a show of hitting him in front of Gaius. "You wish to know how to deal effectively with the Strigoi?"

Gaius leaned forward in his seat. "Of course."

"There is no real trick to it," he informed Gaius. "The secret is to employ combined arms in a unified attack. You have archers, swordsmen, and Greek fire. You plan the defensive area well, and you must have a volunteer to act as bait. When they attack, use your Greek fire and your archers to distract the Strigoi… to wound them, burn them. The swordsmen should then leap in for the kill. Even if the killing blow cannot be struck with the first swing, damage to their bodies will cloud the Strigoi's minds with pain, thereby distracting them from their mind tricks."

Marcus paused a bit to make sure the information sank in with Gaius. Once the other general nodded, Marcus continued. "The Strigoi have been using what appears to be an uncontrollable madness attack. However, we recently encountered a small group that seems to be experimenting with a more focused projection of their madness."

Gaius' eyes widened. "You are saying that they are developing the ability to single out their targets and concentrate energies on that target?"

"Yes, but even with this change in their tactics, they can still be killed."

"It must be a successful technique, since you and your associates killed sixty Strigoi. Would you be able to demonstrate these tactics to my soldiers and train them to employ it?"

Marcus tried not to feel annoyed with the request. "Only if the Lady Consul consents," he told Gaius.

Amata looked up from her nails. "Hmm? Oh yes, certainly, by all means. Assist with this training, Marcus," she ordered while smiling at him.

"Thank you, Lady Consul," Gaius replied. "Well, I shall assemble my soldiers in the Imperial parade grounds at eight. Would you care to meet me for drinks at dusk, so we can discuss the training in more detail?"

Marcus looked at Gaius and then turned his eyes back to Amata. "With your permission, Domina."

"You have my leave to do what is necessary to fulfill the terms of this bargain, Marcus," she answered.

"In that case, Gaius, where shall we meet at dusk?" Marcus asked.

"There is an inn near the parade grounds called the Rusty Gauntlet." The other general then stood up. "Well, I must see to my Lord."

Marcus arose and clasped arms with him again. "I will see you at dusk."

"I am looking forward to it," Gaius answered. "If I may, Lady Consul, we can provide you with lodging here, or you may stay anywhere in town."

"I appreciate your hospitality, Gaius, but, I yearn for open spaces and sky above me. I hope you are not offended by my desire to sleep on the surface."

"I understand, Lady Consul. I prefer that myself. I will have Adrastos escort you outside. By my estimate, you have less than an hour before dawn."

Amata nodded. "That's plenty of time to find a place to stay and attain some refreshments. Marcus, let's find a pleasant place to sleep."

After following Adrastos through the maze of tunnels, Mandubratius joined Marcus and Amata, and then the three of them exited the church. Once outside, they walked past a group of pre-dawn worshippers.

"Where do you think the rest of our party is?" Amata asked Marcus in Gaelic. He noticed, with pleasure, that her coy games ended once they had exited the Children of Ares' stronghold.

"I'm sure at the closest inn," he said. He then sniffed the air. "This way. I smell our friends."

Soon, he found their associates in a large inn. Marcus made a show of asking the innkeeper where their rooms were located, even though he could sense them, and he led his small party into one of the rooms.

While the others began asking Amata more questions about the Children of Ares, Marcus sensed Máire come into the room and curl up in the bedding next to him.

He rolled over, buried his face into her hair, and closed his eyes. "I have to train the Children of Ares tomorrow on our techniques for killing the Strigoi," he mumbled.

"I heard," she whispered. "Have you fed?"

Marcus shook his head.

Máire pulled aside her hair, exposing her neck.

Marcus felt his teeth extend at the thought of taking her. He pulled her in closer, and within moments, the taste of her vitae awakened him and brought him out of exhaustion. As he encircled her in his arms, he remembered the first time he had tasted her. Soon, the frightening terrors of the Strigoi faded, and sleep welcomed him.

chapter nine

ianait considered her traveling companions and wondered whether anyone had fed, although most seemed a little drunk. She looked on as Marcus took a sip of his wine and turned towards Patroclus, who sat opposite Marcus. Most of the group shared a long table.

Marcus seems to be in better spirits. Perhaps he slept well this past day.

"So, would you and Claudius join me in conducting a training exercise?" Marcus asked in Irish.

"Who are we teaching?" Patroclus asked in response.

Fianait smiled as she watched Marcus tilt his goblet of wine and gulp what remained of his drink. A little wine dripped from the corner of his mouth.

"General Gaius Naevius Tacitus Britannicus and the rest of the Children of Ares," he answered, wiping away the trickle of wine with his sleeve.

For some reason Fianait could not fathom, Patroclus seemed nervous.

"Marcus, I'm not sure about this," the Legate responded.

"Oh come, now, Patroclus," Amata cooed while patting his shoulder. "Please show Gaius how this technique works."

"But I... really don't think–" Patroclus sputtered.

"Is this reluctance because Gaius is your sponsor?" Mandubratius asked after walking from the hallways leading to the rooms.

Fianait could see Patroclus fixate his eyes on his wine.

"It has been years... centuries... since he and I met face to face. Not since he rejected our ways and left with the others."

Fianait raised a brow. Patroclus was a mystery to her. He kept a tight grip on his honor.

Marcus placed his chin in his hands and rested his elbows on the table. "Did he depart on good terms with you?" he asked.

Patroclus shook his head. "Alas, the last words spoken between us were in anger."

"I did not know this," Mandubratius stated and then sat down next to him on the bench.

"He wished for me to denounce and kill you and Amata. However, I do not turn back on my oaths," Patroclus stated.

Fianait saw Máire tilt her head to look eye to eye with Patroclus and then asked, "What do you think his reaction will be when he sees you with Marcus and Claudius?"

Patroclus sighed and lowered his eyes to the wooden table. "I doubt he knows that I still draw breath."

As Mandubratius cleared his throat, his stare sought out Marcus across the table. "Well, Marcus. Do you still desire to have Patroclus accompany you to the training exercise?"

"I have every confidence in Patroclus. If he wishes to accompany us, he may do so, but... only... if he wishes it."

Fianait saw Mandubratius roll his eyes a little.

"Well, Patroclus, it seems you have a choice in the matter. You can either go with Marcus or not. It matters not to me which choice you make."

Fianait could sense a hidden meaning in that offered choice.

Patroclus nodded his head, seemingly considering the matter in silence. After a few moments, he looked up and said, "Marcus, the honor is to serve."

What a Roman thing to say.

"An excellent choice of words, Patroclus," Mandubratius replied. "Amata and I will visit the Empress tomorrow night."

"How boring," Amata grumbled, seeming displeased with the plans.

"At least they'll have some good wine and vitae from around the world," Mandubratius murmured before sipping at his wine.

"Yes, but I'll have to speak Greek the entire evening," Amata sighed and appeared out of sorts. "No one speaks Greek in Rome. My Greek is so bad, I may ask for wine and receive a pig instead."

"Máire speaks passable Greek, as do several other members of our party," Marcus said, perhaps as a boast.

Máire laughed. "I have no interest in Imperial feasts."

Mandubratius' mouth opened in apparent shock. "You would pass an opportunity to drink, dine, and dance with the elite of modern society? You are a barbarian!"

Fianait noticed Máire's eyes gleam.

"She does not even have clothing for such an event, Mandubratius," Amata argued. "Let her train the Children of Ares with the men."

Patroclus then blurted, "I'm sorry to say that I don't think the Children of Ares would listen to a female warrior."

"They wouldn't?" Marcus asked.

Fianait wondered whether her confusion matched his.

"Sadly, no," Amata replied. "They are quite misogynistic, like most Romans and Greeks. I only suggested Máire train them in jest."

"So, they don't respect women at all?" Fianait asked Amata after finally getting an opportunity to join their conversation.

"No, they do not," Amata answered before eyeing Mandubratius.

"Well, perhaps Máire can spend her free time having coitus with Mac Alpin, Edward, and the puppy," Mandubratius suggested and then broke out in heavy chuckles.

Máire threw the wine from her goblet at Mandubratius, who closed his eyes and shook himself a little before wiping the wine off his face.

"What did I say?" Mandubratius sputtered, managing to appear confounded. "Now, I'll have to wash out the stains," he whined and then pulled off his tunic. Mandubratius looked up at Máire and then threw the tunic at her. "You wash it, while the rest of us are busy."

In a crisp, fluid motion, which exhibited the grace, precision, and beauty of the Deargh Du, Máire grabbed the shirt with her left hand while punching Mandubratius in the face with her right, knocking him onto his back. She then threw the tunic at him and spat in his face. "Wash it yourself," Máire suggested in a heated tone, before stomping away.

Feeling outraged herself, Fianait slammed her goblet down on the table and stared at Mandubratius.

After pushing aside the tunic, Mandubratius slid his elbows under himself and sat up, as his legs lay across the bench. "What did I do?" he asked her. "Why is she always so upset with me? That's what women do! Wash things!"

"I hope the likes of you will never control the world," Fianait hissed.

Mandubratius merely batted his eyes and smiled. "You're going to help me up, right sweetheart?" he asked in a condescending manner and then extended his right hand.

Desiring nothing more than leaving the presence of this bloody misogynous pig, Fianait grunted in anger before grabbing her goblet and dumping her wine on his face. After slamming the empty goblet onto the table, she attempted to rush away, but Mandubratius managed to reach up and grab her arm. Fianait then kicked him in his side, causing him to wince and let go of her.

"Honestly, why do the women in our party hate me so?" he whined to the others.

She heard Amata begin to answer him with a sharp-sounding reply, but Fianait could stand his presence no more, so she ran outside as fast as she could without drawing undue mortal attention.

Once outside, Fianait took a moment, allowing the dark, new moon skies and the sea breezes, those gusts that didn't bring foul odors, to calm her. She sensed a few mortals wander through the streets and alleys of Constantinople, and then she perceived Máire to her left. Fianait confirmed her senses with her eyes, when she found Máire at the water's edge, staring at the sea.

Once Fianait came within a few paces of Máire, the other Deargh Du said, "Fianait."

"May I join you?" she asked Máire.

"Of course," she answered after turning around and looking at her.

Fianait sat down next to Máire. "It's beautiful, is it not?"

"It may be, but it's not as pretty as the An Mhuaidh," Máire answered. "The air is foul here and smells of burning animal fat. A night in Éire is entirely different. We could smell wildflowers, animals, and the hidden beings." A wistful smile played about Máire's face for a moment before resignation returned to darken her beautiful features.

Fianait nodded. "Yes, that is true. I miss Ard Mhacha, the islands in the west, the view to the northeast where I can see Scotland and the Isle of Man, the waterfalls in the east." She paused and looked at Máire. "We cannot return home... not now, anyway. We must make the best of the time given to us."

Máire patted her hand. "As you know, I have been exiled from Éire far longer than you have, but yes, I know. What I really miss about home is being respected. There, at least during my mortal years, women were not on a pedestal, nor were we treated as cumal."

Fianait squeezed Máire's hand and the released it. "One would think a Briton would have respect for women."

Máire gave her a sidelong stare. "He may have the blood of the Britons in his veins, but Mandubratius has Rome in his heart and mind. In the mind of a Roman, all women are cumal."

Fianait stared out at the sea and watched the waves. She inhaled to take in all the scents. "Claudius and Marcus are Roman, and yet they don't act that way," she commented.

Máire chuckled. "Sometimes without realizing it, they are over-protective or forget that we share some of the chores. Once, in Bath during our winter festivities, we began drinking. We became drunk and rowdy, spilling mead, breaking goblets everywhere, and passing out. When I woke up the next evening, the mess remained." After a pause, she added, "I didn't want the servants to clean it because it was our mess. So, for three weeks the mess stayed. Marcus and the others seemed fine with drinking in their own filth. Finally, I gave up and cleaned the mess, with some help from the servants. When we finished cleaning, Marcus had the gall to say, 'I see you finally cleaned'. I left him a mop and bucket to clean up his shattered teeth and spattered blood."

Fianait closed her eyes and began laughing. She heard Máire giggle and snort as well.

After a few moments, Fianait managed to get her laughter under control. "I take it that this is not a recurring incident then?" she asked.

"No... it's rare," Máire admitted.

Fianait exhaled. "However, your hostilities with Mandubratius seem to keep manifesting themselves." ·

Máire turned away. Her expression seemed dark, distant.

"You have every right to kill him," Fianait stated.

Máire turned her eyes back to Fianait. "Yes. Thank you. I may do so, when this quest is over and the Strigoi are defeated."

Fianait rose. "Don't you want to put him in his place now, at least sooner rather than later?"

"Certainly," the other Deargh Du replied, "but how? Every time I knock him senseless, he gets up, smiles, and insults me again."

"Then go to the feast!"

"What?" Máire looked surprised. "Why would I do that?"

"Because he doesn't want you there," Fianait answered. "He thinks you're a barbarian and uncultured."

"I merely act in accordance with my station," Máire replied and then chuckled a little.

"Fine, then. Let us prepare for this feast. I see a dressmaker down the street. We can rouse her for dresses. Now, stand," she said before taking Máire's outstretched hand and pulling her to her feet.

"Why?" Máire appeared a little cranky but still amused. "We aren't going."

"You convinced both of us that we needed to go," Fianait answered. She then started to pull the other Deargh Du down the street. "We also need shoes, and your hair is dreadful."

As the door to the Rusty Gauntlet came into sight, Marcus stopped walking and then turned to Patroclus. "This is your last chance to leave."

Patroclus shook his head. "I need to be here," he answered.

Claudius walked past Marcus and opened the heavy, wooden door.

Through the haze from the burning lamp oil, Marcus recognized Gaius at a table in the shadows to the back. An unfamiliar blood-drinker sat with the general.

After leading his party through drunken patrons and promiscuous tavern wenches, Marcus arrived at the general's table.

Gaius rose, and his eyes fixated on Marcus. "Marcus?" The general then looked over Marcus' shoulder. At that moment, Gaius' face blanched.

Marcus turned his head and realized that Gaius stared at the Legate.

"Patroclus?" asked Gaius.

"Yes, your eyes have not been deceived," Patroclus answered.

Patroclus seemed surprised when his sponsor embraced him. He returned the hug.

"It is good to see you, after all these years, Patroclus."

Marcus could see pride shining in Gaius' eyes.

"Now," Gaius said before turning to Claudius. "Who is this soldier?"

"This is Claudius Metrius Sertorius... my lieutenant," Marcus answered. "Amata sponsored him as well."

Gaius seemed a little surprised. "So, she sponsored both of you? She must have been very busy. I'm astonished we haven't met before."

"Marcus and I spent most of our time in Britannia and Éire, General," Claudius stated before offering Gaius his right arm.

Both men clasped arms.

Gaius chuckled. "My, what stories you two must have. Oh, forgive me. This is my lieutenant, Sextus."

More clasping of arms ensued.

Once all five former soldiers of Rome sat down at the table, Gaius called for wine.

"So, you two fought under Julius Caesar?" Sextus asked. "That is most impressive. I was merely one of the Praetorian Guard for Marcus Aurelius."

Claudius leaned forward and said, "It must have been a great honor to serve one of the last, truly good, emperors."

Sextus nodded.

"So, shall we get down to business?" Marcus asked while glancing at each former soldier.

After the innkeeper brought forth goblets and poured the house diluted and spiced wine, Marcus willed himself to drink the swill.

Gaius raised his cup and decreed, "Audaces Fortuna iuvat. We shall drink to bravery on the battlefield."

Marcus and the others raised their cups and echoed Gaius' words.

After pulling out a scroll tube, Sextus withdrew the battle plan and unrolled it on the table. He held the map in place while the others placed their goblets on the four corners of the scroll. He then set the case on the table near him.

"From what you described to Gaius, I've drawn up the battlefield movements. Is this an accurate depiction of your method, general?" Sextus asked while looking at Marcus.

Marcus studied the plan and nodded. "There are three crucial elements that must be identified. They are detection, baiting, and contact. Your attack formation needs to be flexible and highly mobile. Strigoi tend to show up unexpectedly," he said.

Gaius leaned over the table and added, "It is as I thought. Reports I received from Nicodemus relay and reflect some of the same tactics. To his credit, he utilized archers, but he did not coordinate their use with swordsmen, flaming arrows, and Greek fire."

Claudius cleared his throat. "My apologies for interrupting," he said. "We've found that instantaneous communication and coordination are the keys to success. This is most difficult when defending yourselves from their mental attack."

"Given the unpredictable nature of the Strigoi, it is also prudent to have an alternate chain of command, in case key leaders are attacked," Patroclus added.

Gaius smiled. "These are very good points indeed. Sextus, tell them what we have planned for this evening."

Sextus reached into the scroll case and pulled out another scroll, which set atop the first.

The four other Romans lifted their goblets again and then set them back down on both scrolls.

"This is a map of the parade grounds," Sextus announced. "The Tenth Legion will be the subjects for the exercise. For the first few hours, you are to train them. After that, we will release felons who are hoping to win their freedom."

"And they are the Strigoi?" Marcus asked.

Gaius nodded. "Yes. We found it best to use felons in these types of exercises."

"'A chance for freedom'," Claudius quoted before meeting Marcus' eyes, and then all five Romans exchanged smiles.

"Freedom from this life, anyway," Gaius muttered. They all chuckled. "Let's finish this wine and then go to the parade grounds."

Marcus believed strongly that Claudius felt as uncomfortable with this practice as he did. However, any objection would probably give away their true identities.

"Wait!" Máire heard Fianait yell as the door of the carriage started to close.

Both women ran, in an attempt to catch the carriage before it left... at least that was Fianait's objective... not Máire's.

"We're coming, too!" Fianait shouted while pulling a reluctant Máire along. Máire tried to hurry, but she still felt unsure about going to the celebration.

Mandubratius opened the carriage door and faced the two women.

Máire could see a most devious grin spread across his face, and his eyes twinkled with mischief. She wondered whether she needed to throw him from the carriage, since he looked entirely too pleased with himself.

"So, you two decided to join us after all?" he drawled. Once Fianait and Máire reached the carriage, Mandubratius hopped down. He then turned and whistled for Maon, who peered from the carriage and smiled at them.

"Maon, two more ladies will be joining us," Mandubratius informed him. He then offered his right hand to Fianait first and assisted her into the carriage with grace.

Máire looked up and thought that Perhaps Mandubratius had decided to behave.

When Mandubratius offered Máire his right hand, she took it, though with great reluctance and trepidation. In the process of being helped onto the small step leading to the carriage door, she felt a hand on her backside. Máire kicked out her heel and landed a blow against what felt like his shoulder. She then pulled the door shut. "Now... this will be an enjoyable evening," she commented, feeling gratified at inflicting some pain upon that... man.

Mandubratius gazed with mischief upon his face through the window in the door, to Máire, but then he chuckled and called out, "Maon, I think this means I'll be riding with you."

Máire sensed him leap onto the top of carriage. Before she could brace herself or sit, she heard Maon shout to the horses, crack his whip, and then the carriage lurched forward.

The sudden burst of motion caught Máire unawares. She fell to her knees on the floor of the carriage, while her upper body settled against Amata's thighs.

Quite unlike a Deargh Du.

Máire felt embarrassed, as she looked up at the Lamia. "Sorry," she whispered meekly. Though inwardly, she fumed at that horrible Lamia up top.

Amata chuckled. "I assumed you would levitate, like Fianait."

Máire looked up from her less than graceful landing at Fianait, who hovered above her head.

Fianait helped Máire up. Máire sat down in a bench seat across from them.

"Fianait, why are you sitting next to Amata?" Máire asked, though the question was borne of curiosity and not any other compulsion. She didn't want to admit to the two women that Mandubratius' antics had gotten her so worked up that she momentarily forgot she could fly.

Fianait looked at Amata and then turned her eyes back to Máire. "I assumed you wanted to sit next to Mandubratius," she answered, "and I think Amata agrees." A nod from Amata confirmed Fianait's statement. "You two enjoy pestering each other so much." Fianait and Amata giggled.

"Why would you two think such a thing?" Máire felt horrified that they believed her alleged infatuation to be true. "Stop laughing!"

"I thought your confrontations were a strange way of showing affection for each other," Fianait added.

"Oh yes! That makes sense. You and he are infatuated with each other!" Amata exclaimed before laughing even louder.

"I knew it!" Mandubratius shouted from the top of the carriage.

"Awvarwy!" Máire raged, feeling as if they were all goading her for their own amusement.

"Yes, my love?" he called.

"I will open the door, fly out there, and strangle you!"

"But… we're almost at the palace," Mandubratius replied. "You can strangle me later. Look out the windows! The sight is amazing."

For once in her life, Máire followed the advice of Mandubratius and looked out. An ornate palace gleamed with torchlight. Soldiers, bejeweled in their uniforms, walked the exteriors. She then watched large gates open. The smells of night jasmine overwhelmed the stench of the city. After gazing for a few seconds at the wonders of the palace, she pulled away, allowing Amata and Fianait to marvel at the Empress' beautiful home.

Within moments, the carriage came to a sudden stop, and then the door opened.

Guards popped their heads in and offered their hands to assist the women to the ground.

Once Máire and the other passengers had exited the carriage, she caught sight of Mandubratius hopping down from his seat.

A guard stared at him, seemingly confused.

A clerk or court secretary soon joined them. "May I see your invitation, sir?" asked the newcomer.

Mandubratius smiled at the secretary and drawled, "I need no invitation."

The secretary's eyes became blank for a few moments. He soon blinked and seemed to focus on Mandubratius again. The mortal smiled, before replying. "I should say not, sir! However, may I have your name for my list?"

"Of course," Mandubratius replied. "Forgive my barbaric rudeness! I'm Michael Tolomei."

The secretary nodded as he wrote down the name on vellum, with the assistance of a small, gilded writing board. "Very good, sir. Michael Tolomei, plus three lovely women." He smiled at the women as he motioned everyone to a side door of the palace. Once at the door, he rapped on it two times. After the door opened, he called out, "Right this way," before motioning them through the entrance.

Máire could hear the sound of music drifting from within the palace.

Once inside, a guard joined them and escorted them towards a beautiful series of rooms. She tried to ignore the gold, but she felt somewhat ill at ease.

I hope that these gilded halls will not give away my true nature.

"This is where it gets exciting," Mandubratius said and then gestured for them to go into the room on the right.

Máire could not understand why he seemed so giddy, but she soon heard giggling and laughter beyond the door.

I find it curious that I hadn't noticed it before… maybe it is because of all this gold around me… or perhaps it's his fault… he has me perturbed.

Once Mandubratius ushered Máire and the rest of the group into the room, Máire experienced surprise upon seeing guests undressing on one side of the room and storing their belongings in boxes and bags, checked in by imperial servants, on the other side. While Máire held few qualms about being nude in public, given her upbringing and culture, she felt shocked to find public nudity in this place, in this time… in the heart of orthodoxy. Still, what appalled her most was that Mandubratius must be up to some scheme… she would not allow him to succeed.

"Why didn't you tell us about this?" Máire demanded. "What kind of feast is this?" All of Máire's and Fianait's new, fine clothing would amount to little, at this celebration.

Mandubratius smiled. "I'm not sure what they call it now, but in my day, we called it an 'orgy'," he replied and then winked at her.

Máire groaned and felt her face grow taut. "You knew this was an orgy, earlier, didn't you!" she accused before glancing at Amata, hoping to see the same outrage in her eyes, but Amata merely shrugged and began to disrobe. Máire then turned to Fianait, who surely must feel some anger at this maneuvering of Mandubratius, but Fianait just sat down on a bench and rested her head in her hands.

Mandubratius reclined on the bench across from Fianait and looked up at Máire. "I thought you weren't joining us, so I saw no point in telling you," he replied. Most of his earlier exuberance seemed to have dissipated, but Máire wagered that it was part of his manipulation.

Fianait spoke into her hands. "You could have said something before we got in the carriage. We spent a lot of time and money buying clothing and having someone fix our hair," she stated.

"You manipulated us!" Máire charged.

An incredulous Mandubratius, with indignation apparent upon his face, glared at her. "What?! That's absurd. I wouldn't know how to manipulate you! It is obvious to me that you are merely looking for excuses to blame me, when this is in fact your own doing." He then pulled off his tunic and began removing his boots.

Something about the smells of wine, food, and vomit intermingled with the sounds of coitus reminded her, to some small extent, of the wild parties she had attended on Beltane. Still, she would not allow sentiment to cloud her judgment.

With a firm set to her jaw, she looked at Fianait and was about to suggest that they leave this place, no matter how interesting it seemed… it was tainted because that Mandubratius arranged it all, when Fianait opened her mouth.

"Well… wait, we're here. Let me think," Fianait said with a sigh before pausing. She then sat up. "People are having fun… we're already here… I want fun, too." After nodding to herself, she rose from the bench and began undressing.

"Fianait! Don't leave me!" Máire pleaded with the other Deargh Du.

How could she abandon me to this man's machinations?

Máire turned to Amata in one last desperate attempt to talk sense into her, but Amata seemed determined.

Amata turned away from the servant, who had finished packing away her clothing, and said, "Well, I'm going to see what satyrs are available. As I recall, I have a choice… long, thick, stubby… whatever I want." She then walked through the double doors and into the incense-filled room beyond.

Open-mouthed, Máire turned back to Fianait, but before Máire could say anything, Fianait spoke. "Máire, since when have you tried to bring a modest amount of joy into life? You're the dourest Deargh Du I know." She followed after Amata.

"But I–" Máire muttered before the sound of a hand slapping bare skin reluctantly drew her attention to Mandubratius, who she noticed had finished undressing and was standing up.

He stretched a little, and as he extended, he shook his hips slightly which spun his man parts around a little.

Máire knew he was trying to tease her, as if the act of playfully jiggling his phallus in front of her would incite her to lustful action, but before she could yell at him… or kick him, he raised both hands in a defensive, placating manner.

"I'm going to see whether I can find someone with red hair at both ends," he commented before winking at Máire. He then looked over the serving girl tending to his clothing. "But first, I want an appetizer." He grabbed the young woman, pulled up her skirts, pushed her against the bench, and penetrated her.

Máire growled in annoyance, feeling a great deal of revulsion at his act of sullying some strange woman. Máire pushed past the doors to the smoke-filled room, eager to enjoy herself despite the pretense of one desperate Lamia, before realizing she still wore her clothes. She grumbled to herself and headed back into the undressing room. Once inside, she began to disrobe, tossing her clothing to another servant.

She didn't want to admit, at least not to Mandubratius, that the idea of an orgy piqued her interest. If nothing else, this would give visuals to the storied tales Marcus and Claudius often talked about… Roman orgies… unlike any other, they would say.

"Mmmm, very nice," Mandubratius purred, as he continued plowing the serving girl.

Máire grabbed one of her shoes and flung it at him, but Mandubratius managed to catch it mid-air.

"I'll make sure it gets packed with the rest of your clothing," he purred.

"Stay away from me," she hissed.

"But Máire, the further you stay from me, the closer we'll be."

Máire vented her frustration in an abrasive vocalization before stalking from the dressing room into a maelstrom of naked men and women, of every skin tone and hair color one could imagine, engaged in some form of coitus or another in every corner of the large space. The smells of sweat, piss, and of sex itself mingled with smoke from incense sconces and oil lamps, bringing a heavy, cloying odor to Máire's sharpened senses.

She decided that she would have fun despite Mandubratius' game. Máire would take every man she came across, and she would be as loud as possible about it. However, when Máire looked around the large rooms and smiled at the mortal men who watched her, she began to judge them. "Too old… too skinny… too fat," she whispered to herself in Gaelic.

Soon, Máire turned towards the raised dais in the back of the room to see a strikingly beautiful mortal woman reclining on a lounge. Her eyes settled on Máire, for a moment, as if judging her. Owing to the affluence of the well-appointed dais, Máire presumed she beheld the Basileus Irene. As Máire stared at the mortal, Irene tossed her radiant, dark curls over her left shoulder before reaching for a golden goblet.

At that moment, Máire felt someone sidle up behind her and press his erection into the small of her back.

"Why not me?" she heard Mandubratius whisper in her ear. "I'm perfect in every way."

"I told you to stay away from me," she groaned. She then raised her left heal in a rapid motion in an attempt to kick Mandubratius in the groin, but the lissome Lamia leaped back a step, causing her to miss. Disappointed with her failure, Máire faced the interloper and murmured, "Shouldn't you be negotiating with the Empress for the mirror?"

"The hour is early," he cooed gesturing to an enclave in the far corner of the room. "Can't you and I go to that dark corner and enjoy each other?" He reached for her again, but she recoiled from his advances.

"Never. I've found my prey," she growled in a low tone. While none of the men here really captured her lust, she felt that she must lower her standards and couple with someone… even if it just provided her with an excuse not to be around Mandubratius… much less with him. With her target in sight, Máire started to walk away, but then she felt Mandubratius' hand on her left shoulder.

"Never is a long time when you are what we are," he said.

Máire shrugged off his hand but otherwise ignored him. She used a little glamoury to ensnare her prey, who seemed possessed of a muscular, if not graceful build, kind eyes, and a chiseled face… not the most attractive, but he looked like he could give her good coitus.

Her prey smiled and even seemed to drool a bit, as she stalked towards him.

"You're next," she informed her first victim. She then pushed him onto the floor, straddled him, and slapped him. "Hit me," she roared, hoping any pain would make her forget the smirk that still lingered on Mandubratius' face.

Marcus surveyed the arrayed soldiers of the tenth legion of the Children of Ares, who stood at parade rest, trying to decide what needed to be said. Thankfully, Gaius had already introduced Claudius and himself to the legion. Marcus cleared his throat and began his impromptu speech.

"I've faced the enemy and been struck by their madness. So has everyone in my company, and yet because of our technique, we have survived. Not only that, but we have killed sixty Strigoi!"

Marcus could hear impressed murmurs from the soldiers, so he decided to continue speaking along those lines.

"Tonight, my staff and I will teach you the technique we have used against the Strigoi."

A few muffled cheers greeted his ears.

There is interest, and even some enthusiasm, but doubt still linters. Hopefully, Claudius can dispel some of that doubt tonight, and then the rest when this technique is tested against live Strigoi.

With his speech completed, Marcus turned to Patroclus, Claudius, and Sextus. "If you please," he said, as a way to kick off the exercise. He then walked over to stand next to Gaius. While Marcus stood, he watched Patroclus march to the center of the field, with Claudius and Sextus flanking him. At that moment, movement in his peripheral vision drew Marcus' eyes to the right a little, enough to see Gaius lean in closer to him.

"How long have you served with Patroclus?" asked the general.

"Not very long," Marcus replied, wondering what web of lies he would have to spin in order to maintain his concealment of his true identity. "I served in covert operations for a long time, and Patroclus worked with our consuls." Marcus hoped Gaius would not pursue this line of questioning further, and in an attempt to discourage the other general, Marcus resumed his focus on the training detail. Somehow, standing here looking over soldiers in well-formed lines felt very strange to him.

Gaius, however, did not seem deterred by Marcus' lack of attention towards him. "Did you and he meet during that ill-fated, badly planned invasion of Éire?" Gaius asked.

Marcus smirked, while adjusting his gaze to encompass part of the other general's face but still allow him to view the exercise. "Gaius. You understand, of course, that I can neither confirm nor deny such an operation."

"Ah yes... the typical answer one expects to hear from those involved in covert operations. I had to ask, as I am curious. I had heard a rumor that the real reason for the invasion was that Mandubratius sought the Phallus Maximus again, as if such a relic would exist and would bring power to all Lamia." Gaius chuckled.

Marcus joined him in laughter, but then he allowed cold seriousness to blossom upon his face. "Must I repeat my previous answer?"

Gaius shook his head. "No, no. You serve your masters well. Of course, your tone reveals much, even though your words do not."

"Despite the change in name, you are a true Lamia."

"I suppose in some ways, I am," Gaius whispered before turning to watch their staff explain the tactics.

Marcus focused on Claudius, for a moment, as the lieutenant directed soldiers around on the field. He could hear Claudius clearly above the din of marching soldiers.

"We have an advantage," Claudius explained. "We can leap up to attack the Strigoi, while they are limited to movements on the ground."

As soon as Claudius finished speaking, Patroclus motioned for some soldiers to begin setting up straw men as targets.

Marcus hoped Claudius could continue to mask his nature, since the Celtic lines didn't leap... they flew. Marcus surmised that should Claudius fail to execute a convincing leap, this legion of the Children of Ares may set upon their instructors.

Once the soldiers finished setting up the straw men, another soldier handed Claudius a bow and a quiver of arrows, while holding additional quivers in reserve.

"Take your position, Claudius," Patroclus called out.

Marcus couldn't help but smirk at the notion that because of this ruse, Claudius, a lieutenant, had to take orders from a legate. Of course, the memory of putting up with Mandubratius giving orders was not far from his mind. Still, he decided to give Claudius a bit of a ribbing afterwards about following Patroclus about like a slobbering puppy.

Claudius set down his sword and walked two hundred and fifty yards to the center of the arrayed targets. He then looked over his shoulder at Patroclus, who shouted, "Execute!"

Claudius jumped into the sky and fired six arrows on his way back to the earth.

Marcus tracked each of the six arrows as they plunged into the torso of the straw dummy.

"Now, demonstrate it with multiple targets," Patroclus called out. "Ready. Execute."

Claudius jumped into the sky again, but this time, he spun on the way down, firing a series of arrows into five different targets, each of them in a different direction.

"You're getting sloppy, Claudius. Work on it," Patroclus called out.

"Yes sir!" Claudius answered.

Patroclus seemed to study the soldiers before him, for a moment and then shouted, "Centurions, arrange your charges for arrow drills. Execute!"

While Patroclus guided the soldiers through a drill, Marcus turned back to Gaius. "This may take some time," he said, hoping this training would not last for weeks.

"Indeed. I must say, your lieutenant is an excellent shot," Gaius commented. His praise seemed genuine.

Marcus smiled. "Well, he has a very good eye," he replied.

I just hope his fantastic aim doesn't give us away and get us all killed.

Máire stared at her latest cup of spiced wine, wondering how she had allowed herself to fall into this predicament. "After seven partners I should be sated, or at least exhausted," she whispered into her drink. She reclined on a lounge tucked away in the shadows, the site of her more recent encounter, resting on her left side with her right knee raised in order to give her more balance.

From her vantage point, the room seemed to writhe as if it contained one amorphous being, whose mottled, contorted body pulsated, twisted, and gyrated, emitting a cacophony of grunting and moaning noises and spewing overpowering, ripe odors, like sweat, cunny, and piss.

Across the way, in the shadows on the far side of the room, Máire spied Fianait enjoying herself with one man, while Amata stretched on a lounge with several men attending to her needs. Máire decided to wait and see who would finish first.

After watching the two women for a few moments, Máire felt someone push his way on top of her and begin penetrating her. She immediately feared it was Mandubratius who fucked her, but a quick glance revealed her fear to be unfounded. Still, this person was not someone with whom she wished to couple. Were this not an orgy, his penetration of her would be an attack... it would be rape... but did this being an orgy not make it rape?

I didn't consent to this. I am being raped!

Enraged that someone would dare plow her without asking her first, Máire reached out with her right hand, grabbed the back of the rapist's neck, and yanked him over, flipping him onto his back on the floor. She then rolled off the lounge and pinned him while pressing her knee into his bladder.

"What made you think you had permission to penetrate me?" Máire asked through clenched teeth. She had to repeat herself in Greek after realizing that, in her anger, she had first asked the question in Irish.

Through whimpers of pain, the pitiful rapist whined, "You were lying there, with your wet cunny in the air, as if inviting the next passerby to fuck you. I did what any man at this orgy would have done."

His flimsy argument made little sense, the fact he did not request consent infuriated Máire to the core. She decided to respond to his attack in kind.

Máire rose into a crouch and rolled the rapist into the same position she had been in. She then got behind him and mimicked someone penetrating him. After grabbing his hair and forcing him to make eye contact, Máire used her glamoury, along with gyrations of her pelvis, to convince the rapist that she was a burly, male Saxon warrior who liked to bugger demure men.

While most Deargh Du did not use glamoury in this way, Máire poured her ire and scorn for this man into hers, hoping to achieve her desired effect. The man's yelps of fear and pain, sounds of abject horror, indicated her success.

After a few moments of tormenting the rapist, Máire felt fatigued. A voice within told her that she needed to feed, so she ceased her glamoury and whispered into the rapist's ear. "Now, feel what it is like to be penetrated without your permission!" She revealed her true nature before crawling up the rapist's back and plunging her fangs into his neck. As she started feeding, fresh warm vitae forced out what remained of her earlier sadness.

As Mandubratius followed Máire, he wondered how she could be so miserable, what with the wine she had consumed and the prevalence of opium smoke in the room. He tried to count the number of couplings he had experienced in the course of the last few hours, arriving at somewhere between fifteen and twenty. He had even found time to play with Amata and Fianait.

Máire, however, had only coupled with seven men thus far... far fewer than one would expect from a blood-drinker race that shared blood ties with those lusty fae. She even managed to appear annoyed with each of her encounters... especially the last one, who ended up running from Máire, out of the room, while screaming and clutching his arse as if the Phallus Maximus itself were embedded within in it.

I had no idea she could be such a licentious deviant! Perhaps I should visit her...

At that moment, a strange flash of realization overwhelmed him.

Máire has experienced no satisfaction from any of her couplings.

He wondered, for a moment, whether Marcus or her associates had been able to bring forth any pleasure in that poor woman.

Mandubratius tried not to stare as another man ran a hand over her, trying to please her.

At least this one asked first... unlike the last.

He reasoned that she tried to gain some gratification from the experience, but failed. Perhaps he needed to devote some time to meeting her unsatisfied needs, and soon. However, the sounds of heavy thumping and slapping of pelvis against buttocks from the direction of the dais drew his attention away from the lovely but pitiful Deargh Du.

Mandubratius looked on as the Empress received entry from a well-endowed slave from Africa, but the look on her face resembled the displeased Deargh Du across the room.

Could satiety be so lacking in this court? I probably have a better chance of my own satisfaction with the still-beautiful Basileus Irene.

Mandubratius treaded gingerly through the throngs of entwined bodies and puddles of bodily secretions towards the dais, watching and touching any attractive female along the way. As he came within a few feet of the dais, the Empress' guards crossed their poleaxes in front of him.

"Who approaches the Jewel of the Eastern Empire?" a ferocious-looking guard growled at him while staring in a hostile manner.

"Someone who can meet the Empress' needs," Mandubratius stated. He noticed that the exhausted slave finished and then left his mistress' side.

"I know that voice," Irene murmured. Her familiar, honeyed voice resonated through the room. She raised her head and smiled coyly in his direction. "Mandubratius," she cooed while meeting his eyes, but then her radiant smile became a dangerous frown. "I shall have my secretary and guards whipped for allowing you into my palace. I am certain you have no invitation." Her eyes traversed his body. "Although, I must admit that I am a little pleased to see all of you... again."

"Imperial majesty, the pleasure is all mine," he said while grinning at her.

"Yes, I can see that," she answered. "So, do you really think you can slake my thirsts, like old times?"

Mandubratius glanced at the impertinent guard, who wisely withdrew his poleax and stepped back, before sauntering closer. "Your passion will burn like the fires of Hades and reach peaks higher than Mount Olympus," he promised.

Irene laughed, sounding very much like the young woman he had met many years ago. She rolled onto her back and continued chuckling. "Then, you may enter."

Mandubratius bounded up the dais, pleased that someone might enjoy what he had to offer. He marveled at the fact that despite her years, Irene's face could still inspire lust.

As he began to pleasure her, Irene's moans of satisfaction, unheard in the room thus far, drew the attentions of everyone else in the room. He saw that everyone turned to watch as if thankful that their sovereign received the attention she needed. Even Máire peered out of the dark shadows. Mandubratius had to wonder whether she felt jealousy.

Of course she does, but is she jealous of Irene… or Irene's satisfaction?

Mandubratius refocused his attention on Irene, giving her more pleasure.

The Basileus moaned and scratched his back as she peaked. Her wide, blue eyes opened and reflected her delight. Once her body finished convulsing around him, she fell back against her lounge and ran her hand over her forehead, wiping away the beads of sweat from her brow. She then inhaled and patted his chest. "Spiced wine!" she shouted while snapping her fingers at a servant, who quickly procured a goblet for her.

As Mandubratius rolled off Irene, he couldn't remember being so sated after having sex… at least, not in recent memory. He pondered what had made this moment of passion more rewarding… perhaps being observed by so many while having sex… the wine… the opium smoke in there… he just couldn't identify a decisive reason for feeling so satiated.

While pondering his satisfaction, he watched Irene swallow a few gulps of the wine before passing the goblet to him. He smiled in acceptance as he took the goblet and sipped some of the wine within. He then caught Irene staring at him, for a moment, with a question upon her lips.

"I have never experienced such a…" Irene murmured breathlessly between gasps of air. "I must retire to my chambers, for a moment. Would you accompany me?" The last part she spoke in a louder voice, presumably so her guards and servants knew her wishes.

"I would be delighted," he said and then rose while offering the Basileus his right hand. As the guards led him towards a corridor, Mandubratius could see the celebrations begin again. Before walking through the Empress' private door, he took one last look at the orgy, fixated his gaze upon Máire, and grinned at her. "It could have been you," he whispered, certain she could hear him over the din of the revelers.

Her cheeks flushed in a most pleasing manner.

Onward, to complete the next phase of my plan.

When Mandubratius arrived at the Basileus' quarters within the 'Porphyra', the room almost took his breath away… again.

Irene walked up the dais to her bed in the center of her chamber, sat down, and then pulled herself up onto her knees. She gave him an imperious smile and gestured for Mandubratius to approach. She regarded the guards, for a moment, before ordering them to leave. As they departed, she motioned her attendants forward. "Bring us my favorite wine." She then waved the women away.

"No guards, no servants," he commented while raising a brow at her. "You are very trusting, Imperial Majesty." As he took the steps up to her bed, she continued to stare at him, but soon he noticed her smile fade.

"Are we playing the silent game?" he whispered. "I shall play by your example."

After a moment of silence, a soft knock at the door interrupted the game.

The Empress' blue eyes jutted from him. "Bring in the wine, serve us, and leave," she ordered her servants.

A servant stared at Mandubratius after passing him a goblet.

While taking a sip, Mandubratius realized that the woman had left the room and the door had closed, leaving him and Irene alone again.

At that moment, Mandubratius sensed sudden movement, but instead of avoiding the oncoming fist, he remained still. A sudden burst of pain erupted over his jaw when Irene hit him. Mandubratius rubbed his jaw, impressed that she had struck him.

"Where in Hades, have you been?" Irene roared.

"Oh, I've been here and there," he answered in a terse manner. He always loved playing games with this one.

Irene raised her hand. "Don't you interrupt me!"

"But you did ask me–"

Irene huffed. "I said do not interrupt me. You've been gone for several years. You promised you would return five years ago. Why do you torture me like this?"

"Torture you?" Mandubratius queried, knowing full well what she meant.

"Mandubratius, you promised me that you would sponsor me!"

"I did?" he asked while keeping his tone innocent.

She hit him again, but this time it seemed more playful.

"Do not pretend to be a simpleton with me!"

Mandubratius lowered his eyes. "You wound me, Empress. Such accusations are truly hurtful." He then grew silent, until he felt a dagger cut across his cheekbone. "You move quickly for a mortal," he commented before running his right index finger over the cheek and licking off his blood.

"I've had excellent teachers," Irene gloated with a smile. "In order to remain youthful, my teachers train me as if I were a warrior. Now tell me, Mandubratius, what made you drag your sorry carcass into my empire?"

Mandubratius took her hand and looked into her blue eyes. "Oh beautiful empress, I have returned to offer you the gift you so desire."

Irene yanked her hand away. "When, Mandubratius? When?"

"In due time," he promised, ever so careful to remain nonchalant.

"It's been seven years!" Irene shouted as she kicked at a marble stand next to her bed. Her words revealed a growing hysteria. "I want the gift now."

"Well, there's no need to be hasty," he informed her.

Irene wiped her left hand over her face. "But I'm continuing to age, Mandubratius. My beautiful face has wrinkles. My hair will turn silver, soon. My... hands have spots! You must sponsor me now!" She grabbed his right arm with her left hand and shoved her dagger closer to his throat again.

Not that Mandubratius feared she could do him permanent harm, he decided to acquiesce, since that would give him leverage to accomplish his mission. "I will," he said with a gasp of defeat.

Irene pulled the dagger away. "You will? Right now?"

"Yes, now," he added and then sighed.

Irene pulled her hair back and leaned her head to her right side. "I am ready. Take me now."

Mandubratius grinned, enjoying how the game had unfolded thus far. "But, there is something I need, first."

"No!" Irene screamed in rage. She then flung the dagger at him.

Mandubratius saw the dagger's path long enough to easily dodge the blade, which sailed by harmlessly before penetrating a cushion.

"Good aim, though I'm sure you knew the futility of such an attack."

Irene began pounding his chest with her fists. "Why do you make demands of me, Mandubratius? Give me what I need!"

Mandubratius wrapped his arms around Irene and stroked her hair. "Dear love, I will do this. However, I wish to have something from you first." He kissed her brow, hoping his manner and touch would soothe her.

"Name it," she spat. Her throaty command seemed little more than a gurgle.

"I need a mirror," he whispered.

Irene pulled back and raised her brow. Incredulousness washed over her face. "Why not go to the bazaar?"

"Ah, but I do not need a simple, common mirror," he explained while pushing strands of hair away from her eyes.

"Surely you cannot mean–"

"I would like to have your bronze mirror… the one with the exquisite engravings."

"You can't take it," she pleaded in a most undignified manner.

"Truly?" He pouted a little in a playful fashion.

"I shall not give up that mirror. It's priceless!"

Mandubratius shook his head. "That is a pity, then," he muttered, rising and turning his back on her. "I will stop by in another decade to see how well you've aged. Perhaps you will make an attractive crone. Only time will tell."

Irene seized his left hand before he could pull away. "How can you make me wait again?" she asked. Her eyes and her face revealed deep desperation.

My, how easy it is to manipulate the vain.

Before Mandubratius faced Irene, he forced his smile into hiding. "I want that mirror, Imperial Majesty. You wish for me to remain and sponsor you, so give me an incentive."

Irene's eyes closed for a moment, as if she were considering her options. She then opened her eyes. "I will give you the mirror, and in exchange, you will sponsor me," she informed him in a most imperious tone.

"I just love it when women think they're empowered," he purred. When he reached out to stroke her left cheekbone, Irene pulled away.

"Do not mock me!" she roared. "I am the Basileus here!"

Mandubratius clucked his tongue. "Silly empress. Do you not understand that when I sponsor you, you will be bonded to me for the rest of your life?"

Irene's eyes widened in horror. "Bonded? Us?"

Mandubratius reached out to touch her again, but this time, she did not pull away. "Yes. I will become your father, in a sense. I will raise you as a Lamia, and when I see fit, I will allow you to roam without my accompaniment."

Well, at least I will say that now.

"And how long do you think that will take?"

"Oh… two or three hundred years," he replied.

"Two or three hundred years before I can travel on my own? Why so long?" Irene pouted.

"It gives me enough time to see which seedlings are beneficial and which are weeds. Then I pluck the weeds," Mandubratius answered, thoroughly enjoying his manipulation of the Empress.

"But the price is so high... my mirror and my freedom? I'm not sure whether this is worth the sacrifice," Irene whined before drinking her wine.

"So, do you wish for me to leave?" he queried. He then leaned back against the cushions of her bed.

"No, no, no! Let me think for a moment. For what purpose will you use my mirror?" Irene set down her goblet and met his eyes.

Mandubratius studied his nails as if he possessed no cares in the world. He thought of yawning, but he decided to hold off any other signs of boredom... for now. "I wish to show some friends their inner beauty."

Irene scoffed. "You lie."

"I assure you that my words are the truth. Would I lie to you, Basileus?"

Irene sighed. "I suppose not," she responded, but Mandubratius found her tone to be unconvincing. "So, you wish to bring out the inner beauty of your friends. Surely, you do not mean those three friends who arrived with you. They all seemed very beautiful." She frowned a little.

Mandubratius smiled. "No, not those friends, my love... some others."

Irene shook her head a little. "Other Lamia?"

"Yes... something like that."

It is so easy to lie to this one.

The Basileus seemed to consider her predicament again. "Yes, I will give you the mirror in exchange for sponsorship."

Mandubratius nodded before lying on his right side, closer to Irene. After resting his head on his right hand, he said, "That is excellent news."

"When will you sponsor me? I want this done as soon as possible."

He rubbed his chin. "That depends. How soon can I have my mirror?"

"The mirror is here," she answered. "You may have it as soon as you've given me your gift."

There is her imperious tone, again. I wish she would talk like that when we have coitus.

Mandubratius chuckled. "If I were a Lamia, I'd suspect that as soon as I give you this wondrous gift, you'd call for your guard to kill me, so you wouldn't have to give me the mirror. Wait... I am Lamia." He stretched his left arm above his head for a bit, in an effort to maintain his veil of nonchalance.

Irene smiled. "Mandubratius, I have no ill will towards you. Why would I kill someone who brings me such happiness and pleasure? Perhaps there is a compromise in timing our order of this exchange?"

"My transport waits in front of your palace. Have the mirror sent to my carriage and placed under my guards. Allow them to send a messenger to me to confirm the arrival of the mirror," he said.

"I suppose I have to trust you not to kill me… or to leave me again," she muttered before sighing in a defeated manner.

Mandubratius sat up and began stroking her hand. "Well, I could kill you now and take the mirror. Of course, this would mean that our delightful conversation would end. I have found tonight to be… most enjoyable. Besides, I've always wanted a home in Constantinople… one I could visit in order to address my eastern interests."

"You have the negotiating skill of a Persian dung merchant with a thriving business," she spat before yelling, "Guards!"

The doors opened and four guards rushed into her quarters.

"Dispatch two men to deliver that covered mirror to…" She glared at Mandubratius and asked, "Which carriage?"

"It's the one with the grays," he answered, pleased to see her so flustered. "Please give it to my guard, Maon, and he will return to confirm its arrival."

The impatient Basileus looked at one of her guards and yelled, "Don't just stand there… go!" She then scooted off her bed and started to pace around it. "I can't believe it! I'll look young again, and I'll feel young. I'll live forever!"

Mandubratius rolled onto his stomach and stared at Irene.

Poor misguided Irene. I'm not a bloody Deargh Du.

"While the guards are gone, we need to talk. There are some things I should tell you before I sponsor you."

"What would you like to tell me?" Irene asked and then sat on the bed. She rubbed his exposed side with her right hand.

Mandubratius reached out with his left hand and stroked her thigh with his fingers. "You will be as fleet as the wind, and you will be able to make any mortal or weak-willed being do your bidding. As a consequence of not being able to age, you will have to disappear in ten years and pretend to be dead."

Irene seemed to pout a little more, but he paid her inner turmoil little mind when he sensed a blood-drinker approach the room. Soon after, Maon entered the room. He appeared to be a little annoyed.

"We have it," he said in Gaelic.

"Thank you," Mandubratius replied in kind. "Return to your post."

The Deargh Du nodded his head before leaving the room.

"Now," he said after turning to face Irene. "We must have some privacy, Empress." He then rolled off the bed and began to pace.

"Say no more. Guards, leave us. Do not come in until I specifically call for you." Once they left, Irene looked at Mandubratius and smiled, apparently enthralled with the idea of becoming Lamia.

Mandubratius could sponsor her in any number of ways, but he wanted to frighten her, so he walked away from her and entered the shadows. He then used his innate abilities to race to another part of the room, also cloaked in shadow, without her becoming wise to his movements.

Irene still looked in the direction he had entered the shadows, on the far side of the room from where he now stood. "How do we proceed with this sponsoring of yours?" Irene asked. A little fear tinged her voice, confirming that his theatrics were garnering their desired impact.

Sensing the time for action was at hand, Mandubratius leapt out of the shadows, grabbed Irene, and bit her, tasting her blood and drinking fully.

Irene wrapped herself around him as if surrendering. Her voice uttered wordless pleasures, but soon the blood loss became too much for her. Her arms slacked, and her cries of delight faded. Her body soon became cold, and she started to shiver.

Before she could succumb to death, Mandubratius bit into his wrist and shoved the wounded limb into her mouth. "Drink," he whispered.

Mandubratius rubbed Irene's shoulder as she started to awake from her brief transformation. "I'm sorry, my love," he murmured in her ear. "I lied about our bonds a little. You don't need me to keep an eye on you. You don't even need to remain here in Constantinople until you are ready to pretend to die as a mortal." When Irene looked up at Mandubratius, he could almost see tears in her eyes.

"You're leaving me again? I thought you and I had to stay together."

"Not now. I will talk someone into keeping you entertained while I am away," he cooed while patting Irene's back.

"Another Lamia?" she asked.

"Well, they call themselves the 'Children of Ares' at this moment, but yes, they are Lamia, and they will take care of you for me," he promised.

"I don't want you to go," Irene whined. "Please stay."

"I promise, Basileus, I will take care of you. I will return when you're ready to journey. This mission involving the mirror is very nasty. You want nothing of it… take my word for it. Besides, your title rules your existence. When you decide to move into the world that succeeds this one, I shall return."

Irene stared at him with doubt evident upon her features. "This is not abandonment? You will return?"

"Of course I will, my sweet Venus," he purred.

"You are an impossible, yet endearing, monster," Irene said with a sigh. "Stay with me for another hour and give me more of your addictive essence."

Mandubratius leaned in closer to Irene and kissed her once more.

chapter ten

While Marcus watched Claudius and Sextus, as they continued shouting orders to the tenth legion, he noticed Patroclus joining Gaius and him.

Patroclus cleared his throat and stated, "The units are formed and ready for some live action training."

Gaius nodded his head and ordered, "Send for the prisoners."

Patroclus turned around, took a few steps away from the generals, and then signaled to Sextus and Claudius.

After a few moments, Marcus noticed Gaius incline his face to him.

More conversation... can we not watch this demonstration in silence?

"I'm most impressed with this technique," Gaius said. "It's simple, yet choreographed."

"Precision and leadership are the keys to success," Marcus answered in a crisp manner. Behind him, he could hear the footsteps of the prisoners marching past them. When they came into view, Marcus looked on as more Children of Ares soldiers escorted the prisoners in two lines.

Marcus glanced at Gaius and noticed a grim scowl had formed upon the other general's face.

"You may notice," Gaius drawled, "that I've added two more prisoners for our demonstration. I think you will recognize them."

Marcus stared into the sea of dirty prisoners, at first confused by the comment, but upon seeing Efialtes and Nicodemus in the back, he understood.

Gaius scratched his chin. "The winds are changing again. The majority of us are finding the old ways of class over quality to be confining. The consuls are not always right, Marcus. However, this plan has been in place for a long time. I'm surprised Mandubratius and Amata did not tell you or Patroclus."

Marcus swallowed his shock. "Who will lead the Children of Ares now?"

"Mandubratius, of course... and Amata. While neither took part directly in this coup, it was done in their names. You see, after the coup in Rome, the contingent that left for Greece appeared strong, but with my assistance, they grew weaker. My associates and I turned all the strong ones against one another. Now, the remainder will accept their place under the Co-Consuls. We will be Lamia, again, and we will be strong."

Marcus lowered his eyes. "I still don't understand, Gaius." He tried to hold back his building rage at Mandubratius' duplicity.

Gaius patted his shoulder. "Marcus, it was a mistake for the Children of

Ares to split away from the Lamia. Mandubratius ordered me to separate with the Children of Ares until we became powerful on our own. Now that he's here, the timing is right to topple these puppets who would lead us into a false tomorrow. This night, their strings will be cut." The Lamia general then returned to studying the tactical exercise.

Unsure of his safety, Marcus felt the need to hold his hands closer to his weaponry, without his movements appearing threatening, but Gaius turned back to him and said, "Do not worry, Marcus of the Deargh Du."

Gaius knows! That bastard Briton!

"You and your companions will not be harmed. There is an alliance between the Lamia and the Celtic lines," Gaius added before smiling.

Marcus felt himself calm a little and forced his body to relax. He turned to face Gaius fully. "You've known?" he asked.

Gaius nodded. "Mandubratius told me some time after his defeat in Éire. He said that you were a most worthy foe. I am pleased that all of these past issues have been successfully resolved." Gaius then turned to his child. "Patroclus, execute the line exercise."

Even though Patroclus, more than likely, had listened to the entire conversation, Marcus noted that never once did he see Patroclus move his head… not even when Gaius revealed that he knew of Marcus' true nature.

Is Patroclus in cahoots with Gaius, or was he also surprised by this news?

Patroclus shouted to Sextus, "Have the men take their positions!"

"The honor is to serve," Sextus answered and then saluted.

"Prepare the prisoners," Gaius ordered Claudius, who then walked over to the centurions and coordinated the disbursement of weaponry among the prisoners. Once the prisoners were armed, Claudius dismissed the centurions.

Many a prisoner looked at the sword or other fighting implement in his hands as if it were a foreign object… something never held before, while a few others executed cuts and blocks as if familiar with the Arts of Mars.

Nicodemus hefted his sword as if it were an old friend, while Efialtes nearly sliced his leg off, wielding it around haphazardly as a child would wave a stick at a tree.

One prisoner, in a despicable show of cowardice, dropped his weapon and started to run away.

As soon as Claudius raised his right hand, a bow loosed an arrow, which shot through the mortal's neck.

The prisoner's lifeless body dropped to the ground.

"Well, that's one less prisoner to deal with, then," Gaius commented.

Marcus swallowed his bile and nodded his head. "They appear ready to meet their fate."

Gaius nodded. "I am quite impressed with their stoicism. I thought Efialtes would not be so brave, but I'm glad to see that I'm wrong."

Marcus watched Claudius wave his arms in an attempt to gain the prisoners' attention. Once all of the prisoners looked his way, Claudius shouted, "The victorious will be freed!"

"I'm starving!" a prisoner, who didn't seem to know his sword's hilt from its point, shouted back.

"If you live, you will eat," Claudius said, though Marcus knew the truth.

Those prisoners who seemed to know how to wield a sword coalesced in front of Claudius. One of them, a burly, barrel-chested man with ham-sized fists, pointed out Claudius' alleged tactical error. "There's one of him and thirty of us. He doesn't even have his sword drawn."

"Get him!" another yelled.

Claudius turned and started running at mortal speed.

The prisoners followed in a mad effort to keep up with the fleet-footed lieutenant, who ran just fast enough to stay two steps ahead of his pursuers. Among them were Nicodemus and Efialtes, who seemed too fatigued to run at Lamia speeds.

All of the prisoners seemed hopeful that they could enact some kind of revenge upon Claudius, but little did they know that Sextus and his men waited out of the view of the prisoners and prepared to strike.

As soon as the prisoners came into the designated killing fields, Sextus gave the command to execute the plan.

On his order, the archers leapt from concealment, and the rain of arrows began. A dozen men fell with the first volley.

As the archers approached the ground, while nocking more arrows, the swordsmen ran towards their former leaders and the mortals. Next, the archers jumped again and launched a second volley of arrows towards their targets. Another fourteen prisoners screamed and fell. The archers leapt and launched a third volley, which sped towards their targets.

At that moment, the swordsmen engaged in melée combat with the first group of fallen mortals and began slicing off heads, as one would do against the Strigoi. The archers then released their fourth salvo of arrows, felling more prisoners. At the conclusion of the volley, arrows pieced every prisoner, including Efialtes and Nicodemus. Swordsmen waded through the bloodied and moaning prisoners and removed their heads with brisk, clinical precision.

Marcus then realized that Efialtes and Nicodemus fed from the dying mortals and began fighting back, but Sextus noticed their actions as well and took their heads before they could restore their strength.

Once the last severed head ceased rolling around on the ground, Patroclus gave the order to sheath weapons and return them to the quartermaster.

Marcus heard more shouts, ordering a detachment of soldiers to begin removing the corpses for disposal.

Gaius cleared his throat, drawing Marcus' attention, and began rubbing his arms. "Again, Marcus, this technique works well against an armed enemy."

Marcus, however, did not feel as delighted about the poor execution of the technique as the Lamia general apparently felt. "Too many of the enemy were not hindered by arrows when the swordsmen came within range of the Strigoi attack. The soldiers would have been incapacitated," he said, reflecting on the cost of this training exercise. While he could do nothing for the mortal dead, part of him at least believed Efialtes and Nicodemus deserved their fate.

Gaius shrugged. "We will increase the number of our archers."

"Or they should be trained to fire more rapidly," Marcus pointed out.

Gaius nodded his head. "I assume you will be leaving at sunset, tomorrow."

"If our other team returns with the mirror, then yes."

Gaius smirked. "I think you and I are both certain that Mandubratius has probably accomplished his mission by now. Aside from his foray into Éire, he is extremely single-minded, and he always seems to accomplish his goals... quite an admirable feat for someone who is not Roman. You might be a formidable enemy, but I do hope you will be an equally formidable friend. You must have been a prodigious strategist to become a general and praetor."

Marcus smiled for a moment. "I think my idea for defeating the Belgae helped me earn that promotion."

Gaius raised a brow. "So, that was your strategy? That is most impressive. When our paths cross again, I will buy you a drink, Marcus."

"Thank you, General Gaius," he said.

Gaius looked surprised at the formality. "Oh, and please ask the Legate to see me before you depart."

"I shall," Marcus quipped before saluting Gaius. "May Mars smite all those who challenge Rome."

Gaius smiled again and called, "And may we feast on their blood," while clasping arms with Marcus in the Roman tradition.

Marcus turned from Gaius and walked across the field towards Patroclus, who continued barking orders.

"Patroclus."

"Yes, Marcus? Oh, how did you like the demonstration?" asked the Legate.

"They need more training, but I think they will be able to improve. Now, go talk to your sponsor. We will wait for you," he said to Patroclus, who paled a little before walking towards his sponsor.

Marcus looked around for Claudius and found him standing with a few members of their party under a tree.

After walking the thirty or so paces between them, Marcus said to Claudius, "You did well. How did you feel, conducting a drill again?"

Claudius chuckled. "I had memories of our war against Britannia. I was somewhat tempted to turn against the Lamia, but part of me remembered the pleasant times of being a lieutenant under your command, facing an unknown death each day. I must admit that I enjoyed it... again."

The sound of trampled grass brought Marcus' attention behind him, and he spied a grim Patroclus approaching them alone. "Why so forlorn, Legate?"

"He asked me to join him. He said he missed my assistance and informed me of the mission he had taken on... how he infiltrated the Children of Ares and killed their leaders. My respect for him has been renewed. Of course, I think I deserved to know this matter sooner," he stated.

"So, why didn't you join him?" Claudius asked.

"I have a mission to complete," Patroclus replied.

"Then, let us go complete it. Good work... all of you. Let's find good beds back at the inn," Marcus said before leading the way.

Máire looked over the dwindling crowd, at least those still conscious, for Mandubratius, but she could catch no sight of him.

How long did securing the mirror have to take?

One glance across the room revealed that Fianait and Amata seemed nearly finished with their respective partners, who appeared on the verge of exhaustion... or death. Most of the mortals who remained slept on the lounges, cushions, or the floor, or they walked to the baths in a daze. A few pockets of people remained humping one another.

As she sat up to reluctantly find a new partner, a horrible smell hit her nose. In horror, she realized that she stank like rank cheese. Dirt even caked her hands and nails. She decided that she needed a good, long soak, so she wandered to the baths. As she approached, she could hear sounds of frolicking.

Once Máire arrived in the baths, she noticed that all of them, save one, contained frolickers. Though Máire disliked the hot bath at home, she needed to get clean, so she grabbed a sponge and walked into the first free hot bath. Máire muttered complaints in Irish over the heat as she slid into the warm water. She quickly doused herself and sank all the way to the bottom.

For many moments, she just sat there, with her head under the water, and contemplated nothing... not Marcus, not Julien, not Mandubratius... nothing. Still, she kept her eyes open and stared in fascination of how the rippling water overhead caused the room above to warp and convulse as if she had inhaled sponnc, or perhaps something stronger. Despite her soaking, Máire still felt dirty. She knew she needed something to scour the dirt from her. Upon pushing the surface of the water with her head, she spied a bowl of salt by the side of the bath. Máire reached out for the bowl, dumped half of the salt in the water, and then began cleaning herself with the remaining salt in a vigorous motion, as if to scour the stinky skin away and send it to oblivion.

As soon as she noticed several people leave the warm and cool pools, Máire decided to take one while they were empty. She climbed out of the hot pool, walked to the warm one, and sank into it up to her breasts. She sighed as she let the warm water soothe her skin. She reclined against the wall, closed her eyes, and focused on thinking about nothing again.

What an absolute joke, but I can see why Claudius and Marcus rave about orgies. Men are such simple creatures.

At that moment, she felt a set of hands begin to massage her shoulders. She assumed Marcus must have found her, since he did give lovely back rubs, and this rubdown seemed just like one of his.

Máire smiled and drifted further away. She contemplated that she should investigate the baths at home and make suggestions as to how the baths could be updated. These baths were simply amazing in their beauty and function.

From somewhere within the murkiness of her waking dream, she heard an unwanted, yet soothing, voice say, "Did you enjoy yourself?"

Máire sat up and turned around with a start, breaking away from the hands that had stroked her so lovingly. She couldn't believe that she had let her guard down and allowed... him... to touch her.

"What?" Mandubratius asked as if surprised by her sudden reaction. He then slid into the warm bath she occupied, but he drifted a few feet away from her. "By your expression, I'd derive that you did not enjoy yourself. Such a pity," he commented. "I, on the other hand, had great fun. However, I do have some good news to tell you." He took her right hand and kissed her fingers before she thought to pull her hand away. "The mirror is in our carriage."

"How, did you get the mirror?" she asked, wondering why his mission had taken so long.

Mandubratius smiled. "How do you think? I simply asked for it."

"That was it?" she queried, doubtful that he spoke the truth.

Mandubratius rolled his eyes. "There are always so many questions with you, Máire," he answered. "It did come with a price."

Máire looked around, half-expecting that Mandubratius had turned them in to the Children of Ares or the Imperial guard.

Mandubratius sighed and leaned back in the bath. "You greatly resemble a fox hunted by a pack of wolves. Why are you so ill at ease? I'm not going to ravage you... now."

Máire said nothing. Instead, she stared at him with what she hoped would be a piercing gaze.

Mandubratius shrugged. "It was an equitable exchange, although I fear my gift to Irene will not feel so much like a gift, as a curse."

Máire sighed. "You didn't," she whispered.

Mandubratius smiled. "Your aunt will just have to learn to accept yet another sibling. Too bad you lost the opportunity to be my child. Oh, no matter. You'd be a rather boring Lamia, not to mention you are much better looking as a Deargh Du."

Máire didn't know whether she should take his rambling as flattery, rebuke, or the inane machinations of a truly demented man. In any event, Máire did not wish to remain in Mandubratius' company, so she waded to the far edge and climbed out of the pool. She could feel him watching her as she climbed out. While the act of climbing out revealed more of her than she would like for him to see, at this point, she didn't care.

"Why are you leaving so soon?" he purred.

Máire faced him and gave him her best glower. "This phase of our mission is complete. We must leave this place and make haste back."

"But I thought we were having fun!" Mandubratius teased before splashing her in a playful manner.

"Fine, then… enjoy a few moments of solitude," she sighed, "but then, we're leaving. I want to get back to the inn soon."

Mandubratius pouted. "I haven't finished bathing, yet."

Máire felt like the stepmother, or nanny, of some impertinent whelp. "Make it quick."

Mandubratius splashed her again. "Fianait is right. You are dour and joyless. Don't I get an opportunity to relax? I did take care of all of the Basileus' needs, remember?"

"Whatever," she muttered before grabbing a sheet and drying herself. While drying her hair, she heard a repetitive sloshing sound coming from the warm tub. When she turned around to find the source of the sound, she caught Mandubratius stroking himself under the water while staring at her with red, lust-filled eyes.

"Slower… I do want to remember this. It all seems somewhat familiar," he murmured. He ran his tongue over his fangs and licked his lips.

Máire sighed and left for the dressing room, so she could finish drying herself without him groping her with his eyes.

"You still stink," Máire informed Mandubratius as soon as he opened the inn's door for them.

Mandubratius chuckled. "I know. I want to keep some memories of this evening fresh in my mind, and what better way than through my senses."

"It's not your senses that concern me," Máire quipped before wandering over to a bench with her family. After sitting down next to Julien, she noticed Edward and Amata, with arms linked, sauntering down the hallway towards the rooms. During their quick jaunt, they passed Marcus, who stormed into the common room looking for a fight.

As soon as her father-in-darkness saw Mandubratius, his eyes turned green and his face darkened. Fear welled up inside of her, for she rarely witnessed him unleash such anger.

Marcus grabbed Mandubratius, lifted him, and slammed him against the wall. A board behind the Lamia broke.

"How dare you initiate a coup while we're on a mission?" Marcus growled.

Máire stood up, as did most of the others.

A coup?

Mandubratius smiled and presented a boyish façade as he gazed at Marcus. "Well, it helped me succeed in obtaining the mirror."

"You set this up. You set up all of it! Just so you could regain control of this branch of the Lamia!" Marcus accused as he shook Mandubratius.

Máire noticed Patroclus remained sitting.

What was his role in all of this?

Mandubratius coughed a little and then smiled. "I'm so flattered that you feel I could orchestrate these events over time and it would end with you holding me against the wall by my neck and tunic. However, I cannot claim that I had any hand in setting the Strigoi off on their murderous campaign." He laughed for a moment, before calming. Soon, the Lamia's face projected seriousness. "But yes, everything else... I did," he drawled.

Máire had no idea that while Mandubratius fornicated and prattled on at the orgy that he was secretly orchestrating the fall of a government of blood-drinkers. She could not help but feel... impressed... in a sick, sad way.

Marcus stared at Mandubratius for a moment, before slowly lowering him to the floor. He then released Mandubratius and backed away. "Couldn't you avoid staging this coup until after we took care of the Strigoi?" he asked.

"Marcus, my birthday is next week, and I wanted a united Lamia empire before then," Mandubratius replied while adopting a jovial visage.

Marcus did not appear to accept the response, for his eyes reverted to their otherworldly green, and he reached out for the Lamia again.

"Before you demonstrate your strength again, Cu Chulainn, there is another, more logical, reason for this coup."

Marcus lowered his arm and glared at Mandubratius. "I'm listening," he hissed, though his eyes remained green.

"Had I not initiated this coup, we wouldn't have the backing of the

Children of Ares when we meet up with the Strigoi," Mandubratius replied.

"Are you saying that, now that you are back in control, they will fight alongside us?" Marcus asked.

"You may depend on it."

Marcus did not look convinced, but his expression softened and his eyes became bluish-gray again. He leaned against the table in a casual manner.

"So, how did you obtain the mirror?" he asked.

Mandubratius smiled. "The Basileus Irene and I traded for it."

"Traded what?" Marcus asked, though worry clouded his tone.

Máire interrupted them before Mandubratius could speak. "He transformed her!" she said with vehemence, though she couldn't decide what aspect of this revelation harmed her the most.

"Sponsored, actually," Mandubratius added. "I made Empress Irene a Lamia. So, what of it? Oh, and she'll realize a few hours after sundown that becoming a Lamia does not increase one's beauty and youth. After looking at Amata, Fianait, and Máire, she seemed to assume that you were all Lamia."

Marcus sat down in apparent shock.

"What are you saying?" Claudius asked.

"I'm saying we must flee at sunset with haste," Mandubratius answered.

"Why?" Julien asked.

"Because, youngling, Irene's vanity is as volatile as Greek fire," Mandubratius answered.

"Won't the Children of Ares protect you?" Arwin asked before taking a sip of what Máire assumed was unadulterated wine, knowing his preferences.

Mandubratius shrugged. "Perhaps, but they owe fidelity to her as well, and there is a rather universal saying about a woman scorned."

Marcus stood back up… always a man of action. "Then, we need to leave now! The Children of Ares know where we are, and I'm sure your new child knows it, too. If we're caught during the day in this inn, the Empress will figure out a way to bring us into the sun, if she's as volatile as you say she is." His tone belied his irritation.

Mandubratius shrugged. "Yes, I'm sure that is a good idea. She has men castrated for not pleasing her. She has executed men for daring to say she was over twenty-five seasons. I mean, look what she did to her own son for daring to have an opinion of his own. Despite what you might think, playing this game was necessary to snatch the mirror."

"That's enough from you," Marcus growled. "First a coup, and now you're lying to the sovereign of these lands about her new gifts!"

At that moment, a disheveled Amata rejoined them. The Lamia frowned at Mandubratius and added, "I truly hope there are no consequences from this ill-conceived sponsorship."

"Ill-conceived? Look, we needed the mirror, and I took the risk. She's mad, but she won't catch up to us, and if she does, well... our friends will carry the Lamia away, Amata. Besides, Irene finds me charming. She'll move past this minor annoyance," Mandubratius answered.

"Let's stop flapping our gums and leave. We'll have to sleep underground, outside of the city," Arwin grumbled before tipping his goblet back and chugging the rest of its contents.

"How about the sewers," Edward suggested, though Máire didn't find sleeping in sewers to be the best option. It required hours of thorough scrubbing to scour the stink away.

Instead, she added her own recommendation. "I remember seeing a cemetery outside of the walls."

"Both places are far too obvious," Claudius answered.

"True," Marcus admitted. "Any other suggestions?"

"How about the ocean," Fianait suggested, but then she seemed to recognize the holes in her proposal. "Oh," she muttered while looking over the Ekimmu Cruitne and shook her head. "Sorry, I forgot."

Marcus sighed. "I think our only option is to fly to the west, as quickly as we can. Then we'll land and dig in when we need to."

So much for feeling clean after my hot bath. You owe me, Mandubratius.

When Irene awoke the next morning, she shivered from the cool, pre-dawn chill. A quick glance around the room revealed that dawn soon approached. She sat up, slid out of her bed, and walked towards the nearest window, hoping the sun might warm her.

She stuck her right hand out the window and waited for the sun to kiss the top of her outstretched hand.

When the sun rose high enough, she watched in awe as its light touched buildings and trees far away. Soon, the wave of brightness rushed closer to the palace. Once the bright wave washed the palace with light, a beam of sunlight pierced through her window and bathed her outstretched hand.

However, instead of feeling a kiss, the sun burned her hand as if she had thrust it into a bed of glowing embers. Irene screamed from the intense pain and stared in stupefaction as her hand began to smoke and crisp.

Servants and guards rushed in. One of them poured water onto her hand.

"Get out! Leave me!" she roared at them, as she backed away from the window into the shadows of the Porphyra. Still, the bright sunlight hurt her eyes, so she looked away from the bright parts of the room.

Once she found a spot of relative darkness, Irene studied her hand again. Thankfully, her clouded mind began to clear. Soon, memories of the celebration last night came back to her. Mandubratius had arrived with three beauties, and he sought her mirror. Then she remembered being intimate with him... one of few men who could sate her needs. The sex was even better after...

He must have sponsored me!

Irene smiled and raced to find a mirror, wishing to see her renewed beauty.

Youth forever!

Giving up the sun seemed a small price to pay. While in the midst of searching through her dressing table, which stood bereft of her prized mirror, she felt her stomach growl, and she forgot about the mirror.

Irene tried to remember what Mandubratius had told her about consuming blood. The thought of drinking blood seemed sickening, at first, but her growing hunger quashed all misgivings. She needed blood... now.

"I need bandages and clean water!" Irene called out, as a means to summon a food source. While much of her experience last night remained blurry, she began to remember some instructions about feeding.

A servant arrived with a basin of water and set it down on the floor near where Irene cowered. She began binding Irene's arm.

Irene stopped the servant and murmured, "Stay for a moment." Her hunger had increased, and she could no longer ignore it. Along with her heightened hunger, she heard a loud pounding echoing in her ears. Irene glanced at the servant and realized that the sound was the drumming of the woman's quickening heart.

Irene experienced no qualms about tasting the blood of others. She could recall a time during another orgy, when someone accidently cut a servant during his throes of passion. Irene had licked the blood from the cut in a moment of curiosity. Before, she had found the taste odd but intriguing, yet now, she found the sweet, appetizing smell to be intoxicating.

Irene knew she could no longer wait... she had to taste blood, not only to fend off her hunger, but also because she imagined tasted like ambrosia.

When she locked eyes on her servant, the girl lowered her gaze.

"Look me in the eyes," Irene commanded in a soft tone.

The servant made eye contact with her again, and Irene witnessed fear.

"Calm down," she said. Almost immediately, Irene could hear the servant's heart slow.

"How may I serve you?" the young woman asked in a low stutter.

"I am hungry," Irene murmured.

"Let me get you some... food," the servant muttered, attempting to step away, but Irene had gently seized the woman's left arm with her right hand.

The Empress smiled. "But you've already brought me food, my dear."

"I did?"

Irene pulled the serving girl close enough to her that mere inches of space existed between the two women. "Yes, silly girl. I mean to feed from you!"

Before the servant girl could scream, Irene grabbed her mouth with her left hand and pulled the girl's body against hers. Then she felt her teeth extend, as if it were some kind of reflex. With her prey effectively immobilized by her newfound strength, Irene bit the servant girl's throat and feasted upon the blood that poured out. With each pulse of blood that passed her lips, Irene could feel energy grow within her. The rush of energy... of power... drowned out all other thoughts.

As Irene drained the servant, she could feel the girl's heart begin to slow, and soon it stopped completely, along with the flow of blood.

Irene stared at the empty expression in the servant's dead eyes for a moment and then tossed her carcass across the room.

With her hunger now sated, Irene sauntered to the dressing desk once again to search for a mirror. Once she sat down, she noticed that the burn on her hand began to fade. "This is a miraculous gift," she whispered.

After searching through three drawers, Irene finally found a small mirror. She giggled at the discovery and held up the mirror, so she could stare at herself and witness the fruits of Mandubratius' gift... eternal youth and beauty.

Instead of a striking maiden, an old hag stared at her in the mirror. She screamed at the unchanged reflection of her face.

I remain old!

"You Liar!" she yelled at the top of her lungs.

Guards and servants rushed into her room to protect her, but when they saw the dead servant, they started yelling.

Irene covered her mouth, unsure of how to hide her elongated teeth, and remembered that she needed to take care of potential exposure before they suspected anything.

"That girl tried to kill me! I punished her. Take her body away and bury it in a pauper's grave!"

Two of the guards grabbed the dead servant's body and hauled it out of the room. Servants rushed in to clean up blood and re-polish the floor.

While the servants busied themselves with their work, Irene thought back to her conversation with Mandubratius, shortly after her sponsorship.

Mandubratius did warn me to try not to kill them.

He had whispered that it would taste exquisite to drain them, but it would give her a headache afterwards because of the problems stemming from death.

"I suppose I should take that advice," she grumbled in, what she hoped to be, an inaudible tone.

"What is your desire, Imperial Majesty?" the guard captain asked.

Irene rolled her tongue around in her mouth to make sure her teeth had retracted. "Leave me," she told him. After a moment of introspection, an idea occurred to her. "No, wait!" Irene threw up her hands and paced through the darkest shadows of the room. "Cover up my windows, then find Aetios!"

As the guards and servants went about their new duties, Irene paced and planned, while waiting for Aetios to appear. Soon, thick blankets tacked over wooden frames, sealed with plaster, held out most of the sun's deadly rays.

What should I do to make Mandubratius pay for abandoning me once again, when I needed his assistance to survive?

Rapid footsteps heralded Aetios' arrival. After closing the door behind him, he kneeled and said, "I am at your service, my Empress."

Irene, at first, didn't look at him. While staring at a distant tapestry, she said, "Aetios. You've served me well as my secretary during my many orgies."

"I am happy you appreciate my service, and I hope to continue to serve you in this capacity," he groveled.

Tedious man, but useful… unlike his predecessor, who feeds the worms.

"You may yet… Do you recollect the man I allowed in my chambers last night?" she asked.

Aetios nodded his head. "Yes, Imperial Majesty."

"Do you remember his carriage?"

"Yes, Basileus. It's from an inn near the outside of town. I think it's called the Byzantine Inn."

Irene smiled. "Well done. Your memory is excellent. Send an army detachment to detain all the patrons, staff, and the owner. Bring them in for questioning. If they offer resistance, subdue them, and if necessary, kill them."

Aetios bowed. "Yes, Imperial Majesty." He then departed the Porphyra.

With her room now empty of servants and guards, living or dead, Irene gripped the small mirror in both hands and stared into its depths. "Soon, Mandubratius, I will hold your severed genitals in my hand and bask in the beauty of my mirror," Irene swore.

Time drifted by with scant change in her appearance. Irene neither aged nor grew younger. She had hoped that perhaps Mandubratius had spoken the truth, that she would be beautiful and young again… that the transformation just needed time to run its course. However, after an unknown number of hours staring at her reflection, Irene felt her hope die.

I am the blithering fool for having such hope.

With as much fury as she could muster, Irene gripped the top of the mirror in her right hand and squeezed with all of her might. The mirror broke with a satisfying crunch. After shattering it, she held the mangled mirror in her right hand and rested her face in her left.

Irene ignored the temptation to stare into the broken shards of the mirror again. She doubted there would be any change. She would always look old. Gray hairs and age spots would remain. This existence seemed torturous.

Even though the pains of age have faded, what difference does it make?

The sound of footsteps running towards her bedroom brought her attention to the door.

In walked a messenger, who bowed and then lowered himself in complete prostration.

"Yes? What is it?" she asked, weary of visitors in her current state.

"Please pardon the presence of your most humble servant, Basileus, but the captain of the guards found the residents of the inn. He has brought them here for you to interrogate."

Irene pulled herself away from her pity and said, "Bring them in here. I shall confront them myself."

The messenger rose slowly, and then he then turned and scrambled away.

Irene fixed her eyes on the largest mirror shard she held and glared at her face again. In her gaze, she focused her burning rage on Mandubratius, willing this bit of mirror to melt. Because the shard didn't obey her will, she flung it as far and as hard as she could towards the far wall.

When the shard slammed into the wall, it embedded itself in the marble.

The staccato of many booted feet and the smell of sweat preceded the arrival of guards, who barged through the door. When they saw that she was not in danger, they looked around, confused.

Irene stood up and yelled, "What is the meaning of this?"

One of the guards, the captain's second-in-command, said, "Basileus, we heard a loud noise and thought that you were being attacked."

"Do I look as if I've been attacked?" Irene growled.

At that moment, another guard raced into the room. "The innkeeper, his family, and patrons are here now."

Irene acknowledged the guard with a nod and then glanced at the new arrivals who walked with solemn faces, eyes lowered.

Once the guards had positioned the prisoners in a line, one of the guards identified each of the prisoners, starting with the innkeeper.

Irene stepped off the dais and studied them more closely. She sensed that they knew something, but she didn't know what... yet. "Look at me!" she shouted at them.

The innkeeper raised his eyes to her for a moment, but then he lowered them immediately.

Irene rushed over to stand toe-to-toe with the innkeeper and roared, "I said... look at me!" While enunciating her words, she felt a strange power surround her, which grew with each syllable.

This time, the innkeeper's eyes locked with hers. "Yes, Basileus?"

"There were foreigners from the west at your inn. Describe them!"

The innkeeper's brow furrowed. "It was a large party of men and women. They were utter barbarians. They wanted undiluted wine. Most of the men were from the north, by their accents, although I think there were a few Romans and one Frank. They got in a fight early before dawn... two men, that is–"

"Where and when did they leave?" Irene demanded, interrupting the blank-eyed innkeeper. In a fit of impatience, she withdrew her gaze from the simple man and began pacing.

"They departed about an hour before sunrise, and they went west, Imperial Majesty," the innkeeper answered. "They all spoke Latin, I think, and perhaps barbaric languages from the north."

Irene nodded to herself before spinning around to face the innkeeper. "You have just saved your family's lives." She then looked over at the captain. "Imprison them until I say to release them."

The innkeeper's wife, servants, family, and the few guests who had stayed the night wailed in a pitch and volume Irene felt most grating to her ears.

"Quiet!" she growled while waving her hand to the guard captain in an abrupt manner. In response to her gesture, the guards led the innkeeper, his family, and their patrons away.

Irene soon noticed Aetios, standing in the far corner, and motioned him forward. "Get my military advisor, she ordered."

"But Imperial Majesty, it's daytime. You know his odd habits," he replied. His eyes revealed fear.

"Just have him meet me in the catacombs, and if he resists, bring me his head!"

"It shall be done," Aetios droned. He then bowed before leaving the room.

Gaius suspected the Empress's proposed conversation to be clandestine, since he couldn't remember the last time they had met in the catacombs. He walked with purpose, while holding the torch to keep his mortal guise intact.

Gaius had nearly killed Aetios for interrupting his slumber, but since the unassuming Aetios seemed to be in the Empress' good graces, such a murder would no doubt bring reprisals to the murderer, and that was one headache Gaius didn't need just now.

When he extended his senses to identify her or any threats, Gaius felt a blood-drinker awaiting him.

Perhaps this is a survivor from the coup. I should deal with him now.

Gaius set down his lamp and drew his sword, readying himself to charge the blood-drinker whose back faced him. After inching forward in the gloom, preparing to strike, he recognized the Basileus Irene. With no other people in range of his senses, he concluded that Irene was the blood-drinker he detected.

Gaius stopped his advance and lowered his sword. He felt great confusion.

How could Empress Irene be a blood-drinker?

Gaius sheathed his blade and cleared his throat. He assumed she had not sensed him, and he certainly didn't want to surprise her.

Irene spun around to face him, fear evident in her eyes for a moment, but then her typical regal calm settled upon her features.

"Gaius, you startled me," she muttered as she sniffed the air. "You smell different."

"As do you," he commented.

The Empress' eyes widened, as if a great mystery had been revealed to her. "You're a Lamia, aren't you?"

"Yes," he replied, deciding that responding to 'Lamia' was a more truthful answer, now, than referring to himself as being one of the 'Children of Ares'.

"What a strange coincidence... so am I." Irene's countenance darkened, and her gaze scrutinized every inch of his face. "You have scars and gray hairs," she commented, practically spitting her words.

"Yes, Imperial Majesty. I had scars and gray hairs when I became Lamia." He felt some confusion regarding her words.

"So, becoming a Lamia didn't make you younger or beautiful?"

"No," Gaius answered. "Those are not the gifts of the Lamia."

What has Mandubratius told her? That she would become a Deargh Du? That man could sell cac to a dung merchant.

"I thought as much," Irene hissed. She then raised her head and raged, "Betrayer!" Dust fell from the ceiling, and the walls nearly shook with her ire.

"Who betrayed you, Basileus?" he asked, hoping that she did not suspect anything of him.

The Basileus turned her bright blue eyes on him and growled, "The man who made me what I am! Mandubratius!"

Gaius felt some relief that he could count himself safe, at least for now. "So, Mandubratius sponsored you?"

Irene began pacing around Gaius in the narrow catacombs, which left little personal space between them. "Sponsored me, transformed me, raped me," she accused before facing him with her blue, fury-infused eyes. "Whatever it is called, General Gaius... yes!" She then grabbed his tunic and yanked him closer, so that mere inches separated their eyes. "You know him, don't you."

Gaius considered his options. He couldn't say no, and he couldn't manipulate her. He could kill her, but Mandubratius might not be pleased. It seemed he had no other choices. "I know him," he admitted.

Irene heaved, as her face grew red in fury. "Are you his friend?" Spittle from her words at such a close distance sprayed across his face.

"No, no, Basileus. He is the Co-Consul of the Lamia. Therefore, he is my superior. That is all," he replied.

"Since you began serving as my military advisor, whom did you serve? Him... or me?" Irene grabbed his arms and pushed him against the catacomb wall. Her strength caught him by surprise.

"You?" he stated in a questioning tone, though his aim was to sound more confident.

"You hesitated, Gaius." She radiated heat.

"I serve you, Basileus," Gaius intoned before lowering himself to his knees, figuring this would be the best way to appease her.

Irene squatted in front of him.

"Yes, you do. Are there others like you? Others who serve you?" Her voice grew louder.

Gaius stared at Irene. "Yes. There are one thousand Lamia that serve me," he replied, but he quickly added, "serve you," to stoke her ego.

Irene inhaled, appearing to calm herself. "You all serve me. Excellent." She arose and then took a few steps away from Gaius. "You may stand."

As he stood, she began walking around him again.

"Since you serve me... and your men serve me..." Irene paused and faced him again. "I have a quest for you. Of course, I will join you on this journey."

Gaius, upon realizing her motivation for traveling with them, felt a sinking feeling in the pit of his stomach.

"I want you to hunt down Mandubratius, and I will be there to torture and kill him myself."

Gaius nodded his head, believing that any attempt to assuage her ire in this matter might cost him his life. "I will obey your command, Basileus."

"Good." The Empress' gaze sharpened as if piercing his soul. "I reward loyalty and punish betrayal." She then closed the distance between them. Her body pressed slightly against his, and the tip of her nose tickled his.

Gaius felt a brush of desire swell from her intimate closeness. He was also aware of her emotions rising, as if the thought of torturing Mandubratius brought her physical pleasure, yet she remained in control and refrained from kissing or groping him.

He just stood there, staring into those eyes, until she made her next move.

"Now," she purred, "there are six hours until sunset, correct?"

"Yes, Imperial Majesty," he replied.

"Then, I suggest that you make preparations, so that when the sun sets, we can leave immediately!"

"Yes, Basileus."

No fitful sleep for me, or my men.

"Then, go."

Gaius turned around, and he was about to take a step towards his quarters, when he felt a firm hand touch his left shoulder. Gaius turned back and looked into those piercing eyes of hers.

"And remember," she stated, "loyalty is rewarded..." The Empress kissed him full on the lips, and he could feel her tongue explore his mouth. After a few seconds, she pulled her mouth way and glared at him with a menacing visage. "... and betrayal is punished," she added before raking his face with the fingernails of her right hand.

"Yes, Basileus," he repeated, unwilling to show weakness by covering the area where she had drawn blood. Gaius nodded, turned away, and began running through the corridors of the catacombs on his way to his barracks.

He hoped Mandubratius would play along with the Empress' machinations.

Yes, this will all work out. The Co-Consul probably planned this little entertainment for all of us.

He frowned, thinking that sometimes Mandubratius allowed too much time for his games. Still, the Co-Consul and Amata were better leaders than their counterparts in the Children of Ares.

Once Julien had pulled himself out of the dirt, he witnessed Amata climbing out of the hole she had slept in.

"I suppose we should begin waking everyone," she said while shaking out her hair. Amata looked at the undisturbed grass in front of her and reacted to something she saw. "This is vile. I have worms in my hair! I never thought I'd want to go back to the inns." She then turned around and scrutinized him. "By the way, you have bugs in your tunic and hair."

Julien shuddered and began shaking himself, running his hands through his hair and over his body. Several bugs fell to the ground and scuttled away. "I suppose the inns look much cleaner, now." He then sat down, crawled to each dirt pile, and began hitting the dirt, hoping to rouse the others.

One of the dirt piles shifted, and Claudius' head pushed out of it, causing dirt and leaves to cascade from his exit. Upon pulling himself out of his hole, he sniffed the air and said, "I smell water. There must be a lake or river nearby. Amata, why don't you take a quick swim?"

Amata chuckled. "I don't think any of us have time for a bath with the Basileus chasing us. Perhaps a gift of some sort would pacify her." As soon as Mandubratius finished erupting from his hole, she glared at him.

Marcus levitated out of his hole as if he were Jesus, coming out of the cave after His Resurrection. Julien felt annoyance at the show.

While brushing soil off himself, the overbearing father-figure sighed and scoffed, "Or wait, is this a plan of yours to make it easier for us to assimilate with the Children of Ares again and have them join us to fight against the Strigoi?" Marcus sighed again before opening a small flask at his belt. He then emptied some water into his hands and washed them, as well as his face.

The rest of the team had crested their burrows now, and were cleaning themselves or tending to their belongings... all save Horatio.

Mandubratius did not glance at Marcus and instead directed his gaze onto Amata. "I didn't bring any golden gifts for Irene with me because of our friends' problems with possessing and carrying gold," he explained, answering her question.

At long last, Horatio pushed through the detritus and climbed out of his pit. He appeared confused. "Who cannot possess gold?"

"The Deargh Du have a reaction to it," Claudius replied as he pulled out his pack and brushed off the dust.

"How so?" a confused Horatio asked while studying the Deargh Du.

"Gold is poisonous to Deargh Du," Marcus replied after settling to the ground. Like the others, Marcus went about getting his gear ready so they could return to their journey.

Mandubratius looked up from his pack and chuckled. "Isn't it amusing, Horatio, that the empowerer of kings is also the bane of the Deargh Du? One would think Morrigan never wanted the Deargh Du to be kings. Fortunately, we Lamia have no such limitations to our greatness."

Julien glanced at Máire, who smiled at Horatio and then caught Julien's eye. "We neither desire to be kings, Horatio... and Julien, nor do we need gold. There is little need for gold when one has the gifts of Morrigan."

"Oh, yes, yes," Mandubratius purred. "Nothing compares to Morrigan's favor, does it?"

Mandubratius' mocking tone and his rather large smile prompted Julien to consider punching the Briton, and he would have done so, but Máire just shrugged and began picking up her luggage.

If she doesn't feel it necessary to respond to Mandubratius' jab, then perhaps I shouldn't punch that bastard.

Julien watched Máire begin digging through the dirt for the mirror and drew closer to her to assist. "Have you been poisoned by gold?" he asked while helping her lift the artifact.

"A few times," she admitted. "The orgy weakened me a little, since gold was woven into everything, but it wasn't concentrated enough to do me real harm." She paused a moment and wiped away dirt with a rag she carried.

"The last time I experienced severe effects from gold, I was searching a hidden fortress, when I bumped against stones and upset a shelf hanging over me. Several golden chalices tumbled onto me from above. My strength ebbed, my skin burned, and pain wracked my body. Fortunately, I managed to sit up and knock the chalices off me. Afterwards, it took me an hour to heal completely."

Marcus strode over to Máire and said, "Arwin is going to see how far the Empress and her friends are behind us. He needs someone to bring down the darkness, so he can be close to them and remain concealed. Who wants to volunteer?" Marcus asked.

Julien could not let a query like that be answered by someone else. He had to do it. "I'll do it," Julien answered.

He saw Máire look up at him and then glance at Marcus.

She shook her head.

Julien felt infuriated that his own mother-in-darkness had such low expectations of him as if he were some infant, who needed to be coddled, and not capable of anything. "I'm tired of you making decisions for me. I'm a man. I've commanded men. I'm not a sniveling child who needs to be protected." He then glanced at Marcus, hoping for support.

"Don't look for my intervention," the other Deargh Du said while raising his hands in a yielding manner and taking two steps backwards. "I'm not getting into this."

Mac Alpin cleared his throat, and then all eyes, including Julien's, fixated on him. Arwin scratched his chin and argued, "The lad has a point, Maél Morrigan. You cannot keep spoiling the boy, or else he'll never grow up. Besides, I'll keep him out of trouble."

"Boy? I've seen twenty eight cycles!" Julien uttered.

Máire sighed. "Alright… go then." She then turned to address Mac Alpin. "If something happens, I'll be after you, Arwin." Julien noticed Máire's mouth twitch into a smile.

"I promise he won't have a scratch, mother," Arwin chuckled before slapping Máire's back.

Marcus sauntered back to the center of the group. "Good," he said while giving Julien a good, long look. He then shared a glance with Mac Alpin. "We'll head towards Hadrianopolis at half speed. It will give you ample opportunity to catch up to us, and be sure to leave a trail for them."

Mac Alpin grunted in response.

Marcus motioned for the others to follow him. "We'll count off in groups of four again to carry the Lamia."

Julien saw Mac Alpin motion for him to follow. "We best be off, then. Ready yerself."

Julien tossed his supply bag to Edward and made final adjustments to his gear and weapon. "I'm ready."

Julien and Mac Alpin hovered above the distant road, surrounded in darkness, with only their eyes and noses exposed. From their concealment, they watched for whatever might approach them from the empty road.

Having stared for several minutes, Julien desired some conversation. After all, 'mam' was not around anymore. "Is Máire always this overprotective?" he asked Mac Alpin.

"Always, lad? What do you mean?"

"Is she overprotective with all of her children-in-darkness?" he asked. When no response came immediately, he added, "Did she lose one?" thinking that may have been the case.

Arwin chuckled loudly before covering his mouth. He then looked around them as if worried that someone might hear them. "You are her first. In fact, she's never been a mother before... not even in her mortal life."

"No wonder she's so protective," Julien reasoned aloud.

"It's only been about a month since you came along," Arwin stated. "It takes a while to learn, to build up trust... to build the motherly bond. Once she begins to trust you, she will be less nervous about it. It's a new experience for her... for the both of you."

Wishing to change the subject to something else, he asked, "How soon do you think it will be before the Children of Ares, or whatever they call themselves, catch up to us?"

Arwin glanced at him for a moment and answered, "I believe we'll have them in sight within the hour."

"Do you think it's wise to face them near where we found the Strigoi?"

"Perhaps," the elder Ekimmu Cruitne muttered before smiling. "This might mean facing two enemies at the same time."

"And that doesn't bother you?"

"Well, Marcus likes to gamble, and I enjoy rolling the dice myself. I think he is wagering that he will be able to turn the Empress into an ally. After all, she's just been duped by the Lamia leech. Perhaps she won't be of use now, but she may be a friend in the future, especially if we rescue her."

"Why don't we just travel at full speed and leave them to their own devices?" Julien asked.

"We could. We could carry our allies and fly as fast as we can to Aachen. However, this Irene is as merciless as her father-in-darkness is, yet has none of his astute political talents. She will probably wish us harm for aiding Mandubratius, even if the two sides of the Lamia have joined forces. It may be too difficult for the former Children of Ares not to support her. After all, her son is probably not the best of leaders. Imagine your own mother blinding you and leaving you in a prison cell." Arwin paused for a moment, and then gasped, "By the Gods, I sound like a Lamia."

"If Marcus is worried about them following us, why don't we just kill the Empress and forget about the Eastern Empire?"

Mac Alpin snorted, sounding like Máire. "Youngling, you are more familiar with the state of relations between East and West than most of us here. Sometimes, things are much simpler at home. You just fight everyone. I fear if we do not rescue the Basileus from something, all the men will be castrated."

Julien shuddered in horror.

Arwin shrugged and then patted Julien on the shoulder. "It's not so bad. They'll grow back." Suddenly, Mac Alpin held up his left hand, and Julien knew that meant the Empress approached. "I recommend we stay where we are until we can determine their numbers," Arwin continued. "Then we shall make haste to catch up with the others. We need to stay in this darkness of yours, for a little while." After a protracted pause, he whispered, "They are approaching. Stay silent."

Julien nodded his head, even though he knew Arwin would barely notice, since so little of their faces extended beyond the veil. At first, Julien could not smell anything, but after a few minutes had passed, he inhaled. He could now detect the scent of Lamia and mortals. Soon, he could hear them.

The party traveled at a good speed, for mortals at least, but even so, Marcus and the others would have a strong lead.

Arwin grabbed his arm and whispered in his ear. "I count around fifty mortals and fifty Lamia. How many did you count?"

"The same," Julien confirmed, "give or take a few."

"We should leave, slowly," Arwin murmured, "but keep your darkness around us."

Julien grabbed hold of Arwin and drifted into the center of the darkness. While concentrating on maintaining the black mist around them, Julien guided Arwin to the west. At some point, he felt Arwin tap his back.

"We are clear of the Lamia,' Arwin grumbled.

As both blood-drinkers accelerated, Julien released the gloom.

Gaius groaned silently at the absurdity of the Empress' plan. Her horse-drawn carriage, around fifty mortals consisting of guards and servants, baggage mules, and other carts prevented Gaius and his moderate force of Lamia soldiers from pursuing Mandubratius and his band at speed.

Can she not comprehend our snail-like pace?

"Gaius?"

The sound of his name drew Gaius' attention to the carriage, and he noticed the Basileus peering from the window in the door. Gaius slowed down to a jog and drew closer to her. "Yes, Imperial Majesty. How may I be of service?"

The Empress' eyes grew dark and glowed red. "Have your scouts told you how far ahead that traitorous Briton and his band of misfits are?" she growled.

His scouts had found disturbed earth, indicating where Mandubratius and his friends had slept for the day. More importantly, however, was the discovery of a mark in the dirt identifying Mandubratius' direction.

Mandubratius and his games.

Of course, none of this would Gaius reveal to the Empress. Instead of providing the Basileus a full status report, he wiped his brow and said, "It seems they've passed this point early this evening."

"How soon until we catch up?" Irene demanded.

Figuring the answer would require time to explain, Gaius raised his right hand and shouted, "Stop!" In response, the party came to a halt. The mortals and beasts seemed eager for the rest, but the soldiers looked impatient.

Gaius walked over to the carriage, grabbed the hand-holds, and hefted himself up to the step, so he could meet her eyes and converse in a softer tone. "Imperial majesty," he whispered, deciding to be honest with her... at least on this point. "At this rate of speed, we will not."

"How can that be?" Her voice belied her annoyance.

"Mandubratius and his band are like us and can travel at high speeds," he informed the Basileus. Of course subtleties, such as the differences between races of blood-drinkers, could wait for another conversation.

Irene leaned in close and whispered, "Faster than our horses can travel?"

"Yes, Imperial Majesty, much faster."

Mandubratius did not tell her much. Pity.

The Empress waved her hands about as if confusion were at war with frustration within her head. "Well then... let's travel much, much faster! Now, General!" she whispered in a loud, exasperated tone.

Gaius felt contempt at her demand, but he hoped the expression he revealed befitted a confused man. "What about the mortals and horses? They could not keep up with us, even if they continued to travel without rest. Your men would have similar limitations… unless, of course, they were no longer mortal, but then there would be other limitations to consider."

The Basileus sighed, revealing more impatience. "I'm not quite sure I want to subject my men to that without giving them a choice, Gaius. However, if I did that to them, they could only travel at night, correct?"

"Regardless of deciding whether or not to sponsor the men, the road ahead is sparsely populated for many miles. We'll have to feed off animals. We may also have to shelter ourselves within freshly dug pits in the ground."

I know of few occasions where the Basileus has left the protection of the city. This experience will surely be a rude awakening for her. Delightful.

Her eyes snapped open in obvious shock. "We will sleep in the ground?"

"Yes, Basileus. We have done this when there is no appropriate shelter. If that is the case, we find a shady spot, dig a hole, and bury ourselves. We sleep in the earth until sunset. Then we dig ourselves out and find sustenance."

"That sounds perfectly ghastly. I can imagine the odor one develops. It's so unclean," she complained. A deep frown of disgust graced her features.

Gaius hoped this meant she had changed her mind on this endeavor, and that she and her mortal escorts would head back to Constantinople. "Well, Imperial Majesty, there is no guarantee that we can find shelter on the way, so it may come to that. The choice is between cleanliness and catching your sponsor."

Irene slammed her hand on the carriage door and cursed her fate to the Gods. "Fine. I choose to chase the betrayer."

Gaius tried to rein in his disappointment. "Very well then, Basileus, but what shall we do about the mortals?"

Irene closed her eyes for a moment, as if considering the situation. "In your opinion, General, is there any chance that they will keep up with us?"

"No, Imperial Majesty."

"Then, they will return to Constantinople," she said. After appraising his face, she added, "I shall trust that I have your protection and loyalty."

Gaius leaned through the window and whispered directly into the Empress' ear. "Imperial Majesty, we are Lamia, as is your sponsor. However, we protect our kind in positions of mortal leadership. You have my word to serve as your protector."

A small smile won a great victory over the frown that had preceded it upon the Basileus' face. "Well then, give them their marching orders, and we'll go. I hope you will teach me to move fast."

"You will find it very easy to learn this skill," he promised her.

chapter eleven

hile scanning the surrounding forest for any sign of the Strigoi, Marcus sensed Julien and Mac Alpin return.

Mac Alpin crept up to Marcus and spoke in soft tones, as if concerned about discovery. "The Children of Ares and the Basileus are very close. They left their mortal escorts behind and have been traveling at nearly their normal speed, as the Empress seems to be holding them back, but only slightly"

"And the Strigoi?" Marcus queried, having not detected them himself.

"Not a sign," Mac Alpin whispered back, shrugging a bit.

Marcus felt a light touch on his left arm, and upon turning around, he noticed it was Amata, trying to gain his attention.

"What are we going to do?" she asked.

Mandubratius, who stood nearby, said, "I would advise not to attack them."

Claudius smirked while adjusting his gear. "Why not?"

"Because they're Lamia, no matter what silly name they used to have," Mandubratius answered.

"And my sponsor is among them," Patroclus added.

"Let us not forget that the ruler of the Eastern Empire also runs with them," Julien added.

The boy seems frightened… or nervous. Perhaps as a Frankish noble, he knows her reputation better than most of us.

Marcus raised his hands to quell discussion. "If we can delay engaging the Children of Ares, Greek Lamia contingent… whoever they are, we should do so. The goal is to allow the Strigoi to attack them and then we can rescue them." He sighed.

The plan sounds easier than it will be to execute.

"What if the Strigoi do not attack?" Edward asked.

At that moment, Mac Alpin waved his arms in a mad motion above his head to shush everyone. He then closed his eyes and whispered, "It's the Lamia."

"Give us our–" Claudius began to say, but he grew silent as arrows began to rain on them.

"Take flight," Marcus said in a quiet whisper, hoping not to give away their exact position. He took note of a few members of the party who took hits.

Within seconds, another volley of arrows flew towards them, but this time, one of them struck his left shoulder, piercing his skin under his collarbone. While not significant an injury, the pain distracted him. "Shake off the wounds! We need to fly!" He then grabbed Julien with his right arm and positioned him to levitate. Marcus looked on as Máire and Fianait flew away with Patroclus, while Mac Alpin and Claudius pulled up Horatio.

Mandubratius rushed up to Marcus and poked him below his unwounded shoulder. "You won't leave me behind this time." The Lamia shoved himself in between Marcus and Julien, while clutching the mirror to his chest. "Damn the Legate for his good fortune."

Marcus latched onto Mandubratius with his right arm. "I think Máire tires of your mind games," Marcus stated. "And she's not the only one. If you were not carrying that most precious cargo..." Marcus let his voice trail off, making his point known. He then nodded to Julien, who gripped Mandubratius as well, and the two Deargh Du flew into the sky, carrying their annoying ally with them.

Marcus glanced down at his burden and noticed the Lamia's mouth open to make some sort of witty reply, but then the blood-drinker winced before shutting his mouth and eyes.

"You and she live for causing me anguish," Mandubratius uttered in a pain-filled tone. He laughed as another arrow pierced his right leg.

Another volley of arrows missed them by inches, reaching higher than many of the trees.

The next barrage plunged three arrows into Marcus' right leg and thigh at once. With effort, he tried to ignore the ensuing flash of pain, but the loss of blood made him tire. Upon hearing a gasp and soft cry to his far right, Marcus looked over and saw six arrows protruding from Julien's back and legs.

Mandubratius uttered a loud, tortured scream and winced, causing Marcus to remember the cruel torments he and his fellow Romans had inflicted upon the Briton on the coast of Éire, so many years ago.

All conscious thought left Marcus, for a moment, but he managed to clear his head and refocus on his surroundings. Air whizzed by as his body plunged towards the forest below, and he could no longer feel either his grandchild-in-darkness or that Briton holding onto him.

Just then, Marcus felt a hand grasp him, and he opened his eyes to see Julien directly to his right, after having regained control of himself.

Together, Marcus and Julien reduced their descent. Marcus then looked towards the ground and saw Mandubratius still plummeting to earth. The Briton held the mirror to his chest, as if trying to protect it from the arrows and from his inevitable landing.

"Curses on both of us for forgetting to cloak ourselves in darkness," he whispered to Julien, who looked at him for a second but said nothing. Marcus noticed pain and shock showing through Julien's widened eyes. "The others are higher than us," he murmured to Julien. "I must swallow the pain and see what happens to our ally and the mirror."

Julien nodded a bit. "I will join you... in case."

Marcus didn't wait for Julien and, instead, covered himself in darkness and dove. After reaching about twenty feet off the forest floor, he stopped and levitated in place. He then peered from behind the darkness at the scene below him.

In some other date and time, he would have found the scene below him most amusing. Mandubratius lay flat on his back with a few dozen broken arrows peaking out beneath him. The Children of Ares surrounded the Co-Consul and stood menacingly with drawn swords. A dark-haired woman, whom he presumed to be the Empress, pushed her way through the ring of soldiers. She would have been most breathtaking, if it were not for the fierce anger extending from her form.

After the Basileus Irene snatched her mirror away from Mandubratius, she passed it over to Sextus. She stepped on the fallen Lamia's stomach, while wielding a dagger.

Julien soon joined Marcus, and he looked up to see the young Deargh Du peer down at the bloody circus below.

A soft whimper drew Marcus' attention back down, just in time to see the Empress stomp her foot on what appeared to be Mandubratius' broken and twisted leg. She then leaned over, pulled down his trousers, and grabbed something Marcus couldn't see around his crotch area.

Marcus heard a scream of pure agony and looked away from what seemed to be a most painful castration. He then glanced at the boy.

Julien looked ill and pulled himself back into the gloom.

After gazing down again, Marcus watched the Empress toss aside a bloodied mass of tissue. While the theatrics played out below, Marcus realized that a soldier had looked up and recognized him.

"Deargh Du!" he heard someone shout.

"Where?"

"In the area above us where there are no stars!"

"Nock arrows and fire!" Gaius ordered.

Marcus rushed into Julien's darkness. "I think you heard... it's time to go," he said, but he became distracted by the sound of a torrent of arrows singing towards them. "I think I taught them too well. You maintain your darkness, and I will guide us toward the others," he whispered, before grabbing Julien's arm and flying the two of them skyward.

Pain ceased all thought for a few minutes.

Mandubratius had felt agony many times in his long life. The most pain he recalled feeling was when the black-eyed Maél Muire, or Máire, crushed his chest and broke his spine. Back then, his diminishing senses allowed his pain to fade, but this time, the torture did not ebb away.

He closed his eyes, for a moment, while assessing his wounds. Upon landing, he suffered acute anguish as the arrows broke and shoved deeper into his body. Although he couldn't feel his left leg, he sensed that it lay contorted underneath him. His head throbbed with dizzying pain as if cracked open. Of course, his groin also suffered injury. "By Mars," he whispered in shock.

Mandubratius inhaled a painful gulp of air and tried to sit up, despite a smashed left shoulder and arm, which he just noticed, but the pain was too much for him. With his agony-infused skull back on the compacted ground, Mandubratius turned his head and spotted the Empress, who moved her mouth. He attempted to decipher those movements but gave up because of the agony it caused.

Soon after, he felt several sets of hands roll him over onto his right side, which seemed to be less damaged than his left, but the increased aching from being shifted around made him cry out. His cries were stifled when someone shoved a wooden stick into his mouth. He bit down upon feeling someone else begin to extract an arrow from his back. After feeling the arrow shaft break, several fingers dug into his open flesh, trying to get a grip on the arrowhead embedded in his wound. At the same time, he felt tugging around his left leg, suggesting that they might be applying a splint in an attempt to immobilize it. Throughout their butcher-like ministrations, extracting one arrow and then another, his vision grew darker.

I must be losing a great deal of blood.

Thoughts of his mortal days and immortal nights soon overtook the pain, and he could feel his face contort in a smile, but then his current situation with his old enemies brought forth new and conflicting emotions.

Perhaps it would be easier to concentrate on my desire for power.

In a far off, darkened part of his mind, Mandubratius could detect hands upon him, rolling his body onto his back again, but this time, the ground felt different. It seemed softer, and he could feel himself centered between two ridges.

At some point in his journey through his semi-conscious mind, he felt someone forcibly part his lips and then a salty, warm substance covered his mouth.

Perhaps they wish for me to live.

He considered spitting away the blood to spite Irene and her cronies, but his craving for life won out, so he sucked at the vitae. With each hungry gulp, Mandubratius felt warmth radiate through him, melting away the frozen depths of his body. As energy returned, his wounds began to heal, though he knew it would take a great deal of time to recover completely.

Before Mandubratius had consumed his fill of the blood, the arm he suckled upon pulled away. Despite his inner protest, he allowed it to leave.

Soon, his vision began to brighten. Instead of seeing nothing but blackness, blurry images danced around his open eyes, but the light caused pain. He tried to blink away his discomfort, but the stinging sensation led him to close his eyes. His ears, however, fared far better. Instead of just hearing his breathing and the slow beating of his heart, he could detect the sound of the wind blowing through the trees, owls hooting, and crickets chirping amongst themselves.

When Mandubratius opened his eyes, a face came into focus… Irene's.

She stared at him for a moment, before lowering her eyes to her left forearm, which she cradled with her right hand.

Ahh… she fed me. The Empress must desire for me to remain alive… for now, at least.

Even though Mandubratius knew her reason for keeping him alive, he asked her why anyway. When he spoke his question, his voice sounded like it came from a pitiful mortal on his deathbed.

In response to his question, she began to smile in a manner he recognized as his own. "So I can torture you for eternity because of what you did to me," Irene replied. She then turned towards one of the Lamia and nodded.

Before Mandubratius could provide some kind of pithy comment in reply, a crack of blinding pain shot through his skull, and all became darkness.

Amata patted Edward's shoulder as they flew, grateful for his help. She found herself surrounded by some sort of strange luck of the Gods during their escape from the Basileus, since no arrows had pierced her. Curious how everyone else fared, she looked around for her traveling companions.

Upon spotting Máire, Fianait, and the others, Amata's body demanded its nightly meal, and she hoped that no one heard it growl. To voice any kind of complaint after someone spent his or her own waning energy to save her would be humiliating.

All of her companions struggled, and she could see Fianait nearly pass out. Máire had to grab hold of her before she could fall.

Edward must have noticed as well, since he called out to the others, "We've got to land soon."

She heard murmurs of assent, and immediately, she sensed a slow descent towards the ground. They soon touched down on the outskirts of a brightly lit town.

What town could it possibly be?

After giving Edward a brief kiss of thanks, Amata looked around for Mandubratius, but she could not find him.

Perhaps Marcus and Julien fell behind.

With her Co-Consul and his escorts missing, Amata decided to circle back and talk with Fianait, who seemed on the verge of collapse, and Máire, who plucked an arrow from her body, barely revealing any pain or emotion. Amata, lost in a strange fascination, watched the Deargh Du go through the process of healing herself.

Máire shook back her plaited hair over her right shoulder. She then placed her hands over the wound in her leg and began to hum softly with her eyes closed. Once she removed her hand, red skin covered the wound.

"Why do you hum?" Amata asked. She could not remember hearing the Deargh Du sing during the healing process before.

"To focus," Máire drawled, "and I do not care for my singing voice. Others will sing sometimes. Marcus does not, but everyone has their own methods to focus their will. Do you need healing?" Máire turned towards Amata, appearing to be earnest.

"No, thank you for offering. I was spared by the grace of the Gods, for reasons that are not clear," Amata answered.

Máire nodded before turning to Claudius and assessing his wounds.

Amata looked about and witnessed other Deargh Du, and even blood-drinkers of the other Celtic line, hum and begin to sing while healing themselves and others. She then returned her attention to Máire, who removed an arrow he could not reach.

After plucking the arrow, Máire cupped the wound as she and Claudius whispered the song together.

In reciprocation, Claudius turned Máire gently, facing away from him, to remove the last of the arrows that remained in her back.

While receiving Claudius' ministrations, Máire stared at Amata for a moment before asking, "Have you seen Marcus, Julien, or Mandubratius?"

Amata bit back her surprise at the obvious look of concern on the other blood-drinker's face as she mentioned Mandubratius. Undeniably, she would be concerned for her father and son-in-darkness, but tenderness for a nemesis?

I will have to tell Mandubratius, though in a manner that makes it seem like a joke.

"I have not seen them," Amata admitted. "I hoped that you had."

Claudius took Máire's arm and said, "Forgive my intrusion, Amata, but we need to heal our friend. Arwin says he needs your steady hands, Banbh

Ceanúil."

As Máire led Claudius towards the others, Amata trailed behind them. They soon joined the remainder of the large party, who all stood in a circle. Curious as to what they were gawking at in the center of their circle, Amata squeezed past a few of the taller blood-drinkers to get a better look.

Inside of a smaller ring of blood-drinkers, Amata saw Mac Alpin squatting on the ground, but she couldn't tell why he sat there or why his solemn presence drew so much attention from their fellow blood-drinkers.

Despite the crowd, Máire seemed to have no effort getting to the center, as both rings of blood-drinkers moved aside for her. Máire then kneeled in front of the Ekimmu Cruitne.

Amata assumed he bore a wound, but she could not see it.

"What causes you pain, Arwin?" Máire asked.

Amata crept around in order to get a better view of Mac Alpin, but upon getting a step closer, she felt a powerful strum of magic envelope her, making her feel weak.

Mac Alpin grunted before speaking. "There is an arrow lodged in my neck, as you can see. The arrowhead is in my brain, and it will not come out."

Amata leaned forward a little. She then gasped upon seeing the arrow protruding from the back of his head and the trail of gore, which dripped down the shaft and along his back.

How could he not be paralyzed? Perhaps the magic I sense is Mac Alpin creating pleasure within himself.

As Amata watched in fright, she observed Máire looking around Mac Alpin's head for a moment.

"If we extract the arrow," Máire said after finishing her inspection, "it may injure you in a way that we may be unable to heal. Of course, we could break the shaft, but that will cause other problems."

"Maél Muire," Mac Alpin murmured. "You have to get it out, and there are only two ways it can come out."

Máire sighed before nodding. "Yes, you're right, elder."

Amata couldn't fathom what they meant, and she had to know, so she decided to voice her question. "Two ways?" When she noticed several stares looking her way, Amata added, "I am sorry for interrupting, I… only wish to help those who aided my escape."

"We can either crack open Arwin's skull like a nut, fish around his brains with our fingers, and pluck out the arrowhead, or we can shove the arrow out of one of his eye sockets," Máire answered with steady resolve.

Amata felt herself cringe at the thought of being in Mac Alpin's situation. *What if the arrow were stuck in my head? How would that feel? Would my friends help? Would I be so calm while being faced with two horrible solutions?*

After silencing her thoughts, she asked, "What will you do?"

Mac Alpin chuckled before responding. "I wish Máire to shove it through my eye socket."

"But the pain–" Amata whispered before being cut off.

"I am using pleasure to combat it, but I have little energy left," Mac Alpin replied.

Amata felt a strong hand upon her left shoulder, and she looked up to see Edward breaking through the others and around her.

"I will give you my energy," he said to Mac Alpin.

Despite Edward's bravado, Amata saw that unhealed wounds remained on the young Ekimmu Cruitne's back.

Mac Alpin must have noticed Edward's state, for he grimaced and said, "Lad, you are not fully healed, are you..."

Amata reached up to Edward's right shoulder and drew him closer so she could whisper into his right ear. "Feed from me," she said. "I have no healing skill."

Edward smiled at her and took her wrist.

Amata experienced the gentle caress of his fangs as they pierced her arm. As he drank from her, she fell to her knees.

After what seemed like hours of bliss, Edward released her. "I have energy now," he said to Arwin.

Amata felt Patroclus heft her up to her feet, and then he guided her outside the inner circle towards the outer circle, but she didn't want to leave. "I wish to see this," she whispered to him.

He patted her right shoulder before wrapping his arms around her and maneuvering her into a position where she could keep her vigil. He then supported her weight... a good thing, since she felt so weak. Like most of the others... she hadn't yet fed, and with her donation to Edward, she felt on the verge of unconsciousness.

A few members of the outer circle briefly rubbed her back, in what she felt must be a sign of appreciation and camaraderie.

As Amata looked on, Máire prepared herself for the extraction. She then turned to the others. "Get ready to help us heal him," the Deargh Du requested.

After returning her attention to Mac Alpin, Máire pulled aside his dark hair. To Edward, she said, "Gently restrain your father-in-darkness," before motioning for others to join him.

While Edward and a few others grasped hold of Mac Alpin, Máire stood and began to walk around Arwin, examining every angle of the arrow. She returned to Arwin's back and started peeling away the fletching. After

Heather Poinsett Dunbar & Christopher Dunbar

stripping the fletching from the shaft, she placed her right hand on the shaft of the arrow. She seemed to be on the verge of shoving the arrow through, when she stopped herself and backed away.

"I must do something first," Máire murmured before stepping around the blood-drinkers holding Mac Alpin. She sat down in front of him and said, "I'm sorry, Arwin, but I have to do this."

The Deargh Du's hand moved with the speed of lightning. In one deft motion, she plucked out Mac Alpin's eye with just enough force to pull it out and not sever it.

His eye dangled against his cheek, held in place by veins and nerves.

Máire looked into his good eye and stated, "It's painful, I'm sure, but you won't have to waste energy creating a new eye now."

"Good thinking, chroí," the Ekimmu Cruitne gasped.

Something about Mac Alpin's only expression of pain thus far caused Amata's thoughts to drift to Mandubratius. She worried again for him... and the others.

Where could he, Marcus, and even Julien be?

Máire's return to Mac Alpin's back brought Amata out of her contemplations.

Máire kissed Mac Alpin's right cheek before saying, "You realize this may sever things, and you may die."

"Just do it, Banbh Ceanúil, and for once... give me no lip!" Arwin chuckled, as if he sat upon a bar bench with a goblet of bloodmead in one hand and a bar wench upon his knees.

Máire crouched behind him, placing her left hand on Arwin's forehead and her right hand on the arrow shaft. Then, with one quick yet calculated motion, she pushed the arrowhead through, so its point stuck outside of Mac Alpin's vacant eye socket.

Mac Alpin closed his good eye, but he said nothing... didn't even cry out... although Edward did wince, as if he were working through Mac Alpin's pain.

Máire stood and walked around to Mac Alpin's front. Once she assumed what looked to be a comfortable position, she reached out with her nimble fingers and gripped the gore-encrusted arrowhead. She then started pulling at it with her right hand while bracing Mac Alpin's forehead with her left hand.

Amata felt a little wheezy as she watched Máire pull it out, inch by inch.

It's just blood... you've seen worse.

Slowly but surely, the arrowhead and part of the shaft protruded a few inches from the eye socket. Máire then pinched the base of the shaft with the fingers of her left hand and gripped the shaft just below the arrowhead with her right hand.

"Here it comes," Máire warned. "Claudius, grab a rag, get in here, and keep his brains in here when I pull out the arrow."

Once Claudius pressed the rag against Mac Alpin's eye socket, Máire removed the rest of the arrow in one swift tug. Her movement produced a disgusting sucking sound, as the arrow exited the wound.

Gore dripped from the socket, until Claudius applied pressure with the rag he held in place.

After tossing away the arrow, Máire pushed aside the rag and gingerly began to urge the nerves, blood vessels, and the eye back into the socket. Once she finished, Máire cupped her hands over the eye and started murmuring.

Several other blood-drinkers moved in to place their hands upon her and Arwin.

Amata closed her eyes as the soft healing song rose again. She recognized a few words, such as 'channel' and 'Brigid', but the song seemed to waver between lamentation and joyous triumph.

The Celtic blood-drinkers swayed with the tune.

At some point during the song, Mac Alpin and Edward each uttered a moan in unison and collapsed. Both Ekimmu Cruitne fell face forward into the dirt.

Amata shoved her weakened body out of Patroclus' hold and staggered towards the circle, fearing the worst, but then she got a good glimpse of the back of Arwin's head, and it had healed completely.

"Let's roll him onto his back," Máire murmured softly. After helping Claudius, Horatio, and others roll over the burly Ekimmu Cruitne, Máire began to touch various spots on Arwin's neck. "He yet lives," she called out to the gathered blood-drinkers.

Amata echoed the soft murmurs of relief that everyone else expressed upon hearing the good news.

"Cover the eye with your rag, Claudius, while I prepare something to hold it in place." She ripped the bottom edge of her tunic and began wrapping the material around his face to hold the rag in place.

Claudius held the rag until Máire finished wrapping it down.

Amata, who could barely keep her feet, collapsed next to Edward and stared at him, while others rolled him onto his back. He appeared passed out as well. She felt as if she might join him soon, but then Patroclus shoved his left arm in her face.

"Drink this, Domina... please," Patroclus murmured to her.

At that same moment, Máire addressed the group as if assuming the leadership role in the absence of her sponsor. "We must feed and heal ourselves now," she suggested.

Amata bit into the Legate's arm and began feeding. She could already feel some strength return.

"However," Máire continued, "four of us must remain in position around the town to watch for Julien, Marcus, and Mandubratius, as well as the Basileus and her friends."

Well before Amata had slaked her thirst, Patroclus pulled his arm away. Part of her wanted to latch on and suck all she could until she was sated, but she realized that Patroclus shared her fatigue and hunger. Despite his condition, he had given her what he could, enabling her to stand on her own.

How noble.

Meanwhile, Máire continued her announcements. "I'm going to get rooms at the inn for us, once I feed a bit. However, let's try not to overtax our hosts. I smell livestock on the breeze." Máire looked over the party for a moment. "Claudius, would you and Fianait watch over Edward and Arwin for us?"

With help from Patroclus, Amata got to her feet. "I will assist," she stated to Máire before taking a few unsteady steps closer to Edward.

"Excellent," Máire responded. "Horatio and Patroclus, go gorge yourselves, return, and share with Claudius, Fianait, and Amata."

At the mention of her Co-Consul, Amata felt a flood of worry wash over her. She needed reassurances from Máire. She needed hope.

"Afterwards," Máire added, "meet up with me in the inn. Pretend the lads are drunk."

Horatio extended his left hand, which Máire accepted, and helped her rise to her feet.

Before Máire could leave, Amata ran towards her and grabbed her left arm.

The Deargh Du turned to face her.

"What do we do about Mandubratius, Julien, and Marcus?" Amata asked. She heard the anxiety in her voice grow.

"Your brother-in-darkness is a stubborn bastard, Amata," Máire said. "All men are stubborn. They will survive, merely to annoy us. However, we cannot do anything now. We must sleep."

Máire touched Amata's arm with her hand and squeezed it in a gentle manner for a brief moment. "Edward may recover tonight, but Arwin will need more time. He may not wake until he's fully healed. By then, those boys will return to us."

"I understand," Amata murmured, having found some hope in the Deargh Du's words.

Máire released her hand and started for the town again.

Amata rejoined the others and squatted by Edward's unconscious form.

She then picked up his right hand and squeezed it lovingly.

This is indeed a strange situation.

Julien and Marcus touched down near the door to a barn, which lay a few miles from a nearby village. "I think we have half the night left," Julien murmured to Marcus while glancing around, looking for possible threats. "Shouldn't we attempt to find the others?"

As soon as Marcus opened the creaky door, they wandered into the barn.

After closing the door behind them, Marcus shook his head and limped to a place where he could brace himself. He then started to pull out arrows stuck in his legs and arms, though a few arrows necessitated him to break the shafts before pulling them out. Marcus did not heal himself.

Julien walked over and used the same beam to brace himself as he removed arrows clinging to him.

"Tomorrow night," Marcus said through gritted teeth, "we will heal, but tonight, we need to feed, sleep, and recover.

Julien felt the urge to contradict his father-in-darkness, since they could both feed and heal, but Marcus interrupted him before Julien could say anything.

"No healing. It would expend too much energy."

A moo interrupted his words, and Julien glanced up to see the cow he had sensed.

Marcus glanced along with him and added, "We will feed from this cow a few times and then feed from the farmer that takes care of it."

After looking back to Marcus, who seemed to be preparing to pull out another arrow, almost hyperventilating at the effort, Julien asked, "What about our friends? Should we not try to reach them?"

"Worry not, Julien. They will not leave without us," Marcus drawled before yanking an arrow from his right side. "Besides, I doubt the Basileus and her friends will move right away. Mandubratius' condition is grave, and Irene will wish to torture her prize a bit. He must recover for her to punish him again."

Julien felt confusion over Marcus' words. "You do not think they killed him?" he asked.

Marcus did not respond to his question at first. After looking Julien over, however, Marcus turned the boy's body so he faced away from Marcus. He then plucked an arrow from between Julien's shoulder blades.

Julien felt a shot of pain, as if both fire and ice raged an intense war in his left shoulder. Then, with the arrow gone, Marcus clamped his left hand on the wound.

"Irene is not the kind of woman to let mere death get in the way of vengeance," Marcus said while pulling out a rag with his left hand. "She will want to remove that portion of his anatomy again and again." He then pressed the rag into Julien's wound.

As Julien took hold of the rag and held it in place, he felt distaste over the Empress' cruelty. "Thank you," Julien stated before sinking onto a pile of hay. "Yes, I have heard of her barbarity, and I agree with your conclusions." After a brief pause, he asked, "What about the mirror?"

"We will reclaim it when the opportunity presents itself," Marcus stated. He then bound some of his wounds with other rags he kept in his kit.

"By force?" Julien queried.

"I do not wish to confront Gaius. After all, this may be some plan of his and the Co-Consul's. Our kind needs every ally, if we are to stay here on the continent," Marcus explained as he settled on another pile of hay.

"How can you say that?" Julien asked, concerned Marcus was being too soft in the face of betrayal. "His forces attacked us. You said yourself that you taught them too well."

"They did not want to kill us, just make it look so," Marcus commented. "They were deadly accurate after their training. Our wounds were intended to be superficial."

"And our friend, Mandubratius?" Julien asked. He felt a smirk grace his face.

"A bargain for the Empress," Marcus answered with a yawn. "I am certain Mandubratius will come out of this situation smelling of wine and roses. He will probably charm her all over again."

Julien chuckled. "Perhaps you are correct," he reasoned aloud, but then a thought occurred to him. "Don't you believe there is a chance that they will return to Constantinople?"

"No. I believe they will follow us," Marcus replied while leaning back into the hay. "In fact, I am certain of it. Irene must be mollified. If things play out as those Lamia wish, the Basileus must believe that she cannot survive without their assistance. It's easy enough to do when they can save her imperial arse from the Strigoi. The Lamia will do whatever it takes to keep Irene following us… that is, until the Strigoi arrive. After we meet up with the others, we will watch their movements."

"Impressive," Julien replied before gingerly getting to his feet. "But what if you are wrong?" Julien walked over to Marcus while clutching his bandage to his wound.

"Then, we will hunt her down and retrieve the mirror. Sometimes, there can be no alliance," Marcus replied.

Julien strolled over to the cow and began rubbing its side. "Máire told me to feed before sleeping, if I need to heal," Julien commented. He then coaxed the cow closer to where Marcus sat. "So, the main concern is the mirror, correct?"

Marcus nodded. "Yes, that is our main concern." After a bit of a pause, he added, "I remember when I taught her that... about feeding before sleeping. Yes, it will help heal our wounds without our having to use our gifts. Tomorrow night will be difficult. Gorge yourself if necessary. We will need extra vitae to heal."

Mandubratius longed to sit up and scratch himself. The blood he had been fed helped with the healing process, but it did not provide him with enough strength. At this moment, he found himself feeling as strong as a mortal might, but it would not be enough to rip through the ropes.

He looked around, but all he could see from his fully reclined posture were trees, clouds, and stars, which shifted with each clumsy step of his Lamia stretcher-bearers. Soon, the sound of cows and sheep drowned out the usual nighttime noises. Mandubratius extended and twisted his neck, so he could see where they headed, and he managed to catch a glimpse of a barn and small house.

Thank Mars. No sleeping in holes in the ground for me today.

Despite the good news of an above ground rest, he could feel his earlier regained strength begin to melt away. His vision grayed, as he faded in and out of consciousness. Still, bits and pieces of conversation, in both Latin and Greek, filtered through his mind. He heard Gaius speaking to the Empress about the others in his party. Memories gathered in the corners of his brain again, and he could remember his plans... their plans. He hoped that Marcus wouldn't decide to try to steal the mirror.

"If Marcus did that, I would probably be the first casualty," he whispered to himself in his native tongue. He stopped muttering when he heard wood shatter, and then screams echoed into the night, followed by a deadly silence.

He could see Irene pacing in front of the house.

When she traversed past him, her eyes locked on his.

He gave her his best gracious smile, as if she had just bestowed upon him the greatest gifts of the Eastern Empire.

"Move that idiot inside," Irene growled to the soldiers carrying his stretcher.

Someone doesn't like sleeping in such humble accommodations.

Mandubratius smelled freshly spilled blood as they moved him into the house, past the dead bodies. He could not fathom, however, why Irene or the Lamia hadn't fed from them.

A large fire in the hearth lit the house.

Irene followed them inside and closed the door behind him. "Hold him steady," she ordered the Lamia, before crouching down next to him and returning his smile. After fixing her gaze upon his, her face twisted and her smile grew strained, becoming unflattering.

Provocation came to mind immediately. "You shouldn't smile that way, sweetheart. It brings out your wrinkles," Mandubratius murmured. Pain shot through his recovering chest when she punched him, breaking a rib. He felt his smile widen despite the pain.

"Do you know why I'm keeping you alive?" she queried.

"Yes," Mandubratius answered.

"No, you don't, you smug, ignorant bastard!" Irene punched him in the chest again, breaking another rib or two. "How can you know my designs for you?"

"Well," he began to explain, "you're not unpredictable, Irene. You would rather torture me than kill me outright."

For that truth, Irene pummeled him in the stomach, causing him to cough up blood.

"You are an infuriating man. How I fell for you, I cannot fathom. And you... you twisted my body into this form!" For emphasis, the Empress pulled up her tunic, revealing her beautiful breasts.

"You look the same gorgeous self as you did when you were a mortal," Mandubratius answered while feeling a little tingling in his budding groin.

"You said I would look youthful, as those Lamia you were with at the orgy!" Irene grumbled.

"No, you merely assumed they were Lamia. Two of them were Deargh Du, and they become radiant in their transformation. I am sorry you misunderstood me, but know this... I thought you were most breathtaking as a mortal, and I still believe you to be beautiful."

Irene growled and punched him in the jaw, bringing him more pain, which diminished his other aches.

Mandubratius turned aside and spat out a tooth. "It's far more satisfying to make mortals believe you are beautiful through the use of manipulation. Besides, I have arrested your aging. You will not grow older," he added.

"But I'm hideous! Look at me," Irene spat. She then leaned her bosom in closer to his face.

Too far away to suckle... if only my hands were free.

"Have you tried looking into your beautiful and precious mirror?" he purred as she released her hold on the bottom of her tunic, covering her breasts again.

"No," she answered. "I have not looked into it since I turned for–" She stopped herself mid-sentence and stared at him. Finally, she added, "I have not looked into it for some time."

"But this mirror of Aphrodite reveals the inner beauty. Inner beauty does not diminish with age."

"My inner beauty," Irene muttered.

"Yes," he uttered, pleased that his own manipulation skills worked so well.

If I can get her to look into the mirror, then perhaps I can talk her into other things as well. Maybe not my freedom, but perhaps she might allow me to keep my genitals.

"Go get the mirror," he urged her, while trying not to expose his growing weakness from using his manipulation gifts. "You may like what you see."

Irene nodded her head, which disappeared from his line of sight.

"Bring him," she ordered his stretcher-bearers.

When he heard the door open, Mandubratius closed his eyes. He could feel his stretcher being jerked around as they carried him, and then he felt his feet lowered. He began to feel dizzier than before. When he could open his eyes, he saw the mirror leaning up against a cauldron on a table.

Irene turned the mirror to angle towards both of them. She then focused her attention on the mirror. Her features soon softened in the light of the fire.

"You see, Irene. You are stunning," he purred while grinning at his own striking reflection in the mirror.

Irene turned towards him, a look of ironic contentment upon her face, and quipped, "Just for that, I think I will restrain myself from punishing you… for now." To her soldiers, she ordered, "Lower him to the ground and leave."

After sitting down next to him, Irene fixed him with a foreboding look. "Before you go to sleep, I must warn you of one thing. Do not betray me. If you do so, I will have more than your genitals… I will have your head."

Mandubratius decided to say nothing else, thinking she might hit him again if he did so. Instead, he gave her a kind smile… not too strained or boisterous.

The Empress rose and took a step back. "Go to sleep, for we have a long night ahead of us," she said before leaving the small room.

Mandubratius closed his eyes and drifted off into slumber. The effort of manipulating the Empress had drained too much energy from him.

Szeged

After feeding, Claudius walked into the room Mac Alpin and Edward rested in. A sleepy-eyed Amata shrugged when asked whether there was any improvement in their condition.

She tried to wake Máire, who slept next to the hearth, but he stopped Amata, telling her to get some rest.

Claudius did not feel like sleeping, so he walked down to the common room, ordered a drink from the serving wench, and sat down on a bench near his conscious cohorts. When he noticed shadows in front of him, he took a moment to look up from his drink at the few farmers and tradesmen who stared at him and his companions as if they were freaks of nature. Not wishing to provoke a confrontation, Claudius just smiled at them and returned his attention to his drink.

Unfortunately, none of the blood-drinkers could pass for merchants, owing to their bound wounds. He reasoned that their condition was why the locals were paying them so much attention.

If some kind of fight did break out, Claudius, and the few blood-drinkers who sat with him, would be outnumbered. While drink had raised spirits the prior night, it did not take long for all of them to tire. Many still slept in their rooms, exhausted from healing.

The smell of freshly cut wood, sweat, and honing oil soon caught Claudius' attention. He sensed that a mortal, who spent most of his time chopping wood, stood behind him. His annoyance peaked, as a pair of insistent fingers began tapping him on his left shoulder.

Claudius turned around and stared at the stranger, a tall, grizzled woodsman, which confirmed his senses. "Are you in need of something that I can provide?" Claudius asked while trying to swallow his impatience and worry.

The great man stared at him, while scratching at his dark beard.

"What are you doing here?" the woodsman asked, in atrocious Greek, before belching. The smell of cheap wine and the remains of dinner washed over Claudius' face.

Claudius refrained from waving away the stink. "Just traveling through, on our way to the west. And you?" he purred, believing a gentle phrase or two would soothe the troubled giant.

"I'm asking the questions," the woodsman countered.

"There are more? Do continue," Claudius drawled while trying to smile.

Lovely, now I sound like a Lamia.

"You are a stranger here," the man grumbled.

"I'm no stranger than you," Claudius answered. Mentally, he went through his options. Considering that the other blood-drinkers in the room were as weak as he thought, if a confrontation were to break out, somebody might feel compelled to feed.

What an appalling prospect in a crowded common room.

The giant woodsman turned a hard, brown eye on him and did not utter a reply.

Claudius believed that perhaps the woodsman understood him, although sometimes, even a Sugnwr Gwaed's honeyed phrases could not work on a drunk.

Deciding to ignore the brute again, Claudius turned to sip on his wine, when one of the woodsman's great paws began tapping him again. He turned to face the stranger.

Before Claudius could ask the woodsman why he was so insistent, the woodsman demanded, "Did you take our people?"

"I am not taking anyone's people," Claudius explained. "What do you mean?" His dwindling energy levels kept his own form of glamoury in short supply. He felt he could no longer keep the beast from striking him, if the woodsman so chose.

"Did you take my wife?" the giant woodsman demanded.

Claudius sensed the approach of two more strangers. He set his wine down and pondered whether they needed to fly Edward and Arwin to a new, safer location.

If we have to feed here, in public, there will be no safe place for us around this town... or this land.

Claudius glanced at the newcomers to the conversation and noticed that they wore uniforms. The strangers appeared to be the guards of the local lord.

One of them placed his right hand on the woodsman's left shoulder. "Nestor, why don't you give the stranger some space," the guard warned. "I don't think he's the one that took your wife."

Nestor appeared flustered. He faced the uniformed man who had addressed him and stated, "But this man is a devil! The devil killed my wife!"

"Don't be silly, Nestor," the guard countered. "This stranger looks human. Go home, Nestor. I will send Damaris to comfort you and keep you company tonight. Does that sound fair?"

Nestor lowered his eyes and nodded his head. "Good night, Dorian," the big man said before turning away.

"Rest well," Dorian replied and then nodded to the other guard. "Evander, walk Nestor home."

Evander saluted Dorian, walked over to the entrance to the inn, and held the door for the woodsman.

With the confrontation over, Claudius picked up his goblet of wine and began to sip at it again, but then he realized that the remaining guard still stood behind him.

"May I join you?" the guard queried after a brief pause.

Claudius set down the goblet and looked over his left shoulder at him. "Yes, you may," he answered.

"I am Dorian, deputy to Lord Corydon," the guard stated, as he walked around the table and took a seat on the bench across from Claudius.

"Claudius Metrius Sertorius," he greeted, although he wondered why he bothered giving his full name. Most of the time, Claudius chose to use Claudius of Britannia or of Bath.

"You must have a well-known family to warrant so many names," Dorian chuckled.

"I suppose," Claudius answered. "They garnered a reputation on the battlefield and in the bureaucracy in Rome and Britannia."

Dorian nodded. "You also appear to be well educated. May I ask why an educated man would travel through our town?" When he leaned across the table, his face grew lined with worries. "We have seen such horrors for the past four weeks."

"What kind of horrors?" Claudius asked.

"I find it hard to believe you have not heard the tales," scoffed Dorian as he sat back on his bench.

"I have heard of so-called demons killing clergy and unlucky souls that stand in their way, but I thought these attacks had stopped."

"Stopped?" Dorian lowered his head. "They ceased for a few weeks, but then they began again."

"I–" Claudius felt dumbfounded and could think of nothing to say. After a brief pause, he added, "They still attack this region?"

Dorian placed his elbows further away from him and leaned in closer. "Well, you are a stranger here, and we are a small town. You must have not heard about our troubles. Our priests are all dead, as well as some of the parishioners. The attacks drove some of our community to madness. That stopped for a short time, but then, the troubles increased."

As if murdering and madness were not troubles enough, Claudius wondered about Dorian's choice of words. "What troubles?"

"The demons returned after two or three weeks. Instead of killing, they captured our families and friends and whisked them away," Dorian answered.

The Strigoi are exhibiting new tactics?

"That is most unfortunate," Claudius commented. "How often do these demons attack?"

"Every night. They rush in, grab victims, and run away. No swords seem to stop them, and no weapon can puncture their hearts. They are truly the spawn of Satan. Now, matters have become worse. You see, sometimes these demons look familiar. In fact, I believe that those who the demons abduct come back as demons. Do you know of anything like this? Have you heard anything like this in your travels or education?"

Claudius shook his head, although he had some idea what was going on.

Dorian closed his eyes for a moment and then opened them again. "This problem seems to be spreading."

"Has your Basileus done anything to allay this?" Claudius asked, despite already knowing the truth. He recognized that this mortal needed an opportunity to speak his fears.

"Nothing," Dorian grumbled. His eyes grew dark before adding, "She ignores our plight and sends no one to help."

The sound of the door opening drew Claudius' attention to the entrance of the inn, only to see Evander wading through patrons to get to Dorian's and his table.

"Sir," Evander greeted Dorian upon arriving at the table.

Dorian turned to face him with a resigned look upon his face.

"It's time," Evander stated.

Dorian nodded his head and rose to his feet. "Attention!" he yelled, capturing the patrons' attention. "Return to your homes. The curfew is in effect!" Dorian bellowed.

The farmers and tradesmen began shuffling towards the door, looking tired and gray, while the innkeeper and his help collected drinking vessels from the now empty tables.

Dorian, along with Claudius, watched them shuffle out of the inn.

Feeling he and the other blood-drinkers still in the common room needed to return to their rooms, Claudius rose from the bench, but before he could wish Dorian a good night, the guard interjected.

"How long do you and your friends plan to stay in our village?" Dorian asked.

"I hope no later than tomorrow night. We are waiting for friends. We were separated from them outside of Hadrianopolis. In addition, two of our party are ill and recovering," Claudius answered. "You will not dispatch us from this village, correct?"

"I would, for your own safety, if you and your friends had not brought us good luck," Dorian answered, but Claudius could not understand how their presence could have brought them luck. "After your arrival last night," Dorian added, "the demons did not attack."

"Nothing more than a coincidence, I fear," Claudius answered.

"No, it's a blessing," Dorian murmured before turning hesitantly towards the door. "I must man the watch for the night. Please pray that this blessing continues."

Claudius smiled, thinking that prayer seemed too passive and that... given sustenance, some of his friends might be able to help out. "Perhaps my associates and I could join your watch during the curfew," he suggested.

Dorian looked relieved. "Yes. We would welcome any assistance, even if it is a quiet night. We have recently taken in people from the smaller villages surrounding us. Perhaps our good fortune will continue." Dorian nodded and then headed for the door.

"Only dawn will tell," Claudius whispered and then walked to the staircase to join the others.

Maon, and the others who had been drinking in the common room, followed.

"I feel–" Julien began to say, but then he shook his head in amazement upon realizing that his wounds had disappeared.

"Surprisingly well?" Marcus interjected, completing Julien's sentence. "Deargh Du can recover quite easily, with the right resources." Marcus resumed feeding from the cow, but he started to shudder a bit and ceased his feeding. He then sat down. "The farmer will be here soon to check on the beasts one last time. We need to feed on a mortal. After he comes in, you go find his wife. Feeding on the animals of this world is well and good, but there comes a point when you begin to become more and more animal-like. I have been unfortunate enough to experience that."

"How did that happen?" Julien asked.

Marcus smiled for a moment and stared at his folded hands in quiet contemplation. "I will share that story some other night, when the Strigoi and an irate Empress Irene are not nipping at our feet."

At that moment, the doors opened and Julien watched Marcus fix a brilliant gaze upon the farmer. The beautiful glamoury radiated around Marcus, and the light he generated turned everything in the barn into a strange, soft dream.

The man stared at the two of them, dumbfounded.

"Where's your wife?" he asked the farmer.

"Inside the house," the farmer replied, trembling. "Angel of God, I am a humble man and do not deserve this vision." He then kneeled.

Marcus sighed and patted the farmer's shoulder. "Once, men and women knelt in my presence for being an agent of Morrigan. Now they kneel to receive a false angel's blessing. Rise. God favors those who are humble, I think."

Julien headed for the opened door and closed it behind him, leaving Marcus and the farmer alone. He then walked towards the house.

---

chapter twelve

ulien's victim, a young woman, slept in her small bed, convinced of a beautiful dream that made no sense.

After making sure to heal her wound, Julien left the house and found Marcus pacing under the moonlit skies, which grew darker with the passing of clouds. He appeared to be in better humor. "So, where are we going?" Julien asked.

"To the brightest spot on the horizon," Marcus answered, while pointing to the west.

Julien gathered up the gear he had left outside and prepared to take flight. "Why there?" he asked.

Marcus checked his kit and then levitated skyward.

Julien followed.

When the two Deargh Du hovered above treetop level, Marcus answered Julien's question. "I know there are no large towns around this part of the eastern empire, but there is a smattering of villages." Marcus pointed towards the brightly lit area. "That village is lit like a great city. There is only one reason a village is glowing like that."

"They feel unsafe at night," Julien stated.

"Yes," Marcus acknowledged before leading Julien towards the luminous village. "I believe we will find our friends there, but the Strigoi may be based nearby."

"How did you come to those assumptions?" Julien queried. "Do you sense the Strigoi, or our friends, at such a great distance?"

Marcus glanced at Julien and grinned. "I know our associates. Plus, I am certain that Amata is tired of sleeping in the dirty ground. As for the Strigoi, you said it yourself... the villagers feel unsafe in the dark... terrified. The Strigoi are near."

"Should we face the Strigoi without the mirror?" Julien asked, as they drew closer to the village. The smell of mortal guards patrolling the perimeter of the village grew as they approached.

"It is all we can do," Marcus said, but then he changed course and landed in a small, darkened clearing in the forest near the outskirts of town.

Julien followed. As soon as his feet touched the ground, he noticed that he had stepped on a strange stick. He removed his foot from the stick, crouched to the ground, and picked up what he realized was an arrow. He sniffed at dried blood, which clung along the underside. "They were here," he stated.

"Of course," Marcus said. "Could you not sense them from the air? This is why I landed here. We must train you on these things when we have the luxury of time." He closed his eyes and inhaled. "I smell... gray matter." Marcus then knelt down and sniffed again, before picking up an arrow, bereft of its fletching. "I smell Edward or Arwin. One of them must have been wounded in the head."

"Was it fatal?" Julien asked. "I mean, you said gray matter... the brain, correct?"

Marcus' face lost its strange glamoury and grew lined in worry. "I do not see enough ash for there to be a body. We should ask in the village." He then motioned for Julien to follow him towards the lighted village.

The two Deargh Du soon came upon a large group of archers and swordsmen who wore different uniforms.

Upon seeing Marcus and Julien coming out of the night, the armed men drew their weapons and nocked arrows. "Hold!" one of the guards shouted before looking them up and down for a moment. "Do you know a man named Claudius?"

"Claudius Metrius Sertorius, lately Claudius of Britannia and Bath," Marcus replied. "Why do you ask?"

"Lower your weapons," the guard said to his men. "These are friends. Welcome to Szeged." While the others returned to their duties, the guard who had addressed them walked up to Marcus and Julien. "Come, let me lead you to your friends."

"Thank you," Julien stated, finally finding his voice.

The guard fixed a warm, hopeful gaze upon Julien and said, "I know that our village was blessed... first with the arrival of your friends, and now with the arrival of an official of the Western Empire. Come, Inspector General, and bring your servant."

Julien realized the soldier believed Marcus to be his subordinate. He turned towards his grandfather-in-darkness and gave him an apologetic shrug.

"Your friends are in the inn," the soldier explained as they walked, with Marcus in tow, towards the inn, "which is closed for festivities by special order. However, we are allowing your associates to have the run of the place. I am Dorian, by the way. I am so glad you have joined us, Inspector General of the Gendarme. Your exploits against the demons are legendary. Now that they have returned, you can join us in the battle to come."

Julien remained silent, unsure of how to respond.

Once they reached the inn, Dorian held the door for them. "I must return to my patrolling duties. Your friends are inside."

The scent of several Ekimmu Cruitne, Deargh Du, Sugnwr Gwaed, and Lamia reached Julien's nostrils. He found great relief in their well-being.

Marcus nudged Julien to go through the door. "This night feels longer than usual. Let's rejoin our family and friends."

After force-feeding a still slumbering Mac Alpin, Máire brought her wrist back towards her body and rubbed it. She prepared to call for Horatio and Claudius, in order for all to make their donations to Arwin and Edward, when she heard Amata singing softly to Edward in the other room. The very act of Amata singing gentle Latin lullabies seemed odd, and yet endearing. She then noticed Mac Alpin toss a bit and open his good eye, which focused on her.

"Banbh Ceanúil, it would seem that your surgical technique worked," he murmured. It was the first time she'd ever heard him this quiet, with none of his usual bluster or bravado.

She felt tears gather in her eyes, and her throat strained. If he had not survived, she would not have forgiven herself, especially since she could not say how much she loved him.

"I am so..." she began to say, but instead took his hand. "It pleases me greatly to see you are well. As you can hear, your child-in-darkness is being tended to in another room. We did not care to separate you two, but Amata had informed us that the room had grown too crowded with her, Claudius, Horatio, and me sharing it with you. Thank the Gods, you two are recovering."

Arwin raised a brow and smiled. "I would have missed seeing you fumble for words, Banbh Ceanúil." He winked with his good eye. In a more robust voice, he asked, "How fares the rest of our group?"

She slapped his arm. "Piglet indeed, old man! We are all healing up. Unfortunately, three of our number are missing. Marcus, Julien, and Mandubratius, as well as Aphrodite's mirror," she admitted before frowning. "I am worried."

"They'll be along soon enough," Mac Alpin countered. "Marcus and Mandubratius have too much to settle between themselves to allow a mere empress to hold sway, and Julien wishes to prove himself. I have a feeling that it would take a great deal to keep the boy from rejoining us." He then sniffed the air a bit.

"You seem to say that with such certainty and conviction." Máire pointed out, but she could not feel hopeful by his words.

"Do you doubt your heart, now?" Mac Alpin's eye stared at her as if considering her motives.

"I do not know what you mean," she replied.

"They will be fine. Trust your instincts," he stated. "If you have hope, good things happen."

Any doubts she possessed faded as the door opened, and familiar scents flooded her senses.

Marcus rushed in and looked over Arwin. "I heard what happened. You are lucky, elder," he chastised.

"Ha! No little arrow will end my life, Roman… especially one shot by one of your Lamia trainees," Arwin boasted.

Máire found herself tackled by Julien, who smelled of cattle, in a hug. She chuckled and rubbed his dirty hair. At that moment, she heard soft footsteps approaching the room. Upon looking towards the door, she could see Amata peering inside. Her ready smile soon became a confused frown.

Máire ignored the frown and said the first thing that came to mind. "I suppose the leech is downstairs, sucking on a flagon of wine and chasing all the mortal beauties." Máire laughed and grinned at Amata, certain the other woman expected such activities from Mandubratius, but then she remembered Amata's frown. She pulled away from Julien.

"I… thought he was here," Amata said softly. "He is not downstairs."

Marcus turned to face Amata and placed his left hand on her shoulder. "He was captured by the Basileus, Amata. I am sorry, but we could not rescue him. I… believe this is part of a plan between himself and Gaius."

Amata sighed. "There is always a plan or a game, Marcus. What happened to keep him from continuing his fun?"

Marcus became silent, as if judging how best to answer her question.

Julien answered, "As we fled, we saw what appeared to be his… castration."

"I thought of doing–" Máire started to say, drawing a stare from Amata, but she stopped herself and said, "I am sorry."

Amata guffawed for a moment, before her exertions resulted in a coughing fit as if to hold back tears. Once Amata stopped laughing, she said, "I have thought of doing that many times myself as well. The only problem is that it will grow back. I am sure they considered this contingency in their plans." When she turned back to regard Marcus and Julien, her features became hard. "How did he become separated from you two?"

"The Basileus probably demanded that Gaius and his men capture him. They seemed to concentrate mostly on those of us carrying him. We attempted a rescue, but I feared that we were far too weak. Julien and I passed out while in flight and dropped him. Mandubratius had about a dozen arrows in him."

"What do we do now?" Máire asked, feeling unusual concern.

Marcus seemed about to speak, when Claudius barged into the room.

"Where in Hades have you two been?" Claudius asked. "No, never mind," he added while holding up his hand. "I have news of the Strigoi."

"I see my lieutenant has kept busy," Marcus quipped. He then sat down on Máire's bed. "Julien and I spent the night and day drinking and carousing with the most beautiful of women."

Despite the boasts, Máire could see fatigue in their eyes.

"Tell us this news," Marcus added.

"I do believe I deserve a promotion for this," Claudius answered. "Where's Mandubratius? I do not want to repeat this for his benefit."

"He decided to spend some time with the Basileus Irene," Amata stated. "Please tell us this news."

"The Strigoi have been attacking local villages. Dorian, he's the head of the night watch, says that they do not seem to be murdering the priests and the poor wretches. Instead, they are turning villagers into Strigoi. I wish my news was better, yet it appears their army grows." Claudius ran his left hand through his dark curls.

"How long have they suffered through this?" Julien asked.

"A few weeks," Claudius replied.

"I do not wish to increase pessimism," Marcus said before stretching a bit, "but I am sure the Empress and her friends still give chase."

Amata nodded her head. "Gentlemen, where should we go from here?"

"We need the mirror and your brother-in...," Marcus answered, before pausing. "My apologies. I am not sure the name the Lamia use for that term. Yet, if we attack, we run the risk of gaining new enemies and not allies."

Máire heard Marcus sigh.

Amata waved impatient hands before trudging into the center of the room. "I understand these inner workings. After all, the Lamia's own political workings are confusing. Do not worry, for you will not gain new enemies. As we said earlier, this is a game."

An unexpected but tired voice suddenly brought everyone's attention, including Máire's, to the door. "Would you all keep it down? I'm trying to sleep," Edward stated, but many of his words were distorted by a yawn. He leaned against the frame of the door, opposite Claudius. To Máire, Edward seemed barely able to stand.

Amata rushed to his side and propped him up. "I'm so glad you're with us," she purred, while taking his left hand and kissing it.

"I've been here for the last hour, wishing to rest, for a change," Edward stated, though with a smile upon his face. "Are we still certain these Lamia will follow us?"

All faces, including Máire's, turned towards Amata.

Her eyes flashed with the realization that all studied her. Amata sighed. "Irene is very angry. She will soon realize, no matter what she does to Mandubratius, that he will heal. Killing him will not soothe her inner rage. She will keep feeding him in order to continue torturing him. I believe she will press Gaius to chase us. We aided him, and Mandubratius allowed her to wrongly believe that she would look as Fianait, Máire, and I do… of course Felician sponsored me when I was still young and beautiful."

"You are still young and beautiful, my dear," Edward drawled, "but how do you know this?"

"I know her acts," Amata answered. "I am certain you all know how she blinded her own son to retain her regency. Strange, though, how the Eastern Church still sings praises of her," she quipped. "Besides, Mandubratius loves to play dangerous games… the more dangerous, the more entertaining."

"Then we make arrangements to leave at dusk tomorrow night," Marcus said. "Edward and Arwin will have recovered by then."

"I think we are forgetting the poor mortals of this village," Claudius stated. "They suffer with the Strigoi attacks. When we arrived, the attacks ceased. Should we leave, the attacks will resume. We owe these people our assistance."

Máire felt Julien's arm move around her back. An almost imperceptible shiver moved through his frame. She met his eyes and smiled, hoping to soothe him. None of them felt prepared to deal with the Strigoi, even the one who managed to exterminate six at once.

"They avoid engaging us to build their forces," Marcus said.

"Then, we should consider meeting them now," Claudius suggested before leaning against the door frame.

Marcus looked around the room as if looking for consent. After making eye contact with everyone, he said, "We need the mirror."

Máire heard footsteps in the hallway, and then she saw Horatio and Patroclus look into the room.

Both Claudius and Edward stepped aside to allow them entrance.

"The mirror will be here soon enough," Julien said.

"Irene has been sheltered," Amata countered. "She will see the Strigoi and give up the mirror."

Marcus rose from the bed and said, "Then we need to hunt the Strigoi."

Though Máire said nothing, she heard grunts and grumbles of assent. Of course, she would rather face anyone else in battle.

Mandubratius smiled at the Empress again as he sat up on the cot. When he reached for her right arm, which bore a bloody wound, she tugged it away.

"I think you've had enough for now," she purred. "Perhaps we will feed you more after our travels tonight."

"Only if you watch over me," he murmured.

Irene laughed. "Oh, I would never let you get away."

"What if we were to make a deal, my love?" he asked as he met her eyes.

"A deal?" she queried.

"I need to return to my allies with that beautiful and miraculous mirror of yours," he stated. "Your friends could join us. After all, my physical pain must bore you by now."

Irene raised a dark brow. "Why should I let you leave with it? Give me a good reason."

"I need it, so that my allies and I may kill the Strigoi," he answered. He sensed Gaius watching, and likely listening, from outside of the house.

"I do not know what the Strigoi are, and my education was a great deal more than yours, I would believe. I had the best scholars of the Western and Eastern realms. What possible education would a chieftain of barbarians require?" Irene scoffed while showing him an arrogant smile. She then slid her left hand under his blankets and began playing with his healing wound.

His budding appendage tingled with the contact. "A mortal chieftain needs more education than you would believe. The mortal Briton known as 'Awvarwy' learned Latin, Greek, Gaelic, self-defense, and many other topics... even the Druidic arts," Mandubratius boasted before chuckling. "However, I doubt scholars would know about the Strigoi. They are a race of blood-drinkers, such as we are. You may know them in different terms. They are the so-called demons that have been attacking churches and creating fear in both yours and Emperor Charles' lands." Irene touched him in a sensitive spot, causing him to wince a little, but then she stopped playing with his wound.

"Irene, in a rare moment of honesty, I will tell you the truth. The Strigoi are not a race that will bargain with you or us. If you help us kill them, you will aid in the salvation of your people and the Franks," he said after looking at her again.

Irene shook her head a bit, breaking the tenuous grasp he held on her thoughts. "I admit you are very talented with persuasion. However, I love that mirror. It will remain with me. Besides, how do you know it will work? You said it brings forth beauty. It will not kill."

"Perhaps," he admitted. "Yet, they assure me it will stop them."

"Who are they? Your traveling companions?"

"Yes," Mandubratius answered.

"And you lead them?" Irene asked with a doubting smile.

"Of course," he purred.

"Mandubratius, you do not lie well," Irene stated with an effortless and radiant smile. "Seriously, who leads this fabled alliance?"

"It is a joint effort. Besides Amata and myself, there are some Lamia, Deargh Du, Ekimmu Cruitne, and Sugnwr Gwaed involved. If there is one leader from amongst these four lines, it would be Marcus."

"Tell me about this Marcus," Irene demanded before running her left hand over her dark brown hair. Her blue eyes then settled on his.

"He is... was... a Roman general, one of Julius Caesar's generals. He was the praetor of Gaul, once. He and I fought in Britannia as mortals, on the same side." Mandubratius felt his mouth turn down in a frown. "We were sailing for the western coast of Britannia and ended up in Éire." He paused for a moment, lost in her eyes, which were the color of the sunlit skies that he could remember from his days as a mortal.

"Continue," she murmured, breaking him out of his reverie.

Mandubratius glanced away and continued his reply. "Suffice it to say, he had his men nail me to a tree for traitorous activities. I was innocent. Amata and our sponsor found me, while the Deargh Du found Marcus. We assumed the other was dead, until over two hundred years ago, when I was in Éire hunting an ancient Lamia treasure. That is a long tale for another night." He then met her eyes again. "When the Strigoi started to attack us, I sent Amata and Patroclus, the Legate, to him, thinking that the Celtic lines would form an alliance with the Lamia. Reality proved my thoughts correct. This coalition has also furthered our other plans. However, the Strigoi proved to be stronger than we all believed. This is why it is imperative for us to have that mirror."

"General Gaius was kind enough to tell me of the world of the immortals," Irene began to explain. "He informed me what a Strigoi was. I just wanted to see if I could trust you. If I release you and the mirror, I must have a new deal between us. You have made me Lamia and were false to me. Do not be false to me again."

Mandubratius met Irene's eyes and forced a serious visage to form on his face. He could not keep that promise. After all, he lied to himself. "What deal do you have in mind?"

"What can you offer me?" she purred.

"I can offer you a position of leadership within the newly reformed Lamia."

She smiled. "That would be lovely. Yes, I shall be known as the Empress of the Lamia. The consuls can go the way of their mortal predecessors. I will be Empress. That is what I expect," Irene demanded.

"I see," Mandubratius drawled while trying not let his serious visage slip, though with little success. He attempted again to look serious as he pretended to think over the bargain. "I will accept on one condition."

"Then, by all means, tell me this condition," Irene said.

"This transition of leadership will only happen after this current crisis with the Strigoi is over. This time is far too chaotic to allow for a change of power."

Irene closed her eyes for a moment, apparently considering his counter-offer. However, like him, she could just be pretending to consider his condition. "Done," she said, after a brief pause. "But do not think you can continue leading long after the deed is done. You are not as well liked as you believe yourself to be."

"Then, you will allow me to heal and release me?" he queried, confident that she would agree.

"Yes. You will go and tell your allies that we will join them with the mirror in tow," she said. She then offered him her other wrist.

Mandubratius pulled it in close to his mouth and bit down. The release of blood into his mouth almost made him swoon with delight.

Outside of Vézelay

Heloise raised her right hand while pulling the reins of her horse with her left, halting her horse, Urbino, who tossed his head and then turned his neck to glance at her. She dismounted and took the reins, leading Urbino on her tour. When Heloise glanced at the others, she noticed Sáerlaith dismount, whereas the other Deargh Du remained with the vassals and the mercenaries.

Heloise walked through the village, noting the condition of the fields, the garrison, and her home in the distance. All seemed quiet and at peace. Not much damage remained. However, when she strolled past the small church and graveyard, she noticed an increase in the number of graves.

After working through what she wanted to say, Heloise turned while pulling Urbino along to face her family, vassals, and friends. She faced a hushed crowd, including the children. "My friends and people," Heloise began. "Our road home has been treacherous, laborious, and full of sorrow. However, we are home." The cheers that greeted her brought Heloise hope. She held up her right hand, requesting silence, and smiled. "We are all tired and want to get to our homes, but we must be prudent. None of us knows whether our homes are safe." She glanced at the familiar faces. "Therefore, we will camp here in the center of town tonight and we will sleep." She witnessed expressions of surprise. "Yes," she continued. "We have all earned sleep."

Heloise noticed Lady Talia standing by Reginald. She tried not to frown, since that woman managed to avoid any work. She only played with Tildy.

"Tomorrow," Heloise continued, "we will work, clean, and repair our homes. Tomorrow night, we'll feast." She heard even more cheers and allowed them to continue. "Now, there's work to be done. Let's begin."

As the crowd dispersed, Heloise watched her people begin their familiar duties of setting up camp.

Amongst the people unpacking, she noticed Dreu pull Lirienne aside and lead her into the forest. Heloise found herself very pleased with that. She hoped they would formally announce their betrothal at the feast.

When Heloise turned to walk towards the campsite, she noticed Reginald staring at the path that Lirienne and Dreu had just taken. She decided that she needed to talk to him. As she drew closer to her son, she saw burning hostility in Reginald's eyes. However, before she could get his attention, an unexpected voice said, "Lady Heloise?" Her heart jumped. She then noticed Sáerlaith standing beside her. "Oh my," she said. "I forget that you can do that!"

Sáerlaith's demeanor turned serious. "My apologies, my Lady, I did not mean to frighten you."

When Heloise took her hand, Sáerlaith's frown softened. "Thank you for all that you and yours have done," she said to Sáerlaith. "I fear that no amount of gold could repay you for the debt I owe you."

Sáerlaith shook her head. "Let's not speak of debt, Lady Heloise," she replied before embracing Heloise. Sáerlaith then leaned toward the mortal's ear and whispered, "Are you certain you wish for everyone to sleep tonight? Tomorrow, we will be unable to protect you in the daylight."

Heloise leaned in toward Sáerlaith and whispered, "Even if we slept during the day, you couldn't protect us."

"Your logic is sound," Sáerlaith replied.

"Besides," Heloise added. "My people need to return to sowing crops and recapturing our livestock. We cannot do those things at night."

"I understand," Sáerlaith murmured before pulling away a little. "However, we will toil in the evening and protect your camp."

"We will welcome the help."

"Please be sure to give your vassals and family reassurances and explanations of why we are working at night and sleeping during the day," Sáerlaith requested.

"I will do so. Thank you so very much," Heloise said. She then leaned in to kiss Sáerlaith.

The Deargh Du embraced her again and kissed her brow, before releasing Heloise and departing.

When Heloise turned on her heel to return to the campsite, she noticed Reginald staring at her with the same suspicion and hostility burning in his eyes that she had seen earlier, but it soon faded.

Reginald veiled his emotions with apparent ease. Her eldest son then turned away from her and walked towards the campsite.

Heloise watched him walk away and wondered what he contemplated these nights.

A well-lit village overwhelmed Mandubratius' vantage point. He wandered towards it, figuring his comrades would be there, knowing Amata's propensity to complain about sleeping in holes and tents... not that he particularly cared for that kind of activity. Even the Deargh Du preferred beds. With a smirk, he remembered how all Lamia believed the Celtic lines enjoyed that sort of communion with some earth Goddess or another.

"Halt!" a voice shouted from the night.

Mandubratius assumed that a mortal had called to him, but when he focused on his senses, he realized the person who spoke was a blood-drinker. Upon turning his head, he recognized a familiar face and felt some relief.

"Dominus," Patroclus called out as he saluted. "What befell you? Marcus and Julien told the most horrific of tales."

Mandubratius raised a brow at the Legate. His concern seemed more than what should be considered necessary, proving Mandubratius' suspicions all the more.

Patroclus prefers the Celtic blood-drinkers to his own kind.

"Greetings, Patroclus. I'm quite well, as you can see. I managed an escape. Where are Marcus and the former Maél Muire?"

"Out on patrol, Dominus," the Legate replied.

"Splendid, and Amata?"

"I believe she is at the inn, taking care of Arwin and Edward. She is upstairs in the last room to the left."

"Thank you," Mandubratius said while projecting a calm, yet curious demeanor. He settled his eyes on the blue-eyed soldier and thought of a way to give Patroclus a good barb. "Legate, have you been reduced to guard duty?"

"No, Dominus, I thought I would—"

"Isn't guard duty more appropriate for a legionnaire?"

Patroclus nodded a bit. "Perhaps, in the old days, but—"

"So, after all these centuries, you've risen through the ranks of the Roman and Lamia armies to the lofty status of… night guard?"

"Not exactly, Dominus. You see—"

"Carry on, guard," Mandubratius interjected once more, satisfied with his performance. He chuckled and shook his head. "I will find our Domina."

Seosaimhín's ecstasy grew as her army increased tenfold.

Her children's appetite for blood seemed never to sate.

She waved to some of her returning children as they dragged in their insensate victims.

Now, they can truly control their madness.

She strolled towards the effigy of Nagirrom and traced her left hand over the carved God. "Our plans are so ripe, almost ready to be plucked from the great apple tree," she informed the effigy. "Our army grows. Now, they focus and can feed without killing. Their chaotic minds have become ordered. Their words now ring of clarity. They learn to fight in your name."

At that moment, one of her children loped towards her. "Beautiful Queen," he drawled, as if choosing words carefully. "Soulless ones are nearby. Do you want us to deal with them?"

"Kill them," she said at first, but a squawk from behind drew her attention back to the effigy, and she realized Nagirrom perched upon it.

"Do not attack them," said the white crow.

"Hold," she said to the Strigoi. To Nagirrom, she added, "We shall obey, but may we ask why?"

"Because they are a threat. They bear a device that can destroy your army."

Seosaimhín scoffed little. "What device is this?"

"Long ago, a Greek God made a beautiful mirror for a Goddess. All you need to know is that the mirror will destroy the Strigoi. Do not go near them. If they search for the Strigoi, hide. If they attack, flee. Is this clear?" Nagirrom asked before fluttering His wings.

"Yes, Nagirrom, but sooner or later, they will use this tool. How can we protect ourselves from it?"

Nagirrom flew from His effigy and cried out, "The wave is already in motion, and the tide is rolling in." He then cawed before flying out of the cave and into the night skies.

Máire stood on a rock outcropping with Arwin, Marcus, and the others who had accompanied them to scout out the Strigoi cave. While surveying the countryside, she occasionally glanced at the elder Ekimmu Cruitne, who sniffed the air.

"I think there is an entrance to this cave below us, although I do not smell or sense any Strigoi," Mac Alpin said.

Marcus stepped up next to Máire and said, "Let's take a look at the cave. Arwin, unless you are not well, would you lead? You have the best nose."

"I'm as strong as I've ever been," Mac Alpin retorted with a nervous chuckle. "Now, move aside." He then studied the entrance of the damp cave before motioning for the others to follow him down the slope.

Along the way, Máire caught a whiff of noxious vapors, and she watched the others contorting their faces at the stench emanating from the cave. Upon taking another step, she nearly tripped over an animal carcass, or at least it looked as though it had been an animal.

"It appears that they exited here in a hurry," Mac Alpin stated, drawing Máire's attention away from the carcass, for a moment.

"Any signs as to where they exited?" Claudius asked.

Julien, who scouted the different pathways leading from the cave, replied, "Many different directions."

"They scattered," Máire reasoned aloud. Soon, she and the others found bodies at the mouth of the cave.

Mac Alpin sniffed at the air and said, "I believe most exited through the other entrance we had discovered to the east." He then kicked at the body of a newly dead Strigoi, which lay next to a dead mortal, not too far away.

As the group continued stepping cautiously through the damp footing and foul smells, Mac Alpin gestured towards the bodies scattered in the front entrance of the cave and said, "These Strigoi and mortals may have been a diversion for us."

"When have the Strigoi had the necessary brain capacity to create a diversion?" Máire asked softly.

"The attacks of late have deviated from their typical pillage against men of the church," Arwin replied.

"It's as if they are being trained to fight effectively," Claudius added, "and have increased their numbers."

"We should continue before we come up with any kind of conclusion," Julien recommended. He then gave Máire a bit of a gentle nudge.

"Youngling, have you taken a good whiff of this place?" Mac Alpin asked with a chuckle. "I will wager there are horrors down there that you have never seen, and ones I may not wish to experience again."

Julien puffed up his chest with much bravado and replied, "Yes, it smells bad... much like the churches they desecrated. However, I do not need to be sheltered," he added. Julien then pulled at a bag on his belt.

"You better not be thinking about bringing out that peppermint oil," Mac Alpin warned, "It will overwhelm all of our noses. Besides, if you're going to face the horrors here, you'll do it like us."

Marcus came up to Julien and touched his left shoulder with his right hand. "I have smelled enough and plan on having my senses dulled. Hand me that peppermint oil when you are finished with it, Julien."

After Julien and Marcus dabbed oil under their noses, the others passed the oil around.

After dabbing a few drops under her nose, Máire felt it burn, but it was a far sight better than the smells near the cave.

"I didn't know the Sugnwr Gwaed and Deargh Du were such girls about bad smells," Mac Alpin grumbled. "Let's go."

As they wandered into the cave, Máire felt a heavy presence weigh upon her. She stared at Marcus' back, not wanting to imagine what she stepped over or see the walls of the cave.

"With this oil," Mac Alpin stated, "one cannot properly use any senses. All I can smell is damned peppermint."

Once they reached the first chamber within the cave, something caught Máire's eye, and she knelt to study it. Crude designs, painted in blood, covered the walls and floor.

"Spirals," Claudius said. "Is there anything notable about these spirals?"

"Nothing," she informed him. "They are protection spirals. Many different peoples draw them."

"Máire, there are many more here," Marcus called to her from the far wall before following the others down a large passage.

Only Máire and Mac Alpin remained within the first chamber. She rose from her crouch and snaked her way towards where Marcus had stood. Once she arrived, she sucked in a surprised breath at the realization that the pictures and designs improved in clarity, intricacy, and artistry. "These were drawn by Strigoi?" she asked.

"So what of it?" Arwin said while perambulating the chamber.

"You've seen them and fought them," Máire explained. "They have no control. They do not have the focus to paint these. Each of these improves, revealing coordination, skill, and thought."

"Hurry up, Máire," Arwin grumbled. "There is much to explore here. Not just these scribbles."

"You never had an eye for artwork, even though it flourishes in your home," Máire teased. When she chuckled, she heard nervousness in her laughter.

"Artwork is for the Greeks," Mac Alpin countered, though with some humor in his tone. "Let's continue."

Arwin lead Máire down the passageway. They soon caught up to the others.

"A focused Strigoi must be a formidable enemy," Claudius murmured. "Lights are ahead."

Once the group reached the large, torch-lit cavern, Mac Alpin sniffed the air. "Stop. There are mortals down there."

"Are they keeping them as food?" Julien asked.

"Or perhaps they are in the process of becoming new Strigoi," Marcus suggested. "Let's split up. Claudius and Julien, go down and see what you find. Be careful. I see and sense something here," he whispered before sidling off towards an altar bearing a strange statue.

"Máire, do you know what this is?" he asked after touching the statue.

Máire joined him and studied the statue for a few moments. "I believe it is an effigy... a God or Goddess represented by a white crow, but I am unfamiliar with it." She touched an outstretched wing. "Perhaps Julien–"

Marcus interrupted her. "No, do not bother. It is not a local deity... I know who this is." He met her eyes.

"Who is it?" Mac Alpin asked with some impatience.

"Nagirrom," Marcus answered.

"Who is Nagirrom?" Máire asked. She had never heard of such a deity.

"This must be an ancient Roman God or Goddess that Máire and I know nothing about, right?" Mac Alpin asked with a nervous chuckle. "Or Gallic?"

Marcus shook his head. "No, I do not believe that Nagirrom is either. Nagirrom was the personal deity of your... your husband-to-be's... Connor's mother." Marcus paused, as if in thought and stared at Máire.

"Seosaimhín? She's long dead," Máire answered with a slight shudder. "I killed her myself, after the battle. Why do you mention her?"

Marcus stared at the crow effigy again. "It seems odd that in all my travels, I have only seen this crow in Mhuine Conlon in Seosaimhín's disgusting hovel, after our battle with the Lamia." He then leaned in closer as if to study the base of the altar. "Look, Ogham, around the base."

Máire knelt down to stare at it.

"Tell us what these symbols mean," Marcus urged her. His eyes blinked green at her, for a moment, before returning to blue.

"Why do you ask me about these symbols and writing?" Máire asked, knowing his familiarity with these matters.

"You are the linguist and historian in our party," Marcus answered and then returned his attention to the statue.

She chuckled and asked, "Who is older?"

"I... wish you to feel useful, and I need my suspicions confirmed," he murmured.

She sighed and shook her head a bit. "These symbols are in a very strange pattern." A quick glance of the floor and walls of this part of the cavern revealed many carvings. "They are copied here and in circles over here and there," Máire said while pointing to each group of carvings. She then stood up and examined the carved symbols closest to her. "Strange," she murmured. "It's almost a combination of several magics. I see Indian and others–"

"Why would Aphrodite's star be of use in here?" Marcus interjected while nodding towards a five-pointed star.

"The same reason I see a six pointed star of David?" Máire asked, after meeting his eyes. "I believe these are summoning circles. Some magicians of various beliefs summon beings forth from the Otherworld. However, if what they summon cannot be controlled, protective elements, like these Ogham carvings and the stars, may be necessary. It would confine something to this circle, perhaps. I have heard of a few Jewish and Christian magicians working in this manner."

"Yes, but why the Ogham?" Marcus asked.

"I do not know. Druids part the mists to see things. They see no need to summon. Perhaps someone has had Druidic training passed down from an ancient." She felt discomfort discussing these matters.

Marcus held up his left hand and grinned. "Do not worry, Máire. I know you do not do this kind of working."

"What do you think it would summon?" Mac Alpin asked, interrupting Máire's thoughts.

Máire kneeled on the floor, closed her eyes, and ran her hands over the carvings. A palpable tingle coursed up her arms. "Energy," she whispered.

"From where?" Marcus asked.

"The Otherworld, perhaps," she answered. "Or it could be another realm outside of this reality. This symbol," she added while pointing out a particular carving, "could provide focus. The room is itself a big circle." She then crawled towards the altar. After a quick search, she found a small cloth bag and a scroll case hidden behind the stones. Upon opening the sack, she felt a strange dread, even though no spiders or scorpions awaited her... just a bag containing a strange, dark powder. Máire dipped one finger inside and brought it to her nose. The scent of herbs and unknown things made her start coughing, despite the peppermint oil. While holding the bag away from her nose, Marcus snatched it from her grasp.

"What is this vile concoction?" Marcus asked. "Damn that weak peppermint oil."

Mac Alpin drew closer, took a whiff from the bag, and gagged.

Máire inhaled the dank air of the cavern, in an attempt to settle her coughs. "Psilocybe, I think, mushrooms, and perhaps some other herbs," she answered. She then opened the scroll case, extracted a few scrolls, and unrolled one of them. Several incoherent scribbles greeted her eyes. "We will have to translate these later," she said, yet some words seemed to reveal themselves to her.

Arwin started to pace about the cavernous room. "There are more circles here," he called out.

"Someone used massive amounts of magical energy," Máire said, after rising from the ground. She then stuffed the scrolls back into the bag.

"For what purpose?" Marcus queried.

Máire looked at Marcus and said, "Given the changes in behavior, I would say someone is transforming the Strigoi." She then noticed Arwin about to ask the inevitable, so she looked at him and added, "They are being changed into a formidable enemy."

At that moment, she heard Julien yelling for Marcus. Nervous fear gripped his voice. She had forgotten, for a moment, about the possible dangers in earthen walls around her.

Marcus grabbed her elbow, and together, with Arwin keeping pace, they raced down the passageway, deeper into the cavern.

When they arrived, darkness from a Deargh Du embraced them, and then something at their feet stopped them. Soon, the darkness faded from her eyes, and Máire looked down at the freshly killed bodies at her feet. Ichor and blood oozed from severed heads. The sounds of more yelling echoed through the passages, urging her forward.

When Máire, Marcus, and Mac Alpin arrived in the next chamber, she saw Claudius and Julien leaning against a wall fending off people with oddly contorted faces, who reached for them despite swinging blades.

These must be the mortals the Strigoi left behind... the ones in the middle of their transformation.

The corrupted mortals growled and crawled over themselves to get to the two hemmed in blood-drinkers who could not flee due to the low ceiling.

Máire waded in with the others, cutting a swath through to Julien and Claudius. Then, they split into two groups and killed every last contorted mortal. The dead littered the floor, and their blood pooled on the floor.

Mac Alpin slapped Máire's left shoulder in a manly fashion and grumbled, "I guess they didn't develop enough to affect us with madness," while still holding his sword.

Marcus turned to Julien and Claudius, who to Máire seemed uninjured, and said, "Yes, we are fortunate tonight. Did you two find anything else?"

Julien wiped blood from his face and answered, "Nothing more than rags that could be used as blankets."

Claudius, who also wiped off his face, muttered, "Maybe five hundred reeking rags. They were scattered everywhere."

"The sun rises soon," Marcus announced. "I will leave it up to you four. If we leave now, we should make it back with darkness to spare, or we can continue searching and sleep here when the sun rises."

"I am no coward, but it stinks in here," Mac Alpin stated. "I'd rather wind up ash than spend the day here. Not to mention, we could be caught here if they return."

"I agree, in that I do not wish to be caught sleeping if the Strigoi are hiding in part of this cave," Máire chimed in. "Besides, there is something here that makes me feel most unwelcome."

"I only smell mint, but this cave is unsettling," Julien added. "I say we go back to the village."

"To defend ourselves here would be difficult," Claudius mentioned. "Low ceilings would keep us from any aerial attack."

Marcus nodded. "Good, so I'm not a coward for wishing to go to the inn. Well, let us go, then."

As the group walked cautiously amongst the dead, towards the passageway back to the surface, Máire said, "Wait, there was one other thing on the altar that I wanted to study before we left."

"You want to examine the pictures again?" Mac Alpin asked.

"No. I'm going to write down the symbols. Perhaps others have knowledge of these," Máire stated. She led them back into the main cavern. When she reached the symbols, Máire extracted vellum and ink and began to draw.

"Hurry please," Arwin warned before pacing, as if nervous.

"Yes, Máire... perhaps you could study this another time," Claudius suggested while looking around the cavern.

"Magic is important," she murmured, as she rushed to draw each symbol accurately. "At the least, it seems to be essential to the Strigoi, now. Don't any of you find this fascinating?"

"If I can't drink it, kill it, or fuck it, then I don't care about it," Arwin grumbled.

Máire smiled despite her haste to finish. "How do I fit into those categories?" She then used another sheet of velum to create rubbings of some of the carvings in the ground.

"The real question is: how do Claudius, Julien, and I fit into those categories," Marcus said with a chuckle.

"You don't. I could care less about you three," Mac Alpin groaned before winking. "Let's be rid of this place. You have enough scrubbings, I think." He offered Máire his left hand.

Máire quickly bundled everything up, grabbed Mac Alpin's hand, and allowed him to pull her up. As they started to leave, she noticed Marcus lagging behind. She caught Claudius' eye and stared at him, fearing her concerns.

It is nothing. Marcus is as fine as he ever could be.

Claudius stared back at her. His intense dark eyes turned gold in contemplation, or perhaps hunger.

"Tomorrow night," he murmured. "We'll speak to him about it tomorrow, or perhaps you should tell him your worries. We must deal with this apprehension soon."

"What apprehension?" Marcus queried, as he came up behind them. "My lieutenant and my child-in-darkness look very worried. Fear not. Although things are dark now, the balance swings both ways."

chapter thirteen

andubratius strolled into one of the rooms at the end of the hall and found Edward sleeping, while Amata slept next to him on the edge of the small bed. He nudged Edward and watched the Ekimmu Cruitne wrinkle his forehead in annoyance.

"So, Edward, where are my dear friends, Marcus and the former Maél Muire?"

Amata opened her eyes and stared up at him, for a moment. She then jumped out of bed and rushed over to embrace him. "She didn't kill you. I figured you'd manage to charm her again."

Mandubratius kissed her brow. "I had to give up my genitals a few times, but Irene decided it was too much work."

Edward grumbled and turned on his side. "They went out to hunt the Strigoi," he said.

"That does not seem like a fun, leisurely activity for either Máire or Marcus. I would have suggested hunting mortals. When will they return?" Mandubratius quipped.

"Perhaps it will be three or four hours… well, before sunrise at any rate." Edward sat up, looking confused. "Where is the mirror, Mandubratius?"

"That is a very good question, Edward. Now, pardon me for a moment," Mandubratius stated, before slapping Amata's backside, eliciting a gasp of surprise. To Amata, he said, "When you're tired of dealing with Edward, come to my bed." He then glanced back to Edward. "The mirror will arrive with the Empress very soon. I had to leave it with her, for the time being. Where did the noble Roman general and the warrior chieftain go?"

"Due north," Edward grumbled in reply.

"Thank you," Mandubratius said. "I shall go accost them."

After the time I've had, I could use some entertainment.

Marcus heaved a soft sigh upon exiting the cave, which had brought forth the strangest of contradictory feelings. While walking with the others towards the village, Marcus contemplated his whirlwind of emotions. He had experienced near asphyxiation upon entering the cavern, yet a strange exhilaration burned within. Perhaps Claudius and Máire noticed this, as indicated by their nervous glances. Still, there were so many other worries.

Why the good fortune of no mature Strigoi?

As they neared the small village, he pondered the luck of this night, when the strong, spicy scent of a Lamia infused the air. When he looked up, Marcus noticed Mandubratius smiling and waving at them from his perch upon a large rock.

"How fortunate to see you all again," Marcus heard Mandubratius say. His words on the wind revealed pleasure.

"Who let him live?" Máire muttered under her breath, appearing to be ill at ease, of course that was her normal aspect when Mandubratius was near.

Once Marcus and his small party reached the rock that supported the smiling Lamia, Mandubratius leapt down and joined them on the solid earth. "You look well," Marcus commented.

"Thank you. I feel well enough," Mandubratius replied. "However, you five appear to be exhausted and in need of refreshment. I gather you managed to escape unscathed from the Basileus and the former Children of Ares."

Mac Alpin muttered something in an old tongue Marcus didn't know and scoffed, "Hardly. Máire had to shove an arrow through my eye socket."

"But other than that, you appear to be in fine shape. Why didn't you come back for me?" Mandubratius asked.

"We thought it best to wait for you," Marcus answered. "I believed it was some plan between yourself and Gaius."

"But the Children of Ares shot at us," Mandubratius demurred.

Marcus could sense Máire's impatience rise.

"Cease your verbal attack," she warned. "You knew not to expect us. Once again, you just love hearing yourself talk."

Mandubratius still faced Marcus and didn't even give Máire a single glance. When he replied, he kept his gaze fixed on Marcus. "I merely wanted to make sure that this was the reasoning behind your lack of action." He then finally faced Máire. Pleasure loomed in his eyes, indicating that he enjoyed this game.

"How did you escape?" Julien asked, drawing everyone's attention to him.

Mandubratius chuckled, for a moment, and then glanced at Julien. "Ah, but I did not escape."

Marcus felt suspicion rise. He allowed his senses to expand over the village. "If you did not escape–" he began to say, until Mandubratius interrupted him with an impatient motion.

"Let's go inside," the Lamia advised. "The sun rises in half an hour, and we could all use some rest."

Marcus nodded and began leading the party back towards the village.

"I made a deal," Mandubratius continued. "It is simple enough. Irene brings the mirror tomorrow night. If we are successful in our endeavors, I promised her leadership of the Lamia. However, I have a feeling that she may have not considered how difficult it would be to influence the Lamia of Rome when she is an empress, and not an emperor. She will need a Co-Consul. I would be there to assist her. So, I manipulated her. She will get tired of the title, soon enough, and Amata will take her rightful place."

As they continued trudging towards the inn, Marcus heard a soft grumble. He turned his head towards the source of the noise and discovered Máire shaking her head a little from side to side.

"You manipulate the Empress to make her miserable enough to acquiesce to your demands," she grumbled. "Why does this not surprise me?"

This admission caused the Lamia Briton to start laughing. "No, no, no. I manipulate people for my own entertainment and self-gratification," Mandubratius clarified. "She's no different from the others I've manipulated, including you." He chuckled again. "Besides, I like getting my way."

Once the small party stopped outside the inn, Marcus ignored the prattling of Claudius and the others and focused on an agitated Máire. He reasoned that her reaction might relate to that imperial orgy, but perhaps her attitude towards the Briton was because of her innate frustration.

Máire then glared at Mandubratius and muttered, "I suppose your right hand cannot handle your needs for self-gratification."

"Manipulation only one way I reach fulfillment," Mandubratius quipped.

"Do you often need to employ these self-gratifying diversions?" Máire asked with a chuckle.

Mandubratius smiled in a manner befitting a lioness about to pounce upon her prey. "Only amongst women who fake their pleasure."

Marcus watched Máire's mouth open in an 'o' of shock. At the same time, he heard Claudius, Arwin, and Julien stop their conversation.

Marcus knew Máire's secret. He could remember pleasuring her, but the others never knew she had ever faked anything. Gods knew why she did. Perhaps she thought she could make herself believe it and it would happen. Either way, Marcus attempted to ignore her lack of fulfillment because he wanted to forget it and pretend that they shared bliss as they had during her mortal days.

"How did–" she murmured as if admitting to the accusation, but before she could ask her question, Mandubratius interrupted her.

"Oh please, Máire. I watched you all night at the orgy in Constantinople, and I've been with enough women to know when they're faking it. Now, Banbh Ceanúil, what was the question you desired to ask?"

Máire stared at Mandubratius. "Are you implying that I've been faking my orgasms?" she asked in a loud tone.

The Lamia grinned and cooed, "Oh, no. That's not the case, my dove."

Heather Poinsett Dunbar & Christopher Dunbar

His tone reminded Marcus of a cat hunting birds.

Máire's features became a strange mix of confusion and calm.

"Rather, I am shouting it from the rooftops of this village!" Mandubratius yelled. "You haven't had one! Have you ever? Now, that doesn't seem like I'm simply implying anything, now does it?"

"I have had…" Máire paused before adding, "orgasms. Lots of them!" she shouted, matching his volume.

The night watch even came running at all of this yelling in a foreign tongue, but Marcus told them in Greek that all was well and that they should return to their patrol. Still, Marcus watched in shock as Mandubratius locked eyes with Máire and drew closer to her. While staring into each other's eyes, the lecherous Lamia reached his right hand to Máire's crotch and caressed it through her trousers, but she did not react to his invasion at all.

"You see? Not a rise," Mandubratius said in normal tones before retracting his hand.

Máire kneed him in the crotch. "Yes, not a rise. What a pity."

The Briton collapsed to his knees and started laughing, albeit hoarsely.

"I've had hundreds of orgasms, thousands," Máire insisted. "You've been misinformed. Good night." She turned and walked back towards the center of the village.

Mac Alpin, Claudius, and Julien walked around Mandubratius and into the inn. Marcus assumed drinks would be needed after hearing such harsh revelations regarding their lack of skill.

Marcus took a few steps towards Mandubratius and stared down at him. He then leaned over the Briton and smiled. "Sometimes, you just can't get your way," Marcus advised before turning and walking into the inn.

Máire stared upwards, as the purple sky lightened and became nearly blue, wondering whether it would be better to risk the sunshine. Her secret truth now probably entertained everyone in the village. Máire's eyes began to water… not from the sadness or frustration, but from the rising sun. Her body began to ache in warning, and the pain became unbearable.

This is not my time.

She ran for the inn instead of flying, since villagers were about. Once she reached the temporary safety of the common room, Máire swiped at her eyes. The scent of burnt clothing, hair, and skin infiltrated her entire being. As she sniffed, she felt angry with herself for appearing weak, as well as embarrassed that her eyes still watered.

The innkeeper's servants pretended to ignore her as they grumbled to themselves about the hours, though she assumed fear made them snap at each other, not to mention the slovenly behavior of her male traveling companions.

Máire tossed five sou onto the nearest table before climbing the stairs. She paused in the hallway and stared at the long rows of doors. After creeping to the room she shared with those overgrown boys, she closed her eyes. She had no desire to listen to Arwin, Claudius, and Marcus jest at her expense, all the while receiving that sad-eyed, puppy dog stare from Julien. After all, they all partook of her generosity.

Why should I have to share a room with them?

With her mind set, Máire drew her sword and then kicked open the door. "Wake up. Everyone out!" she yelled, not noticing until afterwards that the boys had been preparing to go to sleep. They all stared at her, for a moment, as if she were not quite right in the head.

They must have been discussing me.

"What?" Mac Alpin did not yell his query this time, managing to decrease the volume of his voice.

Máire heard several echoes from the others.

"Calm down, Maél Morrigan. Things will work themselves out during sleep," Claudius grumbled. He had always been stubborn about ignoring her patient requests.

When he rose up in an apparent attempt to placate her, she slapped her blade against his stomach.

Claudius made an annoyed grunt. "You can be such a demanding harpy! This isn't right," he bellowed before gathering his clothes.

At that moment, she heard footsteps from behind and the sound of a blade being loosed from its scabbard. Máire turned and slapped the flat of her sword against Mac Alpin's backside. "Get out," she raged.

The men exchanged the confused stare they normally shared whenever they did not understand something she said or did.

However, Marcus merely shrugged and started grabbing the blankets from his cot. "Where are we supposed to sleep, chroí?" he asked. A bare hint of a smile creased his features.

Sometimes he can be as annoying as the Lamia.

"I don't care," Máire answered while shaking her sword at him.

"Can't I stay?" Julien asked.

"No," she answered, continuing to feel snippy and petulant. "Go sleep on the floor in another room."

Once the men had dragged their tired, dirty bodies and their necessities out into the hallway, Máire turned away and let the door close behind her. Then she lay down in a cot and rolled onto her side, too exhausted to undress, and rested her sword next to her legs. Her fingertips cupped the pommel.

Soon after she closed her eyes, she felt that oblivion would take her, but she heard the door open again. "I told you four to leave," Máire muttered while keeping her eyes closed.

Instead of a man's voice interrupting her slumber, a familiar feminine voice oozed over her. "I believe that is the first time you've mistaken a Lamia for Sugnwr Gwaed, Deargh Du, or Ekimmu Cruitne," Amata greeted in a voice that floated through the air, sounding like a soft peal of bells.

Máire opened her eyes and glared at the often dual-meaning Amata. "Oh, it's you. Where are my manners?" she asked, hearing the sarcasm in her voice. "I want to be alone!" Her shout led to knocking from other rooms next to hers.

"No, you don't," Amata answered with a soothing and sibilant purr.

"Did Lamia suddenly develop the ability to read minds?" Máire asked, wondering whether they actually possessed such a gift.

Has Mandubratius been reading my mind all this time, hence his innate knowledge about what I think?

"No," Amata countered and then smiled for a moment. "It would be most amusing, unless I could not learn to ignore the constant annoying voices in my head. However, I know you wish for someone to talk to… a sympathetic ear."

"If I wanted a sympathetic ear," Máire began to argue, but she trailed off, wondering from where she could find one.

"Awwww, you do not have a confidant," Amata pouted, sounding less satisfied with herself. She then trailed into the room, like a gliding serpent.

"So, the ear of the handmaiden of Mandubratius is sympathetic towards the child-in-darkness of a past lover?" Máire asked. "That is very confusing."

Amata grinned. "I'm hardly a maiden." Her face lost its sharp edges and became gentle and lovely. "There are few of us women amongst these children who call themselves men. Our gender needs to stay together, where feminine issues are concerned."

"And you came to gloat and report back to Mandubratius how successful his jibes were?" Máire released her weak grip on the pommel of her sword and shifted her body into a more comfortable position for conversation.

"Not specifically." The Lamia's face turned from tender placidity to poignant distress. She slinked closer, as if afraid that someone might be listening. "I have had the same problems with a lack of fulfillment."

Máire wondered whether Amata attempted to manipulate her, yet the sad look in Amata's eyes made her feel pity. She tried to fight it off, since the last time a Lamia had made her feel compassion and sympathy, he'd wormed his way into her dreams.

"Tell me, Amata of the well-patronized bower, how long did you have this ailment?" Máire stared into Amata's limpid blue eyes, preparing to judge the Lamia's reply.

"Until I met Edward, it had been nearly one hundred years since my last climax," Amata answered in a whisper. "And that was of my own doing."

Máire watched Amata clench her hands as if nervous. She seemed to be an expert at twisting truth, and perhaps this truth made her nervous. "What caused it?" Máire asked Amata. "Was it a curse?"

"No." Amata shook her head. "Mandubratius and I shared delights of the flesh, once, but it faded. Until Edward, the only pleasure I remember experiencing was with…" Amata smiled for a moment before gasping out, "Marcus." She uttered a soft chuckle, but then her face darkened. "Ever since Mandubratius made a show of raping me in front of the Lamia leadership after killing Felician, well, our relations were not as fulfilling." Amata paused again and stared at the wall as if remembering that moment.

As Máire watched the other woman redden, she realized that the Lamia had probably admitted a deep secret that no one knew. "Who is Felician?" she asked. Máire knew she had heard the name before, but she could not remember the context.

"Our sponsor," Amata whispered.

"And Mandubratius killed him?" Máire tried to not look or seem surprised.

"Felician wanted all Lamia to leave Rome and return to Greece, whereas Mandubratius did not agree, and neither did I. He and I formulated a plan to take over the leadership of the Lamia. So, Mandubratius killed Felician… and… so forth. To prevent civil war between his faction and mine, we agreed to a compromise where we would be Co-Consuls. As part of this compromise, he had to show his male superiority. I allowed him to rape me, though I suppose it was not rape because I consented to it. Of course, the other Lamia were horrified, so our ploy worked."

Máire's earlier trepidations with this conversation began to melt away. "Amata, I do not believe that you consented to be treated in such a manner. I hope you received compensation for such a demeaning experience."

She watched Amata's darkened visage stretch into a conspiratorial smirk.

Amata then crouched next to the bed and leaned towards Máire's ear. "I received compensation by wearing a wooden phallus and mounting him," Amata whispered directly in her ear.

Máire covered her mouth in shock. "By Morrigan's strength," she whispered, aware of the implications.

"Now a third person knows of this," Amata grinned.

"I am most humbled you shared this. Why did you tell me, Amata?" She turned and whispered in Amata's ear. "I could damage his reputation amongst the Lamia."

"We women have to take care of each other," Amata whispered back. "As much as I truly like Edward, I could not tell him these truths. Sometimes, the men that oppress us need to be shamed."

"Sometimes, the women need to be shamed as well," Máire replied softly.

"Shamed?" Amata looked confused. "Do you mean me?"

"The Empress," Máire whispered. "Not you."

"I do not understand." Amata's tone belied her confusion.

"She is to replace you as consul," Máire whispered. "It was the deal Mandubratius brokered with her for the mirror. She wants to be the official leader of the Lamia, but he plans on aiding her as consul. Of course, he plans on staying on as the true leader of your line."

Amata's eyes revealed her shock, before fixating on the floor.

A nagging voice reminded Máire that this could be some intricate act, yet Amata seemed so genuine. Máire hoped that she was not foolish for allowing this to continue.

Amata gazed into Máire's eyes and asked, "Am I to be k... killed?"

"I do not know," Máire admitted, "but, it would seem unlikely. Your dismissal will only be temporary, if Mandubratius' rambling is to be believed."

Amata at first did not answer, at least verbally, but she did close eyes and tighten her lips into a thin line.

Wishing to be supportive of her new found friend, Máire grabbed Amata's arm at the elbow and said, "I offer my assistance, if needed."

Amata's clear eyes opened and fixed Máire with an amicable stare, and her face revealed a gentle smile. "Should any be needed, I will ask. Either way, I am sorry for what happened in the past."

"I somehow doubt that you were the person responsible for the deaths of my family members and of my betrothed, Amata." Upon realizing that she indeed wanted company this day, Amata's company, Máire asked, "Would you prefer to sleep in this room?"

Amata smiled and pulled a cot towards Máire's and pushed it against the other cot. After sitting down, Amata yanked the blankets and lied down.

Máire picked up her sword and set it to her other side. She soon felt the tentative touch of one of Amata's hands upon hers. She squeezed it gently.

"Thank you," Amata whispered. "Sleep well, Máire."

"You, too," Máire replied. As she drifted off to sleep, she wondered how she could use this information against Mandubratius.

Seosaimhín stared in rapt horror at the severed heads, which lay scattered across the floor of the cave. Somewhere in the logical recesses of her mind, she reasoned that her new children couldn't fight effectively because they had not finished the change. However, the maelstrom part of her mind wished for blood and vengeance.

Seeking retribution, she stomped towards the altar and effigy. She felt gladdened when Nagirrom hopped onto the altar and began grooming Himself. To Him, she cried out, "Our hearts seethe with the fury of oceans crashing against distant cliffs. We must quash the soulless ones for this murder of our children."

Nagirrom's deep eyes settled on her, and then His somewhat disembodied voice countered, "They are not ready, Druid."

Seosaimhín felt stupefied… even angered… by the unexpected response. "Nagirrom would have us wait?! Bah! We shall strike against those who have wronged us. Retribution shall be our guide."

"I forbid it!" Nagirrom's voice shook the cave.

Seosaimhín seethed. "Why would Nagirrom forbid retribution against the soulless ones who murdered Nagirrom's children?"

"They are not ready, and many will die. I do not desire that you seek revenge. However, I do not forbid you from seeking vengeance," He told her.

"Then, tomorrow night, we shall seek our vengeance," Seosaimhín hissed.

Vézelay

Talia sensed Reginald stretch his arms over his head in their tent. She closed her eyes in a vain attempt to ignore the heat of the morning. She also felt a little annoyed, since Reginald stared at her in the same manner as so many of the blood-drinkers here. They always lived by their stupid, precious rules and oppressed anyone who dared to think differently.

The sensation of one of Reginald's fingers tracing over her shoulder blade, tickling her, kept her from sleep's seduction.

"I cannot wait to get back to Divio," Reginald murmured before sliding in next to her. He then began to fondle her.

She decided to return his caresses, figuring it would wear him out, so she could get some sleep. "Do you need to return to Divio so quickly?" she purred. "I can assure you that you would be most welcome in my home. I am the Lady of Époisses, after all." She giggled as the tickling continued.

"Is that an invitation?" he asked while nibbling at her ear.

"Why, yes, it is," she replied before tickling him back. She allowed Reginald to pin her to the ground.

Reginald's touch turned from tickling to pleasuring. "You would ask a man, who is expected at his home, to allow his vassals to be without their leader?" he asked with panted breath.

Talia felt him firm against her thigh, reveling again the ease of manipulating weak-willed widowers. "I'm certain they will behave themselves," she informed Reginald. "You could always cast out the troublemakers. Besides, there are rewards for joining me." She began nibbling on his neck. Her hunger rose as she moved her fingers around Reginald.

The widower pulled away and grinned. "What kind of rewards?"

She felt her face twitch into a pout, and she squirmed a little in a playful manner. "What kind of rewards do you want?"

Reginald stared down into her eyes and said, "Well, you, of course." He then leaned in and kissed her.

She returned his kisses briefly, but then she pulled away to regain his attention. "That is most flattering, but you already have me," Talia cooed. "What else do you want?"

"I could always use more wealth," Reginald replied with a shrug.

Talia nipped at his throat and cooed, "I know what you really want."

Reginald pulled back. He seemed less playful, now. "Then, what do I want, Talia?"

Talia stretched her legs and basked in the power she wielded over him, even without her manipulative gifts. "You want power over more people, land, and the wealth that comes with power," she answered.

Men are such simple creatures.

Reginald's eyes hardened for a moment, but then he chortled, "Are you saying that if I go to Époisses with you that you will grant me more power?" He started laughing, so Talia joined in.

"No. What I'm saying is that if you come home with me, I will help you gain that power."

Reginald's face revealed confusion, and he became limp. In a subdued voice, he asked, "How?"

Talia smiled at him, reveling in his confusion. She then wrapped her legs around Reginald, rolled him onto his back, and straddled him.

"I have friends," she informed him. "More importantly, I can help you gain enormous amounts of territory from people who are illegitimately in possession of the land."

"Which territories?"

"Why, Auxerre and Vézelay," Talia replied.

Reginald shifted his weight and pulled away from her. He then sat up and stared at the far wall.

Talia covered herself with a blanket, toying with him, hoping that he could still see her.

Reginald turned back to her, with mouth agape, and asked, "My mother and my brother? Their lands?"

Talia tried not to sound annoyed. She considered Reginald to be a fool, if he didn't notice that his brother, sister, and daughter shared no resemblance.

Is Reginald blind to the obvious?

"Have you not noticed that your father's features are not in your brother's or sister's faces? Nor does your daughter resemble you at all. Does this not tell you that your mother and your wife both committed adultery and produced bastards?"

Reginald seemed offended. "How could you say such a thing?" he spat.

She reasoned that, had he been standing, he would have slapped her. She stared at him again and continued to focus her mind on changing his. "Picture them in your mind," she urged Reginald. "If you can see it with your own eyes, then confront your mother." She held back from manipulating him, knowing the effects might fade too quickly before her plan came to fruition.

Reginald knelt in front of her and covered his eyes with his hands.

Talia placed her left hand on his left shoulder and whispered, "You do know the truth. It's hard for your heart to accept it, but look what your mother and brother did to you, the humiliation you have suffered. Do they deserve this bounty? No. This is rightfully yours."

Reginald sobbed a little.

Talia dropped the blanket, embraced him, and moved in such a way that she rested his face against her right breast. "Do you want the rewards I offer?"

"What rewards were these, again?" he asked with a sniff.

"I will help you gain what is rightfully yours, but you must join me in Époisses. You will join me, won't you?"

Reginald wiped away his tears and met her eyes. "Yes... if my mother breaks when I confront her again, I will leave."

Talia knew he would leave for Époisses, regardless. She reached behind herself and pulled out a letter of introduction from under her blankets. "I will depart tonight, as soon as I make my excuses. I'll leave you with this, in case you arrive before I do. Present it to Rosamund, my head servant. I left instructions for her to take care of you."

Reginald took the parchment scroll. "Thank you."

She grabbed Reginald, rolled him onto his back again, and straddled him.

"You may thank me by taking my mind off this sorrow," she whispered, allowing her hair to trail along his neck. Mandubratius would be so proud of her for this cunning manipulation, without wasting her Lamia talents.

Caoimhín rested his head against the cold ground in the grove as he stared up at the stars. He soon closed his eyes and allowed himself to become part of the grove and its standing stones, but then he heard a woman clear her throat,

Heather Poinsett Dunbar & Christopher Dunbar

and his eyes snapped open to confirm the woman's identity. He noticed Lady Talia staring down at him, and he felt some annoyance at the interruption. He also felt embarrassed that not only had he not sensed her, but also that his tools lay some distance away.

"Caoimhín, I'm sorry for startling you."

He sat up and motioned for her to join him.

She looked uncomfortable at the thought of sitting on the ground, but she finally relented and sat down. "I believe it's time for me to return home. I have come to ask your leave for safe passage."

The grove pulled on him, requesting his full attention. Talia served only as a distraction. "Hmmm," he muttered, trying to re-center his thoughts. "You need to speak with Sáerlaith. She is now the lead Councilor again... either her, or perhaps one of the leaders of the Ekimmu Cruitne or Sugnwr Gwaed." He leaned back against the ground and smiled. "I am her assistant, again, and I have no other duties."

Talia leaned in closer and murmured, "Sáerlaith seems busy and unapproachable. I don't wish to disturb her."

"I could interrupt her on your behalf," Caoimhín answered. "That will ensure that she hears your request." He smiled and closed his eyes, but then some strange harmonious noise drew at his mind. "Can you hear the music here? I must find more sponnc." Before he could rise, he felt warm lips cover his, and a strong tongue probed his mouth. He allowed himself to be drawn into the moment, thinking that he did not need the sponnc. The kisses led to passionate touching, and soon he lost track of himself.

"Oh, I don't wish to disturb Sáerlaith now," a breathy voice informed him. "Just give me your permission to return home. You're her assistant, so you have some authority."

"Of course," he heard himself say, as the kisses continued. "You can go home. I'm sure you miss home. I know I do."

"Yes, I do," a voice murmured in his ear. "I'm so grateful to be allowed to return there. You will tell the Ekimmu Cruitne to let me pass, right?"

"Certainly," he whispered before inhaling, as a tongue and teeth moved along his throat. Fangs soon traced over him and began to scratch his skin.

"Thank you. Please do so," said the voice, but then the fae departed, leaving him confused and quite aroused.

Caoimhín rubbed his eyes and realized that only he remained in the grove and that his throat itched. He scratched himself and sat up, knowing he felt a strange compulsion to find the Ekimmu Cruitne and tell them that Lady Talia planned to return to Rome. He felt relief that she would be gone, far from Vézelay and the rest of the Celtic lines. However, part of his muddled mind suggested withholding the news, at least for now.

chapter fourteen

Szeged

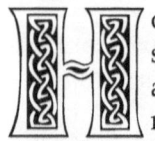oratio could not sleep, what with the loud talking in Máire's room, so he passed the time by watching Edward yawn, while Fianait and the others in the room seemed content, despite the noise from next door. Before he could drift off to sleep, the crash their room door slamming against the wall woke him and the others, from various stages of slumber.

In stomped Marcus, Mac Alpin, Julien, and Claudius, who all grumbled and seemed in no mood for questions or conversation.

Claudius muttered something about Maél Morrigan having her monthlies, before sinking onto the floor with his blankets, whereas Julien and Mac Alpin remained silent and went directly to sleep.

Horatio thought to question Marcus, but the Roman Deargh Du merely stared off into space. With no one to talk to, and with exhaustion weighing upon him, Horatio decided to go back to sleep, still curious at the reason for the disturbance.

When he woke that evening, no one wanted to talk, at least not in a language Horatio could understand. After gearing up and feeding from a mortal patron of the inn, Horatio followed the rest of the various races of blood-drinkers, who prepared to meet with Empress Irene of the Eastern Empire, into the woods. Each man and woman of the party clutched his or her sheathed weapons.

After traveling about a mile east of the village, the party entered a clearing. The woods lay in the distance, shrouded in a magical mist.

Marcus held up his hand, signaling the others to stop.

Soon, the mist faded, leaving behind several figures. A tall woman with regal bearing stood in the middle, and he knew without a doubt that it was the Basileus Irene. The soldiers behind the Empress parted, and a proud, stern figure offered her an arm. Another figure moved to his left side. All seemed strangely amicable.

"Mandubratius," the Empress shouted in greeting. Her smile became sharp. "It would seem you have brought friends to meet us. How very gracious of you. Please, bring them closer."

Mandubratius and Marcus exchanged glances, and then Marcus waved the party closer. Still, despite the seeming casualness of the meeting, all of the other blood-drinkers constantly watched the surrounding trees.

As soon as the party came to a stop, Empress Irene studied the faces in front of her.

Horatio felt her eyes dwell on him, for a moment.

The Empress continued meeting the eyes of everyone in the party as she spoke. "This is a most momentous occasion, I am told. I have learned from General Gaius that the Lamia have been at war with the Celtic lines for many years. Now, there is an alliance. The Children of Ares will rejoin their western brothers and sisters. We are most interested in this alliance with the Celtic lines and any subsequent treaties."

When Mandubratius cleared his throat, the Empress ceased speaking.

Horatio wondered what sort of game existed between them.

"Would you like to meet your new friends, Imperial Majesty?" Mandubratius asked. His mouth twitched into an impish smile.

The Empress strode closer to Mandubratius and examined the gathered blood-drinkers more closely. She appeared to be in her forties, but no one could deny that her beauty had not passed with age. Her glossy, brunette hair blazed under the luminous moon, and her blue eyes, which radiated a combination of power and mischief, sparked with a gleaming fire.

The Empress then walked a few paces to her right, paused in front of Marcus, and turned to face him. "You, you're the one Gaius and Mandubratius speak of in such… glowing terms. You must be Marcus, the Deargh Du."

Marcus nodded in response.

"Do you always come to meet with friends armed in such a manner? It is as if you expect an attack."

"Yes, Imperial Majesty," Marcus replied. "It is the custom of my people to be prepared for battle, and with the threat of the Strigoi, we must maintain our vigilance."

The Empress chuckled. "Your people are Roman, Marcus. These people would have been your slaves in your days of mortality, if I am not mistaken."

Marcus barked a laugh. "Doubtful, as I'm only half Roman. This is my real family, and they are slaves of no one."

Marcus turned and began to introduce each member of the Celtic lines. He paused, for a moment, after introducing Horatio, which left him feeling grateful for the inclusion.

Before Marcus could finish, Amata chimed in and said, "Do not forget me, Marcus." She chuckled a little. "Though I'm not a member of his family, I must say that I truly enjoyed your orgy, Empress."

Horatio watched Amata's eyes flash at Mandubratius and then lock on the Empress.

All the Lamia, save Mandubratius, shuffled his or her feet in indecision while watching Amata and the Empress challenge one another.

Mandubratius merely smiled at the two women.

Finally, the Empress broke her glare with Amata, smiled, and said, "It is a pleasure to meet you all, but I feel you already know who I am." The Empress' smile turned deadly as she studied Amata, again. "Now, I suppose you wish to see my precious mirror."

Before Amata could utter a reply, Horatio heard Arwin and Edward shout, "Strigoi to the north!"

Horatio felt pangs of fear, as Marcus began shouting orders.

"Prepare! Get into positions," he yelled. Horatio noticed him turn to General Gaius. "Stand with us," Marcus said to the Lamia, who nodded.

Gaius rejoined his lieutenant and began shouting orders to his soldiers.

Horatio nervously clutched at his sword, unsure of what exactly he needed to do. He was a cavalryman, not a foot soldier.

At the perimeter to the north, he saw several blood-drinkers fall, clutching at their heads, and then a loud blast echoed through the village and surrounding forest. Horatio looked on as Edward lobbed a series of incendiaries towards the north and west, resulting in a bright spray of fire and loud, concussive force. The earth burned where they struck.

In the aftermath of the explosions, Claudius ran by, handing out incendiaries amongst their party.

Horatio took the offered incendiary in his left and switched it out with his sword.

A few Strigoi fell from the incendiaries tossed by the other blood-drinkers.

The combined group of soldiers formed into a defensive circle, with the archers protected in the center. Horatio stood his ground in the perimeter and prepared to meet the beastly Strigoi running towards him with their weapons drawn. He pulled his right arm back to throw the incendiary, when he heard a sound that made him cry out and close his eyes in exquisite pain. Still, duty demanded he throw his burden. Through his pain, he put all the strength he could muster into throwing the container, but it was not enough. The blast overwhelmed him.

In her wildest nightmares, Irene never pictured herself in a field surrounded by madness. She tried to convince herself that demons did not exist, yet a needling voice in her brain reminded her of tales of these beings who could cause mortals to rip out their eyes and go mad.

Did not the church make up these tales to keep power? Why can't I even defend myself?

As the screaming demons ran towards her, she felt the long-gone emotion of crippling fear. The heat from a massive ball of fire, a small distance away, pulled her out of her morass. She could see the gathered warriors throw clay jars at the demons... Strigoi... whatever they called themselves, but then a strange darkness seemed to overwhelm her and grow thick.

Lamia and the former Children of Ares leapt into the air and loosed their arrows upon the Strigoi, though Irene had no idea why they would do such a thing. At that moment, an intense screeching noise made Irene wince in pain and close her eyes. When she opened them, she saw that only a dwindling circle of soldiers surrounded her. She had forgotten the basic tenets of her training that kept her youthful and strong. Irene covered her eyes. Despite her crying bloody tears, she noticed the arrival from the sky of another of those Celtic blood-drinkers.

"Where's the mirror, Basileus?" demanded the impertinent interloper.

Irene blinked her eyes open and stared at the woman who stood in front of her. She thought she recognized Máire from her orgy, possibly the one Marcus referred to as his daughter-in-darkness.

Máire? Is this her name? Such an odd name. Why does she need to look at a mirror?

The blood-drinker exuded the beauty and grace of the ancient statues of Aphrodite, except that soot, blood, and dirt smudged the woman's features.

"You want to look in my mirror?" Irene queried, wondering why Aphrodite would want to look at Herself in a mirror during this battle.

"The mirror is a weapon that can stop the Strigoi," the other woman explained in a harsh, impatient tone.

"Weapon?" Irene whispered, unable to grasp her meaning.

"Damn you, Mandubratius," Máire grumbled. "I'm certain he left out these important details. Just tell me where it is, please."

Unsure why she should keep it hidden, Irene glanced over her shoulder and said, "Under my cloak, strapped to my back."

Máire hefted her up and began to unfasten the mirror. "Lamia, always making things difficult," she fumed before disappearing with Irene's mirror.

Out of the blackness, a demon settled its eyes on Irene and smiled a horrific grin, allowing its maddened eyes to overwhelm all else. Its stare drove pinpricks of fear up and down Irene's spine. As the beast walked towards her, it chanted a strange phrase over and over again, and each time, it grew louder. "Nagirrom. Nagirrom! Nagirrom!!"

Irene covered her ears and screamed, and the memory of her sins during her reign engulfed and devastated her. The screeches of her only son echoed in her mind.

Máire watched the Strigoi's freshly severed head roll down the hill before glancing at the Empress, who still remained curled up in a fetal position with her arms covering her face. Máire shook her head a bit.

Defending the Basileus is the job of the Lamia, not mine.

After taking to the air to find Marcus, she found him swooping down to decapitate an arrow-riddled Strigoi. Máire could not help but notice the strange mixture of blood and tears on his face. She found consolation in hoping that the Strigoi were the cause of this peculiar behavior.

"I have the mirror," she shouted before landing next to him. Edward and Mac Alpin landed a few feet away.

Marcus wiped his face with his sleeve. "Wonderful," he answered while giving her a nervous smile. "Do not hesitate, chroí, use it."

She shook her head. "I am not sure how to use it, Marcus. The Empress is in no state to talk about it, and I cannot find the leech."

Mac Alpin came forth to study the mirror she gripped. "While it is a lovely mirror, I see nothing that seems magical about it. Perhaps it is like other mirrors. We need a light source to have an effect. It will be impossible to use in the dark," he added.

"How do we do that?" Marcus asked. "Oh, we Deargh Du can illuminate it with our glamoury." In an instant, white light surrounded him, and he stared into the mirror.

When Máire looked into the mirror, she could see a vague hint of Marcus' shadowed reflection, but she saw no light reflected from his glamoury.

"It's a magical light," she mused. "Perhaps glamoury does not work with this mirror." She then stared back at the other blood-drinkers and asked, "Any other suggestions?"

Arwin cleared his throat and answered, "We can throw every incendiary we have left at the forest and set it on fire. It will create light and we will aim the mirror at the enemy. They will see a reflection." His tone seemed reluctant.

Marcus chuckled a little. "I can't believe I'm saying this. Edward, start a fire."

"Don't worry, Marcus. Everything is in my control," Edward answered. He then took their offered clay pots and left to gather more.

Arwin shook his head a bit and said, "I hate it when he says that," before running off towards a group of Strigoi attacking the archers.

"We are most lucky that the Strigoi are slow," Marcus muttered as he returned to the air to continue the fight.

Few of their party remained standing. However, the remaining archers and the flying blood-drinkers kept the Strigoi from succeeding in the battle.

A series of several explosions, which made Máire unsteady, cast a bright light, illuminating the forest to her left, but then a guttural growl made her turn towards the forest.

Several Strigoi, smelling of foulness and burning wood, staggered towards her.

She aimed the mirror towards the forest and then adjusted it to reflect a beam of light from the fire into their eyes. She felt a moment of shock as they screamed and dropped to the ground, writhing in pain. Hope surged in her heart, and she adjusted her aim to cover another group. She tried to ignore the steadily increasing attacks. Máire closed her eyes as the attack on her senses started to fade, but then she gasped upon feeling an unbearable pain in her stomach. She glanced down towards her feet and saw a sword tip emerging from her abdomen. Máire squeaked and collapsed to her knees, still clutching the mirror to her chest, cradling it. She prayed that it would not shatter.

She looked up and saw a Strigoi lean over her, his orange eyes locked on hers. She uttered another frightened squeak as its image shimmered and became Connor. He smiled at her in a demonic way before kneeling at her side and ripping her tunic to shreds. Máire screamed as he reached for her chest, knowing what he sought for his revenge. She couldn't move. The pain of him tearing into her flesh engulfed her entire being. She felt Connor rend through her rib cage and pull out her heart.

While holding it overhead, he squeezed it in his fist and drank the spurting blood.

"Why aren't I dead?" she moaned while waiting for Morrigan to arrive and take her from the pain.

"If you think this is the end of your suffering, you're very mistaken, mhuirnín," Connor hissed. "It's just begun."

Everything faded to black.

Her heart... her heart remained in his hand. Her body refused to die, and she heard herself utter a sad gurgle, as Connor continued to drink from the bloody tissue. He soon lost interest in the now dried husk of an organ and tossed it aside. Connor's eyes settled on her again and he grabbed the skin from the wound in her torso and gripped her right shoulder. He leaned in and clamped his mouth on hers.

Máire felt Connor begin to peel back her skin, and she gurgled into his mouth. As she looked around the church, Máire witnessed the guests begin cheering and laughing. She soon found the strength to study them, and she realized that the Tuatha dé Danann surrounded her. Morrigan applauded the loudest.

She could say nothing, as Connor's mouth remained latched on hers. His tongue began choking her throat.

Máire uttered a stifled sound as he began flailing her skin again. He grabbed her intestines and began to pull them out. After a few moments of tortuous agony, Connor broke off the kiss and pulled away, but his face changed and now Marcus stared down at her, his hands slick with her vitae. "Are you happy about your decision to join us, Banbh Ceanúil?" he asked as he tugged at her intestines again.

"Yes," Máire answered, upon finally finding her voice, but then sharp pain exploded across her face as her father-in-darkness backhanded her. A warm wetness encompassed her cheek. Máire turned her head, and now Seanán stared down at her.

"Are you sure?" he asked.

She felt a pang of regret for not being with Seanán. "I'm sorry that I made myself forget what we had," she answered in a harsh hiss.

"Sorry? Sorry!?" Seanán started to laugh, and his hands grasped her shoulders. "Do you want to know what became of me? Do you?" he demanded while shaking her.

"Yes," she sobbed. "Please tell me."

Seosaimhín peered at her from behind Seanán. The old crone smiled at her, stinking of vile refuse. "I tore him to pieces, and I ate his morsels for my supper," she purred. Seosaimhín then leaned in closer to Seanán, grabbed the right side of his hair, and yanked, exposing his throat. When she bit a hunk of the exposed skin on his neck, fresh blood sprayed over Máire.

"No," Máire heard herself whimper.

After Seanán's body fell to the ground, Seosaimhín kicked him aside. "It's too bad you didn't want to be our daughter," she informed Máire. "I would have taught you how to bring him back and become your slave."

Máire began shaking her head vigorously.

Mandubratius strolled through the ring of Tuaths and tilted his head to study her. "Yes. It's too bad that I am not your sponsor. I could have molded you into a leader of millions, Maél Muire. But no," he cooed as he crouched down next to her and stared into her eyes. "You made a different choice."

"A very bad decision," Seosaimhín agreed with a chuckle.

"And now, you must suffer the punishment," Mandubratius added.

"Please don't," she whispered.

"Now, now, it's too late for pity from me," Mandubratius teased before standing up and glancing over at Seosaimhín.

"Roll Maél... Máire..." He stopped and laughed for a moment. "Well, whatever her name is, roll her over, Seosaimhín, and hold her down."

"Please don't do this, Awvarwy," she heard herself cry out, hoping the use of his real name would bring forth mercy. Instead of mercy, cold air hit her skin as they pulled off her dress. She felt his weight cover her. She screamed as the painful penetration commenced. The pain and agony began to blind her, and soon, Máire slipped into darkness once again.

Heather Poinsett Dunbar & Christopher Dunbar

chapter fifteen

ulien wondered why someone would ignite the forest. He decided to demand an answer, if he could find anyone to ask.

Brilliant light and intense heat, akin to the fires of the sun, burned the trees at the north edge of the clearing, setting the open field and the surrounding trees aglow.

He took to the air, trying to find the others, when a bright, focused light nearly blinded him, for a moment. After blinking away the glare, he realized the light came from the mirror Máire wielded. It reflected the light and images back to the Strigoi. He felt relief as they fell, but the reprieve ended, when Máire dropped to the ground while clutching the mirror. Her screams pierced his soul like daggers.

He yelled to get the Strigoi's attention, but it ignored him and began to feed from her. Before Julien could think, he flew towards the Strigoi and stabbed it in its left eye. After landing, he yanked out the sword and beheaded the wounded Strigoi with a swift cut. He watched the body collapse, joining the gleefully smiling Strigoi's head, which rolled through the grass, leaving a crimson trail.

A wordless squeak drew his attention back to Máire, and he saw that she had closed her eyes tightly. He watched her body slacken as her hands lost their grip on the mirror.

Julien pulled the mirror out of her limp fingers and began shining it towards the attacking Strigoi, which began to fall. At the sound of a growl behind him, he turned around, grateful the light from the fire burned brightly and allowed for a reflection. He saw ten, then twenty, fall.

Suddenly the Strigoi turned towards the south, as if a distant force commanded them, and they loped off.

The remaining allies, who could still stand or fly, rushed toward Julien.

As soon as Marcus arrived, he began to survey the area before studying Máire, for a moment, as if assessing her health. He then turned back towards the others and said, "We need to try to keep the fire contained, as if that's not obvious already."

"That won't be necessary," Edward pointed out while holding up several larger clay pots.

"So, you plan on stopping one fire with another?" one of the Children of Ares asked.

Edward gave Julien a quick glance before replying to the Greek Lamia. "These incendiaries are specifically designed to snuff out fire."

After rubbing soot away from his face, Mac Alpin said, "Please explain how that might work, Edward. My brain is… still recovering."

"I will demonstrate," Edward countered in an overly confident tone.

"Gods, here we go," Mac Alpin muttered under his breath.

"I'm not so sure about this," Marcus murmured, and Julien, for once, agreed with him.

"Look, we have no time. The fire will spread to the village, if I do not try. I know I can put it out," Edward stated.

Marcus studied the field before looking back to Edward. "Try it, but please do not kill our friends."

"Thank you," Edward said and then turned to Mac Alpin with a smirk. "You'll see."

"Let's start carrying our friends away from this explosion," Fianait suggested. She then picked up Amata and hoisted her over her shoulder.

Julien turned around to pick up Máire, when the first explosion nearly knocked him off his feet. He rolled onto his back, shielding the mirror. A second explosion caused his ears to pop. Several more followed in rapid succession, causing waves of strong wind and deafening rapports. Once the blasts had ceased, Julien sat up and stared at the results.

Flattened trees surrounded the clearing, while blackened holes and craters dotted the landscape. Ash scattered with the wind, and yet, no fire burned within the darkened void.

In the midst of the cataclysmic panorama, Julien saw a naked figure, crawling out of one of the craters. "Edward!" Julien cried out. Once he reached his friend, Julien noticed that Edward bled from his ears, eyes, nose, and mouth, while blisters covered his body. Edward seemed to be oblivious to his own condition.

"Edward, it's me, Julien," he said, trying to gain Edward's attention by shaking the alchemist's shoulder.

Edward opened his eyes and blinked them in obvious pain. "Julien, did it work?" he asked with his pain-ridden eyes staring at Julien.

"Yes, it did!" Julien chuckled. "The fire is out."

Edward laughed. "Arwin will consider this one for the history scrolls. I stopped a fire!"

"What happened to you?" asked Julien, concerned for his friend's wellbeing.

Edward studied himself, for a moment. "I was probably standing too close," he commented. "I'll have to remember that, the next time I do this."

"Close your eyes," Julien requested, thinking he could heal him, but then he noticed Edward's bloody ears. "Edward, how can you hear me?" Julien asked.

Edward stared at Julien and said, "I can't. I'm reading lips. I've lost my hearing before. Arwin," he added while looking over Julien's shoulder. "You owe me, now."

"What was the wager?" Julien asked with a smirked, as Mac Alpin grabbed Edward and hefted him over his shoulder. Julien shared the burden, and then the three blood-drinkers rose.

"I bet him he'd never stop a fire on his own," Mac Alpin teased. "I've got him. You take in that mirror."

Julien released his hold on Edward and turned towards Máire, in time to watch Marcus pick her up. "What about the dead?" he asked Arwin.

"They will become ash with dawn's light," Claudius said, after swooping in. "The real question is what to do with these Strigoi that remain."

"Strigoi?" Marcus asked while balancing Máire and her gear. "What Strigoi?"

Julien located the Strigoi who had fallen after looking into the mirror and pointed at them. "The ones that did not leave. They looked into the mirror and witnessed their beauty," he answered. Through his peripheral vision, he saw the others turn to face the twenty former Strigoi, who merely appeared to be regular people lying in the dirt, bereft of any monstrous or disgusting features.

Mac Alpin sniffed the air for a moment. "They aren't mortal."

"But what are they?" asked Julien.

"A mystery for now," Marcus stated in a weighty voice. "We'll place them inside the lord's barn and the Children of Ares' tents, and then we shall draw lots for volunteers to watch them, after we take ours to the inn. We will sort this out later, Julien." He then turned away and flew Máire towards the inn.

As Julien picked up the mirror, he looked again at the power it wielded, and he felt awestruck.

Julien, upon landing outside of the village, caught glimpses of weakened Lamia attempting to manipulate the mortals to let them pass and return to the lord's home. Even the other races appeared shaky on their feet, as they carried their friends. Because of their weakness, the blood-drinkers could not influence the mortals, so arguments broke out between the frightened soldiers and the blood-drinkers.

He impatiently grabbed a torch and whistled, hoping that the soldiers would still respect him. After yelling, "We fought the demons," they all turned to face him. "Look at us!" he continued, adamant to persuade through words and not magic. "We are lucky to walk still, yet there are many others of us on the battlefield who will not rejoin us. Now, help us carry our friends into the inn and barns."

"Yes, my Lord," one of the guards shouted, before barking orders at his men.

Julien caught a half smile, which brightened Marcus' face, for a moment. The other Deargh Du saluted him, in what must have been an ancient Roman salute, before carrying Máire into the inn. Julien pondered with whom he should trust the mirror, when a voice interrupted his contemplation.

"How many demons did you destroy?" Dorian asked.

Julien turned to face him and answered, "Perhaps a hundred." He stared at Dorian and added, "There will be more." At that moment, he heard a man cry out, "Maria!" Julien turned and recognized one of the Strigoi that witnessed her beauty.

A man, who carried an axe in one hand, ran over to see the former Strigoi. "That's my wife," claimed the woodsman. "Maria, are you well, Maria? The demons had taken her. How can she be back? What did they do to her?"

Marcus interceded, exuding soft glamoury. "We'll know for sure later. For now, she needs rest, as do you," he replied.

The man started to sob. "No, she needs me."

Julien looked at the guards and said, "Help this man. He needs rest, as does his wife."

As the guards led the woodcutter away, he babbled to them.

Dorian drew Julien's attention away by saying, "Sir, there are others here I recognize." He gestured to other prone forms. "Are these strangers your friends?" he asked while studying the party of Lamia.

"Close enough," Julien admitted. Upon seeing Fianait, he decided to entrust the mirror with her, so he handed it to her.

Marcus added, "They did fight the demons with us."

"How did you ever defeat them?" Dorian asked.

"The Eastern Church and the Empress gave us the use of a holy relic, which can drive evil demons out from the innocent," Julien stated. "There is no more time for questions, for we must evacuate the field."

While surveying the triage area set up in the inn and adjacent barns, which swelled with those recovering, Julien felt a hand latch onto his arm.

The owner of the arm looked up and whispered, "Where am I?" He seemed more like a frightened child, rather than a monster.

Julien leaned in, patted the man's shoulder, and whispered, "You are in the village of Szeged. Do you remember much from your… illness?"

"Beautiful, bright white light," the man murmured before smiling, for a moment, "and the voices of angels. So hungry."

"Bring forth some of that stew," Julien called out to one of the village volunteers, before sitting down next to the man. As he took the fragrant bowl, Julien tried not to inhale the scent of spices and garlic.

The former Strigoi sat up, took a whiff of the spicy stew, and gagged before turning away.

"I'm sorry," Julien said, putting away the vile substance. "Is there anything you would prefer to eat?"

The man shook his head. "I have strange desires," he whispered. He then latched onto Julien's left wrist.

Julien prepared to listen to whatever this man had to say, when a conversation between Marcus and Arwin caught his ear. Both blood-drinkers stood a few feet away from Julien.

"You notice these people smell differently, not like the Strigoi anymore," Mac Alpin whispered.

"Are they mortal?" Marcus asked.

"I don't think so," Arwin replied.

Just then, Julien heard the elder man utter a cry of frustration before a sharp pain made Julien hiss. He looked in shock as the man began to feed from him.

Screams of fear echoed in the large home, followed by screams of, "Destroy the demons," and so forth.

"Calm down!" he heard a voice command. Julien looked over at Marcus, expecting him to be issuing orders, and observed the Deargh Du walk purposefully into the center of the room. At the same time, Julien felt the former Strigoi release his arm.

Marcus took in the crowd and began his speech. "Among us is the emissary of His Holiness and the Basileus Irene. The Basileus herself sleeps under this roof. The Basileus' sacred mirror allowed God's own angelic forces into our realm. These angels helped rescue your friends and family from the grips of Satan himself. They will spend the rest of their lives suffering, but you will not kill them."

Julien noticed several Lamia swallow their laughter.

Mandubratius cleared his throat and added, "When our brethren have healed, we will lead you to sanctuary. That is, if you do not harm these very special children of God."

Julien heard a shuffle, as the former Strigoi, who had fed from him, sat up.

"My friends, what they say is true. I witnessed those demons. They took me from my church. They changed me!" He lowered his eyes. "I did horrible,

horrible things that only God and Jesus can forgive, but an angel of mercy with wings of bright light appeared, and this angel cast out the demon. Yet, my body has changed. I can no longer eat food to live. Instead, I must subsist on the lifeblood of others, but I can do this without killing anyone that I feed from. I do not see this as a curse. God has granted me life, and I feel better than I've ever felt before. Many of you know I've suffered from stiffening joints, but look now at my useful hands, which can continue to do the Lord's work on earth. Now, I ask you, my friends, to not condemn us, for God has delivered us from evil, and goodness has prevailed."

Mandubratius nudged Marcus while adding, "As further proof of this miracle, one of the angels will fly."

Marcus glared at Mandubratius and uttered something in a northern tongue. The elder Deargh Du then raised his arms and revealed his glamoury. He levitated a few feet off the ground and then landed. He seemed rather vexed with the entire procedure.

In response to the display, the people kneeled and began loudly begging for forgiveness. A few even grabbed Marcus' tunic and asked for blessings.

Mandubratius smiled and said, "So, who wishes to help revive these angels?"

Vézelay

As Reginald prepared himself for the feast, he found himself grumbling about his wet clothing. His mother had insisted upon wearing clean clothes, leaving him with few alternatives. He gathered and packed up his clothing, thinking there may be little time to do this after he approached his mother with his questions. In the midst of packing, he could feel a hard frown settle upon his brow. Reginald sat back down and pulled on his boots.

Why does Talia have to leave again? What is this business with Sáerlaith? Why would Caoimhín agree to step down?

Reginald believed that a man would never step down in leadership, but these mercenaries were a strange lot… stranger than most mercenaries should be. They seemed to bother Talia greatly as well, as if they shared an odd familiarity with her.

Once he left the house, he could hear music on the wind, so he decided to investigate the feast. Torches lit the outside of his mother's home. Many vassals drifted in the direction of the roasted meats, stews, and the spiced wine, where as the majority of their children slept in his mother's home.

Reginald strolled in the direction of his mother, when he witnessed her speaking to Sáerlaith. Her mother's hand rested on Sáerlaith's arm in an overly familiar manner.

Giggling interrupted his train of thought, and Reginald turned towards the laughter, only to see his sister sitting in Dreu's lap. When she leaned in to whisper something to him, Reginald stalked over towards the couple and grabbed Lirienne's left arm with his right hand.

"What are you doing?" Lirienne demanded while trying to pull away.

"That is exactly what I want to ask you," Reginald replied. "What are you thinking? He's beneath you, and you're bringing shame to our family."

The sound of footfalls brought his attention to his left side, where he discovered his mother's scarlet, rage-filled face glaring at him.

"You're hurting me," his sister hissed, drawing his attention back to her.

"I'm certain mother would agree with me that you're embarrassing us," Reginald charged.

Instead of agreeing with him, his mother pushed her way between his sister and him, gripped Reginald's right arm with her left hand, and growled, "Let go of your sister."

"Why, Mother? She's misbehaving." Reginald glanced around a bit and then stared at his mother. "You are defending her?" In his periphery, he could see Dreu stand up. "Stay where you are, Captain," he said.

His mother leaned in and slapped him with her right hand. "Let her go," she ordered.

He released Lirienne in shock, before staring into his mother's eyes. "Did you just hit me?" His left cheek burned, so he ran his left hand over his beard.

His mother turned towards Dreu and said in a calm voice, "Please take Lirienne to the mercenaries for medical attention."

Reginald stared at Dreu and was about to order him to back away, when he felt another slap.

"Pay attention to me," his mother uttered in a growl. "What right do you have to pull your sister away from her betrothed?"

"B-betrothed!" he sputtered while trying to swallow his bile and rage. "I was never asked permission!"

"Julien and I gave him permission," his mother replied. "You weren't around."

"But I'm the head of the house!" Reginald insisted. He then grabbed his mother's right arm.

His mother yanked both of her arms away. "I am the head of this house! As head, I can select who my daughter marries."

"That's not what father would have wanted. He would have wanted a marriage with another noble family, but what family does he have to offer?" Reginald shouted back at her while pointing at Dreu's and Lirienne's departing forms.

"He's an officer, a captain of the garrison, and he has far more respect amongst those who matter than you do, my son." His mother's words became a terse whisper.

"How well do these people respect you and my sister?" Reginald replied, but then he realized what he needed to speak. "Oh, forgive me, mother! Lirienne is only my half-sister!"

A momentary look of shock, which rolled over his mother's face, revealed the truth.

Reginald spun towards her vassals who stared at him in mute shock. Even the musicians had stopped playing mid-note.

"You should all know my mother is an adulteress." Despite feeling a mild slap of pain on the back of his head, he continued. "Do you deny that you fornicated with someone who is not my father?" When Reginald turned back to face his mother, she stared at him through tear-rimmed eyes.

"By your silence, you have confirmed your guilt. Know this, then. Your bastard children learned well from your example." He looked back at their audience and shouted, "You see, my daughter isn't even my daughter! She is my niece!" After returning his glare to his mother, Reginald added, "So, you see that your sin is propagated through your bastards and theirs. You've admitted your guilt. Therefore, I demand that you return your title and your lands to the proper male heir."

His mother's blue eyes turned dangerous and dark, and the hue of her face burned even brighter than before. "You will never, never have my lands, even after I die. Now, leave my home. You are never welcome back."

Reginald leaned in towards her and seethed, "I'll return when these lands are mine."

"Go… now," she hissed in a voice devoid of all emotion save rage, before spitting at him.

As Reginald backed away from his mother, he noticed bright eyes staring at him. The mercenaries' eyes appeared frightening in the torchlight. They seemed almost mesmerizing, yet he turned away.

Reginald headed towards the house to find his packed bag. Afterwards, he grabbed a horse from the barn, saddled it, and left. Despite riding off into the night, he still felt those eyes on his back.

As Heloise watched her son leave the feast, she felt rage gnaw at her heart. Her legs began to weaken, but she felt steadying arms wrap around her. She glanced back at Sáerlaith in thanks, and then some of the other blood-drinkers assisted her to a chair.

"Wine," Caoimhín requested, turning to one of the vassals.

Soon, Heloise held a cup of the red, spicy warmed wine, which met her lips. She grasped the cup and began gulping it, ignoring everyone's suggestions to sip it. She closed her eyes as she finished the wine, and she began to feel warmth creep back into her bones. When she opened her eyes, Heloise realized that everyone stared at her. While their sympathy grated on her, she decided to speak up. After all, Reginald had pushed her to a point of pain, and she felt humiliated. After placing her empty cup on the table, Heloise announced, "My sincerest apologies for my lack of restraint and my son's hurtful allegations. Resume the music! Dance and make yourselves merry. This is a feast, damn it all! Bring me more wine!"

Heloise leapt to her feet, grabbed her cup, and began to serve herself. The cheers of her people lifted her spirits. However, she could see Sáerlaith, Caoimhín, and other of the mercenaries watching her, whispering amongst themselves. She didn't care. She knew she had done nothing wrong, but she decided not to tell the whole truth to anyone.

Lirienne soon returned, after visiting one of the mercenaries, and she bore no outward signs of Reginald's abuse. Of course, now that Reginald had left, either she or Lirienne would have to raise Clotilda.

By the merciful Gods, what shall I tell Clotilda? That her father wasn't her father and that he left her because he no longer cared about her?

The sensation of a gentle but firm hand resting on her shoulder caused Heloise to feel as if her heart leapt into her throat. She looked over her shoulder into Sáerlaith's concerned eyes.

"Lady Heloise, would you like me to escort you to your home?" asked Sáerlaith in a soft, musical, yet stern voice.

"Now, why would I want to go there?" Heloise argued before hiccupping into her hand. She then refilled her cup and began emptying it again. "There is a feast here, and I plan on enjoying it." She heard herself drawl the words.

"Heloise, your people are watching you. They witnessed you strike and cast out your eldest. I'm certain the actions were justified, but everyone is worried to see you in this inebriated state. You should rest," Sáerlaith whispered. After patting Heloise's shoulder, she added, "You need to sleep on this, so tomorrow, you will have a clear mind and can decide what to do next."

Heloise lowered her cup and gazed over her gathered family. She could see a few stares directed towards herself and Lirienne. She felt her face flush, and she realized how foolish she must appear. Heloise dropped her cup on the table and turned to Sáerlaith.

"Please help me," she whispered. "I will retire, but please continue the celebration."

As Heloise wrapped her left arm around Sáerlaith, she heard the musicians begin to play again. With assistance, she began to walk towards her home, but she managed to stumble a little on the way. She could sense Lirienne following her, and she felt guilty... not just because of her drunken performance, but for the truth behind Reginald's claims.

As soon as the door closed, Sáerlaith picked up Heloise and carried her, as if she were little more than a child.

"Lirienne, could you pull back the covers on the bed?" Sáerlaith requested in her musical voice.

Heloise heard her daughter rush around them and go upstairs.

"Do you wish us to pursue Reginald?" Sáerlaith asked in a darker tone.

"Hmmm?" Heloise realized how sleepy she felt. "Pursue Reginald? Why? What would you do when you caught him?" She heard a door open and close. She soon felt someone removing her shoes and loosening her hair.

"Whatever you wish us to do, Lady Heloise," the other woman answered.

"Leave Reginald to his own devices," Heloise whispered. "I don't wish any harm upon him, Sáerlaith." To accentuate her point, she looked up into the Deargh Du's beautiful face.

Sáerlaith nodded her head. "Then, we will allow him to find his own path."

Heloise closed her eyes and drifted off into sleep.

Szeged

As the darkness enveloped her... rather them, the overwhelming blackness of the Strigoi-induced nightmares disappeared, leaving only still shadows and absolute bliss. A thrumming pulse of pleasure made Máire thrash about a little, but then a sudden thrust of movement made her close her eyes in rapture at the feeling of invasion. She muted her cries for a moment, before giving in and moaning in joy as the rhythm and movement in and around her body continued. Máire had no idea who blessed her with such pleasure, but who cared? It had been over two hundred years since she neared completion. Only someone she loved must be creating this ecstasy. After all, she could sense her desire beginning to peak. She never experienced this before. Not only did her body wallow in delight, but also her mind soared like a raven into the moonlit heavens.

Her lover's pace quickened for a few moments, but then it slowed down, as if teasing her with the promise of pure ecstasy. She felt him thrust into her again. He cried out in blissful agony and released into her. His continued movements made her start to climax.

Her voice caught in her throat, and she managed a breathy sigh, before succumbing to crying out her pleasure. Despite her climax, he continued his movements.

She could do nothing but wrap herself around him. Her toes curled in absolute satisfaction, while her hands stroked his shoulders and back.

After a time, he began to slow and eventually rested himself against her body.

Máire continued to rub him, feeling the swell of his backside under her hands, as he remained within her. She felt sated for once in this life after mortality. She could only describe the experience as glorious and relaxing. She kept her eyes closed, wanting to continue enjoying the pleasure after the act. "I love you. Thank you for this," she whispered.

He said nothing in reply, which left her somewhat bewildered. Then she felt him shift, and with that gentle movement, his limp phallus slid from her body. As he moved down her form, he began to kiss her, beginning at her navel, licking and nibbling his way up her torso. His ministrations left such pleasant tingles, as his teeth rasped at her body, leaving bloody scratches that he gently suckled.

She writhed again, impatient with the tender torture.

His mouth reached her chin, and then he devoured her lips. His tongue dueled with hers, and a new erection teased at the entrance of her body.

She kept him from entering her again, wanting to hear a word or two of acknowledgment. "Didn't you hear me?" She heard herself sound desperate for recognition and reward. Máire hated herself for that weakness, but she could not help it. "I said I love you."

"If you expect me to reciprocate and voice my utter adoration for you, all you need to do is ask," a familiar voice murmured in her left ear.

She focused her eyes on the dark figure and witnessed Mandubratius' grinning face staring down at her.

Watching Máire open her beautiful, green eyes, Mandubratius saw them swell with a strange and heady combination of desire and fury. He smirked at her, as he sat next to her cot, thankful that the puppy, otherwise known as 'Julien', had left to go feed. That meant he could rest next to Máire and push his way into her dreams… and what a satisfactory dream it had been. After pulling out his hand from under her blanket, he examined the wetness from her body gleam on his digits. Mandubratius licked his hand, before sticking one of his fingers into his mouth and closing his eyes. He continued to smile, reveling in the sweet taste on his fingertips, until he heard a low growl, so he prepared himself for the verbal onslaught.

Instead of launching a verbal assault, Máire sprang from her cot and grabbed the back of his neck, slamming his head against the wooden wall of the room. The loud knock echoed in the small chamber. He could not help but feel surprised by her sudden movements.

How could a blood-drinker recover from the Strigoi's mental attack so quickly?

Máire pushed her knee against the hollow behind his knee, causing Mandubratius to collapse over the side of her cot. She knelt next to him, augmented her grip on his throat, and pushed his face to her cot.

He chuckled, before uttering a tormented gasp as she grabbed his backside and squeezed a sensitive area with her fingernails. The dull pain twisted into a strange, growing pleasure.

Máire leaned in and began to whisper in his left ear. "Now that I have your attention, Awvarwy, I did not appreciate feeling your fingers inside me. Do you feel this?" she asked as she squeezed her hand. Her fingertips grew slick with his vitae. "Do you know what I will do to you?"

"I cannot wait to find out," he answered, disappointed that her blanket muffled his words.

"I'm going to attach a wooden phallus to my belt, and I'm going to ravage this," she hissed, while squeezing his backside again. "I will make you bleed, I will make you beg for me to cease, and I will let every mortal man, Lamia, Deargh Du, Sugnwr Gwaed, and Ekimmu Cruitne, and even the Strigoi, watch me rape you. They will see that you are not a man... that you have allowed yourself to be penetrated by a female."

He spat aside the blanket and tried not to smile.

Apparently, Amata has seen fit to blab our secret.

When he looked up at her, Máire's eyes appeared as black as a starless and moonless night. Though he recalled too vividly the last time he had seen those strange eyes staring from her face, their appearance did not deter his bravado. "I only wished to let you experience pleasure. I'll wager it's been centuries. You were so eager–"

"No more words, Awvarwy, save a yes or no." Máire's voice seemed a bit strange. "Would you like me to do this?" she asked, as she pulled back on the nape of his neck.

He heard a cracking sound, and pain shot through his back. Despite the throbbing ache that started to fade, he could not help but smile again. "Yes. Please do so."

Máire emitted another furious growl, and her eyes remained that strange and soulless black, as she turned her arm and slammed her elbow against his spine, just above his left hip.

Mandubratius cried out in pain, realizing that this was no longer the exciting and pleasurable stimulation her attentions had bestowed earlier. He collapsed at her bare feet. After a brief pause, he felt her shove a blanket into his mouth. He whimpered, which he hadn't done when Irene tortured him.

Máire picked him up and dropped him into another cot. "I need to sleep. Kindly keep your sniveling to a minimum."

Mandubratius opened his eyes and witnessed her irises return to emeralds. She slid into her now vacant cot and pulled the blanket over her head, only leaving a pale bare foot exposed.

The radiating pain, as well as his exhaustion, grew, and Mandubratius finally gave into the darkness of unconsciousness.

chapter sixteen

hen Máire felt someone pull away the blanket, she mumbled, "Go away, Awvarwy. I'm too exhausted to deal with this, again." After feeling the hand move away, Máire looked up to see Julien kick Mandubratius, to no avail, since Mandubratius remained unconscious, asleep, or perhaps he pretended to sleep.

"Bastard," Julien sputtered. He then turned back to her and knelt at her cot. "Are you alright?" he asked, stroking her hair. "I heard you cry out."

Máire glared at Julien and muttered, "If you were trying to catch my assailant, it is too late. If you truly believed me to be in danger, you would have flown here as fast as you could. Instead, you walked in with the speed of a mortal." Somewhere in her sleep-befuddled mind, she reasoned that perhaps Julien had indeed hurried to her side, but she felt isolated and violated after that dream.

"He forced himself into my dream. Perhaps my well-being is not as important to you, or perhaps it is, because you sensed him here." She sat up and met Julien's stare. She then held up her right hand, silencing him before he could speak. "No matter," Máire added. "I am not your wife, or even your mistress. I have whomever I want, whenever I want. This is the way I've been, how our family, the Deargh Du, have been since our mortal days of romping in haystacks. Besides, you've lain with many women. In your narrow, Frankish way of thought, as a woman, I cannot fight, nor can I fuck. Oh wait, I can fornicate with you, but no one else." She slid back against the cot. "Admit it. There is pettiness in your eyes when I see you watching Marcus and I, or any other man."

Julien sighed and stroked her hair again. "This is the remnants of your past attack talking. Perhaps you confuse me with some man in the past, sweetheart. I am concerned for you. Mandubratius would harm you in these dreams or in your waking state. I am sorry I left your side and rendered you vulnerable to his entertainments."

"Ha!" Máire cried out, without an ounce of mirth. "Do you presume to stand between Mandubratius and myself? Are you defending me from him? Do you think me so weak? I was possessed by Morrigan Herself and nearly killed him, once. I have nothing to fear from him, and I do not need your protection."

Julien's eyes grew sad, and she could swear she witnessed tears. "You needed my protection a few nights ago, Máire."

"What?" Her anger faded, and she found herself confounded.

"Some Strigoi stabbed you from behind. Then, he started feeding from you. He would have killed you, if I had not killed him first. I picked up the mirror... thank the Gods it had not shattered... and I turned it on a number of Strigoi, but I continued to watch over you and keep you from harm." Julien's voice sounded of deep sorrow. "Marcus brought you here, but I healed you. Why don't you have a modicum of respect for me, when I feel love and respect for you?"

Máire felt her eyes water, and she began to sob into her hand. "Julien, I do respect you. I am so sorry. I am so confused, and I'm making no sense. First, during the Strigoi attack, I felt my dead husband-to-be tear my heart out. Then, he," she added while gesturing to the other cot, "sneaked his way into my bed from my dream. It felt as though I were raped, because I never would have had coitus with him. I did not intend to say the things I said to you, Julien. I love you. Please forgive me for being so hurtful." Máire sniffed and wiped her face. When she felt Julien's hand encircle hers, she opened her eyes and stared at him.

"Did you say you love me?" he asked.

She stared back at him, dumbfounded by his claim.

Did I say that? Impossible.

"I'm sorry," Máire whispered. "You must be mistaken. I'm cursed, remember? Seosaimhín's curse is so strong, chroí." She grasped his hand and sat up before feeling dizzy. "I must rest," she whispered, sliding back into her bed, "before I say anything else that offends you, my love." She closed her eyes, as incoherence overwhelmed her. Passing into sleep again, she woke for a moment, as someone slid into the cot and held her. He smelled of mistletoe, wine, sweet honey, and ginger. She felt Julien kiss her brow and nuzzle her neck with a few day's worth of beard growth. Máire smiled as the tickling sensation continued.

Julien awoke, upon hearing the door close. He had collapsed into a deep sleep, along with Máire, after their conversation, but he could not tell how long he had slept. When he slid out of the cot, Julien noticed that Mandubratius had left them. Part of him wished to be selfish and continue holding Máire, but the other part of him wanted desperately to find that Lamia and cleave his head from his neck.

While still in a sleepy daze, Julien walked out of the room, ambled down the stairs, and found himself leaving the inn. An early evening greeted him. As he glanced around, looking for that bellicose Briton, Julien noticed that the villagers and the guards moved about their homes listlessly. He extended his senses and found his quarry. After drawing down darkness around him and creeping into the forest towards his prey, Julien heard a familiar voice, which shot daggers up and down his spine.

"So… she loves you." A soft chuckle echoed in the glen.

Julien turned towards the voice and released the darkness to the shadows. He tried to hide his shock of being discovered as he spied Mandubratius leaning against a tree. "You had no right to listen in on our conversation," Julien argued. "You also had no cause to enter her dream and antagonize her."

This will come to no good. How could I possibly forget all of those warnings from the others about dealing with this particular Lamia?

Despite his previous blustering, Julien decided to turn away and return to the inn. Before he could take two steps, Mandubratius' jovial voice shattered the silence between then.

"Antagonize?" Mandubratius laughed again. "I see. Máire lies. She truly enjoyed the experience, but she would never admit to it. Besides, I had every right to listen in to you and her making idiotic declarations of love for each other. Although, I must admit that hearing your mutual avowals of love made me laugh… hysterically. Know you that, like the Appian Way, Máire's cunny has been tread upon by thousands of travelers."

Julien lost all conscious thought. He clenched his fists and turned to strike the other blood-drinker, but his disappointment and frustration grew, as Mandubratius easily dodged and ducked every punch, all the while continuing to smile and occasionally laugh. Soon, however, a loud voice startled Julien.

"Why in Morrigan's name are you two fighting?" demanded Marcus in an officious tone. He frowned at them both. "I am certain you started this," Marcus accused Mandubratius.

"My apologies, General… Praetor… whatever your title is these nights." Mandubratius laughed before clasping his left hand on Julien's right shoulder. "And I am most regretful if I've offended you, puppy. I was merely surprised by your lack of proper perspective. After all, while Máire is a sweet and delicate flower, she is a flower that has been plucked often. Just ask Marcus. He's plucked her the most."

Julien watched Marcus glare at the Lamia with a growing intensity, but after a moment, he returned his gaze to Julien, and his stare faded into a placidity. Marcus said nothing at first, but after another brief pause, he said something surprising. "He is not lying. It is in her nature to behave this way, Julien. Mandubratius, you cannot possibly understand what it means to have fae blood, as a Deargh Du, and feel the inclination for acts of coitus, so leave it." Marcus turned away.

"He is lying," Julien yelled at Marcus's back, furious that his grandfather-in-darkness would say such things about his own family instead of defending them. "How can you, of all people, sully her name by siding with this… uncouth boor?" Julien watched Marcus shrug a little before turning back to face them.

In a calm voice, Marcus retorted, "Julien. When you have known Máire long enough, you will find that she prefers extensive varieties and high frequencies. It is not an insult… rather, it is normal for Deargh Du to behave in this manner. It is just the way she is, the way we all are. To deny this behavior in others, or yourself, denies the blood in your veins. I will say no more." Marcus then walked towards the gathering night guard.

Mandubratius crossed his arms over his chest and smiled in a smug manner.

Julien puffed up his chest and said, "I don't care what you and Marcus say about Máire. She has the bearing of an innocent."

"Innocent my arse!" Mandubratius crowed. "Máire will have coitus with any living man or blood-drinker. Then, if her blood thirst has not ceased, she may sate herself by killing her mate."

"She should have killed you when she had the chance," Julien hissed.

"Is that so?" Mandubratius queried, laughing again. "Perhaps Inspector General Julien de Divio, newborn Deargh Du, desires to remedy that unfortunate turn of events." His eyes gleamed with a red luminosity.

"Perhaps I will… someday," Julien replied. He then glanced back at the inn. "Leave my mother-in-darkness alone. Máire is consumed with her curse and does not need you to augment her anguish." After speaking, Julien turned back to face the Lamia, knowing that he must, otherwise it would be nothing more than a game. As he glared at the Lamia, he noticed that Mandubratius' ready smile soon faded into a reflective frown.

Mandubratius shifted to contemplate the moon with a studious fervor of an astrologist of antiquity and murmured, "Go home, puppy."

Julien felt a moment of confusion before moving away to return to the inn.

Did the mention of the curse subdue Mandubratius or was it something else?

Vézelay

Heloise closed her eyes and considered allowing herself to sleep.

Clotilda had fallen asleep early, after wearing herself out playing and demanding to know when her father, and now uncle, would return for her.

How does one explain to a child that her newly-found father wasn't mortal? Perhaps Marcus might be able to find a solution. Surely, such a thing was not that unusual.

Lirienne's moods had been vacillating between pouting over Reginald's insults and contentment over her upcoming nuptials. Both her daughter and granddaughter now slept in her bed.

Heloise placed another blanket over them and decided to rest in front of the hearth. After walking downstairs, she sat down with a basket of sewing. However, a sound made Heloise turn away from the warmth of the fire, and she noticed Alais staring at her with a small smile. "Does Lirienne need my assistance again?" Heloise asked with a smirk. "My daughter needs to develop fortitude."

"No, my Lady. Sáerlaith returns and wishes to speak to you."

Heloise nodded to the regal woman who had walked up behind Alais. "Sáerlaith? How may I be of service to you?" Heloise queried.

"Lady Heloise, I may be of service to you," Sáerlaith answered. "May we speak?" she asked politely while nodding towards Alais, indicating that she wished for privacy.

"Alais, I will call for you if we need you," Heloise said before motioning for Sáerlaith to join her at the hearth. Both women, leaders of their respective groups, then sat down in front of the warm flames.

Heloise glanced at the beautiful woman, who seemed ageless in the firelight, and asked, "Have you come to tell me news of Julien?"

"Unfortunately, I have not heard from him," Sáerlaith answered. "However, I am here to speak to you about something else."

Heloise watched her guest's eyes dart about as if nervous. "Please continue," she persuaded Sáerlaith.

"This is regarding Reginald," Sáerlaith answered. "The woman that he was with, that Talia, as she is called now, is Lamia. That is the same race as Amata and Legate Patroclus, whom you hosted earlier. The Lamia are quite proficient at manipulating mortals. Some can even influence us. I am concerned for the protection of you, your family, and your vassals."

Heloise leaned forward. "Is this Talia evil? Does she harbor designs on Reginald?"

"Yes. She has designs on many, but it's not because of what she is, but because of who she is, that may be the reason behind her actions. She's a Brugundian of a noble family, I am told."

Heloise felt her throat constrict in shock. "She's that old?" she whispered.

"Many of us are older than her," Sáerlaith replied. "I have seen over a thousand cycles."

Heloise tried, and failed, to fully grasp how this woman, who looked a decade or more younger than Heloise, could actually be older than Jesus... or even Methuselah, for that matter. "And what is this Brugundian doing with my son?" Heloise asked while grasping the arms of her chair.

"Well, it could be absolutely nothing, but they could also be plotting something."

"He demanded our lands," Heloise muttered. "That's what she wants, but why does this concern you? You're head of the council of the Deargh Du."

Sáerlaith smiled. "I have an interest in my extended family, Heloise.

Marcus is not my child-in-darkness, but he is my family, thus so are Máire and Julien. However, there is an ulterior motive I have for coming here."

Heloise nodded her head. She knew there must be some reason for the generosity of these so called mercenaries. "Go on, please."

"Lady Heloise, my people are homeless," Sáerlaith admitted, before leaning in and taking Heloise's right hand. "You have taken some of us in during our time of need, and we are most appreciative. You know who and what we are, and you accept our existence without hatred or fear. You are the lady of these lands. I am hopeful that you and I can negotiate some sort of agreement, where in exchange for keeping your family in power and Reginald and Talia at bay, we could build a stronghold within your lands and feed from your people."

Heloise arose from her seat and began to pace the length of the room, contemplating this enormous proposal. The Deargh Du offered protection to her family, but that would require a sacrifice of blood and land. Yet, sharing her blood with the Deargh Du had been a most pleasurable experience. They healed their victims. Heloise's feeding experience seemed like a pleasant dream. She reasoned that if this activity occurred in Éire, surely these other Deargh Du control their bloodletting and have perfected their methods of feeding.

"Sáerlaith, you said the Deargh Du would protect my family, but for how long? Until the end of this crisis, until I die–"

"Until no descendant of yours draws breath," Sáerlaith interjected. "We are long-lived, after all."

Heloise pondered the answer and weighed the costs and benefits. Finally, with her decision made, she said, "Sáerlaith, you and your friends have done so much to assist us. I couldn't begin to repay you. Since you seek a home and food, I will do my best to provide you with the needed resources."

"Thank you, Lady Heloise," Sáerlaith said, "perhaps–" The Deargh Du paused and smiled.

Upon hearing tiny footfalls, Heloise turned and saw Clotilda peer into the room.

"Where's papa?" Clotilda whimpered, rubbing her eyes. "I want to see papa. Will he return with Lady Talia?"

Heloise picked up her granddaughter and carried her to the hearth. She met Sáerlaith's eyes, for a moment, and embraced Clotilda. "Your aunt Lirienne and I will be taking care of you, now. Clotilda, that man is not your father, and Lady Talia is an evil crone that eats children." Heloise wiped her granddaughter's soggy eyes, which were the clear blue of the summer skies, much like her father's and grandfather's.

"But she was nice to me." Tildy's chin wobbled.

"No, my sweet pumpkin. She used us all to get to him," Heloise explained to Clotilda.

Sáerlaith handed Heloise a piece of cloth and backed away, as if unsure of her place.

"No, please stay," Heloise said to the Deargh Du. Her granddaughter found the others of that race to be fascinating. They murmured ancient tales and fascinating stories to little Clotilda. In turn, Clotilda had said that she believed they must be a group of fae. The young child insisted Máire must be their 'fire queen'. Marcus was simply 'The King'.

Gods know where children come up with such things.

Sáerlaith smiled and drew closer to Heloise and Clotilda, who sniffed.

Heloise placed the cloth over Clotilda's nose. "Blow," she directed the child. After Clotilda blew, Heloise wiped her nose and tossed it into the hearth.

"What do you mean?" Clotilda asked while sniffing again. "Who's my papa, then?"

"Your uncle Julien is your father, Clotilda. He isn't your uncle. You will understand when you are grown."

The girl sniffed again. "Uncle Julien? He's nice. He tells the best stories. So, what is my pa...?" Clotilda's face revealed her confusion.

Heloise looked over at Sáerlaith, who nodded her head in understanding. "Reginald is your uncle," Heloise explained.

"He made me cry," Clotilda whispered. "He didn't save mama. He said it was my fault that she and my brothers died. I want my mama." Clotilda began sobbing again.

Heloise watched Sáerlaith wince as if she may start crying herself.

Sáerlaith hugged Clotilda, stroking her back. "There, there," Sáerlaith said in gentle tones. "Your real papa loves you very much. He will be back soon."

"He will?" Clotilda asked.

"Yes, very soon," Heloise answered. "Now, you go back to grandmama's bed, my little pumpkin, and I will tuck you in."

"Will the Fire Queen, her King, and their court return?" Clotilda asked.

"Yes, pumpkin," Heloise said, hugging her granddaughter.

Once released, Clotilda wiggled down to the floor and raced for the stairs.

As Heloise sighed, Sáerlaith offered her another square of cloth.

Heloise accepted the offered cloth and sat down. "Thank you," she murmured before blowing her nose. "She's lost her brothers, mother, and in a way her father. If Reginald has his way, little Clotilda will grow up as a pauper or nun, not the lady of these lands. I would sorely like your help in preventing Talia from taking what she desires."

"Talia owns much of Burgundy," Sáerlaith replied. "If Reginald wrests control of your familial properties, she will practically have all of Burgundy. She is trying to regain the legacy of her grandfather, or so I heard. She escaped to Éire after the conquest, vowing one day to return and possess all that she claims belongs to her."

"Why haven't you killed that beast?" Heloise queried, clenching her fists.

"Her life is not mine to take," Sáerlaith answered. "You see, the Fire Queen," Sáerlaith paused with a smile, "who I assume is Máire, is her niece. Talia betrayed her and her family during the days when Máire was Maél Muire, a mortal chieftain in Éire." Sáerlaith grew silent for a moment. "After over two hundred years, this is the first opportunity she has had for vengeance. I cannot take that from Máire."

"Can you thwart Talia's plans?" Heloise asked.

"We can attempt to capture her and your son," Sáerlaith answered.

"If we take Reginald away from Talia, will he be himself?"

Sáerlaith rose again. "I don't know, but we'll try to find him and free him."

Heloise inhaled and yawned a little.

Sáerlaith smiled at her. "I do believe it's time for you to go to sleep. My associates and I will make plans to travel to Époisses."

Heloise nodded before ambling from her chair and ascending upstairs, where Clotilda would be waiting. She hoped her granddaughter would come to terms with having a new father.

Szeged

As Marcus sipped at his wine, he stared down at the full plate in front of him. A whimpering dog caught his attention, so he hid a portion of his lamb and then tossed it to the dog. The mortals seemed oblivious to his actions. He sat in a large dining hall with seven other people, including the lord of the village and his family.

The spacious and solid house exuded signs of past wealth under a current ugly exterior and interior. However, it served to protect many, now. The people of the village congregated here for protection. He could hear them speaking to one another during their meal.

"So, where is the inspector general?" Lord Elias asked. "I was hoping he could join us this evening."

Before leaving for this meal, Marcus had searched for Julien and found him healing some of the blood-drinkers recovering from their battle wounds.

"He is helping heal some of the wounded angels," Marcus answered. While he knew his answers were the worst of lies, he could not fathom how else he could explain blood-drinkers.

Doris, the lady of the lands, spoke up and said, "If only that fool of an empress had the dedication of these angels and the inspector general."

"You and your angels have blessed us by keeping these demons at bay," Elias added. "How can we ever repay the angels of God for this? Even churches and missions to convert heathens seem small compensation in comparison."

Marcus sighed, wondering why mortals always demanded to know this. He decided it may be best just to tell them to attempt to be kind to others. "Do not judge what you do not understand. Try to be compassionate to all beings on this earth." He felt ridiculous for saying such a thing, as he could not remember being compassionate about anything as a mortal.

The mortals fell silent, for a moment, but then one of the lord's sons asked, "Do you still believe that we must leave our home?"

"Yes, I do," Marcus answered, grateful for the change in topics.

"But why?" another family member asked. "The demons have not struck again, since your successful defense of our home."

"Because they will return," Marcus said, after finishing off the dregs of wine. "We must all retreat to the west."

"Why the west?" Elias asked.

Marcus thought over his options on revealing the truth, but he instead decided to lie, as if the habits of the Lamia had now become his own.

How could one protect the innocent and not frighten them with the reality?

"There is an army of angels in Aachen," he began to explain, "waiting for the holy relic. This army can send the demons back to hell and repair those mortals under their sway." Marcus gave up on further explanations and wondered whether they would believe this tale. He summoned a bit of his glamoury to confuse the mortals.

"Will we be lucky enough to see this glorious army of angel-kind?" Lady Doris asked before nibbling on some bread.

"Perhaps," Marcus chuckled. He started feeling overwhelmed with their questions, but they did serve as a distraction from those strange dreams the Strigoi had brought with them.

While the family members discussed darker subjects, Marcus sensed Julien moving through the house, and he hoped his arrival would distract the family and their vassals. Marcus questioned whether his and Julien's earlier quarrel could be considered finished. Julien seemed dedicated to protecting Máire's virtue, which Marcus considered to be a truly noble pursuit for a man in this day, but Máire's talents lay in her skills, not in falsified assets, such as innocence and incorruptibility.

Perhaps soon, Julien would realize that her baseness in virtue did not make her a bad person. Marcus thought that a further explanation of these matters could help smooth the situation between them, yet they may not have the luxury of time. He decided that their discomfort would pass during their travels, but then Lord Elias interrupted Marcus' musing.

"Never in my lifetime did I expect to see a single angel, yet an entire army is a true blessing. Inspector General, what a pleasant surprise. Marcus informed us you were helping God's angels. Please join us." Elias stood up and gestured for his family to make room for Julien.

As Julien turned towards Marcus, his eyes still reflected that earlier rage because Marcus would not defend Máire against the harsh truths that Mandubratius loved to exploit. "Máire is awake, again. She is weak, but the others are taking turns feeding her."

Marcus nodded and then paused for a moment. "Do you believe she will be able to travel by tomorrow?"

"Tomorrow night, yes," Julien answered before sitting down in the offered chair. "She says she needs you to sit with her. She has ominous dreams that you may understand."

Marcus nodded. "I will do so." He paused mid-thought, considering the care of the mortals, instead of Máire. As he thought of their predicament, he watched one of the servants pour Julien a goblet of wine and pass over a plate of food. With Máire's improved condition, his course of action was clear. "We must leave tomorrow at dusk," Marcus announced before facing Elias. "My Lord, could you start gathering the remainder of your vassals here?"

"You wish us to travel at night?" Elias queried. "Perhaps it would be best for the people of this village to travel from midday to midnight."

"We can protect the people at night only," Marcus said. "The demons are subject to the whims of the sun and cannot abide the light."

"In order to be able to fight the demons at night, we must rest during the day," Julien recommended.

"I see," Elias answered. "I would rather have the protection of your family of angels during the darkness. If that means traveling at night, so be it."

"Then, we must make preparations to travel at dusk." Marcus closed his eyes for a moment, hoping all would go to plan.

Lying in the cot, curled up in a fetal position, Irene tried to forget the experiences and memories from the last few nights. Nightmares had come to her on winged horrors at all times of day and night. She heard whispers about the dreaded thoughts all those attacked had suffered, yet they seemed to muddle through their fears. However, her own qualms overwhelmed her sensibilities.

"Nagirrom," she whispered to herself, as if inciting shivers to move up and down her spine. She wondered whether the other blood-drinkers would arrive and shout that single word at her when they took turns feeding her or placed their hands on her wounds.

Irene's eyes swam with tears, upon remembering the anguish in her dreams. She wiped her face with the woolen blanket, hating it for its scratchy texture and yet grateful for the warmth, when she sensed the presence of someone. She looked up and saw Mandubratius peering at her from the open door. A strange, strong odor of honey and herbs swelled as he neared.

"Empress, I'm so glad to see you well," he murmured.

"You stink," she accused. "How dare you approach me? You did little to protect me."

"My apologies, love, but I believed you to be well protected by your guard." Mandubratius pulled a stool over to her cot and sat down next to her. He then stroked her hair. "I must admit some relief that the Celtic lines were here to heal you. You should feel quite honored, since Marcus spent more time healing you than he did his own child-in-darkness. Of course, many are willing to heal the endearing piglet."

Irene grumbled under her breath. "Healing me, how?" She suddenly felt as though someone had violated her.

"Oh, you were unconscious. Most of us were lucky, love. The Strigoi only chose you and Máire to feed upon." Mandubratius took her hand and traced his fingers over hers. "After the Strigoi struck you with their madness, they sliced you open. We brought you here to recover, and Marcus and some of the others healed you."

"And now I'm bound to him… them." Irene stared up into those large green eyes, dejected by the prospect of owing her life to others.

Mandubratius shrugged a little. "Doubtful. Marcus considers saving lives his duty. He is disgustingly good and fair. The Deargh Du are a strange race, Irene, and he is one of the strangest. Also, the villagers here believe us all to be angels, thanks to our efforts and the effects of your mirror."

"My mirror," Irene whispered. "The last time I saw my mirror, that red-headed Deargh Du took it from me… that woman from my orgy, who you tried to make jealous." Irene chuckled weakly.

Mandubratius smirked while placing his right pointing finger over his mouth and sucking at the digit. After a few moments of silence, he removed the finger from his lips.

"Returning to the mirror," he explained, "it removed the ugliness and madness from several of the Strigoi. They became something different. While they are still blood-drinkers, they have grace and minds of their own, now."

"How long have I been unconscious?" Irene queried, still drowsy and weak from her ordeal.

"Two nights," Mandubratius answered. "Since you and Máire have recovered, we will travel to the west at dusk and leave this village behind."

"Have they attacked us again?" Irene asked, clutching his hand. She feared another onslaught.

"No, not yet," he murmured while his other hand began stroking her hair again. "Yet, they will retaliate soon." After a brief pause, he added, "Empress, I know you have received some training, but how astute are you in the arts of Mars?" His face seemed concerned.

"I can wield a sword," Irene answered, "not as well as the soldiers, but well enough... well enough to become empress of the newly-reformed Lamia... Empress of the Lamia!" She watched him smile and chuckle a little in response to her statement. "Do not laugh at me," she ordered him, feeling her rage rise.

He stopped and studied her with an alluring stare that made her burn.

"You are trying to manipulate me again," she stated. "I know this should make me angry, and it does. However, it is also most impressive. You must teach me to refine these skills, Mandubratius."

"Perhaps I will," he purred, sliding into her cot. He then smiled at her in that omniscient manner of his.

"You think I need you to help me rule the Lamia after we defeat these Strigoi." She could not help but wonder if that were possible, now.

Mandubratius' left hand slid over her hip. He leaned in and began to nibble at her throat.

She shivered in growing excitement at the feel of his mouth against her neck. She inhaled at the sensation of his teeth breaking through her skin, as he began to lick and suck at the bloody wound.

"Empress," he whispered in her ear. "You will never want to be rid of me. You do need my guidance, and I need a woman such as you to entertain me."

Irene smiled for a moment, as he resumed nibbling her throat and caressing her breasts. He soon began to rub himself against her thigh. She felt him begin to toss aside his clothing.

"I daresay you need me as well," Mandubratius advised. "No one in this village or amongst our party is as entertaining or exciting as I can be." His breath made her quiver again.

"Mandubratius," Irene sighed, wishing she could talk them both out of this. "Damn this, I'm weak and I do need you now." By her reckoning, Gaius possessed the rough, callused manners of a soldier, and Sextus reminded her too much of her son. She couldn't trust those strangers in their party. Irene rolled over to face Mandubratius on the small bed.

He pulled off her simple dress and grinned at her. His fingers then danced over her again. "Then, all you need to do is ask," he said in a gentle and soft undertone. He traced one of his fingers over her swollen nipple and then palmed her breast gently.

She heard herself utter a sigh, and soon a strong burn raced through her body. Irene slid her hands down the resilient muscles of his back. At the same time, she felt a rock hard erection slide over her sex, promising sweet delights, but only if she allowed him access. She felt his hands lift her up, teasing the soft folds of warmth at the apex of her legs. Irene heard Mandubratius utter something she did not understand as he rubbed in eager anticipation against her damp center.

She wondered whether it was his ancient tongue for a moment, but she forgot about those thoughts, when the torrent of sensual gratification continued. His firm flesh made her breathless as he stroked her, teasing them both. She wrapped herself around his body and ground against him in a silent plea for satisfaction.

With a push, he thrust himself into her, filling her.

Her hands stroked down his back as she took all of him within her. Impatient with his movements she rolled him over. She arched her body against his in a frenzy of yearning, easily forgetting that she shouldn't be doing this. She knew Mandubratius would use this to his advantage.

He arched towards her, increasing the tempo of their movements, before slowing. He then moved his hand between them, and he started stroking her.

The hypnotic attention of Mandubratius rubbing against her in slow, insistent circles made Irene cry out and increase the depth of each thrust, unable to keep herself still. She sensed his hands glide to cup her backside, and she heard herself begin to groan in completion. As their movements became frantic, she wrapped herself around him tightly, feeling herself begin to peak again as he convulsed inside her.

He bucked within, filling her in staccato spasms. The movement brought her back to the edge as she came again, and Mandubratius stroked her body with his hands.

Irene slid against him and trembled a bit, as she leaned in to feed from him. Mandubratius tasted of honey, flowers, and spices, which seemed odd to her, somehow.

As he leaned forward to scratch at her throat, he ran his hands through her hair and suckled blood from her again.

She licked at his wound and stared down at Mandubratius, while he stared up at her with those impish green eyes. When his eyes closed, she stared down at his thick, long eyelashes. She wondered whether she would ever truly control their kind, or whether he would simply manipulate the situation to his favor.

Irene sighed, knowing the truth, and slid off Mandubratius. She felt his arm envelope her and pull her in closer. Irene reasoned that she may as well admit to the fact that he would always try to find ways to manipulate her into bending to his will.

chapter seventeen

Vézelay

s Sáerlaith wandered towards the grove, she heard the soft echo of a heartbeat. Her eyes soon revealed the silhouette of Lady Heloise, who stood in front of the altar, making an offering of some sort. Sáerlaith paused, lowered her head, and waited for the Lady of Vézelay to complete her ritual. After some moments, Sáerlaith sensed the mortal complete her ceremony… the mists had departed, allowing Lady Heloise to see the landscape and her guest.

Sáerlaith cleared her throat. "You have a beautiful grove here," she complimented, taking a few steps closer to her host. "You and your family must have done your best to keep it clean. It is most impressive. In Éire, so many of our groves have fallen into disrepair. It breaks my heart to see what has happened to some of our holy places."

Lady Heloise gave her a gentle smile. "Thank you. A group of like-minded women in Burgundy meet here with me for the sacred rituals."

Sáerlaith closed the distance with the other woman and spoke in more conversational, secretive tones. "Sometimes, it is up to the women to keep our sacred knowledge. So, what have you learned, Lady Heloise? I assume that this has been a life-long study for you."

"It feels like several lives," Heloise chuckled. "My family has had a hand in ancient knowledge for some time. I have discovered that many were Druids. They may have gone to Britannia or Éire to further their studies, but I am not certain. However, we broke with tradition and began to write things down."

Lady Heloise wrapped her left arm around Sáerlaith and began escorting her to the house. "My family felt fearful about the threats from Rome, so we began to document our rituals and practices. I have translated some, but due to limitations in linguistic skills, some of our group rituals are merely ancestral memory, intuition, and our own ideas." She sighed and then studied Sáerlaith. "However, I believe that you are not here to discuss Druidic practices."

Before Sáerlaith could respond, an Ekimmu Cruitne ran towards them, calling her name. She turned towards the blood-drinker and asked, "Yes?"

"There is a messenger here for Lady Heloise. Shall we allow him to pass?" asked the newcomer, looking at Heloise.

"Yes, of course," Lady Heloise replied.

Sáerlaith waited with Lady Heloise in silence, while the Ekimmu Cruitne ran towards the house to retrieve the messenger. In anticipation of the dreaded news, she forgot her response and her reason for seeking Lady Heloise.

As soon as the messenger came within earshot of them, he called out, "Lady Heloise?" When he reached them, he opened his pouch, revealing an official document from the imperial court in Aachen. With a nod from Heloise, he passed her the scroll.

After reading it, she closed her eyes. "It is as we feared. Reginald is challenging Julien and I for our lands."

"And what do you intend to do?" Sáerlaith asked.

"I will fight this," she spat, rolled up the scroll, and turned back to the messenger. "Inform Ercanbald that we will go to Aachen and defend ourselves against these charges."

The messenger bowed his head and then raced back towards the barn.

Heloise looked at Sáerlaith and said, "I will speak to Reginald and try to convince him that such action against his own blood would be unwise." She then studied the skies, for a moment. "The sun rises soon. But, of course, you know this."

Sáerlaith nodded in acknowledgement.

"Funny," Heloise continued. "Julien told me that so much has changed in the course of his transformation to Deargh Du, such as how some things became innate knowledge for him... the time of sunrise and sunset, for example." She seemed introspective, for a brief time, before focusing back to Sáerlaith. "There is something I wish to show you. Let's go inside to the cellar."

Curious, Sáerlaith followed Lady Heloise into the house and down into the basement.

When Heloise reached the far corner, opposite the basement stairs, she started to feel along the wall at the level of her hip. Soon, she stopped at a particular point, before pushing in a loose stone. A hole then opened below the stone. Heloise reached within and pulled out a thick scroll case. When she depressed the stone again, the hole closed. The elder mortal then kneeled and tossed loose dirt onto the stones.

Heloise presented the scroll case to Sáerlaith and said, "You may find this interesting. These are the remembrances by my family of Germanic Druids. As I said earlier, some of these are in languages that I know... some I do not know. However, someone who has lived a long time and traveled may know these words."

Sáerlaith could feel the age of the knowledge inside. How she wished Ruarí could read these. To Heloise, she said, "This is most gracious to share this knowledge with me." She smiled, remembering his fondness for ancient literature. "I would like for you to travel with us. We can protect you and reach Aachen quickly," she added.

"You will carry me by yourself?" Heloise asked.

"No, but I'll have help. My associates will assist us."

"Thank you," Heloise murmured.

"We'll retrieve you when we are ready. Be certain to pack food and clothing. These manuscripts deserve my full attention, and I will do my best to read them, but not until after this matter with your eldest is settled."

"Keep them," Heloise offered.

Sáerlaith felt surprise at the suggestion. "Really? Are you certain? These manuscripts are priceless, Lady Heloise."

Heloise smirked. "Each generation of my family makes, at least, one copy of these scrolls. I have a few copies in the house, as well as a few copies buried in the grove. You may find this useful."

"If Ruarí were here," Sáerlaith whispered before pausing. "Ruarí was Arch Druid and knew many languages. However, the next best person to translate this would be Máire or Marcus, who are well traveled and are educated in more cultures than I am. I know that Máire actively practices Druidism. Marcus, however, avoids magic, other than what all Deargh Du can accomplish, such as glamoury and bringing down the darkness, for reasons that I cannot comprehend." Sáerlaith grew silent, believing she knew the truth.

"Odd," Heloise murmured. "He seemed so comfortable in the grove. Perhaps, he practices it in a different way. In studying my associates, it seems that some people's talents in the magical realm are innate. Sometimes, Sáerlaith, those with powerful gifts fear the talents they can wield."

Sáerlaith smiled and chuckled. "I am glad that you honor me by calling me by my name, instead of saying 'Lady Sáerlaith'." She then felt her smile fade. "Yes, he may fear his talents. Marcus is unlike most Deargh Du," she added.

"I thought that might be the case," Heloise said before scrutinizing Sáerlaith's face. "You look tired, Sáerlaith." She leaned in and kissed Sáerlaith's cheek. "We should both rest, if we are to leave tonight. Sleep well."

"Thank you," Sáerlaith said, returning the kiss. She watched the elder Lady of Vézelay ascend the stairs to the ground level. Soon, those very same stairs echoed with the wearied footsteps of Deargh Du seeking the basement for the day.

Outside Szatymaz

Amata grumbled and rubbed her forehead, as the noises of a man and woman voicing their pleasure grew. Edward had avoided her during the tent assignments, so she threw in her lot with Marcus and Máire. So far, they did nothing more than speak two sentences to each other in quiet tones, as if trying to allow Amata sleep. She found herself a little disappointed that Marcus wasn't even attempting to talk her and Máire into sharing his blankets... not that she planned on a threesome, but the offer would have soothed her ego. Still, the noises continued unabated, and she felt irritated for not making them herself.

Máire rose up, not bothering to cover her thin tunic, and grumbled, "Who is that?"

"Who else but that woman," Amata replied before sitting up. "The Empress has to put on a show and scream the loudest. It doesn't help that Mandubratius loves to hear himself, whether he's speaking or moaning in pleasure."

In a sleepy voice, Marcus muttered, "I remember many times when you two had been so vocal." He then sat up.

Máire groaned and said, "You cannot judge the experience based on a woman's screams, or lack thereof." After lying down, she added, "Perhaps we should start making noises and give them the hint."

Amata chuckled, before saying, "At the most, Mandubratius might pause in the midst of all this love, cheer us on, and make promises to join us tomorrow. At the least, he won't care."

Máire rolled on her side, facing Amata, and grumbled, "Can I ask why you aren't staying with Edward?"

Amata shrugged, knowing they were bound to ask. "He's been a little distant," she said. "I think he is upset that I was so happy to see Mandubratius again. As much as your leech disgusts me, Máire, I cannot deny that he is a most charming scoundrel. Edward and I care for each other, but Mandubratius makes me laugh."

Marcus looked at her and quipped, "Honestly, Amata, you can hire a fool or village idiot to make you laugh. Hire the fool and leave your brother-in-darkness, while you can. If the Empress wants your place, let her take it. No one can rule forever. Sooner or later, the praetorian guard will assassinate the emperor."

"I know," Amata said with a sigh, hoping that would never be her fate. "However, I should not abandon the Lamia. You two must understand… you are both considered outcasts, in the eyes of the Deargh Du in Éire, right? Yet, you cannot deny what you are. You will always be Deargh Du. I will always be Lamia. I should not abandon those who may need a stable leader. Perhaps Mandubratius will change, one night, and I will feel secure leaving the Lamia to his leadership without me."

Marcus smiled at her. "After this is over, if you desire retirement, I will extend you an invitation to my home in Bath. Yet, I fear my home may be endangered, soon. I have the feeling that the Deargh Du of Ard Mhacha will not be satisfied with just Ard Mhacha for long." Marcus pulled his left hand from his blanket and took Máire's extended right hand. "One night, the Deargh Du of Ard Mhacha may decide to cleanse the earth of the Roman bastard and his slut," he added, sighing.

"Let's worry about that after we survive the Strigoi," Máire suggested, before emitting muted chuckles, which turned into a nervous snort, causing Amata to realize why the men referred to her as 'endearing piglet'.

Amata, however, thought one might describe Máire's giggles as amusing and appealing.

"Why is Mandubratius my leech, Amata?" Máire asked. "I have no claim to him, nor do I wish to have a claim to him."

Amata laughed. "He is your leech, Máire, because he wishes fervently to be attached to your side. Perhaps you should consider sleeping with him. Maybe the game will bore him, and he will turn all of his attentions to his new toy."

Máire snorted again in laughter and shook her head. "I am not sure which I would prefer to deal with," she replied.

Amata looked over at Marcus and, in a wistful tone, said, "I hope your home will be safe. I enjoyed my visit there. You never know... I may show up on your doorstep as a deposed consul of the Lamia, if the Empress has her way."

Marcus patted Máire's hand. "Gods willing, we will survive this Strigoi infestation, since we have the tool to do so. If the Empress deposes you, I will look forward to your visit, Amata. I will also speak to Edward on your behalf, if you wish."

"Your kindness shames me," she said. "Please tell him that I am sorry, and that I only wish for his happiness. If that means we do not have any kind of relationship, I understand." She lowered herself to her blankets and closed her eyes. "Good night, my friends," she murmured. She wondered whether she could rely on them. When a firm hand caressed her shoulder, the act only added to her worry that they might be as duplicitous as Mandubratius.

Vézelay

While tightening the thin leather strap on the scroll case, Sáerlaith could sense the dimming power of the sun as he faded to give deference to the growing moon.

The other Deargh Du continued to sleep, but a stir of motion caught her attention, and she looked across the basement to see Caoimhín open his eyes and give her a small grin.

She smiled back at him, while trying to take a moment to center herself from the sounds of mortals moving about upstairs, which grew too distracting. Sáerlaith closed her eyes and wondered where Talia and Reginald decided to hide in Aachen and how long it would be before Reginald found himself hiding during the day and imbibing blood. She soon opened her eyes, rose from Julien's bed, and walked to the staircase.

As soon as Sáerlaith reached the door upstairs and opened it, a young woman stopped her activities and lowered her brown eyes to the floor.

"Lady Sir-la," the servant murmured. "Lady Heloise asked me to feed you, if necessary. I have done so before." The young woman's eyes met hers for a brief moment.

"Ah, perhaps you've fed Julien?" Sáerlaith ascertained.

The servant shook her head and blushed. "I wished to, but he fed off others, so I offered sustenance to his companions."

"An unselfish act," Sáerlaith said. "I will make this fast for you." She then took the young woman's left arm, applied a little glamoury to cover the pain, and bit into the underside of her arm. Sáerlaith did not want to be greedy, but the soothing taste of the servant's blood made her lose herself. After a satisfactory meal, Sáerlaith licked at the thin delicious trail of blood drips and began to heal the young woman. "I presume Lady Heloise is awake, Alais," Sáerlaith stated.

"Yes. How did you know my name?" Alais asked before giggling softly.

"I learn things through your essence," Sáerlaith said while patting her arm.

"Will I need to be available for the others?" Alais asked with a smile.

"Perhaps. They will join me soon." Upon seeing Lady Heloise descend the stairs from the upper level, Sáerlaith bowed her head towards the elder of Vézelay, who beamed a smile. When the others arrived from the basement, she turned to face her party and said, "You may feed as necessary, but do it quickly, after I dismiss you. We must leave as soon as possible. Caoimhín, you will stay in my stead with the rest of the three thousand to watch Lady Heloise's residence and her family."

"Thank you," Heloise said before going down the stairs into the basement.

Caoimhín uttered a nervous laugh. "Be careful with Talia," he warned, grasping Sáerlaith's left arm. "She had no trouble influencing me in the grove."

Sáerlaith patted his arm. "She has a very strong and gifted sponsor. I promise to be careful, Caoimhín. However, I do have some good news. The Lady of Vézelay and I have agreed to a mutually beneficial arrangement for the protection of our families. She will give us a new home."

The beautiful Deargh Du appeared to blink back tears. He then lowered himself to his knees in gratitude and kissed Lady Heloise's hands.

"This is truly kind of you, but not necessary. You are the brood of Morrigan," Heloise said. "I should bow to you. However, I feel that as we are equals in this arrangement, we shall be equals otherwise."

Sáerlaith hugged Heloise. "When the others are ready, we will leave."

Outside of Szatymaz

The slow pace of the mortals' march through the woods gave Marcus increasing aggravation with each step. He soon sensed Julien come up next to him. The young man seemed a little upset that Máire had chosen to stay with Marcus during the last day instead of him. However, Máire and Amata spent most of their day giggling like old friends. Marcus did not find the experience exciting, but he did find it a relief... a distraction from the desperate dreams about the battle against the Helvetti and his mother. He found the silly giggling of women to be a welcome respite.

Marcus felt such gratitude for their aid that he cornered Edward early in the evening and spoke to him about Amata's situation. Now, Edward and Amata appeared to be speaking again. He reasoned that whatever came from the effort would be a surprise for all involved.

Marcus glanced at Julien for a moment and said, "As I informed Claudius and Arwin earlier, I did not have the opportunity to enjoy coitus with Máire and Amata at the same time. The noises you heard were from the Empress and her sponsor."

"It is not my business, but I do believe you," Julien said, sounding sheepish about the matter. "We should move past our disagreements and deal with them... when we are not in immediate danger."

"Agreed," Marcus assented. "We will have an honest talk with Máire."

Julien nodded his head. "I must admit, Marcus, that I grow weary of this slow pace, and now I worry that we may endanger our mortal associates."

Marcus stopped walking and closed his eyes to consider the situation. After a moment, he opened them and rejoined the march. "We could take the people of Szeged to the next village we come across."

"I know," Julien said, "but is it right to discard them like that?"

"They will be safer at the next village than they were in Szeged. As much as we should take care of the weak, Julien, we must also consider that we cannot do our other duties, now."

"True, but it may be difficult to convince them of that," Julien said.

Marcus patted Julien's left shoulder. "I am certain that you can persuade them, even without glamoury."

The young Deargh Du uttered a half-hearted laugh, and then both men became silent for several steps.

Julien ended the stillness. "I will do my best." The younger Deargh Du seemed introspective for a moment. "Marcus, have you ever wielded a magical object like the mirror?"

"I have held objects of antiquity, some of which were said to have been forged by the Gods themselves, but I have never wielded anything that emitted the power that mirror does." Marcus gave his arms an impulsive scratch, finding nervous energy to spare.

"So, I have done something in my short lifetime that you have not," the youngling boasted, grinning.

"Time has not yet ended, and neither has my life," Marcus drawled before chuckling. "Perhaps I will have an opportunity to use a magical implement soon. I hope it will be something impressive, like a sword."

At that moment, Mac Alpin landed a few feet away from them. "Finally," the Ekimmu Cruitne muttered, "I've found you two at last."

"Arwin, with your nose, you could have found us in a bog, buried under a bull's carcass," Marcus said.

"Yes, that is true," Mac Alpin agreed with a smirk.

"Is there an emergency?" Julien asked.

"No. However, Claudius and I found a village twenty miles ahead of us, which the locals call Szatymaz. It is larger than Szeged."

"It sounds like an excellent place to drop off our fares," Julien said. "They may find safety there, if we are of more interest to the Strigoi."

Marcus shrugged. "Unfortunately, we cannot protect all the mortals in this region. We must hope that we are a better target."

"The Strigoi are still slow. At least this village is some distance away from the other," Mac Alpin affirmed.

"Someone needs to inform them of this plan," Julien said.

Marcus smirked. "Why, that sounds like an excellent duty for the Inspector General of the Gendarmes."

"Perhaps, but I have no legal authority over inhabitants of the Eastern Empire," Julien said.

Mac Alpin barked a loud laugh. "Julien, your emperor's gendarmes never let simple things like borders stop them before."

"As I told you earlier, these people know and respect you. You freed some of them from a hopeless curse," Marcus added. "Besides, you can use glamoury to aid you, if necessary. These mortals wish to be led, Julien."

After a pause, Julien said, "I'll speak to Lord Elias and Father Xofer."

"Ask Father Xofer if his new flock wishes to continue with us," Marcus said. "This new group may aid us in defeating the Strigoi."

"As long as they are not as slow as the Strigoi," Mac Alpin added. "I feel the need to move at our normal speed."

"Yes, yes, I feel the same way," Julien said before heading for the middle of the mortal party.

"Lord Elias, Father Xofer," Julien greeted, nodding to the two men and matching their pace.

Both the Lord and priest inclined his head in respect. "Inspector General."

"If we could speak in private, for a moment," Julien said, while motioning for them to follow him away from the others.

"How can we be of service to you?" the priest asked with a serene smile.

"Szatymaz is a day's journey away. We would like to take your people there, Lord Elias, and leave you in their care."

As Julien watched Elias' lined face grow worried, he concentrated on exuding glamoury and radiance.

"I don't understand. You intend to leave us?" Lord Elias asked. Soon, however, his fearful eyes seemed to drift into relief.

"We were on a mission, my Lord. Before we encountered your village, we were on our way to Vézelay and Aachen to complete this mission. I am afraid that our pace has slowed so much that if we continue to escort you, we may lose the chance we have to meet the rest of the Angelic army. We have traveled far enough away from the demons, and we are now their true target." At least, he hoped that would be the truth.

"But, if the demons do attack us, we no longer have you to protect us," Lord Elias whispered.

Father Xofer put his left hand on the noble's right shoulder. "Have faith, my Lord. Faith will protect us." He smiled another gentle smile and then met Julien's eyes. His eyes glowed a strange orange for a brief moment, before becoming hazel-brown.

Lord Elias blinked and then asked, "Did you say Szatymaz?"

"Yes," Julien answered.

Elias beamed, while his eyes studied the stars, lost in their brilliance. "My nephew is lord of the lands, there. He has three hundred soldiers. Perhaps they can take care of us, Inspector General. Yes, we should do well there." He then met Julien's eyes. "Inspector General, this is a most acceptable plan. My nephew will protect us well, until your forces overwhelm Satan's army."

"Then, you will tell your vassals at dawn?" Julien asked. He studied Father Xofer, wondering whether this was a talent of the new race of blood-drinkers.

Will they bring good spirits and encouragement now, as opposed to insanity?

"Yes," Lord Elias said with a smile. "When I do, I'd like you, Marcus, and Father Xofer at my side."

"It would be our pleasure," Julien answered.

"And mine as well, Lord Elias," the priest added. "I need to speak to Lord

Jul... I mean the Inspector General for a moment, my Lord."

"Of course," Elias said. He returned to his family and took his wife's arm.

The priest watched Julien for a while, as if analyzing him. "I am sorry if I interrupted your workings on Lord Elias. I merely thought that giving him a good thought about the future may be of use to us. I had need of your ear."

"No, it was no interruption," Julien replied. "Thank you, Father Xofer. I am grateful for any assistance. I am a stranger to this new life, as much as you are. I fear that my training is not complete."

"I understand, but at least you have a family that wishes to teach you. I feel as though I am an unsure shepherd of a flock of wayward sheep," the priest said, but the deep air of piety around him seemed to fade like the mist.

"My friends and I wish for you, and the others who were demons, to join us," Julien said.

"We were not demons, my Lord," the priest replied. His eyes turned a deep brown as they settled on Julien, revealing his composure. "Nor are you and your friends angels."

Julien inhaled sharply, trying not to reveal his shock.

"Do not worry, young Deargh Du," the priest said. "I understand the need for deception. If the mortals knew what we truly were, they would fear us and likely try to do us harm. God allowed us to survive."

Julien could find no words.

"Yes, I was Strigoi. I know not what we will call ourselves now. However, I do know that you are Deargh Du, and there are Ekimmu Cruitne, Sugnwr Gwaed, and Lamia in our party," added the priest, while using his head to point towards some of the blood-drinkers.

"How did you know?" Julien whispered.

"The Strigoi are able to have some knowledge when a mortal is transformed to Strigoi. That intelligence is shared by all."

"You remember–" Julien began to say, when Xofer interrupted.

"Yes, even through the transformation you and Máire wielded with the mirror," the priest answered. He then turned with alacrity and faced Julien, before dropping to his knees. "I am forever indebted to you, as are the others like me, for restoring us from madness. I have a clear memory of every evil and atrocity that I committed against my flock and others. Yet, I know Madness controlled me, as if Madness were a person. Even though my mind screamed no, I still performed Madness' bidding." The priest's voice shook, and he began to shed tears.

Julien kneeled, to be at Father Xofer's eye level. "You say Madness was, in essence, a person?"

The priest wiped his face with a sleeve. "Yes, I do."

"Do you know if it was a man or woman who held the reins of Madness?"

"Madness is a woman," answered the clergyman.

"Can you describe her for me?"

"It will sound like lunacy," Father Xofer warned. He stopped crying and focused for a moment. "She had the most beautiful skin of ebony I have ever seen," he began to explain. In a feverish manner, without pauses, he added, "Yet, I have seen dark-skinned tradesman before, and she was nothing like them. She was black as the starless sky, my Lord, with hair like the moon. Her eyes would, at times, become nothing but pure white. I sensed madness in that beautiful woman, but she was not Strigoi. She told us rambling tales of other races, but she had the oddest names for them. Some she referred to as 'Soulless ones'. She said they were all to be hunted down and killed. She said Nagirrom wished it to be so and that we owed fealty to Nagirrom. It was our duty to spread Nagirrom's name throughout all of the empires. My Lord, do you know who this 'Nagirrom' is?"

Julien shrugged. "That name is not familiar to me, Father Xofer." As Julien rose, he helped the priest to his feet. "Yet, I believe the statue we found in the cave could be Nagirrom."

"The cave, yes," the priest drawled. "That is where Madness harnessed her powers through strange, Pagan rituals... no offense to your kind," the priest added quickly. "I sense a great many beliefs that I have no knowledge of within your family and yourself."

"No offense taken, Father," Julien said. "How much do the others know?"

"Everything that I do," Father Xofer answered. "I have given them some comfort in knowing that they should not judge themselves for what they did in Madness' grasp. God forgives, and I pleaded with them not to reveal what we... and you... are to those who were not touched. It is better to be a false angel than a burned and dead demon."

Soon, they started to walk again in order to catch up to the rest of the party.

"So, will you join us?" Julien asked.

"I will, as will the rest of the flock," the priest answered. "We can travel–"

Julien heard the sound of wind whispering around him, and with his Deargh Du eyes, he tracked the priest, as he shifted into an accelerated speed and circled around him. Julien blinked at the unexpected display and found the priest directly behind him, grinning.

"I daresay we can move as quickly as any Lamia," the priest answered.

"I will tell the others the good news," Julien said, but before he could take another step, he felt a hand reach for his shoulder. He looked back and met the priest's eyes again.

"Thank you for taking us with you, my Lord," Xofer said. "You have every right to kill us for what we did to you and yours. I know what fears Madness instilled, nurtured, and brought forth in the others. I am not sure whether we can assuage these fears, but we are sorry for what we did."

"Then help us, Father," Julien whispered, "and use your newfound skills to give peace to those who are troubled."

Julien felt the hand squeeze and release his shoulder. He then quickened his pace, so he could walk to the head of the line with Marcus and Mac Alpin. Behind him, he sensed the priest return to his place with Lord Elias' family. After a few steps, Gaius and Mandubratius joined them.

With the leaders together, Julien announced in quiet tones, "They have agreed to stay in Szatymaz."

"Excellent," Marcus said with a grin. "Well done."

Mandubratius chuckled and said, "So, that means we can finally increase our pace and be on our way. Well done indeed, puppy."

"Don't call me puppy," Julien hissed.

Arwin cleared his throat and said, "There was a puppy called Setanta, once, who grew up to become the hound and champion of Ulster. Cu Chulainn gained a reputation that you must know of, Awvarwy." The elder blood-drinker then smirked at Julien and winked.

"Let's forget this disagreement for now," Marcus advised. "What did the priest say, Julien?"

"He says that all of the changed Strigoi are most grateful to be asked to continue the journey, despite what they did, and perhaps because of it. They wish to continue with us."

Máire, Julien noticed, walked along the periphery of their group, keeping her distance from the Lamia. When he wasn't looking at her, he felt her fingers trace over his hand for a brief moment, but then she pulled away... too soon.

"Are you certain this is wise?" she asked, while looking at Marcus.

"It suits us to learn what they can do," Mandubratius purred, before Marcus could speak.

Máire's face grew pinched at his words. Her mouth became a tight line, but she said nothing.

"Yes, true," Marcus murmured. "Was there anything else that you learned from this interaction?" he asked Julien.

"They have a gift of inducing a happy peace into mortals and us," Julien continued. "They can also communicate without words between themselves."

"Fascinating," Gaius murmured. "So, they pass information this way?"

"Yes," Julien replied.

"I suppose it is not a surprise that they commune that way," Marcus said.

"They pass a shared knowledge, too?" Máire asked.

Julien nodded. "He says that from their creation, they are given intelligence in such a manner."

"Such an amazing trait," Mac Alpin murmured. "Perhaps they are not as brainless as they seem."

"And they still do so after our spell... or whatever you wish to call this transformation of ugly wretches into themselves again," Mandubratius said. "Do they read the minds of others, or merely themselves?"

"I know not," Julien admitted.

"And what other traits do they have?" Máire asked.

"They are as fast as the Lamia. Any other skills or traits are a mystery to me," Julien replied.

"We must be wary of them," Mandubratius stated, with a conspiratorial smile. "We don't know their skills or motivations. They may become a threat to us. We should consider exterminating them."

"They are under our protection," Marcus hissed in an impatient whisper. "And I would not wish to enrage their patron or patroness, whichever God, or Goddess, that is."

"They seem to be no threat," Julien commented. "In fact, they seem to feel indebted to us for removing the curse."

"I merely suggested they may be a danger," Mandubratius said soothingly.

"No harm will come unless their actions warrant it!" Marcus growled.

"Oh, very well. You two are being most rude." Mandubratius practically chuckled. "Come, Gaius. I am certain the Empress wishes to know this new intelligence." The two Lamia pulled back and walked to the end of the line.

"Mmmmm," Arwin muttered. "I'll inform the rest of our comrades and tell them to prepare." He took to the air.

Julien watched Máire move closer to Marcus and smile at him.

"He's gone for now, so we can rest," she commented. "You did very well, Julien." She smiled in his direction.

"Yes, first rate," Marcus added, sounding distracted again.

"Should we teach these Strigoi to fight?" Julien asked.

"I think that is a grand idea," Máire stated.

"I wonder... if we train one to fight," Marcus asked in a murmur, "will the others innately know the skill? Either way, this sounds like a good duty for the Inspector General."

"I have never trained troops before," Julien admitted.

"Assess them, and then we can help you train them," Marcus added.

Julien sensed himself blushing. "Thank you for your confidence," he said. "I will endeavor to not let you down."

chapter eighteen

Szatymaz

áire leaned back against the wall in the common room of the inn and watched the boys enjoy a bit of mirth, at the expense of a mortal serving girl, while discussing their predicament.

Mac Alpin grumbled in Irish, "I never heard so much sniveling from a noble. You would think this Nestor had to take in a town of thousands." He then turned to smile at the serving woman who tended to the needs of the inn visitors. In Greek, he said, "I can eat no more, my sweet. However, that wine is most refreshing."

The woman smiled, turned bright red, and scampered away.

As Máire watched the mortified woman scurry, she thought of the other blood-drinkers, who slept in the rooms above… too tired to cavort or hunt.

Claudius drew her mind back into the conversation. "At least, his uncle showed some decisiveness," he stated while resting his cheek against his hands. After yawning, he looked over at Arwin, with understanding evident within his eyes. "You didn't." He began to chuckle.

"As if you wouldn't," Arwin replied with a smirk. "Better than your fumbling attempts at goosing women."

Máire watched Marcus stare out the window. Somewhere, from the depths of his mind, he muttered, "Plenty of building materials here. They should be fine. Finer than the Hel–" He then fell silent.

She left from her place against the wall and sat next to him. Máire then rested her head against his shoulder. She wished to feel his comforting embrace, but he had been ignoring her. She wondered whether she had done something to warrant this. When she pulled back, he finally noticed her presence.

"Forgive my distraction," he murmured while patting her hand.

"I believe we are all trying to compensate for feelings of guilt," Julien said.

Máire stared at him, and she noticed the others did as well.

Leave it to Julien to be as blunt as I can be.

"These people are in as much danger as any of the mortals in these empires. We cannot be everywhere," Horatio muttered.

"Do not feel guilty for what you can't personally control, Horatio," Máire said. "I, for one, have no feeling of guilt." After she spoke, however, she noticed Claudius hiding a smile.

Before she felt driven to yell something unpleasant at these men, who certainly deserved a taste of her emotions, Máire decided she needed to leave. As soon as she stood, she felt Marcus' hand upon her left arm.

"Where are you going?" Marcus asked, finally paying attention to her.

"I need air," Máire stated. "This place has an unhealthy smell." She walked to the door and left the inn, though she could still hear the conversation about duty through the closed door. She felt relieved to miss a discussion on philosophy.

Máire avoided Lord Nestor's home, where the Lamia, save Horatio, slept. She reasoned that dealing with the leech would be a bit difficult, given her present state, so she took off into the nighttime sky, pleased to feel the wind at her feet. The clear view of the stars beckoned to her, drawing her to rise up level with the thin, wispy clouds. Once there, she hovered above the town and positioned herself to stare down at the lights far below. In the distance western horizon, she could see specks of brightness, which she reasoned to be the Emperor's palace in Aachen.

Her frustration faded as she rolled in mid-air to stare at the stars, but an insistent thirst reminded her that she needed sustenance. Cloaking herself in darkness, she plummeted towards the earth's surface, letting gravity take her most of the way. When she reached a point mere feet above the ground, Máire used her innate abilities to hover, and then she landed gently in the dark alley behind the inn. She was maintaining the cloak of blackness around her form to hunt, when a loud commotion near the Lord's home caught her ears. Máire flew towards the noise. She soon heard a gaggle of young boys shouting to each other, as well as the persistent yowl of a cat in pain. She hastened her flight, landing near the corner of a building opposite the source of the commotion.

"I shot the monster!" she heard one boy shout.

"Let's finish it," another replied.

As the sound of footsteps neared, she wondered what she should do. Just then, she spied a large, short-haired, black cat darting around the corner. His big, green eyes revealed fear and pain, while several white fairy hairs graced his throat and chest. She noticed a small arrow protruding from his right hindquarter. As she looked on, he started to limp, obviously tiring in his escape. The cat stared directly at her and uttered a soft, anguished meow.

Máire ran towards him, upon hearing an insistent command within her heart. Brigid demanded the protection of Her children. Once she reached the cat, she stood over it and turned to face the mortals. She felt her face contort in a growl. "How dare you chase one of My own?" she yelled in a voice that was not her own.

The two horrid boys fell on their backsides and screamed in terror.

"Never harass innocent creatures again for your amusement, especially My cats, or you shall feel My enduring wrath!"

She watched the boys run out of the alley, bawling, leaving their weapons.

With the threat over, Máire leaned over the cat, which purred softly and nuzzled her leg. She then reached down and picked up the cat. He seemed massive, for a tom… not fat, but well-muscled. She wrapped her arms around him and lifted him. She reasoned that he would have been too heavy for most mortals to carry.

He stared into her eyes with odd directness, whereas most cats abhorred such familiarity. The cat batted at her left cheek with its right fore-paw before mewing again. The wounded animal continued to bleed, slicking her hands.

While holding this poor, dying cat, she felt her hunger fade away. Then, for reasons she could not fathom, Máire actually sensed the cat's desire to live. The only means she knew of to save a cat this close to death would be to change him, but she worried that Morrigan might punish her for trying to rescue this hurt beast.

On impulse, she shifted the weight of the cat to her left arm and then drew her right hand to her lips. When she licked her hand, something tasted strange, but she decided that was not important. "I have never heard of a Deargh Du cat," she whispered. "I am not sure if it can be done."

"Please do this," a voice whispered.

The vision of a blonde maiden flashed in Máire's mind, giving way to a host of other women at various stages in life, each bore golden hair and green eyes. "Brigid?"

The blonde Matroness stared at her and commanded, "Do it."

Máire looked at her burden and watched the cat's eyes flutter open and shut. "No chance to feed more from you," she whispered, thinking the poor cat could offer little blood now. "Dear Goddess, please let this work," she murmured before biting her right wrist and sticking it in front of the cat's mouth. She soon felt a rough, scratchy tongue lick at her wound.

Máire sat in the alley and placed the cat in her lap. It moaned again softly, so she fed it some more. "You are such a beautiful man," she cooed.

His ears pricked at the compliment.

She touched the simple arrow in his rump and slid her right hand around the shaft, drawing a moan from the cat. "Yes, so beautiful, strong, and fearless," Máire sighed. She quickly plucked out the arrow and started to heal him, yet a strange sensation warmed her hand.

The cat appeared to be healing himself, faster than any Deargh Du could. The cat offered up another deep, throaty meow before standing up on her knees and nuzzling her.

"What a skillful and beautiful kitty," Máire said with a smile, stroking his brow, yet still confused at how this cat managed to heal himself.

"Thank you," a masculine voice echoed in her mind. "You are beautiful as well, Deargh Du."

"You speak?!"

"Do you see my mouth moving, except to say 'meow'?" The cat uttered a mew, revealing his teeth.

"No, I don't," she answered. "How can I hear you speaking in my mind?"

The cat narrowed his eyes at her. "Silly Deargh Du. I am not a mere cat."

"This is because of the transformation?"

The cat laughed a strange and sibilant half-hiss of a chuckle. "No, you didn't transform me. I just needed the blood of a fae, or some other being with magic in its blood. Frankly, I am a little surprised that a Deargh Du would not recognize me by my blood."

Máire licked the rest of the blood on her hand and closed her eyes. The flavors now came into focus. "Yes, you are more than just a cat," she murmured. The sight, sounds, and smell of rolling green hills, copses of trees, streams, flowers, and frolicking animals overwhelmed the scents of Szatymaz. "You are a fairy cat."

"Yes. You and I share some common blood," the cat clarified before settling into her lap.

She felt the compulsion to pet him and enjoyed the chore.

He soon rolled onto his back. "Yes, rub there," he instructed firmly, as she started to pat his belly. "Oh purr, purr," the cat chortled, closing his eyes.

"So, what shall I call you?" Máire asked. She felt herself smile more than she had in days.

"I am known by many names," the cat answered. "Why don't you give me a name you like?"

"Perhaps I should get to know you better," Máire replied before ceasing her petting. "That way, the name will suit you. So, why were those monstrous children chasing you?"

"I am a cat," the cat replied tersely, staring up at her. "You are not to stop rubbing," he commanded.

Máire resumed petting his stomach.

"Anyway," the cat continued, "I'm a black cat, and these mortals fear what is black. They believe me to be a demon."

"Mortals can be just as stupid as blood-drinkers… sometimes more so," Máire stated.

"Indeed, but I daresay you have a brain between those pretty ears. You must have been quite the smart young mortal," the cat said.

"Flatterer," Máire cooed.

"For now, you may refer to me as 'Cat', until you find a suitable name for me," he said. He then rolled onto his feet.

"I should show you off to my family," Máire said. Knowing cats preferred to select their mode of travel, she set him on the ground and rose.

"Are they Deargh Du as well?" the bundle of curiousness asked.

"Some are," Máire answered, as she began to walk towards the inn. "However, my family also consists of some Ekimmu Cruitne and a Sugnwr Gwaed. We are also accompanied by Lamia and some new blood-drinkers that used to be Strigoi."

"Mmmmm, most of these names are unfamiliar," Cat said. "I know of the Sugnwr Gwaed and Ekimmu Cruitne. Unfortunately, none of those races will hear me, other than the Deargh Du, but sometimes the Lord of the Hunt likes to give His hunters a chance to speak to His animal companions."

"Perhaps you can scare Claudius then," Máire suggested with a chuckle. "Let's be on our way."

"Alright," the cat agreed. "Scaring blood-drinkers is quite amusing."

She was shocked to sense him leap and land on her right shoulder. He curled around the back of her neck and plopped down, with his forelegs draped over her breasts.

"You may walk, now," Cat instructed her.

"Does his majesty wish to snack upon my ear as well?" Máire asked with a laugh, before she started walking back to the inn.

Cat batted one of her plaits with a soft paw. "Perhaps I shall take you up on that kind offer later," he replied.

Máire smiled and shook her head a bit. "You remind me a great deal of a Lamia I know."

"Is he as beautiful as I am?" Cat asked with a hissing laugh. He stared sideways into her eyes and appeared to flutter his eyelashes.

"Hardly," Máire replied with a smirk.

"Not surprising," Cat retorted. "Most Lamia are the height of tedium. Unlike them, I am quite eye-catching. I have these lovely green eyes and my shiny black coat." He yawned and revealed his teeth again.

"You sound more and more like this Lamia," Máire quipped. "That, or he is very cat-like. Perhaps his name would suit you."

Cat pricked his ears forward. "And what is his name?"

"His real name is Awvarwy, but he goes by Mandubratius," Máire answered. "It is best, however, that I do not give you his name. I can little bear uttering his name. You deserve something better."

"Indeed. Those names are long and unwieldy," Cat said, wrinkling his nose. "I prefer shorter names."

Once Máire reached the inn and opened the door, she realized that the morning sun began to turn the skies purple.

Claudius and Mac Alpin appeared to be passed out, and next to them slouched the Legate. She wondered whether he had been cast out of the Lord's home. Patroclus also appeared to be half-asleep. Marcus, awake and alert, still played with his cup and dice.

Cat stood up on her shoulders, stretched, and then leapt towards Claudius, landing on his back.

Claudius grumbled, "What now, Maél Morrigan. Am I sitting in your seat?"

"No," Máire answered, while patting Claudius' back.

"Is that a cat?" Marcus asked, looking up from his dice. He grinned, as if returning to his old self.

"No, I'm a walking pillow," Cat answered, before climbing up Claudius' back towards his neck, where he began licking Claudius' ear. "Hey, drunk Sugnwr Gwaed. That's right. I called you 'drunk'. Wake up! Has Cernunnos allowed you to hear my words?"

"Cernunnos?" Claudius murmured.

"I have come in this form to smite all hunters who disappoint me," Cat forewarned.

"What?"

Cat nipped Claudius' ear in a playful fashion, and in response, Claudius sat bolt upright. The action caused Cat to fly through the air and land on another table. He shook himself and groomed an inky paw before leaping off the table. Cat then trotted towards Máire and jumped onto her shoulder.

Máire heard Marcus start to laugh.

"Thank you," Cat said, as she steadied him.

"Cernunnos?" Claudius queried, rubbing his eyes. "I heard the Lord of Beasts speak to me. Marcus, stop laughing."

"Mmmph?" Mac Alpin looked up, bleary-eyed.

Marcus shook his head and continued chortling.

"I see no god," Arwin blurted, examining the room. His eyes then locked on Máire. "What is that around your neck? Is it a fur collar?"

"Hardly," Cat answered.

Claudius started chuckling and soon joined Marcus in gales of laughter.

Mac Alpin stared at them both.

"Does this cat speak?" Claudius asked, before breaking out into a large grin. "He is a most verbal cat. My communications with cats have mostly been limited to 'get out of my sight, stupid Sugnwr Gwaed,' and 'you're boring me'.

They only understand my thoughts and never my words... most of the time."

"Bloody vermin cannot speak," Mac Alpin muttered.

Cat hissed and growled, startling Arwin.

"Elder, this is a special cat," Máire said while patting Cat.

Marcus stood up and walked to her side. "Where did you find this handsome cat?" he asked.

"She rescued me from some uncouth children in the alley," Cat answered. "Yes, you may pet me."

"I am obviously drunk," Claudius announced, as he joined them and scratched the cat's chin, "but speaking to a cat in this manner is most amusing."

"I hear nothing, young Claudius. You are drunk," Arwin stated. "Patroclus," he enunciated, while elbowing the Legate, "tell these three fools that their joke is a foolish one. I see Marcus' mouth moving."

"Claudius is not that drunk," Marcus answered. "I hear a cat talking. You're extremely drunk if you believe me to be speaking for the cat."

"Yes, it is I, unnamed Cat, speaking. It appears that Ekimmu Cruitne and Lamia cannot hear my words."

"Such a smart cat," Claudius cooed.

"Yes, I know I have a dizzying intellect," Cat chuckled.

"Cease this madness," the Legate grumbled. "Animals do not speak as we do."

"Nonsense. He just doesn't wish to speak to you," Claudius jested while winking at Máire, who found this exchange humorous and quite uplifting.

"So, what is his name, really?" Marcus asked.

"Soldier, you may address me directly. It would be more polite," Cat demanded.

"Yes sir," Marcus said, before saluting him. "How shall I address you?"

"Which name do you feel is appropriate?" Cat asked. "I go by many names. You may choose to call me one thing, but it would not be my only name."

Marcus grinned. "You remind me of Lucius Corvus, the first spear centurion who liked nothing better than to humiliate us spoiled senators' sons when the lesser classes in the cohorts showed greater courage than us. Does 'Lucius' suit you, Cat?"

"It does, thank you. I suppose you are wondering how I can speak." Lucius gave them a superior cat-grin.

"I know we have all encountered many strange things in our travels. A talking cat is within the realm of possibility," Claudius answered.

"Indeed," Marcus chuckled. "I mean, we are a sterling example of strange things."

"Stop playing this game," Mac Alpin muttered.

"Somebody's tired and crank-y" Máire drawled. She then walked over to him and patted his shoulder. "Arwin and Patroclus look very sleepy. They need to go to bed," she teased while stroking Arwin's hair.

"I suppose," Mac Alpin sighed. He rose from the bench. "I won the bed, aye?"

"No. We agreed it was my turn for the bed," Patroclus said, "but I sold my claim to Claudius."

"Patroclus, my sweet, it is bedtime," Máire said.

"Mmmm, say that again," Patroclus purred. "I have been kicked out of my rightful place for being too friendly with the Celtic lines," he complained.

"My poor chroí," Máire said, rubbing his back. "I shall tuck you in, if you like."

"Sweetheart, if I were not so tipsy, I would require more than a simple tucking in," Patroclus answered. He captured her right hand, brought it to his mouth, and stuck her index finger in it. His teeth caressed her in a rough scratch, causing her finger to bleed. Patroclus suckled at her blood.

Máire felt herself redden. The Legate never appeared interested in her before, in this way.

He released her digit and kissed her hand before rising. "Come Arwin, let's join the others," he said.

Claudius smirked. "I'll follow them upstairs, but I'm not tucking Patroclus in. Sleep well and enjoy the bed, Chieftain and General… oh, and Lucius." He scratched Lucius' head and followed the two other blood-drinkers up the stairs.

"My lieutenant bought me the use of the bed," Marcus said with a chuckle. "I mention ill-dreams, and he thinks I need a good night's rest. So, Lucius, I suppose you are not an ordinary cat, if you are even a cat. In fact, your scent is quite familiar, in some way."

"I am a fairy cat. Perhaps our common blood makes me familiar to you," Lucius suggested.

"So, what brings you to Szatymaz?" Marcus asked.

"I was curious about that myself," Máire added.

Lucius stood up on Máire's shoulders, stretched, and then jumped to the table. "I wished to experience this world and have fun," Lucius answered. He began to groom himself.

"Since you answer to Lucius, may I call you 'Lugh' sometimes?" Máire asked. "You brought us the dawn, as the Light-Bringer does, and you have many talents and skills, like Lugh Lamfada."

"Now you are the flatterer," Lucius chortled. "Yes, I will answer to Lugh. It is a most pleasing name." He stretched his front legs and next his back. He then uttered a squeaky mew, as he yawned.

"I agree," Marcus chuckled. "Besides, 'Loo' sounds like it is short for 'Loo-cius'. Lucius, would you care to share the bed? This is a very special occasion."

Lucius took a running leap and landed on Marcus' shoulder. "That is a most kind offer." Lucius waved his tail and wrapped it around Marcus' neck, as Marcus started for the staircase.

Máire followed. "Will you continue with us to Vézelay?" she asked while rubbing Lucius' back.

"I have never been to Vézelay. Yes, I will join you. I just realized that we have not been properly introduced." Lucius fixed his green eyes upon Máire. "So, what is your name, beautiful lady? She is lovely to behold, isn't she?" he asked, pawing Marcus' shoulder.

"That is Máire, Lucius," he said, turning a charming smile on her, "and yes, she is wondrous to behold."

Máire cleared her throat and said, "This honey-mouthed, young soldier is Marcus Galerius Primus Helvetticus. He is my father-in-darkness."

"That I knew," Lucius purred. "It is indeed an honor to meet you both. Now, open the door, and let's examine this bed. I do like a large bed. I need stretching space."

Máire chuckled and opened the door. "What do you think, Lugh?"

Lucius bounded off Marcus' shoulders and onto the bed. After kneading it for a moment, he said, "It is acceptable."

Marcus tugged Máire into the room and closed the door behind her, all the while grinning at her.

"You seem to be in excellent spirits," Máire commented as he leaned in closer for a kiss. "What about our companion?"

His lips moved against hers for a moment. "I think Lucius will enjoy having the bed for himself for some time," he murmured to her neck.

An enticing shiver coursed through her body as his mouth hovered over her throat, before biting her and drinking. Máire closed her eyes and pulled Marcus in closer. She smiled as she felt his hands begin to toss aside her clothing. She had started to believe that he found her boring in bed.

Marcus slid into bed next to Máire, which nudged Lucius towards the edge. Marcus knew she had not reached a climax, but she seemed to enjoy herself otherwise. He pulled her in closer to him and played with her nipples.

"That was most entertaining," Lucius commented. "I give it a score of 'noble and passionate effort'." He stood up and stretched. "If you don't mind,

I will lie between you. I am certain that exertion has made you two warm."

Marcus heard Máire snort and snicker, but her laughter ended in a squeak of pain, as Lucius stomped on her left breast, and he simultaneously scratched Marcus' right hand a little.

Lucius then stepped onto her shoulder and hopped off her. After climbing to the top of the blanket, he dove under the covers and burrowed through the maze of folds.

Marcus yelped like a young boy, as Lucius stomped on his groin.

"Ah, this is most satisfactory," the cat said while leaning up against Marcus' leg. "Did I hurt you?"

"No… not really," Marcus squeaked.

"Sleep well, boys," Máire said. She then turned and leaned in for a kiss. "I love… good night." She kissed Marcus gently, slid back down, and then closed her green eyes.

As he stroked a strand of her hair and watched her drift off into dreams, he heard again the words Máire started to say… 'I love'.

Outside of Savaria

While in flight, Máire adjusted the sling Claudius had made out of a blanket from the inn to aid her in carrying Lucius against her side and back. However, Máire decided to wrap an arm around and under him as they flew.

Lucius took advantage of his accommodations and peered out of the sling.

"Be careful," Máire advised him. "You don't want to fall… again."

Lucius met her eyes for a moment. "Thank you for catching me, Máire."

"You are most welcome," she answered, "but you must be more careful. You could have been killed."

"I was not worried. You would have saved me. After all, I bring you and Marcus luck."

"Is he behaving himself now?" Julien asked, after moving in next to her. "I can carry him for you, if your back and shoulders grow weary."

"I am quite content where I am, my Lord," the cat tittered. "Besides, I am a fairy cat. It is not in my nature to behave."

She sensed Marcus, who wore the mirror strapped to his back, swoop in next to them. "It amazes me that the transformed Strigoi can keep up with the Lamia," he said.

"What else can they do?" Lucius asked.

"They bring feelings of warmth to those nearby, Lucius," Julien answered. "However, I plan on taking some time at the next break to learn more."

"Best of luck to you," Lucius said. "I know I tend to hide my secrets. They may not wish to reveal all these skills to you, or to any of us, for that matter."

"Trust is an issue for all of us. We will all make compromises," Marcus answered.

"I have a feeling that it is not so much that they do not trust you, Julien," Lucius said before stretching a little in the sling. "They seem to highly revere you and Máire for your assistance in removing Aphrodite's curse through the mirror that Marcus carries."

"You know about that?" Máire asked.

"I am a fairy cat," Lucius said with a chuckle. "Yet I sometimes tend to soak up information like a sponge. In the Otherworld, I have heard mention of this curse. How does the mirror work?"

"It reflects the inner beauty of the Strigoi, or any other person, towards them," Máire explained.

"Unfortunately, the biggest limitations of this mirror are that it needs a strong light source and that it only delivers a narrow field of vision," Julien added.

"So, what awaits us in Vézelay?" asked the fairy cat.

"That is where Julien's mother and sister live," Marcus answered. "Lady Heloise practices the ancient ways and may be able to help us use this mirror, as I am somewhat certain our own Druidic sages know little about it. Some of us will bring forth the remainder of our forces from the surrounding area."

Lucius purred. "It is wonderful that the Deargh Du have so many friends. I remember a time when Deargh Du isolated themselves from the rest of the world, after the creation of the Ekimmu Cruitne, as if that matter could be the fault of the entire race, instead of just a single Deargh Du and a single Ekimmu." He wiggled his nose for a moment. "How is it that the Deargh Du are now more worldly?"

"I must return to the front of the group," Marcus said before departing.

"Marcus made many friends in the world of blood-drinkers," Máire answered. "He brought ideas and his friends to Éire. In some ways, I feel closer to these friends than those who share my bloodline. When the Lamia and the Celtic lines were at war, Marcus trained the Deargh Du to fight as an army. The combined army of races drove the Lamia out of Éire, yet we now have an alliance with them."

Julien interjected and said, "I should continue ahead. Let me know if you require my assistance." He leaned in and gave her a quick kiss on her cheek.

"I will," Máire called out, as he darted through the line.

"Julien is your brood, is he not?" Lucius asked, while staring up at her.

"He is indeed. He has done very well, considering how little time he has had to learn our skills. I wish I could have prepared him better."

"No, you did well," Lucius reassured her. "He is quite happy to be your child-in-darkness. He craves responsibility, yet in some ways, he is very different than you or Marcus." Lucius stretched again in the sling. "Sweet Máire, who carries me so gently, I'm going to take a nap. You may wake me when it's time to eat." He then closed his luminous, green eyes.

"Yes, your majesty," Máire said before laughing.

"I love being called that," Lucius purred. The fairy cat grew warm and began to snore.

The Wilderness between Reims and Aachen

Sáerlaith stared at the growing skyline of Aachen in the distance. So far, they had not found Reginald or Talia.

"I wish I could understand how we have not found him," Lady Heloise commented. "We seem to be moving so quickly."

The elder mortal had expressed joy regarding their method of travel, saying she found it invigorating. She kept laughing in absolute pleasure as they flew, almost to the point of distraction.

"They may be hiding from us, my Lady," Maon answered. "It is difficult, but not impossible. Still, I grow hungry, and I smell food nearby."

Sáerlaith sniffed the air. "As do I. We shall take a quick break before continuing. Ask at the village if anyone has seen Talia or Reginald." She motioned to the others, and they headed towards the surface of the Great Mother. After landing, the other Deargh Du headed towards the small village.

Sáerlaith decided to feed on some nearby cattle, but Heloise's insistent hand kept her from leaving.

"Feed on me first," Heloise beseeched. "Julien told me that feeding on animals for too long brings out animalistic tendencies in the Deargh Du." After a pause, she asked, "Do you think he is well?"

Sáerlaith smiled and took the proffered arm. "I am certain he is fine, Heloise. His companions are warriors of great renown. He will be safe." She then bit into Heloise's arm and started to feed. After a satisfactory snack, Sáerlaith licked her lips.

Heloise asked, "Do you think the Strigoi will return?"

Sáerlaith raised her head and said, "I know they will, but not soon enough to cause harm to Reginald."

At that moment, an excited Maon and Dubhghall landed a few feet away. "Reginald and Talia were here," Dubhghall said. "They arrived near dawn this morning and left four hours ago."

"We will continue after you two feed. Make haste! We will run the risk of meeting the sun if we do not hurry," Sáerlaith warned.

Heather Poinsett Dunbar & Christopher Dunbar

Vézelay

Julien's impatience grew as they waited in the grove for those who could not fly. He wished to see his family, and yet the others lagged behind. He hoped he would not be found a rude host for wishing the Lamia and the transformed Strigoi to hurry.

While he looked on, some of the Deargh Du, including Máire, paced around the altar, murmuring things in their own language.

The mild winds of the early summer paused, for a moment, and at last, he could detect the scent of the other blood-drinkers growing on the wind.

Upon arriving, they stopped in front of him. Each blood-drinker appeared exhausted from the night of running. Even the usually verbose Lamia remained silent and complaint-free.

Julien cleared his throat and said, "Please feel free to feed from our cattle."

"I'd sooner drink blood from swine," he heard the Empress grunt.

"The swine are in the back fields," Julien informed her. Soon, he could smell someone else nearing them. He looked to the back door and saw a familiar-looking, cloaked Deargh Du approach them. He could also see Marcus grin.

"Caoimhín," Marcus called out. "Where is the rest of the welcoming party?"

Caoimhín laughed. "Sorry, Marcus, but the celebration will be a quiet one tonight," he said before embracing Marcus.

Julien could see the Lamia and the transformed Strigoi watch them curiously. At the same time, the other Deargh Du ceased their contemplation of the altar and neared Caoimhín.

Caoimhín touched the frame of the mirror on Marcus' back and said, "You were successful. We shall speak of my mission when necessary. Who are these new companions?"

Marcus turned towards the Lamia and the former Strigoi. "This is General Gaius Naevius Tacitus Britannicus of the Greek branch of the Lamia, previously known as the Children of Ares. This lovely woman is Her Imperial Majesty, Empress Irene, the Basileus. This is Father Xofer, of the recently transformed Strigoi. Everyone, this is Caoimhín of Ard Mhacha."

Caoimhín bowed his head. His silvery-blonde hair gleamed in the moonlight. "I am most honored to meet you all. May the Great Queen bring us…" he called out in prayer before pausing. While looking at Father Xofer, he said, "Forgive me. I forget that sometimes our practices alienate others."

The priest gave a small shrug. "I see no harm in good tidings, Caoimhín. Thank you for the welcome."

"Is 'Great Queen' in deference to me?" Irene asked with a smirk.

"No, Imperial Majesty," Caoimhín beamed at her, as if bemused. "Until now, I had no idea you were a blood-drinker."

"It was necessary for this mirror," Marcus interjected.

Caoimhín returned his soothing gaze to the Strigoi. "Please explain to me how you changed from the Strigoi to this... this beautified state."

"Julien and Máire wielded the mirror Empress Irene has donated, which Marcus carries. It transformed us and freed us from our madness."

Julien heard a throat clear from an unmistakable Briton.

"Greetings again, Caoimhín. You can thank me personally for obtaining the mirror," Mandubratius stated while staring at the Deargh Du.

"I am certain all made sacrifices, Mandubratius, but you are to be congratulated for this gift," Caoimhín added in a diplomatic tone. "I am sure the transformed are grateful."

Julien interrupted the other Deargh Du, hoping the others would not judge him harshly. "Caoimhín, please excuse my rudeness, but is my mother well? I thought she would have been here to greet us. Is my sister here?" As he asked his questions, many of the others departed to find food.

"Your sister and... niece are with Dreu, the commander of the garrison," Caoimhín stated.

"Clotilda is still here?" asked Julien, confused. "Is Reginald staying?"

"My Lord, there is much to tell. If it pleases you and Marcus, feed first, and then we can discuss our news in the basement. You two are pale, and you need your strength."

Julien nodded, although he remained bewildered. He hoped that feeding would bring ease and order to his mind.

A cheerful Alais greeted Julien, as he wandered into his home. "Welcome home, my Lord," she said. Her eyes gleamed, as if under the influence of glamoury from a Deargh Du that had fed from her. She took his arm and beamed at him. "Your friends are waiting by the hearth. Others are gathering in the basement. They requested that I let you know."

"Thank you, Alais. You look exhausted. Perhaps you should rest."

"Oh no, my Lord, I'm far too excited to sleep." She then bounced back into the other room and, from the sounds of her work, began to pour wine into goblets. She traipsed around the room, handing goblets of wine to each person in turn.

Julien found Marcus and Caoimhín quietly chattering in Gaelic by the hearth. He experienced some frustration, in that the others always seemed to lapse into Gaelic, or the old tongue of the Britons, as if they forgot... or ignored... the fact that he had no knowledge of those languages.

As soon as Alais handed Caoimhín a goblet, he purred in Latin, "Thank you, Alais." He then took a sip of the wine. "I miss mead, but I am beginning to enjoy these local beverages." Alais handed Julien the last goblet, as Caoimhín said, "Your mother is accompanying Sáerlaith towards Aachen in an attempt to prevent your brother and Lady Talia from usurping you and your mother's lands. A summons was sent, accusing you and your mother of various crimes."

"What?!" Julien exclaimed. He drank his wine in a few gulps and then fumbled with the goblet. "What would make Reginald try such a thing? The Emperor gave me those lands, and Vézelay belonged to my maternal grandfather, not my father's family."

Caoimhín fixed his gaze upon Julien and said, "Lady Talia's words drip like poison. She convinced your brother to turn against his family. She may have even manipulated the Emperor into hearing her case without your presence."

"I appreciate Sáerlaith's efforts to prevent harm to our family, but why are the Deargh Du interested in aiding us?" Julien asked.

"We've lost Ard Mhacha," Marcus explained. "We have no place to go. We have no home in which to interact with each other."

"Thus," Caoimhín continued, "we have no identity, until your beautiful and benevolent mother provided us with the opportunity to create a home, here. Some of us will go to Britannia and Scotland with the Ekimmu Cruitne and Sugnwr Gwaed, but the majority of us will remain here," he explained. "Your family has saved our race, Julien. In return, we will protect your family. When we adjourn to the basement, I will inform the others." Caoimhín paused for a moment. "If Sáerlaith does not find Reginald on the way to Aachen, she plans to intercede in court with your mother."

Julien paced in front of the hearth, feeling the warmth grow as he walked. "I wish to join them in court, if it comes to that. At the very least, I must question Reginald and ask him why he turned traitor to his own flesh and blood. He and I may never have seen eye-to-eye, but our mother loves us all."

"Don't be too hard on him," Marcus advised. "Lady Talia is a grand manipulator. She has been plotting to regain the lands her grandfather lost when the Franks annexed Burgundy."

"I will judge him appropriately. Thank you for not making this public knowledge," Julien said to Caoimhín. To Marcus, he said "I know you both realize we need to keep this information from the Lamia for as long as possible."

"Yes. That is the plan we discussed earlier," Caoimhín answered. "However, they will notice that you have left."

Marcus stood and said, "The best thing to do is to give you a head start. They tend to discover secrets quickly, but you can fly faster than they can run. In addition, I think, as a whole, that the Lamia could care less about these lands, although Francia and the empire as a whole are another story. However, they already have an empire in the east, now, and hopefully, that will keep them busy." Marcus closed his eyes and yawned. "The sun rises soon." Marcus finished his drink and handed the goblet to Alais. "Let's go downstairs."

Julien walked down the steps into the basement, where cots and bedrolls lay scattered all over.

Everyone shared jugs of wine.

"May I have everyone's attention please?" Caoimhín called out. "Everyone is aware of the difficulties in Ard Mhacha. Nearly one thousand of the Deargh Du have been exiled from our home, yet our friends here are our saviors from a vagabond's existence. Lady Heloise and her family have granted us a new stronghold in exchange for the protection of her family. We have already found a suitable site for our home. We all owe Julien and his family our fidelity and support," Caoimhín added, before smiling.

All of the Deargh Du faced Julien and began offering praises. Many walked to him with tears in their eyes and whispered utterances of soft blessings, while others kneeled.

Julien was embarrassed for the outpouring of affection, unsure of whether he deserved their expressions... it was his mother's decision, but were it his, he would have made the same choice. Still, he felt embolden by the outpouring of gratitude. "Thanks are not necessary," he said. "You are my family." Julien soon felt a soft form rub against him. He looked down and saw Lucius looking up at him, for a moment, before nudging him again.

Mandubratius shouldered his way through the Deargh Du and clapped his right hand on Julien's right shoulder. "This is a most pleasant surprise, that our allies will be near to us," he said, smiling. "I will gladly offer our allies any assistance."

Julien watched the Lamia's eyes gleam with the opportunity to calculate plans and rain discord on the Deargh Du. Of course, for all Julien know, Mandubratius could simply be pleased to have them closer, as they would be easier to watch.

"Thank you for your kindness, Mandubratius," Caoimhín replied, thankfully negating the need for Julien to reply.

He smiled, as other Deargh Du offered more thanks. Soon, someone passed him a bottle of mead, and he realized that they now presented him with their most prized possession. He took a few sips and stretched a moment, feeling exhausted, before handing the bottle to someone else. He then went to his bed to sleep, but he found the Empress reclining in it, while Lucius sat on a pillow and waved his tail about, as if expressing his irritation.

"This beast insists upon dirtying our bed," Lucius grumbled.

To Irene, Julien said, "You may be the Empress in the east, but this is my bed." He missed this bed, after weeks of sleeping in dirt and on disgusting mattresses. Unfortunately, Irene kept her eyes closed and continued to ignore him, so he decided to take action.

While avoiding bedding and other blood-drinkers, Julien stepped gracefully around to her side. He then slapped her backside... hard.

The Empress squealed in annoyance and rolled over to stare at him. "Inconsequential Frankish gnat, if this is your attempt at foreplay, you had better try again."

"That wasn't any kind of play," Julien replied. "You're in my bed, and I'm here to reclaim it."

The Empress sighed and sat up, revealing herself. She smiled for a moment, yet her eyes revealed her annoyance. "You are rather handsome for a barbarian. I will promise you pleasure if you share your bed. Please," she pleaded, though in an unfriendly manner.

The thought of pleasure seemed enticing, but he had the feeling that if he didn't give her the gratification she expected, he might lose his genitals.

"I'm tired," he answered. "Stay if you wish." He then sat down, kicked off his boots, lied down, and tugged over the blankets.

After settling himself, Julien felt Lucius stomp on his stomach and finally lie down between the Empress and himself.

"I'll scratch her if she rolls over me," Lucius said, while nudging Julien's hand for a rub.

"Understood, Lucius," Julien answered, scratching the cat's chin.

"Stupid cats don't talk," the Empress muttered. "I wish you and the rest of your kind would stop this game–" A muffled yelp and a thud interrupted her sentence.

Julien sat up, upon feeling the bed settle, and glanced at Lucius, who appeared to be asleep and snoring contentedly.

"That black monster scratched me," the Empress fussed, as she rose from her place on the floor.

"He's asleep," Julien said while smirking at her. "Get under the covers and go to sleep, Empress." He patted the other side of the bed.

"I'm sleeping elsewhere," she mumbled. "Keep your familiar away."

"Suit yourself. Nudge one of the beautiful women you pass and inform her that there is half of a bed available." He chuckled at his unexpected humor. Julien then leaned back into bed and patted Lucius' stomach. "Well done."

A green eye stared at him. "Just do not make the mistake of calling me 'stupid cat', 'black monster', or 'blanket hog'."

"I shall not," Julien whispered before closing his eyes.

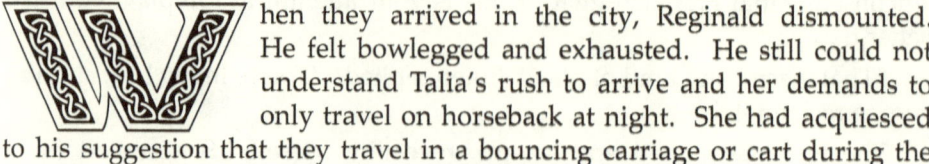

chapter nineteen

Aachen

When they arrived in the city, Reginald dismounted. He felt bowlegged and exhausted. He still could not understand Talia's rush to arrive and her demands to only travel on horseback at night. She had acquiesced to his suggestion that they travel in a bouncing carriage or cart during the day, but their nights were a frenzy of riding at full speed through the ancient Roman roads. Because of the scant money he had brought with him, Reginald barely had any money left for a room and food. Helping Talia from her horse, he said, "I am sorry, but our accommodations will be poor."

She smiled and gifted him with a tender and gentle kiss. "Once the fool on the throne realizes his error, we will have the accommodations of our choice."

He grabbed the reins of both horses and escorted them to an awaiting stablehand at the inn. After leaving the horses and a sou with the hand, Reginald walked back to Talia, took her left arm, and led her towards the inn. Along the way, he saw her golden tresses blowing free in the wind, and he could not help but stare at her, for a moment, but then he remembered why they had traveled here.

"Why the sad frown, Reginald?" asked Talia in the manner of a parent. "We are here. Things will be righted. Your family has done you wrong, and now it's time to correct these problems."

"I know," he answered. "I still cannot believe what my mother and sister said in front of you."

"Do not worry yourself, my love. You'll be done with them, soon enough. You can toss them out of your houses, force them to work in the fields, or do away with them entirely."

"Are you implying that we should kill them?" he asked, pausing outside of the door of the inn. Something within him found a growing depth of horror at that prospect.

"I'm not suggesting a method to deal with them, Reginald," Talia cooed, as her left hand rubbed at his back. "I am saying… if they resist, you may have to deal more harshly with them."

A small voice within him raged at the suggestion that he should harm his family. However, a stronger voice soon reminded him of their treachery.

"Forgive me, Talia. I spoke rashly. It may be necessary, as you say."

"No need to apologize, Reginald," Talia stated before opening the door. Walking inside, she asked, "Are you hungry?"

Reginald chuckled a little. "All I wish to do is sleep with you in my arms, at least until midday." He placed money in front of the sleepy-eyed innkeeper and said, "We wish for a private room."

"Third door to your right," the innkeeper said, pointing towards a dank hallway. He then handed Talia a lit candle.

Reginald pulled Talia towards the designated room and opened the door. Upon peering into the darkness, he shivered a little. "Once again, I am sorry for the state of our accommodations," Reginald said before inhaling and walking into the room. As he sat on the bed, he felt relief because he could not hear the scurrying of rats.

Soon, Talia began to undress him. "You poor, exhausted man," she cooed. "Reginald." She paused after speaking his name.

"Yes?" he asked.

"Have you ever wondered what it would be like to walk the night? To run faster than any deer? To have the ability to see over the treetops?"

Reginald chuckled a little. "Such abilities are not possible."

He felt coldness encircle him. Then he noticed that Talia had disappeared. A split second later, he felt a cold and gentle hand touch his shoulder.

"I'm behind you," Talia murmured.

When he turned, he saw Talia, standing across the room, bent over, with her hands resting on her knees. She cocked her head to the side and gave him a ready smile. Then, without warning, she vanished again.

He turned back towards the door and found her staring into his eyes with a great intensity and directness. Her blue eyes seemed to glow red.

"How did you?" he whispered, fearful that some demon had possessed his Talia.

"I can move faster than most people," she boasted. "Now, look down at your right hand."

Reginald felt a small, cold object slide into his hand. When he looked down, he realized that he held a dagger.

Talia took his burdened hand and caressed it gently. "Now, do as I say, Reginald." She positioned the dagger over her heart and commanded, "Plunge your dagger into my chest."

He gasped at her words, but her eyes pleaded with him. Some compulsion, other than his own, drove him to thrust out with the dagger. Sticky, cold blood gushed over his digits. "God, no," he whispered. He closed his eyes, released his grip on the dagger, and waited to hear Talia's body hit the floor, but he heard no such sound.

After a scant few moments, she commanded, "Open your eyes." Reginald felt forced to stare at her. He watched Talia wrench out the blade and toss it aside. When her hands tugged apart the rip in her dress, he stared at the wound.

"It will heal completely by tomorrow night," she reassured him.

"Are you..." Reginald heard himself squeak. "Are you like what Julien has become?"

Talia laughed outright. "We are similar creatures, I suppose, Reginald. However, where he and his kind seek an irrational balance, my kind strives for power and glory." He watched her smile, revealing long teeth. "Would you like to become one of us?" she purred.

Part of him wanted to run into the night and beg for assistance at the palace, but a stronger desire for the glory Talia mentioned dwelled within him. "This will help me regain my property?" he asked.

"Of course, my love," Talia answered.

"And you are not demons?"

Talia stroked his right arm. "I assure you that we're no demons," she murmured, reaching for the simple, small cross he carried in a pouch. Talia held it up and showed it to him. "Would a demon handle a cross without some sort of pain?" She then kissed the cross in reverence.

Reginald nodded his head. "You are not a demon."

"We are not demons," Talia intoned. "Do you wish to become one of us and live forever? You will learn skills through this gift, skills that will gain you influence, power, and glory."

Reginald lowered his gaze and stared at the dirty floor, while a battle warred in his head.

Demon or not, would this transformation create evil? I remember evil done in the past, but why not pursue it? God appears to have no interest in my pain, and He has done nothing more than test me. Perhaps God does not even exist.

"I wish it," he answered, after losing the battle with his conscience.

Talia's eyes glowed a deep red.

Reginald's fears grew, as he felt himself freeze in place, unable to move.

"I knew this would be your choice," Talia murmured. Her teeth grew again. As she leaned against his neck, her cold breath made him close his eyes.

A dizzying pain caused him to collapse backwards. He could feel Talia straddle him. Weakness festered within him, as energy and warmth drain from his body.

The pulse of aching emptiness brought Reginald back into the present.

A burning pulse of pain echoed through Reginald's body. He attempted to rise from the bed, but after an unsuccessful endeavor, he fell back to the thin

Heather Poinsett Dunbar & Christopher Dunbar

mattress, exhausted and overwhelmed.

"Drink," Talia ordered.

Reginald parted his lips and felt a warm, sweet, and salty fluid pool within his mouth. On impulse, he gulped down the salt-laden substance.

"There, there, my sweet child. That is all for now." Reginald felt Talia's arm move out of his grasp.

"Rest now, and after sunset, when you're able, we will find you a suitable meal. We must feed, after all." She stroked his face with one of her warm hands. Talia leaned in for a kiss. "I am now your sponsor, and you are my child," she whispered.

"What do you mean 'feed'?" Reginald asked, but he already knew the answer... he just desired to hear the truth.

Talia chuckled softly. "Feed, as in we find a willing mortal and drink his or her blood. Don't you remember, my love?"

The memory of her feeding from him, only a few hours ago, made his senses reel. He leaned over the other side of the bed and fought the urge to vomit, but darkness overwhelmed him, soon enough.

Vézelay

Julien sat up in bed and surveyed the basement full of sleeping blood-drinkers. A growing chill in the air revealed that the sun had faded to the west. He pulled up the covers, slid his feet over the bed, and began preparing to leave. After pulling up his left boot, he caught a glimpse of Lucius opening a sleepy eye, studying him in silence, and going back to sleep.

Julien rose carefully, examining the rows of sleeping guests. He thought of using Máire's lessons in the forest, which involved moving in silence, but in the end, levitating seemed more appealing. So, he rose a few feet above the floor, angled his body, so he would not bang his head on the cross-beams, and drifted to the stairs. No one seemed to notice his passage.

While ascending to the first level, Julien considered whether Lirienne could aid him in understanding why Reginald had turned on his family. Despite Caoimhín and Marcus' assurances that Lady Talia was a master in manipulation, he knew that Reginald could have controlled his actions... at least, he hoped he still possessed control over himself. After silently closing the door behind himself, Julien saw a beaming Alais glide towards him, wordlessly offering him her bare, left arm.

"Thank you," he murmured. Julien took her arm and turned it over, stroking her pale skin with his thumb, and then bit into it. The sensation of feeding from her filled him with warmth. During his meal, he noticed Alais' breathing grow harsh. He ceased feeding and kissed the wound. "Don't let the others take too much," he advised before rubbing her arm and healing her.

Alais' eyes glazed in pleasure, and she beamed at him. "If I am ever needed for anything else," she cooed, voicing her desires that he had sensed during his meal.

He smiled. "I will find you. Go sit in front of the hearth until you feel well, Alais." Julien then crept towards the front door.

To Julien, the well-lit garrison served as a welcome beacon. As a soldier saluted him, Dreu appeared in the doorway.

"Welcome home, my Lord. Lirienne is most anxious to see you again." Before Dreu could say more, Julien's sister rushed out and embraced him.

"You are home, and you will sup with us," Lirienne demanded, kissing his cheek and chuckling.

"Lirienne, I would enjoy nothing more than to join you and Dreu, yet I must rush to Aachen to protect our home." At that moment, a thought occurred to him, and he realized how long it had been since the last time he had spoken with his sister. "Forgive me. How are you two? Are you married yet?" He let his lips curl in a smile. They both appeared to flourish together.

"No, not yet," Lirienne said with a propitious smile. "We will when all this bad... all of the nastiness surrounding us fades."

Julien changed the subject and said, "The village, from what I've seen since I awoke, is little short of amazing."

"Thank you, my Lord. Rebuilding and trade are thriving again, due in no small part to your family's efforts."

Julien watched Dreu rock back and forth on his heels. "You're practically family now, Dreu. Stop the 'my Lord'," Julien said with a chuckle. "I am most impressed with these improvements."

Dreu cleared his throat. "My apologies, my... Julien. I should return to the watch. I wish you the best with your business in Aachen. If you require my sword, I will join you."

"Thank you, Dreu," Julien affirmed while nodding his head. "I require your sword here to protect my... our family." Before he could utter another phrase, he let Lirienne drag him into the small living quarters of the garrison.

"We can speak inside," she informed him. "Leave us," she said to the servants.

The smell of food grew, as they neared a table set for the evening meal. He became aware of the rapid pulse of a child and quick, light footfalls. He then saw Clotilda, racing around the corner.

She embraced his legs and cried out, "Papa," before bouncing up and down.

Julien felt his jaw grow slack in shock.

"Now, Tildy, Papa's been traveling for many days and nights. Go ask cook to cut an apple for you," Lirienne directed Clotilda.

"Yes, Aunt Lirienne," Clotilda answered before turning back to Julien. "I've missed you, Papa." She beamed up at him and then bounded towards the kitchen.

"Why is Tildy calling me 'papa'?" Julien asked with what sounded like a squeaky voice.

Lirienne's blue eyes settled on him. "She calls you 'papa' because you are her father, Julien."

"I don't understand," he murmured.

"Honestly, Julien. Stop lying to me and to yourself," Lirienne challenged while patting his left shoulder. "You and Flor were sweethearts. Whenever Reginald left Divio, you'd visit her. She confided in me, knowing that I was in a loveless marriage. Reginald did not love her and she hated sharing a bed with him. Flor came to you for comfort…. I know this."

Julien inhaled sharply and stared at her. "Yes, we did have coitus," he murmured. "Yet, she never said the children were ours."

"She never told you," Lirienne explained.

"Flor would have told me if that were true."

Lirienne sighed, as if exasperated with him. "What would have happened to her if she had said such a thing, Julien? You would have insisted on running away with her. Reginald would have gone after you two, and then if caught, you might have ended up dead, and she would have been sent to a nunnery. Reginald would have also shunned the children."

Julien turned away from her and sat down at the table. Long-forgotten sorrows came to the fore in his heart. "She should have been my wife. Reginald knew we loved each other. Why did he have to marry her… I became furious when I discovered how our brother treated Flor. He had so many mistresses. He spent all his spare time in pursuit of them. I thought that if I could give her the pleasure she lacked in the marriage bed, her life would gain meaning. Flor would become as sweet as she had been before their marriage."

Julien took a goblet of wine and drank down a gulp. "When our daughter was born, I suspected that Clotilda might be mine, but Flor seemed so pleased. Her life had purpose after the children, and Reginald gave her a modicum of respect. I knew the consequences, if Reginald had known the truth, yet the risk of seeing her and the children was worth it. No one seemed the wiser." He wiped his tears away with his right sleeve.

Lirienne swiped at her eyes, as she crouched down and embraced him. "Thank you for finally voicing the truth, little brother," she said.

"It was difficult for me when I heard that they had… died," Julien whispered. "I could not mourn Flor, Ledger, and Jakelin as a husband and father. I had to hide my feelings. I have even hidden them from my new family."

"I know," Lirienne whispered as she handed him a piece of cloth from the table, "but at least you still have Tildy. She's part of Flor."

Julien took the cloth and dabbed at his face again. He always felt ashamed when he cried. "I'll be a proper father to Clotilda. Once this mess is over, she and I can move to mother's home, until the stronghold is complete. Then she can travel with me when my family and I are needed." He sniffed and tossed the cloth into the blazing hearth.

Lirienne frowned for a moment. "Do you really think that is wise, Julien? You are not human anymore."

"My family likes Clotilda. For Morrigan's sake, she refers to Máire as the 'fire queen'. Clotilda loves hearing their stories."

Lirienne interrupted him. "I know, Julien, but you are now part of a tribe that travels the world and maintains the balance. As you live, your daughter's children and grandchildren will continue to live and die, while you remain youthful. You cannot leave her each time there is some new and horrible monster to defeat."

"But I always wanted this," Julien pleaded, taking Lirienne's right arm. He stared at her and whimpered, "I thought my chance to be a father had disappeared after that attack. But now..." He paused a bit, before continuing. "Look, I love my daughter. Why can't I take care of her?"

Lirienne sighed. "Julien, we know you will be there for her, but she needs to be raised with consistency. You cannot travel and take her with you. How will you two get along? She loves to play in the sun, and you are mired to the night."

Julien released Lirienne and turned towards the table, pondering why Lirienne's words rang of the truth. How could he think of taking Clotilda? "Who will raise her if I cannot?"

"Her Aunt Lirienne, Uncle Dreu, and her grandmother will raise Clotilda. We will instruct her in the ancient path." Lirienne smiled. "Perhaps one night, she will be able to understand what you are and appreciate the sacrifices you've made."

"Thank you," Julien murmured while smiling back at her.

"I also know that you did not come here for just a visit. Is there something else you need to tell me?"

"I'm sure mother already told you about Reginald's plan. I'm going to Aachen to join her. If that Lamia thinks she can take our home from us, she will be disappointed with the outcome. I love you. Take care of my daughter and your family," he said before rising up and embracing her.

"I love you too, little brother." Lirienne squeezed him and patted his back.

"Tildy! Your father wishes to speak to you," Lirienne called out, backing away.

Once Clotilda had run back into the room, Julien squatted to her height. "I'm sorry, Clotilda, but I have to leave for Aachen, again. I'll return very soon. Be good for your aunt and uncle." He smiled at her and blinked back his tears.

"I'll be good," Tildy replied. "Can I go with you the next time? Please." When she grinned at him, he could almost see Flor in her face.

"We'll see," he murmured, pulling her in for a hug. He then kissed her hair, which smelled of apple.

"And you'll teach me to ride a horse, like you promised the last time?"

"Good Gods, you remember me promising you that?" Julien chuckled. "That was a good six months ago. Yes, my love. I'll teach you to ride a horse when I'm home. Be good, and remember that Papa loves you very much." When he released Clotilda, she grinned at him again.

"I love you too, Papa." She waved at him and headed back for the kitchen.

As he turned, he jumped a little upon finally seeing Máire and Edward standing in the doorway. Either his own senses lied, or his daughter had distracted him.

My daughter…

Julien turned and waved at Lirienne before following Edward and Máire into the yard.

"I thought you would never see us," Máire commented.

"I needed to say goodbye to Lirienne and my daughter," Julien said. "I will tell you about it on the way to Aachen. I figured Marcus would send someone to keep an eye on me."

"You don't seem surprised in the least," Edward remarked.

"Marcus is a busybody," Máire quipped.

"Yes, that he is," Julien rejoined, "yet, I'm pleased he sent me a great escort. Let's begin our journey."

Aachen

Reginald woke to the sounds of crickets chirruping to each other.

Have I slept through the day? Impossible. What a strange dream.

As he rose, he noticed Talia had risen and left her side of the bed rumpled. He pulled back the fur covering the window and stared out into the star-filled night, when a strange sensation nearly forced him to his knees, and an unknown pain began to grow. Reginald doubled over and moaned. His stomach throbbed with a perplexing demand. He had never felt this hungry before. After walking out of the room, he smelled something rancid in the air, but his stomach informed him that any food would do.

He walked down the hall and into the common room, where the innkeeper's wife fretted about with chores. "My Lord, would you like some supper? It will be ready in half an hour."

"That's not soon enough," Reginald insisted. While his stomach demanded food, he did not know the punishment for disobeying. In search of sustenance, Reginald ran out into the street. The cold air outside quelled his hunger pains, a little. He soon spotted a food stall across from the inn, which looked promising. He walked up to the distracted attendant and hissed, "Food. Now."

The startled attendant handed him a greasy joint of mutton. "Will this suffice, my Lord?" he asked.

Reginald dropped a coin into the attendant's hand and scurried to a nearby alley with his prize. He then started to devour his meal, as if he had not eaten in weeks.

After nearly a dozen bites, the pain in his stomach increased triple fold. He fell down into the alleyway and began to vomit. Reginald prayed in silence that no one would see him in this condition. He continued to heave, until all the mutton lay splattered in the alley. He soon heard laughter in the distance. Reginald wiped his mouth and turned in the direction of the laughter. "You do not know me," he said to the stranger, who stopped his laughter and stared at Reginald.

The stranger shook his head after a moment of intense study and then turned away.

Reginald rose from the alley floor and started walking. Every few steps, his pain caused him to lean his shoulder against a building for support. After lurching several steps down the alley, his intake of breath detected someone ahead.

As he neared, a strong stench enveloped him. His sharp vision revealed a prostitute, standing at the corner of the alley and road. Her smell and appearance brought forth the compulsion to vomit again, but then the smell changed from noxious to appetizing.

When she turned to face him, her features conveyed a difficult life. She seemed sharp-boned and sallow of skin, while her dark eyes followed him. "Are you interested in my company?"

He said nothing at first, but he reached for her.

The prostitute backed away and said, "You may touch me when you've given me sufficient coin. Five sou."

As Reginald followed her, she continued to back away. Finally, he pleaded for her to stop.

The prostitute ceased her movements and stared at him. Her rate of breathing rose, with each breath increasing in volume. She then emitted a strange beating, as if from a drum.

As he approached her slowly, her breathing steadied. Reginald could now smell the illness that exuded from her, and yet a stronger smell swelled about her. He could almost taste it. A strange compulsion drove him to try to imbibe it. Without much thought, Reginald embraced the prostitute. As he stared at her, her eyes grew fearful. He leaned in and sniffed her face, drawing his nose down her cheek. When he reached her neck, the scent intensified. After licking her throat, a strange energy built within himself, as realizing that the scent of this delicious smelling substance dwelled inside the prostitute.

He opened his mouth and bit her throat, feeling his teeth plunge through the skin. Reginald's thoughts washed away, as the first pulse of blood passed his lips. He closed his eyes, dwelling on the absolute pleasure of this strange act. He could sense the prostitute's ecstasy grow as he drank from her. As her body temperature decreased, her movements escalated into a wild frenzy. Soon, however, she became limp, like a sleepy child, and the drummer ceased tapping the beat.

While Reginald's hunger had eased, his own euphoria raged within. He tossed away the prostitute into the alley, as if she weighed no more than a mere loaf of bread, but then he heard a familiar voice from behind.

"Did you enjoy your first feast?"

Reginald turned and witnessed the smiling and radiant Talia. "It was... yes, it was most pleasurable," he answered, after finally finding words, yet they still seemed inadequate to describe the entire feat.

Talia looked over the prostitute and commented, "A pity. If you had let her live, you could have fed from her again. I will teach you that skill, in time."

He stared at her, confused by her statement.

Talia's blue eyes met his. "We can feed without killing," she explained. She then proceeded to walk around him in a small circle. "You already have a prodigious talent for manipulation."

"What do you mean by that?" he queried.

"We Lamia have the ability to alter the perceptions and memory of mortals," Talia said. "We can also influence other immortals, to a degree."

Reginald watched her eyes flash red.

He remembered red eyes in the carriage and at other times. She had altered his thoughts and perceptions. Reginald felt a building fury within himself. "You have been manipulating me."

"Of course I have." Talia beamed at him. "You're so hungry for power, Reginald, yet you didn't realize that for yourself. I've manipulated you because, deep within, you wished to seize control of your family's lands. You even believe Julien and Lirienne are bastards, and that it's your right to take over their property and your mother's for her adulterous affairs."

"How did you know of these suspicions?" he asked Talia.

"Emotions are in the blood. Emotions are shadows that remain from memory. They are not fully complete, but they can paint a picture of someone's past," Talia said as she took his arm. "You will see this soon enough. You may have experienced it already."

Reginald closed his eyes and recalled what seemed to be the emotions of the now-lifeless prostitute. Her two emotions wavered between sadness and fear... fear of an abusive father and overwhelming sadness at the passing of her mother. Yet, he also sensed an enduring bitterness that increased with each day of a harsh life. Reginald swallowed away her emotions and hoped they would fade. "I see the truth of your words. I've had my suspicions, and I've desired my family's property. Why did you wish to encourage those thoughts?"

Talia smiled at him, while tracing her left hand over his cheek. "Reginald, I want what you want. I wish to help you in any way I can."

"Then, why did you sponsor me?"

Talia's laughter grew loud in the alley. The sound of her chuckles echoed into the night. "Because you wanted it, silly. We Lamia crave power. Is it not fitting that you became one of us? Besides, your brother is a Deargh Du. That cowardly lot insists on meddling in our affairs. What gives them the right to be so virtuous and altruistic? Of course, their true motives are that these characteristics lead to their control of every situation. Now, Reginald, you have the same power as Julien. You're on an equal footing, and he's no longer superior. Does this not please you?"

Reginald considered her words, but before he could speak, Talia interrupted him.

"Were you not jealous when you found out that he received these gifts, including that damned beauty of theirs? I mean, you did lose your wife and children."

"That adulteress was not my wife, and those are his children," he spat.

"At that time, you did not realize they were his, so you weren't jealous? After all, you are the elder brother. If anyone should receive those gifts, it should be you." Talia's hands grasped his shoulders.

"Are you manipulating me again?" He felt as though he could not trust her completely.

"No, my sweet. I am merely trying my best to bring the truth out, the truth that resides within you." Her voice became a sibilant purr.

Reginald gave in and kissed her. After the initial excitement had passed into a burning desire, he stroked her golden locks and stared into her eyes. "Does my being Lamia change our approach in this plan?"

"No. This new situation does not alter our plan at all," Talia said, pushing him against the wall of the alley. "I announced our arrival at court. In three nights, you shall have your prize. Now, allow me to teach you the finer points of our skills. We can play later," she said, while caressing him.

Reginald sighed, impatient at the interruption. However, staring into Talia's beguiling eyes influenced him to give in.

"Lead the way, lady sponsor," he said. Talia took his hand and they moved into the streets of Aachen.

Vézelay

After hearing Máire and Edward leave the basement in search of Julien, Marcus dozed for awhile longer, surprised by his exhaustion. His thoughts regarding the gathered forces in Aachen soon faded. When he awoke again, he considered taking the empty bed. Following his compulsion, Marcus rose, wishing to sleep late into the evening. However, when he pulled back the cover, he found a bleary-eyed Amata staring up at him. Her pale hand rested next to Lucius.

"Marcus, have you seen Edward?" Amata asked. "I was sleeping next to him, and when I awoke, he was gone."

"Maél Morrigan and Julien have left, as well," Claudius muttered from his blankets a few feet away. "Where did they go?"

Marcus shrugged, figuring Claudius would understand why he did not wish to answer that particular question, since he had a feeling that their allies would not be pleased.

As others started to rouse themselves, Lucius squeaked a yawn and stretched his legs.

Across the room, Mandubratius sat up in one of the cots and stretched. "Are you quite sure, Marcus? You have no idea where your family has run off to?" he asked.

"Perhaps for a swim," Marcus lied.

"They'll probably return and throw cold water on us," Claudius muttered.

"I have a feeling that the two of you know where they went," Mandubratius purred while looking at Marcus. When Marcus didn't speak, Mandubratius added, "Ah, the general is tight-lipped. Hmmm, let me remember what I overheard. Julien is leaving to chase after his mother. Now, why would Lady Heloise travel? Interesting questions, are they not, Marcus?"

"Is there a point to this interrogation?" Marcus asked.

"Ah, the praetor gives up on silence and retreats to jokes," Mandubratius teased. "Do you really want to have me annoy you for the rest of the evening? Why not tell the truth?"

Marcus considered his options. The prospect of dealing with Mandubratius the rest of the evening made him frustrated beyond belief, but perhaps Mandubratius would be reasonable. After all, what possible interest would the Lamia have in Burgundy, when they had the Empress under their control? A small slice of Francia seemed to be too much trouble to bother with, when they wanted to deal in the fates of empires.

Better to get this out of the way.

"Fine... the truth is this. They went to Aachen to keep Talia from coaxing Emperor Charles and Reginald de Divio from seizing Vézelay and Auxerre."

Mandubratius seemed to consider that information, and then he laughed and shook his head. "Yes, Talia always wanted Burgundy. She is most single-minded about the entire matter. It's a foolish plan, but I must admire her perseverance. She has tried to regain these lands for over two hundred years." He paused for a moment. "Of course, the Lamia have never had any part of these machinations. It seems like a trivial matter, in comparison to our other, more entertaining plans."

Marcus looked over at Amata, for a moment, who closed her eyes. He stood up and strode to Mandubratius' cot, while the Lamia yawned again and stretched. "Then you have not aided or abetted Talia in this scheme? I mean, you are her sponsor."

"I have not," Mandubratius stated. "In fact, I encouraged her not to proceed with this endeavor. However, much like her niece, she is not one for taking advice."

"I think you tried to discourage her, but you allowed her to continue her game. After all, it's entertaining to watch a young child grapple with politics. However, my line promised to protect and defend the interest of Julien's family. So, it is our duty to prevent Talia from completing this plan." Marcus crossed his arms over his chest and glared at the Briton.

Mandubratius smirked. "I have no intention of interfering. By all means, try to stop Talia. However, I feel that I should make a few observations. You sent Máire, or allowed her to go with Julien, as well as your incendiary expert."

"As you said, she tends to follow her own counsel."

"A strange choice, Marcus," Mandubratius said while raising his brows. He then reclined.

"What makes you say that? Please get to the point."

Mandubratius chuckled. "It's obvious, even to my eyes, that Máire and her aunt are hardly on the best of terms."

"Again, what of it?" Marcus demanded.

"Well, Marcus, you see... if Máire were to kill her aunt, which Talia probably deserves, I'm afraid that such an act would rend our treaty to shreds, which would be most unfortunate, wouldn't it?" A calculating smile slid over the Lamia's face.

Marcus leaned in close to Mandubratius. "Are you threatening me and mine, sir?" he asked, attempting to keep his tone light and soothing.

"Oh my, that attempt to appear menacing yet peaceful is most impressive. No, I'm not threatening you or your family."

Marcus watched the Lamia's features grow hard. "I would never dream of threatening you, my old friend," Mandubratius uttered. Despite his even tone, his green eyes belied a perilous warning.

"Yes, I know you wouldn't," Marcus acknowledged before pulling back. "To keep this alliance in place, I'll send Arwin to track down Julien, Edward, and Máire. He will send her here, and he will make sure that Talia behaves. I assume you will tell her that her games need to end to keep the alliance intact."

"Of course," Mandubratius said with a smirk.

"Mac Alpin," Marcus called, turning away from the Briton. He could stand to deal with Mandubratius no more. "See if you can catch up to Máire, Edward, and Julien. Take her place in their party and send her to Vézelay. Make sure Lady Talia knows that her games are no longer an option."

"Thank you so very much, Marcus," Mandubratius drawled from behind. "I feel that this is a wise course of action for all parties involved."

Marcus wondered whether it would be better if he joined Arwin. As he watched Mac Alpin walk to the staircase, a rustling sound distracted him. He sensed the Empress sit up, and she proceeded to study him. He noticed that she had taken over Sextus' cot, after Lucius had demanded her spot in the bed.

"This is a lovely village, but it is too small to meet our needs. Why do we stay here, Marcus of the Deargh Du? All I've seen you do is flee from the Strigoi."

Marcus turned and witnessed the Empress smirk at him, as she joined Mandubratius on his cot. Now their unsettling twin smiles and hard eyes remained fixed upon him.

He sat down on Julien's bed and smiled back at them, deciding to join their intimidation game. "There are a plethora of reasons we stay in Vézelay," Marcus remarked. "One, we are here to recuperate. Two, we are here to prepare for this battle against the Strigoi. These last two reasons have little to do with your personal interests, but I'll say them anyway. Three, as I have mentioned before, we are here to protect this family, and finally, we are here to find our stronghold site. After all, it may be necessary to use. Does this answer your questions, Empress?" He smirked at her. "I seem to recall you cowering during our last meeting with the Strigoi."

The Empress lowered her eyes.

"Awvarwy? Any questions?" Marcus asked, forcing a smile.

"Awvar-ee?" the Empress tried to echo while facing her sponsor.

"Awvarwy. It is a long story, one better saved for another night. That's my true name. Very few can pronounce it correctly, so my title is my name for present." Mandubratius then met Marcus' eyes. "Marcus, do you intend to force us to stay here against our will? Perhaps you wish to force us into laboring on the construction of this stronghold."

"Of course not, Mandubratius, the Lamia are welcome to leave at any time," Marcus said. "Now that you speak for the entire Lamia population, what are your intentions? Do you wish to leave us and return to Rome, so we meet the Strigoi alone?"

"Of course not," Mandubratius answered. "However, I do need to return to Rome and see if I can recruit more soldiers from His Holiness. You have my word that I shall not interfere with the business in Aachen." He paused and then turned to study the Empress before shifting his green eyes back to Marcus. "I will depart with my escorts, Marcus, and leave the remainder of the Lamia here, if that suits you." Mandubratius leaned his chin against the palm of his right hand, awaiting a reply.

"I would appreciate the extra warriors, in case they are necessary," Marcus answered. He heard in his voice a great deal more enthusiasm than he felt.

"Excellent," Mandubratius said, raising his head. "I will leave Patroclus, Amata, Irene, and the remainder, except for my general and a soldier of his choosing. Does this suit you, Gaius?"

"Traveling suits me well," Gaius answered from a cot.

"Splendid. Amata? I know you are awake," Mandubratius added while addressing her.

Amata sat up in the bed and answered, "This suits me fine." She then stared at Marcus, for a moment, with her luminous eyes.

Marcus felt his focus waver when he heard Lucius meow during a yawn.

Mandubratius broke the silence and said, "I'm sure it will, as I'm sure it suits Patroclus." A thin veil of a threat laced his words. He then smiled at Irene and said, "Now, my love, you have a duty as well. Stay here and consider Marcus your commander."

"My commander? I'm the Empress! I will not be subjected to the whims of a mere general!"

Gaius emitted a soft groan of annoyance from his cot.

"Fine," growled Marcus. "If you won't tell your child how to behave," he said to Mandubratius, "I will." Marcus smiled at the Empress, rose from the cot, and forcibly dragged her back to the bed. Once there, he bent her forcibly over his knees.

"Now, stop behaving like a child, Empress, and I'll treat you like an adult. If you decide not to, I'll humiliate you with a beating. Now, adult or naughty child?" he asked calmly.

He heard her grind her teeth in rage. Marcus realized that all eyes stared at him in the silent room. He watched several of his associates, including Mandubratius, close their eyes and begin laughing.

"I said 'adult'!" the Empress stated a tone both emphatic and resolute, yet she still raged within.

With his point made, Marcus released her. "I am so glad we came to an understanding, Imperial Majesty. All I ask is for respect." He then noticed Mac Alpin watching from the stairs. The Ekimmu Cruitne's chortles added to the growing dissonance in the basement. "Mac Alpin, you should make haste to catch up with Máire," he reminded the Ekimmu Cruitne.

Mac Alpin nodded and headed to the door.

"We shall depart as well," Mandubratius said, motioning to Gaius. He started to gather his bag of supplies, as Gaius gestured for Sextus to join them.

Marcus decided to follow Mac Alpin out and make sure there were no more distractions. As he walked upstairs, Marcus sensed Lucius follow him.

Once outside, the dark skies revealed stars and a golden moon. Mortal heartbeats echoed around them. Soon, the scents of the group in the basement faded into the distance, while other blood-drinkers wandered outside.

Mandubratius came up behind him and stood. "Well, Marcus, it appears that we are ready to depart," he said.

Marcus could sense the ready smile on his associate's face. "So, you are. Most impressive," Marcus said after turning to face the Briton. Together, they inspected Gaius and Sextus, as they held their traveling pouches and supplies.

"Do wish us a safe journey, old friend. I'm sure our paths will cross soon, when we meet again to defeat this menace," Mandubratius avowed.

Marcus could not help but be surprised when Mandubratius hugged him and kissed his cheek. He managed to return the squeezing embrace and kiss.

Mandubratius backed away and said, "May your Goddess protect you in this new home."

"And may Mars be at your back," Marcus said, before the Lamia left. Dust flew as they disappeared into the night.

Marcus heard Lucius chuckle at the dealings of blood-drinkers before he grew distracted and stalked an unwary bird. Marcus then sensed someone awaiting his attention. He saw Father Xofer and several of the transformed Strigoi watching him.

"We would like to offer assistance," one of them said.

Marcus nodded. His earlier anger had faded into a warm and soothing peace. "Thank you," he said. "Would one of you go find Dreu, the garrison commander? We need to integrate with his forces. Then, I believe Caoimhín and I will ask for volunteers to help seek out a stronghold."

chapter twenty

While in flight, Edward felt a hand on his left arm. He glanced over and saw Máire looking at him.

"I think I need to take some sustenance," Máire said. "Can you catch up to Julien and tell him to meet us at that small village?" she asked, pointing to a moderately lit area in the distance.

They had flown towards Aachen in a hurry, in order to avoid any further dealings with the Lamia. Unfortunately, their rate of speed began to diminish after a few hours. Only Julien kept up their original pace.

"Of course," Edward said while smiling at her.

Máire fell back and headed towards the village.

As he sped up, grateful for something to do, Edward contemplated why Máire had woken him and asked him to join Julien and herself. He reasoned that his incendiaries might be needed, or perhaps she had determined that some distance between Amata and him might be useful.

Amata seemed to be as confused as he was, regarding their relationship.

Marcus had spoken to him about her lowered status in the Lamia and her resolution to carry on.

Edward found much admiration for her in that matter, yet he wondered how long her lowered status amongst her kind would continue, and when she'd decide to join forces with Mandubratius again. After all, this could be nothing more than a game to Mandubratius. As soon as Edward caught up with Julien, he tapped his shoulder and pointed to a village. "We must feed."

Julien nodded his head and then began to fly towards the village. The two blood-drinkers landed outside of a large farm.

Máire wiped her mouth after feeding from a doe. She then sat down for a moment, while the doe turned and walked toward the two men.

Edward looked into its luminous eyes, which offered to reveal the secrets of the forest, but unfortunately, he could not understand deer-talk. He leaned in and patted it before drinking its blood. When he felt his strength return, he pulled back. "What exactly are you intending to do once we reach Aachen?" he asked them both. He spotted an impressive stag in the distance, which watched them and then trotted forward, nearing them. As it moved towards Julien, Edward noticed the younger Deargh Du grin.

"You called him, Julien. Well done," Máire praised.

Julien held out his right hand to pet the animal and said, "If we get there in time, we'll use whatever means necessary to prevent Reginald from challenging my claims and my family's claims to our property." He then started to feed from the stag.

"And your aunt?" Edward asked, looking at Máire.

"As Julien said, whatever means necessary," she answered. "If Talia interferes, we will deal with her."

Edward smirked. He could sense some of Máire's true motives. "And if she does not interfere?"

The Deargh Du paused for a moment. "We would deal with her still. Edward, she will never stop interfering in this province."

When she met his eyes, Edward could almost see the same cold resolve that settled in Marcus' eyes at times. "You are not here merely to support Julien and his family," he commented. "You seek her death and vengeance."

"Does that trouble either of you?" Máire asked.

Julien stopped feeding and touched the impressive horns of the stag for a moment. "It does not concern me at all," he stated.

"Edward?" Máire turned her green-eyed gaze to him.

"I've known you for over two hundred years," Edward explained. "It is not your nature to maintain hatred. Even Marcus and Mandubratius have pushed aside their mutual desire to kill each other and have some sort of grudging respect. They are allies. Your father-in-darkness and mine were not friends until events made them so. Perhaps, you need to put that hatred aside."

"Our allegiance with the Lamia is temporary," Máire commented. "You remember well that the Lamia invaded Éire. They took much from us. I was born of vengeance, Edward. Just because I am mild most of the time does not mean it does not fester within. Unless there is a compelling argument from the Goddess or another deity, Talia will die. I hope this is not a problem."

Edward shrugged. "As long as it does not become an obsession. I do not wish to lose you to an obsession. Part of me remembers your conviction regarding Connor Mac Turrlough, when we were both mortals."

"I find myself obsessed more with the images the Strigoi laid within my head," Máire said before looking at Julien. "I killed my husband-to-be at the altar because he had killed my love, Seanán, and raped me."

Edward watched Julien sit beside Máire and embrace her, with her head resting against his shoulder.

"The man I was teasing with marriage had conspired with my aunt and Mandubratius. I wished to kill him with my own hands. During my transformation to Deargh Du, I went to my wedding and plunged my hand into his chest. I ripped out his heart and drained the blood from it while he still watched. It tasted of rank bitterness, but it was still the best of meals. Connor soon fell and died. In the ensuing battle between the Lamia and the Deargh Du, Ekimmu Cruitne, and Sugnwr Gwaed, Morrigan possessed me.

I wielded Her strength as I faced Mandubratius. I almost killed him, but the Goddess stayed my hand and said I could not. She then left me."

Máire took an unsteady breath. She kissed Julien's brow and sat up from the embrace. "This is why I was born of vengeance. Now, the Strigoi are showing me visions of them ripping out the hearts of the people I care for. However, in this latest dream, Connor tore me apart and took my heart." Máire looked away as if to will away images from her dream. She then turned back and added, "I will take my vengeance, regardless. She manipulated poor Uncle Cennedi and made him Lamia. He tried to save me from her. I should protect others from her current and future manipulations, so Talia does not destroy as she has done in the past." Her eyes shifted to Edward. "Now, stop digging in my head for answers," she demanded in a playful tone.

"All right, Banbh Ceanúil," Edward said. "I will cease, if you tell me why you nursed Mandubratius during this mission. I understand my feelings for Amata and why I nursed her."

Before Máire could answer, Julien interjected, "It would look bad, if we neglected to aid them in their time of need." His deepening frown implied to Edward that Julien felt uncomfortable with the conversation.

"I have no feelings for anyone," Máire stated. "Marcus asked me to watch over him, since no others readily volunteered." She shrugged a little. "It is always up to the women to care for the men. Besides, I feel badly for anyone attacked by the Strigoi. That's just the way it is, Edward. Enough chitchat. Let's continue to Aachen."

Upon smelling an undeniable scent, Edward turned away and said, "Not just yet, Maél Morrigan. Arwin is about to join us." He pointed to a speck in the distance, which grew in size. In moments, Mac Alpin landed a few feet away from them.

"Is something wrong?" Julien asked Mac Alpin.

"Not specifically. Máire needs to return to Vézelay," Mac Alpin announced while looking at Máire. "Marcus is concerned that you wish to kill your aunt."

"Yes, so what of it?" Máire asked.

"Mandubratius issued an ultimatum. If you kill Talia, the alliance is off," added Mac Alpin.

"And Marcus wants me to let her live, Arwin?" Máire challenged. Edward could see her eyes begin to glow.

Mac Alpin's face softened. "At least until this mission is over, Chroí," he said before embracing her with a playful growl. "We all have to quell our tempers because of the alliance."

Máire pulled out of his embrace and countered, "But my aunt deserves to die, Arwin."

"And you have this same opinion about the rest of the Lamia, such as

Amata, Horatio, Patroclus, and Mandubratius?" Mac Alpin asked. He raised his brows and shuffled his feet a bit while he awaited her answer.

"Amata and Patroclus are more friend than foe now, and Horatio was an innocent tool of war for the Lamia who created him," Máire answered. "Mandubratius is an enemy and an annoyance, but I cannot kill him. However, Talia has given us many reasons to destroy her. We cannot ignore the fact that she is trying to take Julien's family's homes. I have a duty to him. If that means killing her, you can't stop me."

"You cannot stop me either," Julien pointed out. "She is a direct danger to my brother and to the rest of my family. I am with Máire on this."

Mac Alpin grumbled. "Well, wee lass, I've known you well enough to know that when your mind is set so firmly, there are few things that can change it. I also realize that it would be a futile struggle to bind you and haul you back to Vézelay. I will tell Marcus that he swallowed his rage, and sacrificed his desire to behead that bothersome Briton, for nothing."

Máire threw up her hands. "Must you make me feel guilty, Arwin?" She began to pace back and forth, swinging her arms, as she muttered to herself in Gaelic. She soon stopped and turned back to address Mac Alpin.

"Alright, we will seek Talia. She will not die by my hand, nor any Deargh Du's until the time is right," she acknowledged. "However, we will injure her if necessary." Edward witnessed her eyes dart to Julien, who nodded his head.

Arwin grunted and then said, "I will tell your father-in-darkness that you will allow her to live. Now, come and give me a proper farewell, since you did not even say goodbye before leaving." He squeezed her again. "By the Gods, lass, stop picking up the leech's habits regarding manipulation. You've already manipulated all who surround you." He smirked. "Have a safe journey, you three. Edward, try to make those two Deargh Du behave." Mac Alpin then released Máire and took to the skies.

"What should we do with Talia, if we do not kill her?" Julien asked.

"We will destroy her claims and her reputation in court," Máire suggested.

"Isn't that acting as a La–" Edward began to say before silencing himself.

"Yes. It is exactly like the behavior of a Lamia," Máire admitted. "However, if we destroy her reputation, she will be unable to trouble the Empire again. Now, we must make haste. There is a lot of ground to cover."

Vézelay

Burdened with concerns of intrigue, Amata wandered to the grove, where she found the Deargh Du and the other Celtic lines sitting upon the ground. She thought at first that they preformed some ritual in front of the fire, but then she witnessed a little mortal girl, with large blue eyes, amongst them and realized that they were merely gathered and staring up into the skies. Amata cleared her throat to get their attention, and then everyone grew silent.

Marcus turned towards her, as did the pretty pale-haired Druid, Caoimhín, and then offered her a jug of wine.

"Thank you," she said, accepting the jug. She then sat next to Marcus. Amata felt like the odd woman out, the only Lamia, until she noticed that Horatio and Patroclus sat amongst the gathered. She even spied the priest and a few of the transformed Strigoi staring out into the skies.

"This is a most beautiful country," Caoimhín commented. "Not as beautiful as our home, but it is exquisite all the same."

"I think I still prefer Bath," Marcus admitted, "though this place has a comforting wilderness."

Amata saw Claudius, who bore a thoughtful look, turn to Marcus. "Do you feel as though we visited here before?" he asked. "I mean… as mortals. I think we may have campaigned through this area. At one point, I thought that at the end of my military career, I would retire to Gaul and plant vineyards, since they seemed so very fond of wine here."

"Perhaps we did come through here," Marcus said with a chuckle. "My memories of that past have faded, a bit…" As his voice trailed off, Amata could see a frown darken his face.

Even the others, Amata noted, seemed to lose themselves in their thoughts.

Unsure of whether she should stay in this glum group or leave, Amata glanced about, looking for some escape, when she noticed the little mortal girl staring at her with genuine curiosity.

The child ran to her while holding a wreath of night moonflowers. She curtsied and smiled a toothy grin, extending the flower crown to her.

Amata grinned in spite of herself and felt ridiculous, yet she said, "Thank you, sweetheart," to the little girl. Lamia, as a general rule, did not associate with children, unless one planned to manipulate their parents. Nonetheless, Amata placed the crown on her head without fathoming why.

With her gift delivered, the little girl whirled around with the excitement and energy of a frenzied pixie.

How did they exude such boundless energy?

Marcus' word broke her from her thoughts. "Careful, Tildy! Watch out for the fire," he called, sounding much like a fretful father. "In fact, I think it's time for you to go back to your Uncle Dreu and Aunt Lirienne and go to sleep. Think of good things and you'll have good dreams."

Amata closed her eyes and thought about good dreams, as if having only good dreams was so easy. She pondered that perhaps this was why they gathered under the stars, fervently hoping for a gentle dream during the day, and not the haunting nightmares of the Strigoi. They gathered in the grove, she realized, to find peace.

When she opened her eyes, Amata saw the little girl edge her away around the fire with a great deal of care.

"Alright," said the little girl, as she gave a little pout to the circle. She then blew them all kisses.

Fianait chuckled. "I'll walk her home. Come on, Clotilda," she called before picking up the girl. She then scampered away with the girl, towards the garrison.

With the distraction of the little girl dissipating, Amata thought it a good time to lay voice to the concerns that had brought her here. "Not that it's any of my business," Amata said in a quiet voice, "but the Empress plans to study the location of your future stronghold. She and the others wish to follow you."

"Mmmmm," Caoimhín murmured. "We believed this might happen."

"You aren't concerned?" Amata asked.

"Amata, we know where the Lamia have their strongholds in Rome and in Constantinople," Marcus answered. "If the Lamia know, they know. Why don't you gather your line, and we can all go visit the site of our stronghold, if they wish."

"If we remain as allies, Lady Consul, you need to know where we live, do you not?" another Deargh Du asked, as he continued to trim his nails.

"And if we are not allies?" Amata asked, concerned Empress Irene might decide to end the alliance on a whim.

Marcus laughed that glorious loud chuckle of his, and his earlier frown disappeared. "Amata, we have selected a location that is easily defensible. If we are enemies again, we will protect our new home."

Amata smirked. "You have nothing to fear from me. So, why do you all wait here?" she asked. Soon, she sensed the arrival of other blood-drinkers, she assumed to be Lamia, from behind. She took a long draught on the wine jug and turned towards the newcomers. The appearance of Empress Irene confirmed her suspicions. Amata waved them over.

Marcus continued speaking as if he hadn't sensed the arrival of their guests. "We've fed and we're sated," Marcus said with a shrug. "Besides, Máire should be returning soon. I'd like her to be here for the cleansing and blessing of our new home. We find ourselves short of Druids, after all. I take a lot of pride in her magical skills. I must admit to some envy of her skills." Then, without missing a beat, he called out, "Good evening, Imperial Majesty. Please forgive us if we remain seated."

After walking towards the gathering, the Empress announced, "I hear we are welcome to the site of your new stronghold. That reveals great trust."

"Imperial Majesty," Caoimhín greeted with a smile. "We all trust you to be yourself."

To Amata, Irene appeared bewildered.

"Does that mean… you trust that I will not reveal your location?" asked the Empress.

Marcus set his eyes upon the Empress. "Imperial Majesty," he stated. "As I was telling the consul, this site is easily defensible. If you are our ally, you will be allowed inside. However, if we are not allies, then there is no way the Lamia would come close enough to use the intelligence gained." He smiled in a cool, yet amiable manner. "We trust you will do right by your own code, Imperial Majesty." Marcus leaned back against the ground and closed his eyes, but then something seemed to catch his attention, since he sat up and looked around with surprise evident upon his face. "Wait," he murmured.

"What is he doing back so soon?" Caoimhín asked.

"And where is Máire?" Marcus added.

Amata knew what to expect next, so she fixed her gaze upon the bewildered Empress, who then visibly jumped when Mac Alpin joined them from the sky.

"I can answer that question now," Mac Alpin said while smoothing back his windblown hair. His ruddy face grew lined with a wide grin.

"Where is our Banbh Ceanúil, Arwin?" Marcus asked.

Amata noted that the Empress seemed surprised by Máire's nickname.

"Máire promised not to kill her aunt. However, she still desires to prevent Talia from carrying out her plans."

"And you believed her?" Claudius asked, chuckling. "Máire is not deceitful, but she can exaggerate, if necessary."

"She was quite eloquent and decisive. I believe her to be truthful," Mac Alpin argued.

Marcus grinned. "Perhaps, I should judge this sudden onset of eloquence for myself, Arwin. She may believe herself to be truthful, but my passionless child-in-darkness is ruled by her passions, at times. You've experienced it yourself, many times as well."

"Sunrise comes in a few hours," the Empress said, interrupting them both. "I am certain you two realize that already, but I am discovering these new skills. I think we should return to the Lor… Lady's home."

"True, Empress," Marcus acknowledged while nodding. "Caoimhín, I will take most of our group present to Aachen. Gather whomever you feel is necessary to begin work on the stronghold."

"And the mirror?" Caoimhín asked.

"I will take it in case the Strigoi attack." Marcus then addressed the priest. "Father Xofer, I believe you and yours would prefer to join Julien and Máire."

Amata watched the priest's face become slack, and she realized that he communicated with the others of his line.

"Yes, we would like to join you again."

The Empress stepped forward and said, "We will join you, of course." She smiled at the gathered group. "We are allies, after all. I'm sure the consuls would insist upon it."

Amata simply nodded her head in assent.

Aachen

After landing a mile away from the palace, Sáerlaith dusted herself off.

Lady Heloise removed her cloak and said, "I fear we may be too late, or maybe it is just my nerves. It has been many years since I've been to Aachen or attended the Emperor's court." The elder mortal stared at the palace and then gasped. "Gods, it's magnificent at night. I had no idea. The flickering torches make it look almost like…" Heloise paused, as if trying to find words.

"Magic?" Maon asked.

Heloise nodded her head and smiled at the other Deargh Du. "I could not put it better myself."

"It must be quite opulent during the day," Sáerlaith commented.

"No, it seems quite common and dirty, then… or rather it did." Heloise smirked, before growing silent.

Sáerlaith nodded to the two approaching Deargh Du, who led four magnificent horses. "Lady Heloise, I believe these are our escorts." She smiled at the new arrivals.

"We thought it best to bring mounts to make an impressive appearance," Deasún said, leading one of the horses to Lady Heloise. As he turned to offer a boost to her, he added, "The secretary is still working on the docket."

Ailin held Sáerlaith's mount steady, which she felt was unnecessary. "We must get to him soon," he advised.

Sáerlaith nodded, saying no more, and mounted her horse. Once the others had ascended their mounts, she gathered her reins and squeezed the horse's sides, and the dun trotted towards the palace.

Sáerlaith stood behind, as Heloise conversed with Ercanbald, the Emperor's secretary. After a brief conversation, she heard Ercanbald say, "Return in two night's time, my Lady… ladies," before bowing towards them and disappearing down the hallway.

A flustered Heloise pulled Sáerlaith into a cubby and whispered, "Why did you not manipulate Ercanbald into a meeting with Charles tomorrow night?"

How was it that Lady Heloise refers to the Emperor as 'Charles' and nothing more? Perhaps they are or were old friends. Time will tell.

"Manipulation is not a talent for my kind," Sáerlaith murmured, patting

Heloise's left arm. She kept her suspicions silent. "Besides, it would be hard work, in that we would have to manipulate many to keep them from becoming suspicious of us. You are now on the docket to refute Reginald's claims."

"Forgive my impatience," Heloise said as she took Ailin's arm and beamed at him, "but I hate waiting."

"Then, I suggest that we should not be idle in our wait, Lady Heloise," Sáerlaith said, before leading the party out of the cubby and down the passageway to the main entrance.

The elder of Vézelay chuckled. "I am Heloise to you, my friend, and nothing more. What shall keep us occupied?" she asked, staring at Sáerlaith.

Maon stopped just outside of the palace entrance, cleared his throat, and whispered, "Please forgive an old warrior for intruding in gracious conversation, my Lady. However, in all gravity, your son and Talia will soon discover that we are in Aachen. We must prepare ourselves for the possibility that your son will attempt to prevent you from testifying against his claims."

"You mean... Reginald would try to kill me? He would never, ever do such a thing." Heloise's eyes flooded with unshed tears.

"Heloise," Sáerlaith murmured, turning and offering her a scrap of linen she kept for her own tears. She then glanced at the curious guard who eavesdropped and used her glamoury to indulge in his dreams. "Reginald is not himself. He is being influenced by a powerful Lamia. You have only met Amata and Patroclus, and they have not forced their wills upon you. Reginald may even be..." Sáerlaith paused and took Heloise's hands in her own, "Reginald may even be Lamia, now. I doubt he will be able to refuse Talia's wishes. If Talia desires your death, he may not be able to generate his own will to keep you alive."

"Where shall we go?" Heloise asked in a whimper.

In a soothing voice, Maon whispered, "We stayed at the abbey to the south, remember, Sáerlaith? We can find sanctuary there in the catacombs."

"Yes, we can protect ourselves there, if necessary," Sáerlaith agreed. "I will go find our companions hiding here and nearby." She stared at Maon and Ailin. "I know you two. I trust you with my own life, and I know you will protect an innocent mortal with your lives. I will bring forth a large party of Deargh Du and our brethren to defend our friend."

As Sáerlaith inhaled the scents of Aachen, she detected the smells of blood-drinkers in the immediate area. She then ran towards them and felt the familiar gusts of wind that signaled the rapid departure of her line.

Reginald reveled at the sweet taste, as he licked every inch of Talia's delectable, long neck, tracing the thin line of vitae, which dribbled down her throat and pooled at the joining of her collarbone. Feeding made their shared pleasures intensify one hundred fold. Soon, however, he felt his attention wane upon hearing the sound of someone pounding against the door.

"Who is it?" Talia grumbled in a loud voice. Her obvious annoyance faded as she smiled up at Reginald. She wiped his lips with her fingers and stuck her digits in her mouth.

"It is Bernalt," echoed a voice through the door. "I bear news from court."

"Who is that?" Reginald asked.

"Bernalt is an assistant to the Emperor's secretary. I bribed him to tell us should something unexpected occur, in regards to our appointment," Talia explained. She then slid away from him and walked to the door.

Reginald rolled over. He felt disappointed with the interruption. He could not help but feel some shock, as Talia opened the door in her unclothed and aroused state.

"Come in," she bade the stranger. "Did anyone see you, Bernalt?"

"I do not believe so," Bernalt answered. His eyes darted about as if trying not to stare at her. Once he crossed the threshold, Talia closed the door.

Talia cleared her throat, in an apparent attempt to regain the mortal's attention. "Bernalt, give us your news."

"My Lady," Bernalt greeted. His eyes lowered to the floor. "Lady Heloise of Vézelay has added her name to the docket to rebut Lord Reginald's claims."

"Oh, is that all?" Talia chuckled.

"No, my Lady," Bernalt continued. "A party of three accompanied her."

"I see," Talia murmured. "Very well, Bernalt. Thank you for the information. Leave us."

"And my payment?" the little man asked, as his eyes drifted from the floor.

"Bernalt, I already paid you, remember?" Talia's eyes glimmered, as she gestured for the mortal to walk towards her.

Without resistance, Bernalt followed her orders.

Once he drew close enough, Talia slid her left hand over his throat, leaned in, and started to feed from him.

Reginald felt revulsion at her feeding and closed his eyes.

Do I look as she does when I feed?

"Reginald, come feed," he heard Talia say.

"I am not hungry now," he said.

"Very well. More for me then." Talia smiled a bloody grin.

Reginald listened to the sounds of her swallowing as she enjoyed her meal. After a few moments, she pulled away from Bernalt.

"Thank you, Bernalt. Forget this. You may go home and continue to keep us apprised of our meeting with the Emperor."

Bernalt plodded towards the door and nearly fell on his way out.

Talia closed the door behind him. "Now, my child, I have a duty for you," Talia said. She approached him and kneeled in front of the bed. Her eyes gleamed, promising thousands of pleasures. "Your mother interferes with our plans. We must deal with her."

"Deal with her?" Reginald asked. "We can manipulate the Emperor... why bother?"

"We cannot ignore the danger she brings," Talia insisted. "You must kill her."

"You would have me kill my own mother?" Reginald asked. "I can't do such a thing, no matter what she's done."

"You or someone else, Reginald," Talia persisted. "If you do not, little brother wins. Your mother stands in the way of our success. Do you not want the power and wealth I promise?" Talia crawled into bed with him.

Reginald found himself unable to turn from her stare. "Yes," he groaned, "but her death–"

"Reginald, my sweet," Talia purred while stroking his arm. She brought his right hand to her lips and nibbled gently at the palm. "You realize what she will do to you, do you not?"

"I don't," Reginald answered, but some part of him knew.

"It won't be long before she has you killed, Reginald. She will ask her friends, or Julien, to do it. He will volunteer to be your executioner. After all, he is Deargh Du, and you are his enemy."

Reginald swallowed his bile and reluctance. "Talia, I cannot bear to have her blood on my hands."

"I understand, Reginald. Hire someone else to do it, then. The blood will be on their hands, and if you feel it necessary, you can hunt them in the name of retribution." Her fingers moved over his hand and wrist.

The solution seemed so obvious to Reginald. "I suppose you are right," he said with a sigh. "My mother is the queen of liars and must be dealt with."

"Good," Talia purred, as she leaned in. Her lips gently warmed his for a too-brief moment. "I am glad that you see things in the proper light. Your mission is to hire a band of murderous cutthroats that can find and kill her and the members of her party."

"Do you think they are Deargh Du?" Reginald asked.

"Perhaps. They may be protecting her. Tell these assassins to attack with gold throwing-knives. Further instruct these hired killers to leave behind all of your mother's associates, after they are incapacitated."

Reginald rose and began to dress. "How many do you believe I need?" He would need to either convince several people to give him enough coin or manipulate these marauders into believing that he gave them worthy compensation for this deed.

"Twenty or thirty," instructed Talia.

"Why so many?" Reginald asked, "and why golden weapons?" He added.

Talia started to chuckle softly, but soon her quiet laughter grew loud. "Silly boy, have you ever fought a Deargh Du? Gold is their bane. It weakens them. Otherwise, they are excellent warriors, second only to the Ekimmu Cruitne, or so I'm told." Talia rose to her feet and walked towards her clothing. After rummaging through it, she pulled something out. "Here."

Reginald watched in awe as she tossed bags of coin towards him. "Why did you hide this? We could have stayed in better lodgings!"

Talia shrugged for a moment. "I took this from the palace," she admitted. "Sometimes, it is dangerous to spend money in a frivolous manner, Reginald. However, using it to pay brigands is necessary. Take these to the blacksmith to melt down and create the throwing knives. They can keep the knives after the deed is done. The other bag will serve as the remaining payment for the deaths of the three Deargh Du."

"Will there be enough time for all this?" he asked.

"You tell them that you will deliver the knives tomorrow night and that they will need to attack them at noon."

"Very well," Reginald said, before gathering the bags. He felt surprised at their lightweight, or perhaps he was stronger after his transformation.

"Now, hurry. There is not much time to put these plans into effect. Try to return before sunrise, but if you cannot make it, find shelter."

Reginald leaned in for another kiss and then departed the small chamber.

Julien, Máire, and Edward flew, with hands joined, through the palace over the heads of the guards and other passers-by at top speed, while surrounded by shadow. To Julien, the halls seemed no more busy than usual, at this time of night. Sensing that they were near their destination, Julien tugged both hands, and the three blood-drinkers halted in mid-air and settled to the floor without a sound. Through the darkness, he discerned two guards standing in front of the chamber. Julien whispered, "Let me approach them. You two stay here, for the moment." Without waiting for acknowledgement, he left the gloom and marched towards the guards. At sight of him, they lowered their weapons, blocking his entrance into the Emperor's chambers.

He stared at the guards for a moment and then announced, "I'm Julien de Divio, Inspector General of his Imperial Majesty's Gendarmes. This is an emergency that cannot wait for the light of day."

The two guards lowered their eyes and avoided meeting his gaze.

"Look at me when I'm speaking to you," Julien commanded in a whispered hush. "Let me through, or his Imperial Majesty will hear about this and blame you for your blundering."

The guards exchanged glances and then raised their weapons, allowing Julien to pass.

"What I have to say is not for your ears," he commanded them in a loud whisper. "Leave this hallway and return in one quarter of an hour." With eyes locked on theirs, Julien pushed forth as much glamoury as he could muster. "Do you understand?" He watched their eyes begin to glaze over.

"Yes, Inspector General," the guards answered in a meek whisper. They then totted away from the door slowly, as if caught sleepwalking.

Once the guards passed beyond earshot, Julien called out, "Make haste," to his two companions, forgetting himself for a moment. "Please," he added. "They may draw attention to themselves, and others may investigate."

In low tones, Edward asked, "Should we flee when the others arrive?"

"The Emperor will tell them that I have authority to wake him," Julien answered. After opening the door, he led the others inside. He then gestured for Edward to guard the entrance. When Julien reached the Emperor's bed, he leaned over the slumbering ruler, hoping he would not panic. "Imperial Majesty, wake up," he said softly.

"Mmmm," the elder mortal murmured and stretched. "What now? Has Leo found his spine?" He sat up, opened his sleep-laden eyes, and studied Julien for a moment. "Julien? What is going on? Why didn't the guards wake me?"

"I had to speak with you privately, Imperial Majesty," Julien replied.

"I see." The Emperor yawned and then swung his feet over the side of the bed. He seemed to realize now that they were not alone. The elder man smiled at Máire. "Who is with you, Julien? Is that the lovely Máire of Ulster? Is she a gift for me?" he asked with a chuckle.

Julien noticed Máire smile at the Emperor, who grinned back at her, resembling a sleepy-eyed young man, for a few moments. However, the Emperor's fixed gaze upon Máire brought forth annoyance. "No," Julien answered, feeling a small amount of impatience rise within. "This matter concerns my family."

The Emperor faced away from Máire and stared at him. "What about your family? Is Lady Heloise well? I believe she is slated to appear before me tomorrow evening."

"My mother is fine, Imperial Majesty. I am just concerned. I was informed that my brother is attempting to usurp my title, which you had bestowed upon me, as well as titles bestowed upon my mother's family."

"Your brother Reginald makes many disquieting claims, to say the least," the Emperor stated. "These were made in the gaze of the public eye through an intermediary. I must hear these arguments in a public forum and decide which arguments are just."

"Emperor Charles, you cannot believe those baseless accusations," Julien sputtered. He hoped that the accusations would be just that… baseless. However, he knew with a sinking feeling that some would be partly true.

"Have you seen the accusations?" The Emperor's eyes met his. "I remember them, and I think them rather foolish. They include charges of adultery against you and Lady Heloise. It calls into question Lirienne's and your parentage. Oh yes, and something about witchcraft."

Julien inhaled. He feared these would be the accusations. Dizziness overwhelmed him, but he soon felt Máire take his arm and steady him.

"I find it hard to believe that any of these accusations are based in truth," the Emperor said. "One of my gendarmes, a witch, in league with satanic forces? I think not!" Emperor Charles laughed.

"Can you dismiss the charges?" Julien considered pushing forth his glamoury again, but Máire gently squeezed his hand. He stared at her and noticed a brief shake of her head. While stroking his thumb over her left hand, he noticed the Emperor watching them, for a moment.

"I'm sorry. It's a matter of record, and it's my duty to hear these things and try to settle them. I'm sure it will be resolved, and then you and your brother can make peace on it. He did not even come in person to make these charges. I do not understand why he sent Lady Talia. It's most unusual." The Emperor paused and began to pace barefoot across the floor.

"I hate to interrupt, Imperial Majesty, but your guards are returning," Edward said from the doorway.

"Hmmmm? Oh yes." The Emperor pushed past his guests and leaned out the door. "I'm not to be interrupted. My inspector general will find you when you are needed." He then shut the door. "Guards can be such an annoyance."

"Am I to go to the dungeon?" Julien asked the Emperor.

"The dungeon? Whatever for?"

"I stand accused of witchcraft. Is it not typical to send accused witches to the dungeon for questioning?" Julien asked.

The Emperor sat down on a chair next to a table. "Sit, sit, you three," he bade, while motioning them to the table. "Julien, I know well enough that you are no witch. You and your family share some peculiarities, but these peculiarities are not witchcraft." The Emperor fell silent for a moment. "You and your family have an infallible moral character. It's a baseless accusation, Julien. You will not go to the dungeon."

"I appreciate your confidence, Imperial Majesty," Julien said.

"Worry no more on that. We will see these matters cleared up. Now, if you three will give me leave to go back to sleep, I am going hunting tomorrow. Would you care to join us, Julien?"

As the Emperor rose from his seat, the others followed.

Julien found himself embraced and returned the embrace. "I fear I may find myself too exhausted. We raced here from Vézelay."

"Then we will meet up again tomorrow night," the Emperor said, pulling back. "Rest well." He then nodded towards Edward and Máire, who lowered their heads in a bow, before walking towards the door.

When Julien joined them, they started to look for the guards.

"It seems as though these matters will be resolved," Máire said.

"Yes, but what if my actions as a Deargh Du are mistaken for witchcraft?" Julien whispered before becoming silent, as the guards came into view. "Go defend the Emperor's quarters," he told them. The guards nodded and walked towards the door to the Emperor's chambers.

After walking down the passageway a bit, Edward chuckled. "Julien, I think the Emperor gave you his word to overlook those rumors of witchcraft, but what about the questions of adultery?"

"I suppose it is possible that I am not Reginald's true brother," Julien stated. "Unfortunately, the adultery charges leveled against me are the truth."

"Practically everyone in this court is an adulterer, including the Emperor," Máire stated. "This is what happens when children are not allowed to live their own lives and select their own husbands and wives."

"What will happen if these things are proven true?" Edward murmured.

"My mother, Lirienne, and I will be thrown in the dungeon, my brother would seize my mother's lands and mine, and my daughter would be restricted to a life of poverty as a vassal or as a nun, if she is lucky."

"Such things won't happen," Máire swore.

"How can you say that? I am guilty of adultery, and my mother may be as well," Julien argued in a loud whisper.

"We will find a way. Trust me," Máire said as they reached an outer door.

As Julien stared at her, he wished he felt the same confidence Máire exuded.

Prüm Abbey

Odulf felt the spiked hammer swing back and forth from its place on his belt, hidden beneath the voluminous cloak. He grumbled as he tried to nudge his mount into a quicker pace, but the horse refused to move faster. The unseasonable heat made them all feel rather cantankerous.

"Emme?" Odulf called over his left shoulder as he pushed back his dirty traveling garb, which was favored by the repentant pilgrims who visited holy sites to witness the relics.

"I don't see why we couldn't sell these knives and purchase real blades," Emme grumbled, upon catching up to him.

"You informed the others of the plans, again," Odulf muttered while staring at his younger brother. Their associates could be foolish, sometimes, yet the idea of all that coin made him want to make sure things went as planned.

"For the hundredth time, yes!" Emme yelled. "They understand."

"We are almost there." Odulf dismounted and took his horse's reins. He knew that pilgrims never rode, but he assumed the monks would believe the horses to be an offering of thanksgiving. Once he reached the entrance, he shifted his cloak about and then knocked on the main gate.

A small window opened and a young monk stared at them. "Welcome to Prüm Abbey, my brothers in Christ. We can offer you nourishment and a warm place to sleep," the monk greeted while smiling. His guileless eyes settled on them.

Odulf met the monk's eyes. "Actually, we are here to see the catacombs. We do not require sustenance, at the moment."

"Catacombs?" The monk's face showed a moment of surprise and disbelief.

Odulf studied the monk, who continued to remain in a state of confusion. "I must be mistaken then. I wonder if the abbot can find time to see me."

"Oh, Abbot Sigibert is quite busy today," the monk explained. "I doubt he can break away from his duties."

Odulf reached for the money purse on his belt, removed it, and took the monk's hand. He then poured several silver coins into the shaky palm. "I give these alms for those in need. I wish to see the relics." He then released his grip on the monk, hoping the monk would understand. He knew they could sometimes be brainless about these matters.

He unlocked and opened the gate. "Thank you for your generous donation, good pilgrim. God will truly find your soul worthy for eternal bliss. Let me see if the abbot can break away from his duties to see such a generous servant of the Lord." He then padded away towards the inner refectory.

Odulf motioned the rest of their party through the gate. "Remain here," he whispered fiercely.

"What will we do next?" Emme asked.

"The monk has no knowledge of the catacombs. It is as our patron said. The abbot will know of it and reveal its location." Odulf scratched himself, cursing the itchy robes. "After I leave, do what you must. It won't take long."

Soon, the doors to the interior refectory opened. The monk came out and then waved towards them.

"Stay behind. I'll take care of this," Odulf said. As he walked through the fields of grass, he noticed the tidy gardens in the distance. He followed the monk through the cloister towards a smaller building.

A short, squat man with a red face looked up from a simple desk. The abbot presented Odulf with a gracious, genuine, and wide grin. He then stood and said, "Welcome. I am Abbot Sigibert. I understand you and your brothers have come here to see our sacred relic."

"Abbot, I understand that you have more relics within your catacombs. I wish to offer the abbey a fair donation in exchange for my fellow pilgrims and me to see and pray over those relics."

The abbot raised his right brow and puffed out his chest.

Odulf placed his right hand on his belt, waiting for the abbot to lie.

"Catacombs, you say?" the abbot asked. "I know for a fact that we only have a root cellar, here. It's full of rats and is quite a nasty place. No relics are there, good brother. If you wish, I can take you to our relic on display. It has restored sight to the blind and grants peace to those who pray to the Saints and to Holy Mother Mary."

Odulf pulled the hammer from the thin, leather strap and brought it down on the desk, shattering the wooden top, causing the abbot to back away from the ensuing splitters that flew through the air. Odulf then grabbed the cowering abbot with his spare hand and lifted him up. Blood and several splinters dotted the abbot's face. "Tell me where the catacombs are, old man!" he shouted before grabbing the abbot's right hand and holding it on an undamaged part of the desk.

"I don't know of any catacombs," the abbot cried.

Odulf slammed the hammer on the abbot's hand. He heard bones crack, as the abbot screamed in pain. As he shoved the abbot against the wall with a small amount of force, Odulf hoped Emme and the others had gained control of the abbey by now. He ignored the abbot's whimpered prayers to Jesus for mercy. "I will ask one more time. Where are the catacombs?"

The abbot continued in his prayers.

Odulf pinned the abbot against the wall, grabbed the abbot's wavering useful hand, and slammed it to the wall. The sound of broken bones and screams echoed through the office. "Tell me what I want to know," he said.

The abbot stared at him, mid-scream. "Behind the Presbytery," he yelped. "Exterior wall. You will find a small door."

"Thank you, abbot. Now go with God," Odulf said before smashing his hammer against the abbot's face, splattering the wall in gore. He did his best to wipe off the hammer on the abbot's garments, but some tissue remained. After leaving the office, Odulf removed his cumbersome cloak and dropped it.

Emme ran towards him, soaked in blood, and said, "Everyone is dead, save a few monks who ran away. We lost one, another is injured, but his wound is not serious. Did he give you the location of the catacombs?"

"Yes, Emme," Odulf said, while waving towards the other men, who ran towards him. "Follow me," Odulf commanded, marching towards the outer wall. Upon arriving at the entrance the monk described, he motioned for them to form several rows across the width of the door. After staring at the solid entrance, Odulf waved for five men to join him. "Go get gardening tools or suitable weapons to knock down the door," he murmured.

The men raced towards the shed and quickly returned wielding a bench.

Emme started a small fire on the side, and then several men lit torches.

"Now, there are only a few people here, but we must be careful," he whispered. "After we break down the door, we must travel in silence. Kill anything you see. Go!"

The stout men ran towards the door with the bench. After five attempts, the door collapsed.

The men galloped through the wide entrance into darkness. At first, the torchlight exposed the walls and floor, but then gloom surrounded them, even though Odulf could still hear the crackle of fire and feel the heat from his torch.

"Black magic!" Emme called out. "Beware!"

The sounds of screaming and blades made Odulf's earlier bravado fade. He felt himself pushed against a wall by an unseen force. He continued to hear sounds of battle, but everything remained as dark as a moonless and starless night. He soon felt a wisp of chilled air lift the hair from the back of his neck. Odulf thrust his hammer backwards and felt it connect with something. He pivoted, cut across, and felt an impact. He could sense the sound of cracking bone, and after a brief span of time, a shower of blood cascaded over him. The darkness soon parted, and he could see a woman lying on the ground. He could also see his brother and some of the men fighting. However, most lay in blood-drenched piles. Odulf turned to regard the woman and noticed that her eyes opened to study him. He nearly dropped the hammer in fright.

He inhaled, bringing up the hammer in an arc. Before he could swing, he felt a sudden, sharp pain in his back, which made him drop the hammer and stare down at a sword poking through his chest. He turned his head to the side to see who was behind him and saw an elder, bloodstained woman, dressed in the garb of a noble, standing behind him. Her penetrating blue eyes captivated him. As she twisted the sword, he felt a renewed spasm of pain. He started to fall forward and collapsed on top of the other woman. Next, he sensed a boot press on his back. He turned his head weakly to the side and saw that the elder blonde woman held the bloody sword in her hands.

"Well done, my Lady," a voice drawled.

He studied the beautiful and pale women and men before him, as they stared at him with green, burning hatred. Soon, everything faded into shadow.

chapter twenty-one

dward feared the worst, as he drew his blade. The abbey smelled of spilled blood. He stood guard at the open front gate and sniffed the wind. He detected the foul odor of death on the breeze, but he could not discern the smells of the savages who had done this to the group of unarmed monks and their pilgrim guests. From his vantage point, he could see Máire trip over a death-bloated body.

After getting to her knees, Máire said in a low tone, "I found fifty monks and others." She limply wiped at her brow with her left arm. "Something makes me feel ill-at-ease."

"Abbot Sigibert is dead as well," Julien called from the other side of the cloister. "Someone smashed his head in and his hands. It is horrific." After walking to Máire, he patted her shoulder and said, "I'm sure this is just shock."

"No," Máire moaned, shaking her head. "It's more than that."

Edward stared at the body Máire had stumbled over for a moment and then ran towards it to confirm with his eyes what his senses already told him. A gleam caught his eye. "This so-called pilgrim is armed. He is obviously not a monk." After inspecting the body, he said, "I see the reason for your sudden illness." Edward picked up the golden knife he found concealed in the corpse's clothing. After showing the weapon, he heard a sudden gasp.

"They know Deargh Du are here," Julien said before grabbing Máire's arm and dragging her to the other side of the abbey.

Edward dropped the throwing knife and caught up with his companions. Once the three blood-drinkers arrived at the entrance to the catacombs, he noticed that the door had been forced open and that a bench stood in the middle of the path.

"Edward, all I smell is rot and blood," Máire said, as she grabbed him for support. "Please tell us some good news."

From this proximity, he could discern the living from the dead. "Nine Deargh Du and one mortal."

The party entered the catacombs and began probing the lower levels, creeping over blood-soaked stairs and dead mortals. When the ceiling height allowed, they took flight. After a few moments flying, they found Maon, who looked up from his sword. Others came into view nearby.

Maon greeted Edward. "Thank the Gods, they've brought us friends. We could not smell through the reek and feared the worst. We all suffer from gold poisoning." He tried to stand, but he fell, and his blade slipped from his grasp.

Edward saw Heloise drop a bloody sword and race into her son's arms.

"Where's Sáerlaith?" Máire asked from behind Edward.

Edward watched a pale arm rise up in a pained greeting and then drop.

"She's badly wounded, I fear," another Deargh Du murmured. "We could give little of our healing power to her and no blood. Lady Heloise fed her, but she could only give so much. Now, a Druid can aid us." The female Deargh Du, whose name Edward could not remember, gestured Máire forth.

Máire sat next to Sáerlaith and stroked her matted hair.

Edward kneeled next to Maon and began to feed him and the others, hoping it would aid their cleansing. Occasionally, he would pluck a golden throwing knife and toss it aside.

"How would mortals know of our weakness?" Máire asked.

As Edward moved on to another Deargh Du, he noticed Sáerlaith's bashed skull. Máire rolled up her sleeves and began to heal her.

The female Deargh Du with an unknown name murmured, "They threw those knives of theirs as soon as they were in this room. I was lucky. I received a small wound in my arm." She rolled up her left sleeve, revealing her dressing.

Maon stumbled closer to Edward and said, "We lost three, hit in critical places." He then pointed to their heads. "You can see what happened."

"We need to get to court as soon as possible," Julien said. "It's an hour after sunset. We may have missed the opening remarks. We must go. Perhaps we aren't too late."

"We'll return later," Máire said, once she finished feeding Sáerlaith. "There are horses left in the stable."

Maon nodded. "We can go feed." To Edward he said, "Thank you."

Outside Luciaria

Mandubratius stretched his arms overhead and glanced at his companions.

Gaius broke the silence by saying, "It would seem that your friend, Leo, has rearmed his soldiers."

"And acquired new forces," Sextus added before turning to Mandubratius. "Sir," he said, "may I inquire as to your intentions regarding this mortal army? I am curious."

While he found Sextus and Gaius to be more useful than Patroclus, Mandubratius felt a little lonely for gentle feminine attentions. He should have requested the aid of the Empress or Amata, but Amata's rage at his games grew after the Empress joined their party, whereas, Irene would have found the journey south tiresome.

"Would you two agree that the Strigoi represent a threat to the Lamia?" he queried Gaius and the younger Lamia.

"Of course," Gaius answered, while Sextus just nodded.

"Well, my intentions are to convince His Holiness that his emissary should lead his army into battle. I also intend to recruit, rather create, more Lamia."

"That did not seem to work well last time," Sextus commented.

Rage boiled within Mandubratius, and he summoned a ready answer to spit at Sextus. He also considered castrating Gaius for allowing one of the former Children of Ares to have such a loose tongue. He stalked towards Sextus to administer punishment with his dagger, when Gaius grabbed his subordinate's head and yanked on his tongue.

"Sextus, it is not your place to find and state fault in your superiors' actions. Do so again, and you will find yourself speechless for a cycle of the sun."

Gaius released the soldier and allowed Sextus to back away. The general then wiped his right hand on his tunic.

"My apologies, consul," the out-of-breath lieutenant replied. "It was not my intention to offer criticism."

Mandubratius turned away and stared back at the camp, for a moment. "Be mindful of your rank in the future," he warned.

"I will, sir," Sextus stated.

Mandubratius could see the shadow from the lieutenant's salute. "To answer your earlier question," he added, "I will make sure to give these new Lamia a purpose in their waking hours. This will ensure that they do not act like children with swords." After speaking, he adjusted his weapons and dusted away the dirt of their journey. "Now, I will approach the encampment alone. When I am given charge, I will send for you." He heard the young lieutenant begin to ask another question, but a harsh and scornful grunt from Gaius caused Sextus to fall silent.

"We will be ready, consul," Gaius said.

"Excellent," Mandubratius answered. He then proceeded towards the encampment without a backwards glance. As he approached the papal camp, he pondered at the disorder and confusion. In his mortal days, everything in the Roman camps, from the tents to the torture implements, could be found in their prearranged location. Every structure lay in perfect right angles.

Much has changed, and not for the better.

Mandubratius soon sensed the movements of mortal guards, one of whom tossed about in sleep. He decided to announce himself by kicking the sleepy mortal in the backside. "Get up you lazy, fetid, pile of dung!" he shouted at the guard, who leapt to his feet. Mandubratius continued spouting insults from centurions past. "Sleeping while on duty is one of the most despicable derelictions of duty!" He punched the soldier in the chest. "Do you realize you've put us all in danger? Your slumber could have allowed murderers to infiltrate our defenses and kill His Holiness. Do you know what the penalty for neglecting your duty is?" he demanded, while kicking the soldier.

"Loss of rations, sir," the guard squeaked while looking up at him.

"Loss of rations?" Mandubratius spat while laughing hysterically. "In my day, you would have been stoned by your fellow soldiers! Summon your relief! I'm taking you to your commander."

The soldier scrambled to his feet. He then reached for a nearby torch and waved it towards the east. Soon, a replacement, as well as another soldier of greater bearing, walked towards them.

Perhaps this is their captain.

The soldier Mandubratius suspected of being the captain of the watch glared at the negligent guard. "Why are you leaving your shift? It doesn't end for another four hours."

The guard glanced at Mandubratius, as if afraid to answer.

Mandubratius locked eyes with the captain and said, "I caught your man in slumber during his duty." He watched a flash of anger gleam in the captain's eyes. Mandubratius closed his eyes and concentrated on further manipulating the captain. When he opened his eyes, the captain waved the torch towards the north, and within moments, Mandubratius heard the sound of footfalls grow. Three more guards came running and stood at attention.

"Take him for punishment," the captain ordered, pointing at the unlucky guard.

Once the soldiers departed, leaving the relief guard and the captain, Mandubratius addressed the more senior soldier. "Now, you will take me to His Holiness." He watched the man open his mouth, but Mandubratius interjected, "Tell Leo that I am Emperor Charles and that I am here in disguise. I wish to plead with him for aid."

The mortal captain blinked. "I see," he said. "Yes, Imperial Majesty. Please follow me."

Mandubratius strolled behind the marching captain towards a grand tent, which stood in the center of the encampment.

When the captain of the guards stopped outside of the tent, which was guarded at all corners and entrances, he gestured for Mandubratius to wait. The captain then ducked under the flap.

From outside, Mandubratius could hear the guard captain rouse the Pope and then overheard their conversation.

"The Emperor?" the Pope muttered. "What is he doing here?" Leo's voice belied sleep and confusion.

"Shall I send him in, Holy Father?" asked the captain.

"Yes, yes. Send in Emperor Charles, but stay close."

Mandubratius pulled up the cowl of his cloak and lowered his head.

Once the flap of the tent rose again, the captain said, "You may go in, Imperial Majesty."

As soon as Mandubratius walked into the tent, he felt the flap fall behind him, giving him and Leo privacy. He smiled and looked up at Leo, whose back was turned to him, and lowered his cowl.

"Greetings, Imperial Majesty," said the Pope, as he began to turn to face his guest. "I did not expect you to–" the Pope stuttered upon seeing Mandubratius. "You!"

"Greetings to you, Leo," Mandubratius said, bowing.

"How dare you–"

"We have unfinished business, Leo," Mandubratius said with a dark chuckle. He concentrated on Leo's mind but found the Pope closed off. Mandubratius reasoned that it had been too long since his last visit. Still, he hated failure.

"You destroyed my cavalry!" accused Pope Leo III.

"Your cavalry destroyed themselves," Mandubratius countered. "At least, that is what the lone survivor told me. I was not there to witness their demise."

"I heard rumors of blood-drinking and soldiers living despite being run through with a sword or spear," the Pope spattered in a loud whisper, as his face reddened. "What did you do to my cavalry, demon?"

"Demon, you say." Mandubratius smirked at his host. "I should take offense to that."

"With your forked tongue, you convinced me to make you my emissary and you goaded me into getting involved in this mess with Charles. Are you in league with the demons that you claim to fight against, Michael?"

Mandubratius stared into Leo's brown eyes. "Perhaps you should sit down, old man. You may very well burst a blood vessel," he hissed.

The mortal priest struggled a little with the suggestion, but finally, the Pope sat down.

Mandubratius walked to the other side of the tent. After picking up another chair, he placed it across from Pope Leo and straddled it. "I'm not a demon, Leo. Those murderers aren't demons, either," he began to explain. He hoped this clarification would be simple enough for a mortal to grasp. He felt like a teacher dealing with a simple student. "In the early days of the church," Mandubratius continued, "I know there were writings about beings that were not demons. These beings were immortal and drank blood. They could also heal and regenerate themselves, as well as demonstrate other powers."

"There were no such writings," the Pope replied. "This talk is blasphemy!"

Mandubratius smiled. "I'm no follower of Jesus or His holy father. I'm no parishioner, and I'm not one to be lied to. I know as pope you are privy to the truth, Leo, about the birth of Christianity. I know that your priests and monks have sought and recorded occurrences beyond theological explanation."

The Pope's face belied his surprise. He started to sweat and stammer. "How do you know of these things?" he asked.

"I am older than the Church, my friend." Mandubratius continued to smile at his host. "I attended the Nicean Council and not just the main discussions between the participants… no. I associated with the Homoousians. I know all the secrets, Your Holiness… some of which I crafted myself. I am responsible for rewriting much of the Book of Revelations. It aided my faction in scaring others into submission, and made your church wealthy."

"Again, you blaspheme our church," the Pope replied. "These words came from God Himself through His disciples and apostles." The Pope shook his head in disbelief. "There is no possible way you can convince me that you're over five hundred years old."

"No, I suppose I cannot convince you I was alive then, but let me ask you this: do you have a dagger in your possession, Your Holiness?"

The Pope's eyes glimmered as he stared back at Mandubratius. "I have one, yes," he answered in muted tones.

"Pull it out."

"Why?" the Pope asked, as he reached for his right side.

"It's rather simple. I'd like you to stab me."

"I was intending to stab you," the Pope drawled. "I believe I'd like to do nothing more."

"Before you do," Mandubratius said, standing up and shedding his cloak. He removed his belt and his tunic. "I cannot abide stains on my clothing."

While the Pope maintained his stare, he rose from his seat and, in a flurry of movements, shoved the dagger home.

Mandubratius felt a gentle ripple of pain move through him, though he winced a bit when staring down at the hilt of the dagger protruding from his chest. He then looked back up at the Pope and grinned.

Pope Leo almost fell over his chair, but he managed to sit down without further incident. He stared at Mandubratius in shock.

"Do you have a rag or something handy?" asked Mandubratius in a conversational tone, as he began to search for a suitable piece of cloth. "The bleeding is not bad, but once I pull out your dagger, it will be messy."

His still-speechless host pointed towards a small water dish and a cloth next to the cot.

"Thank you, Leo," Mandubratius said, before snatching the linen from the table and wrapping it around the dagger. He then removed the blade with one, swift pull. After wiping the dagger clean, he asked, "Where should I put this, Your Holiness?" As he waved the linen, he tried to keep from laughing.

"You can leave it there," the mortal squeaked while pointing to the basin.

After tossing the soiled linen towards the water bowl, he drew closer to the Pope. "See? It's healing already."

Pope Leo leaned forward to study the wound.

"So, Holy Father, is it possible that a person who can survive and heal themselves from such grievous wounds can live a long time?" After Mandubratius pulled on his tunic, he stared at his nails, waiting for a reply.

"Yes, it is possible." His words revealed a lack of vigor, now, but Mandubratius detected acceptance in his tone.

"I have read early writings describing your kind," the Pope murmured. "I thought they were nothing more than fantasy. You are Lamia."

"And what do these writings say about the Lamia?" Mandubratius queried, without admitting to the truth.

The Pope grew pale. "You consume the blood of others and you are immortal, but you cannot abide the sun." He paused and met Mandubratius' stare. "And you manipulate others."

"It would seem that this information is fresh in your mind," he drawled, enjoying the game.

"After I returned to Rome, I decided to study the ancient texts," Leo answered. "I had suspicions about your nature, and I decided to consult various references to verify my fears. I had some trouble believing what I read, but when I plunged my dagger into your heart, my doubts disappeared."

"Now that you know what I am, Your Holiness–"

Pope Leo interrupted Mandubratius. "These murderers that attack us, they do not sound like Lamia."

"You are very astute, Pope Leo. There are other races, like the Lamia, that live on the lifeblood of the living. These so-called demons are of a race called the Strigoi. My allies and I have been hunting down the Strigoi, and we have managed to kill many."

"I've heard rumors about the people who have killed Strigoi, as you call them." The Pope picked up a scroll and held it like a sword of knowledge.

"Yes," Mandubratius stated. "I'm part of that band of warriors. However, I'm here to seek your aid, Your Holiness."

"My aid?" Pope Leo laughed a dry chuckle. "If what I have read and seen is to be believed fully, you Lamia are powerful and don't require my help. What could we possibly do to assist you and yours?"

Mandubratius looked to the ceiling. "Well, our numbers are few, and the enemy grows by leaps and bounds every night."

Leo appeared shocked with his statement. "Just how many are there?"

Pope Leo asked as he leaned back in his chair.

Mandubratius locked eyes with the Pope. "There were five hundred, the last time we met," he answered. "Perhaps they number in the tens of thousands, now."

"I'm not sure I have so many," the Pope admitted, before straightening up and meeting Mandubratius' ready stare again. "I'm sure Emperor Charles will send a comparable number of soldiers. How many are in your band?"

"At the moment, we have a few thousand. Perhaps we shall have five thousand, when our allied forces gather."

"Twenty-five thousand of us versus tens of thousands of those madness-bringers?" shrieked the Pope.

"Madness bringers?" Mandubratius asked.

"Yes. My personal guard refers to them as such," Pope Leo replied.

"That is quite an apt description of a Strigoi," Mandubratius stated.

"How could this force hope to defeat an army that can rally so many? This madness is a horrible weapon."

Mandubratius smiled. "Ah, but Your Holiness, we have a weapon of our own that takes their madness away. Plus, I and other Lamia can sponsor your soldiers to increase their strength and skill."

"Sponsor? You mean change into Lamia?"

Mandubratius nodded.

The Pope's face turned from gray tones to red. "You've done this before! You changed my cavalry!"

"It was necessary to have a greater force to throw at the Strigoi," Mandubratius explained. "I apologize for not consulting you first. Let me explain. Christians would believe beings, such as the Lamia, to be demons. Therefore, in sponsoring these soldiers, I could not tell them what they really were, so I told them that they were angels recruited by God's representative to remove the demon scourge from the face of the earth. If they knew what they truly were, they may have ended their lives."

"How can you justify taking men and using them for your own machinations?" asked the Pope, as he rubbed his eyes.

Mandubratius took a moment to reflect on that question. "Well, Your Holiness, have you ever been in a campaign where you are facing an army of greater numbers and decided to abduct peasants from farms to add to your own numbers?"

"Yes," the Pope sputtered, enraged, "but that doesn't–"

"I beg to differ with you, Leo, but that is the way I saw it." He attempted to extend his control over the mortal again, and in response, the Pope relaxed.

"I can accept the reasons you had for this sponsoring, but why did you send these men to the Anglo-Saxon kingdoms? After all, they were wiped out in the wilderness, over there."

Mandubratius mulled over that question. "I blame myself for not training them to be Lamia, Your Holiness. However, I did not have time."

"Train them?" Pope Leo queried. "What do you mean?" he asked as he leaned forward in his chair.

"Well, when we sponsor a mortal, the sponsor teaches him or her how to be a Lamia. The training is not merely how to feed and fight, but how to blend into a country, instead of merely conquer." He mused over Talia's inability to grasp this lesson. "For instance, if a peasant found a thousand pieces of silver, he or she would overindulge. The excitement of the newfound wealth drives them to extreme extravagances. If, all of a sudden, a mortal could move faster, see better, and withstand wounds, they would expose themselves for being anything but mortal. This is what happened to the cavalry, Your Holiness."

The Pope grabbed a thin piece of linen and patted away the perspiration on his face. "You sent the cavalry to the Anglo-Saxon wilds, so they could fight the Strigoi there, and by doing so, gave them a duty, so they would not overindulge themselves."

"Yes."

"Did you know they would find death?" The Pope's dark eyes gleamed.

Mandubratius pondered whether he should tell Pope Leo the truth. "I knew of other blood-drinkers in Britannia. These blood-drinkers would not have looked kindly on the unannounced arrival of an army of Lamia. I had not finished training them to fight as Lamia, so I suspected that they would either be captured or killed."

The Pope twisted in his seat, as if trying to restrain himself. "Why did you feel it necessary to send them to their deaths?"

"Your Holiness, they were completely out of control. They fed in public and killed their victims. We Lamia try to protect our victims, as we need them as a food source. Why kill, when we can simply allow them to heal and then feed from them again? Yes, there is pleasure in killing, but I digress. These Lamia engaged in fighting, while in the view of mortals, who witnessed soldiers impaled on spears, laughing and not dying, thus exposing their immortality. I could not let that continue, or else all the Lamia, and the other races, would be in danger."

Pope Leo closed his eyes, as if considering the answer. "So, you've come to me to seek permission to sponsor some of my forces." He then opened his eyes and glared at his guest.

"Yes."

"You feel this is necessary because of the greater number of these Strigoi," the Pope added.

Mandubratius nodded.

The Pope leaned forward in his seat. "How do you intend to restrain their indulgences, Michael?"

"I would like you to tell these newly sponsored Lamia their purpose and how they must behave, Your Holiness."

The Pope laughed, revealing some nervousness. "You wish for me to instruct them?"

"What better teacher of new angels is there, Leo? You are the voice of God on earth, after all."

"I will agree to your proposal, but I must ask one condition," the Pope stated, before stroking his beard.

"Name it," Mandubratius replied in an aloof voice, staring at his nails.

"My condition is that you don't use the cavalry," the Pope stated. "I prefer that you utilize the disposable forces."

"Of course," Mandubratius replied, "but I also wish to have access to some of the archers and swordsmen."

"Agreed," the Pope said, looking somewhat annoyed. "I presume you wish to lead them."

"Actually, I prefer to leave that duty to another Lamia in my company. He will train them."

"And who is this person?"

"His name is Gaius Naevius Tacitus Britannicus. He's a general."

The Pope chuckled. "I see, but of what army?"

Mandubratius shrugged and said, "The army of Rome, under Emperor Trajan." He grew tired of sitting, so he rose and began to pace about the tent.

"He's ancient," the Pope whispered.

Mandubratius laughed and shook his head. "That youngling? Your Holiness, I was present when Julius Caesar first tried to conquer my homeland."

The Pope gulped. "Gaul?"

"No, Britannia," Mandubratius answered.

"I see." The Pope rose and walked over to his desk. "I grant your general permission to train your forces."

"And my commission?" Mandubratius asked with a smile.

Pope Leo stared at him with increased gravity. "I included that in these orders, General," spat the Pope, as he handed the scroll to Mandubratius.

Mandubratius sighed. "A demotion from my office," he said, as he took the scroll. "Well, life will go on." He then kneeled and kissed the Pope's ring. "Thank you, Your Holiness."

Aachen

Charles paced back and forth, trying to think over the current judgment required, yet his mind could only worry about a future matter that he must address. He scanned the room for Julien and Heloise and found many familiar faces, except for theirs. He felt that it would be most pleasant to see Heloise again. In the far corner of the room, he could see Lady Talia, who glimmered in a golden radiance next to Reginald de Divio, which made him feel a modicum of disgust for her. Unpleasantness seemed to surround them. Charles could not fathom why he had promoted Reginald in the military. That mediocre man never deserved such a lofty position.

Charles realized that his family and vassals stared at him as if they were awaiting an answer. He tried to remember the argument between the two parties he currently judged. As he studied them, one appeared to be rich and pretentious, while the other man's eyes were downcast, and his clothing seemed somewhat careworn.

These are probably his only clothes.

"My decision is for him," Charles said, pointing to the poor man, although he wished he could remember the man's name and all that had been said. "I have rendered my decision," he announced to the surprised faces in attendance.

"Imperial majesty, this is not right," the figure draped in fineries implored as the guards took his arms.

Charles motioned forth his secretary. Once Ercanbald leaned in closer, Charles whispered, "Remove him, bribe him not to talk, and tell him to never return to my empire." He watched the secretary nod and leave the room. The Emperor then began to pace about a bit, wishing he could find a reason to lengthen the judgment process.

When the secretary returned, he cleared his throat and said, "I believe the next case is Reginald de Divio versus Heloise of Vézelay and Julien de Divio."

"Are there any other cases?" Charles asked. "With such grievous accusations, I would prefer for all parties to be present."

Ercanbald began to flip through his records. "No, Imperial Majesty, all other cases have been heard."

"Very well." Charles faced the gathered members of his court and announced, "I wish to take a one hour recess."

"You will hear this case now!" a strident voice shouted, grating on his ears a little. He turned and focused his eyes on Lady Talia. His thoughts grew thick, like the early morning fog. Charles willed himself to concentrate. He felt an intense dislike for Talia settle in the pit of his stomach and start to grow. "You demand?" he hissed.

How dare that woman challenge me!

Talia dropped to her knees. "Please forgive me. I misspoke. I only wish to express my desire to get this fiasco resolved. Reginald and I wish to be wed," she explained before fluttered hers at him.

He would have been lost to her charms, if he had not heard a strange sound of compassion emanating from those surrounding him. He could not fathom how and why his battle-hardened family and friends became so soft when this woman's voice trilled through the palace corridors.

When Charles stared down at her again, he noticed something in her eyes that belied a ploy, yet he couldn't deny the compulsion to embrace her and allow her free rein over the proceedings. He bit his lip in confusion and ire, and tasted blood. "I forgive you, Lady Talia. Yet, we need a rest."

"Your wisdom outshines the stars, Imperial Majesty," Talia purred. As she rose to her feet, Talia allowed him to witness a flash of her skin.

Charles turned away, annoyed with his reaction. He had an hour, which would leave little time for Julien and his mother to arrive.

The wine did little to alleviate Charles' mood. A cooling night breeze stirred the tapestry covering the small slit of a window. He knew that his family wished to join him, but he found himself more worried with the immediate issues at hand than the latest gossip from his daughters... and tales of the hunt from his sons. As soon as Ercanbald arrived, Charles asked, "Have Heloise and Julien arrived yet?" He sensed his own impatience increase tenfold.

"I'm afraid not, Emperor, but I have taken care of the matter involving your previous judgment. What do you wish to do?"

Charles closed his eyes. He knew revealing his favoritism would not be that detrimental to his leadership, yet a nagging voice in his head, which sounded very much like Talia, demanded that the trial occur tonight. "I will hear the arguments," he said. "If the defendants have not arrived, I will attempt to rule on the information presented." He saw Ercanbald nod and exit his quarters.

Charles soon could hear Ercanbald calling the court to order, as well as the noisy bustle of his children, which echoed down the hallways. With his mind prepared, Charles left his quarters and walked back into the audience chamber. After sitting down, he declared, "Lord Reginald, I wish to hear these accusations you make from your own mouth. Explain how you deduced these matters, for all our benefit."

Perhaps this could buy more time for Heloise and her son.

Upon landing outside of the palace, Máire, and the rest of her party, ran for the front entrance. Máire soon realized the sorry state of their appearance, but she reasoned that it could aid them. Once they reached the entrance, she and Edward allowed Heloise to stand on her own feet.

"Halt!" shouted a mortal, and then a lit torch drew towards them. "Inspector General?" asked the same voice.

Julien gave the guard a salute. "Yes, Baldric. There is an immediate matter of some importance."

"Have you been waylaid by brigands?" Baldric asked, as he opened the outer doors for them. "Allow this party to pass," he called into the darkness.

"We will discuss it later," Julien answered, before rushing his mother and friends past the guards.

After reaching the doors to the official rooms of state, Máire positioned herself next to Edward, behind Julien and his mother. She could hear a voice, which sounded like Reginald de Divio, echoing through the corridors. She also noticed Edward wrinkling his nose.

Julien waved to the guards, who pushed open the doors to the stateroom.

She heard the Emperor state, "The accused are not present at this time."

"Imperial Majesty," Julien shouted, pushing himself and his mother forward through the crowd.

The Emperor seemed surprised at the interruption, while his face and eyes revealed a strange blending of confusion and gratitude. Máire then caught him beaming at Lady Heloise as if she were the only person in the room.

She soon detected the strong scent of Lamia, and Máire finally saw her aunt, who frowned at the Emperor and Lady Heloise. Deep concentration grew on her aunt's face as she attempted to divert the Emperor's attention.

"Aunt, you are a toothless crone!" Máire yelled in Irish. While everyone at court shifted his or her stares to Máire, she focused her eyes on Talia, who turned and smiled at her.

The Emperor gazed at Talia for a moment, as if confused, but then his bewilderment faded. He returned his attention to Heloise and Julien and asked, "Why are you two so tardy?" He stood from his chair, walked down his dais, and towards Heloise. His face revealed deep concern.

"We were attacked on our way here," Heloise said. "At the least I was, as well as my protectors. Most of us survived."

A loud murmur rose in court.

"Who attacked you?" the Emperor asked.

Máire watched Heloise duck her head for a moment. Then, the mortal steeled herself, and her back straightened. "Perhaps that is a question for my eldest son." Heloise turned to stare at Reginald.

Talia, and not Reginald, screeched, "This accusation is outrageous." Her voice carried above the surprised clamor in the room. "What proof does this ancient witch bear?"

"I know what you've done to him," Heloise accused.

"Silence!" roared the Emperor. "Everyone settle down and give me silence! I will tolerate no more outbursts from anyone present! Is that understood?"

Máire heard a general mumbling of assent from the gathered mortals. Even Heloise and Julien seemed a little sheepish.

"Since there is no evidence to support the accusation that Reginald had anything to do with this unfortunate attack, we will move on. Julien de Divio, Count of Auxerre, you have been accused of adultery and witchcraft. Heloise de Vézelay, Lady of Vézelay, you have also been accused of adultery and witchcraft. Do you two wish to defend yourselves against these charges?"

Heloise cleared her throat. "Imperial Majesty, I wish to challenge these accusations through combat. Let combat determine the innocence or guilt of the parties."

"You wish to fight your son?" the Emperor queried.

"No, Imperial Majesty. My son Reginald died long ago. I am a frail woman, and I cannot fight him. Therefore, I request a champion to stand in my stead," Heloise requested.

"Very well. Whom do you request, Lady Heloise?"

Heloise looked at Máire and stated, "I ask Lady Máire of Ulster to be my champion."

The crowded room drowned in voices, but through the din, Máire could hear the Emperor yelling for silence again in a tone that frightened his guards. Immediately, all present ceased speaking.

"Lady Heloise, that is a most unusual selection," the Emperor stated. "You wish to have a foreign woman fight for you. Julien," he said before facing Máire's son-in-darkness. "Surely, you wish to answer these charges yourself, or do you wish for her to fight as your champion as well?"

Julien looked at Máire and smiled. "I know of no better warrior. I desire her to be my champion as well."

"I accept," Máire stated, before the Emperor could ask her.

"So, it is noted," the Emperor said, motioning to his secretary. He then turned to face Reginald. "Do you wish to—"

"I will be his champion," Talia interjected. "I am embarrassed to admit this, Imperial Majesty, but I am no stranger to the sword."

The din of voices grew again, but this time, the Emperor silenced them with a stare. "Very well. You both have ten minutes to prepare. Guards, have the men-at-arms bring forth two swords."

"Imperial Majesty, I will fight with my own blades," Máire called forth. She watched his face light in a small smile.

"Very well, Lady Máire. I require only one sword, then. You seem dressed for battle, Máire. Lady Talia, do you plan to fight in your courtly attire?"

"No," her aunt answered. "I will change into something appropriate."

"Very well, follow Ercanbald. He will take you to my chamber to change and will provide you with appropriate attire, if desired."

Once Talia departed, Máire quietly approached Julien and Heloise. She handed the sheath of her sword to Julien and her cloak to Heloise and then kissed them both. "Ask Morrigan to grant me strength," Máire whispered to Julien. When he embraced her, she rested her chin on his shoulder and inhaled. Upon feeling Heloise's hands in her hair, she knelt and allowed Lady Heloise to pull back her plaits, while Julien tied them with a leather thong.

After the tender touches, Máire stood up and walked to the far corner of the room. She began to stretch, preparing for battle. Through her priming, she could hear Mac Alpin's warning in her ears. All she needed to do was injure Talia enough to keep her from harming Julien's... her family, yet the rage to kill still burned... all of those deaths bloodied her aunt's hands. When she heard footsteps, Máire turned away and saw Talia's eyes settle on her. As she watched the Lamia's posture, every movement revealed strength.

Perhaps her sponsor taught her more than mere manipulation.

Emperor Charles interposed himself between the combatants and said, "Before we begin, I wish to ask whether you two are certain of this."

When his eyes settled on Máire's, she nodded in assent. She saw Talia copy her motion.

"Very well, then. Fight for honor," the Emperor called out, before backing away to his dais.

Máire held her dagger in an overhand grip with her left hand and raised her short sword in her right. She saw her aunt smiling at her from the other side of the room, wielding the long, Frankish sword with both hands. Without waiting for prompting, both women waded into battle.

Talia held her sword upright, and then, in a swift motion, she lifted the blade over her head, rotated it, and swung it down in a left-to-right arc towards Máire, in an obvious attack.

Máire stepped in and, while using her sword to block the strike, she sliced her dagger across Talia's unguarded abdomen.

Talia stepped back, while arcing her weapon behind her, and launched another strike from the other side.

Máire blocked again by raising her sword, pommel up, but this time, her sloppiness allowed Talia to slice her blade across Máire's right hand, drawing blood.

Talia stepped back and then launched a lightning thrust aimed at Máire's chest.

Máire twisted out of the way, as she used her dagger and short-sword to deflect the thrust. When Máire took a step back, her aunt launched into a series of cuts, diagonal and upwards from the ground. Máire blocked the blows without striking back, in hopes of learning the attacks and anticipating Talia's offensive strikes. While, Talia's attacks lacked mastery, they compensated in ferocity and force.

While Máire knew that she could physically move faster than Talia, neither blood-drinker could afford to reveal their nature in front of the gathered mortals by fighting at super-human speeds. In a burst of mortal speed, Máire began her attack from her high-left block, transitioning into a diagonal cut, but her aunt countered with another thrust to her chest. Instead of lopping off Talia's head, Máire came down fast with her cut and knocked it aside. In the same movement, she pounded Talia's head with the hilt of her dagger. While in close, she pushed her knee into Talia's and pulled on her shoulder, causing Talia to lose her balance.

Talia grabbed Máire's left wrist and brought her down.

While both women tumbled, Máire's dagger slid from her fingers. As Máire attempted to control her fall, she watched the pommel of Talia's sword approach her face. Máire attempted to dodge the blow, but her movements were not fast enough. A jarring pain exploded in her mouth, and stars swam around her, for a moment.

Talia still had a fierce grip on Máire's wrist, and then in one quick motion, Máire soon found herself on her back. Talia pinned Máire's torso and left arm beneath her, while Talia's knee rested on her right arm, keeping Máire from moving her blade. Talia then glared down at her.

Máire grunted, kicked up her leg, and slammed her heel into the back of Talia's head, causing the Lamia to lose her grip. Máire spun away, still holding onto her weapon.

Talia rolled into a standing position, while Máire copied her aunt's motions.

Once on her feet, Talia launched a low-high cut, which Máire easily deflected with her mid-guard stance, before countering with a thrust. Talia drew back from Máire's attack and began a new series of strikes, with success.

Máire felt pain and wetness move down her leg from a gash.

Julien gripped his mother's arm, little realizing the strength in his hand. As she shook off his hand and rubbed her arm, he sensed a large number of blood-drinkers enter the throne room. Loud whispers grew, and he became aware of Marcus murmuring to Edward.

The Deargh Du strode through the gathered crowd to study the fight. Julien saw that a frown wrinkled Marcus' forehead and made him appear to age for a moment. "Why is she fighting her aunt? Máire violates my trust and ignores our concord."

Julien ignored him, knowing Marcus did not expect answers.

Marcus began whispering a diatribe in Gaelic, or so Julien believed, and then the other Deargh Du turned his silvered eyes on him. "Goddess, help us all if she doesn't rein in her passion," the elder Deargh Du murmured.

Julien squeezed his mother's shoulder nervously, as Máire took another hit. He closed his eyes, afraid to witness her death.

"Honestly, Julien, show some maturity," his mother hissed, even though her fear radiated stronger with each blow of the swords. "See? They aren't worried." While his mother turned to study the other blood-drinkers, he hoped for reassurance.

Máire bit her lip, knowing that she could no longer afford to play this game. Without the dagger, she found herself at a disadvantage. Máire launched a weak attack, in hopes of drawing Talia forward and off balance, but the other blood-drinker did not commit immediately.

Instead, Talia took a step back and then lunged a low left-to-right level cut beneath Máire's attack. As Talia leaned through the lunge, she rotated her pommel upwards to connect with Máire's downward strike, while the tip of her sword sliced up Máire's right arm and chest. Off balance, Talia rolled with her momentum, whereas Máire fell to the ground and lost her sword.

Máire felt her dagger underneath her. Reaching around herself to grab it, she saw Talia staring down at her. Hunger and bloodlust radiated in her eyes, turning them red for an instant. Máire knew Talia wished to finish the battle.

Máire beheld her short sword a few feet away, gleaming in the bright torchlight. She gripped her dagger behind her and prepared for the optimum moment to strike.

Talia grunted in exertion as she thrust her long sword towards Máire's chest, but Máire kicked out at the Lamia's knees and rolled away before slicing her aunt's tendons above the heels with her hidden dagger.

Máire continued her roll and then grabbed her sword, watching Talia fall and land unevenly on her knees. Máire then rose to her feet. While staring at her aunt's back, Máire clutched her weapon. She then cautiously walked around Talia and fixed her gaze upon her. "Do you yield?" Máire asked.

"No, I do not," Talia responded while smiling at her. Screaming, she swung her sword in an arc.

Máire thrust her sword through Talia's chest, but Talia's long sword managed to strike Máire's shoulder in a glancing blow as she ducked away from the attack. Máire snarled in pain and kicked away the long sword. Through the sting, she noticed that all of the other distractions of the palace had faded into darkness. Máire grabbed her sword and pulled it out of Talia's chest. She then yanked the blood-drenched Lamia up to her knees and raised her blade, but before she could swing, a strong force grabbed her arm. An intense fury welled up within Máire. She prepared to whirl around and stab the unmovable force, but her hand stilled upon hearing whispered words in her ear.

"You cannot kill her, Maél Muire," Marcus murmured.

"I must," she whispered back. She began to shake in a mixture of rage and sadness.

"The Goddess would not wish it," Marcus countered.

"The Goddess did not stop me," Máire challenged back.

"Through me, she has. You cannot kill her. We've all gone through too much to lose our alliance, chroí."

"You do this for the alliance alone?" Máire asked. She turned a bit and could see his eyes settle on hers. Máire dropped her arms to her sides.

Marcus pulled her into an embrace, and she closed her eyes. "I do this to maintain the balance. Your family would not want you to become like Talia." She sensed gentle and sweet sympathy in his voice. "Besides, look at her."

Máire turned towards Talia, who lain on the floor.

"In the eyes of these mortals, she is dead," he murmured in Gaelic. "She cannot claim Burgundy, now." Marcus released her and extended his hands for her weapons. "That was a most stunning battle, Banbh Ceanúil."

"Thank you," she whispered, handing him the sword and dagger. "I don't feel quite–" Máire's strength left her, at that moment, and she fell. After landing on top of something soft and sticky, she heard footsteps and the Emperor's call for his surgeon, before blackness surrounded her.

Julien watched Máire tumble and then collapse over Talia's corpse. He pushed aside the others and knelt at Máire's side. While he looked at her wounds, he heard the Emperor's surgeon approaching. At first, Julien feared for her life, but he soon could see her battle wounds begin to fade.

"No surgeon," he heard Marcus whisper. "Take these," he ordered a guard before handing over the weapons.

"Get the litter!" the surgeon yelled at the guards. "Make haste!"

Julien felt himself being nudged away from Máire.

The surgeon started to mutter to himself, as he studied her wounds. "You're in my light!" the surgeon snapped at Marcus, but then Julien felt a large amount of glamoury emanating from Marcus before fading. Marcus then backed away.

Once the litter arrived, several of the guards helped them lift her onto the stretcher. Then, the surgeon motioned with an impatient gesture for the guards to follow him.

Julien rose and raced after them. He could sense a Lamia and Lucius following them. When Julien turned, he saw Lucius pivot and slide across the marble floor. Julien walked back and grabbed him, when he witnessed the graceful figure of Amata, who stood in the distance.

"Here!" the surgeon barked, upon opening a door.

While the guards placed the unconscious Máire on the bed of one of the Emperor's daughters, Amata slid into the room. Afterwards, the guards walked out of the chamber.

Lucius dove out of Julien's grasp and leaped onto the bed.

Julien watched the surgeon open his kit, revealing strange and pungent tools, which included a blood-encrusted needle. Julien felt his mouth drop open, and he began to muster his strength, but then Amata intervened.

"Surgeon," Amata cooed while touching the mortal's left shoulder.

"Step back, woman. I'm trying to save her."

Amata leaned in and whispered, "You've cleaned her wounds and stitched her. She is healed. It is a miracle."

"But I–" the surgeon stammered as he stared at his patient. Confusion swelled in his face.

"Your work is done, my love. You've performed very well. Tell the Emperor that she must rest, but she will recover quickly. Also tell them that she needs visitors." Amata's face lit in a smile.

"Yes," the surgeon murmured. "The Emperor will be apprised of these matters. I'll go," he added, walking away.

With the mortal gone, Julien pulled back the sleeve on his left arm and raised his wrist to his mouth, intending to feed his mother-in-darkness, but Amata held up her right hand.

"Julien, might I make a suggestion," Amata asked. Her blue eyes radiated with soft warmth. She pulled a small dagger from her purse, unsheathed it, and then sat next to Máire.

"Allow me to feed her. You heal her. It will be easier."

Julien nodded, agreeing to her logical proposal.

"Sometimes, it is easy to forget what is sensible when someone we love is hurt," Amata commented.

He watched the silver blade flick over Amata's pale skin, and then blood bubbled to the surface.

After watching Lucius crawl up Máire's leg and settle across her knees, Julien placed his hands over the cut in her shoulder. Once he had mended her flesh, he moved on to the other wounds.

chapter twenty-two

Outside Luciaria

From his vantage point under a tree that bordered the assembly area of papal soldiers selected to become Lamia, Mandubratius looked on, as Gaius indoctrinated the new recruits.

"One thousand is a good number to start with," Gaius mentioned with a shrug. He then turned towards the mortal captain, who awaited his orders. "Quiet this rabble."

"Silence!" the captain shouted to the gathered assortment of soldiers. "Allow me to present your new commanding officer."

Gaius, followed by Sextus, walked towards the front of the gathered forces, while Mandubratius remained under the cloak of the tree's canopy.

"I am General Gaius Naevius Tacitus Britannicus. His Holiness has put me in charge of you misfits. This is my lieutenant, Sextus. Over there," Gaius said, pointing to Mandubratius, "is General Tolomei. He is in charge of this detachment. Your first orders are to march towards the west. We will meet with a contingent of soldiers that will begin your advanced training."

As Mandubratius left the cover of the tree to join Gaius, he heard talking from the ranks, but he felt pleased when he noticed Sextus grabbing the offender who prattled with his neighbors.

As Sextus raised the offender overhead, the mortal's face turned blue. "Were you speaking?" Sextus asked the soldier, before shaking him for a moment and then setting him down. Sextus looked to the others and shouted, "No speaking. Is that understood?" A quiet chorus of 'Yes sir' followed.

"I understand you have not slept," Gaius added, "yet, I suffer your fate. This is a soldier's life." He turned towards Sextus. "Sextus, move them out."

"Single file behind me!" Sextus shouted. "Move!"

Mandubratius joined Gaius and filed in behind the last of the soldiers. "Were you able to get everything squared away while I spoke with Leo?" Mandubratius asked.

"Yes. They will be ready for us," Gaius promised. "I must say that I am most impressed with your success in handling His Holiness. I thought it would be difficult to persuade Pope Leo. You said he might have become immune to most of your persuasion."

Mandubratius grinned as he looked over at the other Lamia. "I learned to manipulate long before I became Lamia. How else could I get Caesar to come to Britannia?"

Aachen

Staring at the spreading pool of blood beneath Talia, Marcus watched over her after the guards carried Máire into another room. With her eyes closed in agonized pain, the Lamia lay prone on the floor. However, a greater apprehension at the idea of Talia rising from the bed of gore eclipsed his concern for Máire. Before he could ponder Talia further, he sensed the arrival of another Lamia. He couldn't tell whether Patroclus or the Empress approached, but he doubted they would join him beside Máire's aunt.

Marcus turned and studied the newborn Lamia who stood a few feet away from him. He could sense timidity and fear coming from Reginald, who refused to meet Marcus' stare. Marcus soon had to move, when the guards shuffled their way through and gathered up Talia's body. In the midst of their efforts to lift her, Marcus heard a throat clear. He looked up and noticed Heloise and the Emperor standing a mere foot apart.

In a loud voice, Emperor Charles said, "In most cases, if accusations are proven false, the accuser receives appropriate punishment." The elder leader's eyes radiated mute fury as he stared at Reginald. "However, your mother bade me not to punish you. I can see the loss you have experienced serves as adequate penalty under these circumstances. As for the matter of Lady Talia's property, I grant it to Lady Máire of Ulster to deal with as she deems fit, and I pray that she survives her wounds. These proceedings are closed. Guards, please escort Reginald de Divio out of my palace."

The guards began to walk the silent Lamia out of the throne room. Reginald did not resist as they led him away.

With most everyone's attention on the fallen lord, Marcus caught a glimpse of the Emperor kissing Heloise's upturned cheek and her resulting smile, as if flames were rekindled.

Marcus offered her his arm, and then they followed the trailing line of blood-drinkers.

"She will recover, won't she?" Heloise asked after a time.

Marcus chuckled. "Do you mean Talia or Máire? They will both survive and recover, my Lady. I hope this means that Talia will trot back to Rome like a dutiful child. However, I have a feeling many of us will guard Máire's room during the next few nights. Máire took property from Talia once before, and the granddaughter of Godomer will not be pleased with this outcome."

Reginald felt nothing but mute shock, as the guards dragged him out of sight of the court. He let them tug him towards the servant's entrance at the side of the palace without exchanging words. Once they reached the door, the guards pushed him out and slammed it.

Reginald landed on his back in the mud and dirt. In his mind, he could hear the sound of latches falling into place while the stench of rotting meat made him gag and nearly retch. He then noticed a poor man staring at him.

"This is mine," the beggar shouted, pulling the reeking meat towards him.

Reginald closed his eyes.

If this is my fate, I deserve it.

"How could I have been such a fool?" he asked in a whisper.

When the door to Máire's temporary quarters opened, Julien sensed his mother and a few others loitering in the corridor.

"How is she?" his mother asked, after poking her head in.

"She's still unconscious, Lady H-," Amata answered, but the sound of an enraptured purr interrupted her.

As Julien studied Lucius, he noticed a bloody set of fingernails lovingly scratch Lucius' head. "She's awake," Julien gasped, stepping closer to her.

"Julien," Máire whispered before offering all present in the chamber a weak grin. "And Amata, as well. Weren't you in Vézelay?"

"Marcus made us all run. He has the luxury to fly, while we Lamia are left to the dusty roads," Amata said in dour tones before chuckling. "My feet are about to fall off from the exertion."

"Where's my aunt?" Máire asked.

"As far as the mortals are concerned, Lady Talia is dead," Amata answered. "Praise to your victory at a believable speed." She then moved away, allowing Julien's mother to approach.

Julien felt Máire's head rest against his hand, as his mother took Máire's extended hand in hers.

"Thank you for being our champion," his mother told Máire. "As the victor, you are entitled to her lands."

"I am the champion, Lady Heloise. The lands belong to you. Máire of Béal Átha an Fheadha, Ulster, and lately Bath, does not need property in Burgundy, as long as the Deargh Du still have a home in Vézelay. This land belongs to Clotilda and her family."

"That is so very kind," Heloise praised.

As Máire stretched a bit, Lucius wobbled on his perch. "How long shall I pretend to recover?" she asked.

"A week, perhaps," Julien's mother said. "Anything less and his Imperial Majesty would be surprised, if not shocked."

"What about the preparations for the Strigoi?" Máire asked.

Mac Alpin's loud voice echoed through the wall when he said, "Don't worry about that. Just rest."

Amata chortled a bit and added, "I shall refrain from the usual response, but suffice it to say, we were all concerned when you passed out. Rest and think of the miles I ran for you," she said, winking at him and Máire.

"I do appreciate it," Máire answered. "So, why are those lazy people outside? Come in and visit me!" she bellowed.

The door slammed open, and then a small gathering of blood-drinkers stormed into the room and began to chatter at Máire in various guttural languages that Julien could not comprehend.

"Stop it!" Julien's mother whispered fiercely, before gaping at Máire. "You're supposed to be wounded," she reminded her, giving her a push back into the bed. "The rest of you, subdue your tones. This is not a céilidhe."

Julien detected a note of sheepishness from Máire's guests at his mother's outburst, but then a gentle knock at the door distracted him.

Ercanbald leaned into the room, said, "Lady Heloise, Inspector General, and guests, dinner is served in the private dining hall," and then exited.

"You are all going to dinner without me?" Máire pouted in a playful manner. "I'll be lonely."

"For the love of the Great Mother," Mac Alpin grumbled. "I need a drink after my long journey and seeing that fierce battle."

"Yes, a good drink," Claudius added before patting Máire's right shoulder. "Oh, don't pout, Maél Morrigan. Only the Lamia resort to pouting. Isn't that right, Amata?"

Amata chuckled.

Edward added, "We'll bring you back a jug of excellent wine," as he and the other blood-drinkers, save Marcus, Julien, his mother, and Lucius, scuttled into the hall.

Once the door closed, Marcus passed Máire's sheathed sword to her and kneeled next to her bed. "Your aunt may choose to visit you," he said. "Keep this close."

After Máire accepted the proffered weapon, Marcus leaned in and kissed her before exiting the room.

"Shouldn't you two go to the dinner?" Máire asked her remaining guests.

"We are taking care of our champion," Heloise replied, sitting in a chair.

"No, you maintain the illusion," Máire argued with a chuckle.

"Marcus is right," Julien countered. "Your aunt may return." He pulled a chair to Máire's bedside and sat down. He then leaned in and stroked her hair. "If you're asleep, who will protect you?"

"I would smell my aunt," Máire answered. "Besides," she added, placing her left hand on a lump under the covers, "Our Lugh will be my champion and protector."

Julien watched as the lump moved to the top edge of the blanket, and Lucius peeked from under it before crawling out.

"If Máire wishes, I will be her eyes, nose, ears, and claws," Lucius cooed, plopping down next to her. He then started grooming her hair.

"What will we tell the guards?" Heloise asked, staring at Lucius, for a moment.

"To watch the door," Julien said. He leaned in and scratched Lucius' ears before kissing Máire's brow.

Her eyelids fluttered open and shut, as if she were sleepy.

Lucius paused his ministrations, yawned, and stated, "Bring me a sampling of the feast, Julien, and the champion's portion of meat." The fairy cat then lowered his head.

"Of course, Lucius," Julien promised as he rose from the chair. He offered his mother a hand, but she shooed him aside.

"I did not know you spoke cat," she said.

"The Deargh Du can speak to animals in a somewhat limited fashion, but Lucius is special," Julien answered. He then noticed the cat purring and wiggling its ears in pleasure.

"Take good care of my mother-in-darkness," Julien said.

"Remember our agreement," Lucius stated. "I'm quite hungry, and mice will not sate my palate." He began to groom his paws.

Outside Luciaria

Gaius grumbled to himself, as the long line of soldiers trudged towards the designated barn in the west. "I admit that I am a little surprised that you sought Leo's permission for this," he said to Mandubratius.

"Sometimes we must allow our underlings to make a decision or two," the Co-Consul answered with a smirk. "It can aid in difficult situations. Besides, his assistance will keep our new troops in order."

Gaius saw that the line had reached the barn doors, which immediately opened. He and Mandubratius left their place and meandered past the gathered troop, towards the front. The smell of dirty flesh grew nauseating as Gaius walked past the gathered men.

Sweaty soldiers, exhausted with the long hours of marching day and night, wiped their brows.

At a nod from Gaius, Sextus strode to the front and gestured for the soldiers to watch him. "Before you begin your training, we will assess your skills. I will assemble you into groups of twenty. Disarm yourselves before you enter the barn."

Gaius looked on as a few Lamia exited the barn and began to help the soldiers remove their weapons.

"Once you enter the barn," Sextus added, "you will find members of our contingent from Rome. Follow their orders." Sextus began to count off twenty soldiers and waved them through. He then closed the door behind them.

Mandubratius walked to Sextus, clapped him on his left shoulder, and said, "Well, let's wait for the newly sponsored." The Co-Consul then walked confidently towards the opposite end of the barn.

Aachen

Marcus toyed with the food on his plate for a bit before returning to his wine. He felt almost unwilling to follow the chatter, which moved back and forth between various topics.

The Emperor cleared his throat and said, "Marcus, you know your friends well and have all traveled a great deal with them. Do other women from Éire fight as Lady Máire does?"

Marcus stared down at his plate, attempting to fashion a response worthy of an emperor. However, the distraction from the last few hours, and his exhaustion, kept his discourse subdued. "Yes," he finally blurted.

The Emperor chuckled and leaned in closer to Julien. "Remind me to never attempt to invade Éire, or we will be fighting women such as that." He then took a long gulp of wine.

"If the women of Éire can be trained as warriors, why not Frankish women?" Lady Heloise asked.

Emperor Charles choked on his wine at her question. "Heloise, the average Frankish woman has not the skills or mindset to be trained as a soldier. Let's face it, the women we witnessed in battle today were not typical ladies of the Empire. Besides, the officers would laugh at the notion of women in their ranks. They may even become mutinous." He glanced around the room at the guards in attendance.

Marcus watched Amata smile. Her blue eyes radiated a strange interest in this matter. She almost resembled her brother-in… Mandubratius.

Amata drew the Emperor in with her eyes and said, "I understand your reluctance to allow women into your martial ranks, Imperial Majesty." While she spoke, she played with the fowl on her plate. "After witnessing the skills of women warriors, I am certain your generals would be afraid to control women who could best them in battle." She joined the other blood-drinkers in a few moments of chuckling.

Emperor Charles put down his spoon and knife and said, "I hope that you are not insinuating my generals are cowards if they don't support a measure allowing ladies into the army. Their unwillingness to go against church doctrines would motivate their response. Those doctrines hold that women are the weaker of the two sexes and that their purpose is to raise children. If I were to demand women take an active role in the army, Pope Leo would possess more reason to try to remove me, or excommunicate me and my empire."

"Then it will be Emperor Charles' loss that women cannot aid him in the field of battle," Amata argued with a bit of a shrug and then smiled briefly at Marcus.

Marcus scrutinized Amata, contemplating that this line of questioning was an interesting ploy to find a possible safe house for herself in the future, if necessary.

Mac Alpin grunted and then added, "Imperial Majesty, what worry is it of yours if His Holiness excommunicates you and your people? You are superior to him in battle. Create your own church."

Marcus closed his eyes for a moment at the absurdity of his fellow blood-drinkers reveling in a discussion of politics.

"Rome and her Church are corrupt," Lady Heloise grumbled under her breath.

In a fit of motion, the Emperor stood and motioned for his guards to leave. Then the table became silent. "Were I to be excommunicated, and by extension this empire, the common man and the nobles would both demand my head, in order to return to Pope Leo's flock. My empire would be his."

"Of course," Amata said. "Yet, may I suggest that an elite, secret cadre of women warriors may be useful in the future for covert purposes. No one would suspect a harmless lady, after all."

"How would these women be useful?" the Emperor asked as he studied Amata.

"These ladies could be your spies, assassins, or perhaps a secret personal guard while pretending to be your mistresses." Amata's eyes lit in glee.

The Emperor chuckled and sat back on his chair. "I see a great many benefits to this plan, Lady Amata, but there would be several risks involved as well. While no one would suspect my mistresses of having martial capabilities, how could I allow someone with such training to be so close? If one of these women desires my death, I may end up betrayed."

"Ah, the worry of every Roman emperor," Claudius stated.

"Yes, will my Praetorian guards defend me or destroy me?" Marcus added. "Your guards pose the same threat as they would."

The Emperor closed his eyes, as if considering Amata's plan. "How would I know that these women would be trustworthy?"

Julien set down his wine and said, "Perhaps we could aid you in these matters. We could train them in these skills."

"It could offer protection to me and my family," the Emperor mused aloud. "When circumstances permit, make the necessary arrangements, as long as it's discreet. No one in my family or staff should know of the truth." He then rose, as did the rest of the table. "I appreciate the company that surrounds us tonight. Thank you for joining me in this late meal, but I'm afraid that I need to go to sleep soon. There is another hunt tomorrow that I wish to take part in. Julien, Lady Heloise, could you join me in my chamber for a moment? There are some matters of property that we need to discuss, which will not take too long."

Marcus bowed his head and followed the other blood-drinkers out of the dining hall, curious about this private meeting.

Julien watched as the Emperor shed his courtly coverings.

"Your mother says that Lady Máire is not interested in owning property in Burgundy and that her spoils belong to your family, again." The Emperor sat and straightened his gown. "Please be seated." He directed them to the two remaining chairs at his table. "I must admit that I admire this notion of championship. This means a great deal of property will be vested in your family," he said, while smiling at Julien.

Julien looked over at his mother for a moment. "Imperial Majesty," he said. "I fear that I must ask for my property to be turned over to Dreu de Matisco, my future brother-in-law." Julien watched the Emperor's face darken.

After a few moments of silent rage, the elder mortal asked, "Are you quite sure you wish to turn over your property to him? You do realize that if you were to keep those lands, you would be one of the wealthiest nobles in the Empire. I don't think you realize how much land Lady Talia acquired."

"No, I'm afraid I'm ignorant of the amount of property she owned," Julien stated.

"As am I," his mother added.

"Her lands include a great number of hectares. If you add Auxerre, Divio, and Vézelay, that is quite a slice of Burgundy."

Julien suppressed a gulp and said, "Still, I feel it best that Dreu take ownership of those lands. I have... other duties to consider, now."

The Emperor's frown deepened. "Julien, I'm disappointed in you. I had such high expectations. I mentored you, I allowed you to rise in the ranks despite your position as the third son. Now, after all I've done, you just turn over your property to someone else who marries your sister... who is not even of our status or worthy of our family!"

"Our family?" Julien looked at his mother, who met his stare but remained silent. When the Emperor spoke his name, Julien gave him his full attention.

"I am your true father," the Emperor declared. "I was hoping you'd rise in wealth, high enough to claim you as my heir without causing a rebellion amongst the nobles and my… our family."

"Who…" Julien paused. "My apologies, Imperial Majesty, you are my father? Mother, is this true?" Julien glared at her, unable to believe she never revealed the truth.

"Yes, Julien," his mother stated, nodding her head. "Charles is Lirienne's and your father."

"Why didn't you tell me?" Julien asked her.

The Emperor answered, "Your mother did not tell this to you because I wished it to be hidden from you. My dearest son, Pepin, tried to take it all from me, once. He died in exile for his foolish deeds." The Emperor turned away for a moment. "I wished you to become a man in your own right. I have too many children who would be unfit to govern others in any fashion. Yet now, you tell me that you don't wish to possess these lands. You are forcing me to reconsider recognizing you as my heir."

Julien tried to rein in his surprise at discovering that he could be… could have been… the Emperor's successor. He secretly agreed with his father's reasoning, but one aspect of being a Deargh Du prevented Julien from leaving a proper legacy. "I can't have children," he said, "anymore. My only child is my daughter, Clotilda. I had two sons, but they died with their mother during the papal attack on Divio."

The Emperor's eyes examined the wall behind Julien for a moment. "I thought she was your niece."

"No. Flor and I spent time together when Reginald was gone." Julien smiled at the memory of her.

"So, you have a daughter and had two more sons. Why can't you have more children?" the Emperor asked.

Julien squeezed his eyes shut. "Something has happened to me. I've changed."

The Emperor, his father, rose and began to pace. His face seemed to glow and redden. "Are you telling me that you prefer satyrs to nymphs now?"

"No!" Julien found himself a little startled at that accusation. "No, that is not the case."

"Julien, don't," his mother bade.

"Mother, he has to know," Julien countered. He warned himself to lose the curt tone in his voice.

"Dear God!" the Emperor gasped, as his anger faded and he grew pale. "It's worse… you've joined the priesthood."

"No!" Julien insisted. "Perhaps it is better to demonstrate what I am." He concentrated on drawing down the darkness, and then blackness blanketed the entire room. At speeds only a Deargh Du could muster, Julien stood up, flew over to his father, and removed the Emperor's ring from his hand, as the elder mortal tried to shoo away the darkness. Once back in his seat, Julien let the darkness fade away. He held the ring in his left hand and said, "Are you missing this?"

The Emperor stared at him. "How did you..." The Emperor turned to Julien's mother and asked, "He is a thief, now?"

"No," Julien uttered in frustration. After sliding his father's ring to him across the table, Julien stood and walked over to the wall. He began to crawl up to the ceiling, and then he turned upside down and began floating. "I'm not human anymore," he answered.

His father stumbled backwards and cried out, "Are you possessed by demons?"

His mother took the Emperor's hands and cooed, "No, Charles. Our son is not possessed. He was chosen by a race of magical beings from ancient times to maintain the balance between good and evil."

"Mother, I'm not sure if this is helping," Julien added, as he flipped over and landed on his feet. "I'm a Deargh Du, now. We Deargh Du have been fighting against these demon invaders."

His father turned back to study his mother. "This is your doing, Heloise. I know you and your friends dance around a fire, practicing pagan rituals. Did you bring down these pagan deities to possess our son?"

Julien hesitated for a moment. "Father... I'm not possessed by any being, demonic or benign. I've just been transformed. I'm stronger, faster, and I can fly. I can heal quickly and heal others. I can influence others through my glamoury. I can even pull down darkness and create illumination." He closed his eyes and felt the strange effect of luminous light leave him.

The Emperor, with mouth agape, drew closer. "Such angelic light," he murmured, sitting down again.

His mother patted Julien's shoulder before taking her seat.

"How were you changed?" the Emperor asked.

"I was out one evening with Máire, and we found ourselves attacked by those... murderers." He believed calling the 'murderers' by their true name and explaining them might prove too difficult for his father, just now. "I was dying," he whispered. "They brought forth such horrible madness within me that I wished to wrench my eyes. I may have, though I don't remember much, save the pain they gave," he admitted. "Máire found me. I asked her to save me. She did."

"What did she do?" The Emperor's eyes narrowed.

"She saved me. Máire transformed me," Julien answered.

"So, is she like you, a Deargh Du?"

"Yes," Julien answered.

"And your companions," the Emperor asked. "Are they all Deargh Du?"

"No," Julien replied. "There are other races, each with their own traits. Lady Amata is Lamia. Edward and Mac Alpin are Ekimmu Cruitne. Claudius is Sugnwr Gwaed. Marcus is Deargh Du. There are subtle differences in each of these groups that I could explain, but they confuse me still."

"And who else knows what you are?"

"My mother, Lirienne, and perhaps a few of our servants," Julien admitted.

"God protect us," the Emperor whispered. "And these companions are here to protect us from the demonic murderers?"

"Yes father," Julien answered, now feeling a bit more confident in calling him that.

"Do you realize that if your servants talk about this, you and your friends will be hunted as demons? If I were complicit, they'd also hunt me." Emperor Charles chewed at his lip, for a moment. "When you and your company have driven these killers from the Empire, I think it best that you leave," the Emperor deadpanned, while staring at the door.

"Leave?" His mother queried.

The Emperor stared at her for a moment and then turned his attention to Julien. "It is too much to risk if you remain here in your current state. You could be discovered, or I could be implicated. How His Holiness would love that. It would be best for the Empire, and myself, that you and your friends leave when this task is complete. Go to Rome, the East, Éire or Britannia... wherever."

"But, father," Julien pleaded.

Julien's mother surprised him by standing and shouting, "Charles, shut up and listen! Julien's people, the Deargh Du, have been driven from Éire. They have no home. I have brokered a deal with them. I give them sanctuary, and they protect my family for as long as my family continues. I do not wish for them to leave Vézelay!"

"Impertinent woman! Now I remember why we did not wed!" the Emperor yelled in response. "Fine! The Deargh Du can stay in your lands. Julien, when this business is finished, you must leave and never return. I will grant your sister's husband-to-be your lands. If he proves himself worthy, I may grant him your titles. We are finished. Inspector General, you may go. As much as I enjoy you referring to me as father in private, you may not address me as such in public. I don't wish this to be known, now."

"Of course, Imperial Majesty." Julien felt his own anger rise.

"I must take some time and rest." The Emperor's eyes shifted to the door.

Julien knew the Emperor's statement was a lie, that he wished to think

---

things through.

"Thank you for seeing me," the Emperor said before nodding to them. He then turned away and poured himself a glass of wine.

Julien walked to the door and held it open for his mother. He promised himself to keep his head high and try to forget this ever happened.

His mother frowned during the entirety of their silent walk.

Outside Luciaria

Leo felt nauseous, as the bumps in the road tossed him about. One particular bump caused him to grunt in pain as his head had hit the ceiling of the cramped carriage. The wooden planks that served as seating creaked with each bounce.

"Are you insane?" he yelled at the driver. As if the secrecy of traveling in an unadorned carriage would protect him. The demons, Strigoi or whatever Michael called them, would be able to find him by means of the magic they honed against mortals. What skills these Strigoi used, besides bringing forth discomfort, disease, and death, he did not know. Nor did he know what powerful talents the Lamia and their friends wielded.

He needed to know the truth. Only then could the Church spread the lies necessary to protect their followers and to protect Catholicism itself. Leo shuddered to think what would happen were the fledgling faith to disappear. He had no choice but to accept Michael's word as truth.

At that moment, he felt the carriage jolt to a stop. Leo steadied himself as he heard the sounds of pain-filled moans. When the door opened, the driver offered him a hand. He stepped down and found himself next to a barn. There he saw Michael glance at him and nod, ignoring the men who lay sprawled around them. None of them even appeared to notice him.

Another group of two dozen came out of the barn. Some of them staggered, while others collapsed, but a few of the soldiers appeared to have more control.

Expecting feats of strength, not weakness, Leo frowned at Michael, but Michael merely smiled back at him. The Pope strode over to his new ally, exuding purpose in his every step.

"Your Holiness," Michael greeted him. "Did you have a smooth journey?"

Leo tried to think of an appropriate response to the question. "No, but that is often the case with carriage travel on these ancient roads. How goes this sponsoring process, Michael?"

The Lamia gestured with his eyes. "You can see that we are almost finished."

They both fell silent, as another group staggered forth from the barn. Leo turned to study the other men that stood with Michael, assuming that they represented the Lamia leadership.

The one with a youthful face turned to the elder soldier between himself and Michael and asked, "Your orders, General?"

The elder soldier must be General Gaius.

The general turned to his underling and said, "Give them a few minutes of rest, Sextus. Call our associates to watch over them. We must make sure the newly created do not wander off."

"Yes, General." The young soldier motioned to the others exiting the barn, and then the Lamia fanned out to surround the new Lamia.

"Forgive me for forgetting proper introductions, Your Holiness," Michael stated. "This is my associate, General Gaius Naevius Tacitus Britannicus. Gaius, this is the Holy Father of Rome, Pope Leo III."

"Your Holiness." The general nodded to him, as though they were equals.

Leo decided to ignore the slight. "Michael, what is it that you wish for me to say to these new Lamia?"

"I believe that you have a spiritual sense of these men," Michael said in a soft voice. "You know how they would react to the truth, Leo."

Perhaps he hopes these new Lamia will not hear his words.

"Yes, the truth would be devastating to these soldiers," Leo whispered, adopting Michael's tone.

"Devastating, you say," Michael purred, sounding comfortable with that thought.

"Yes, I fear many would try to commit suicide," Leo answered.

"You are echoing my words from earlier, Leo. Still… before Christianity, it was so easy to sponsor a mortal. These Lamia, including myself, saw our new lives as a gift. My, the times have changed." The Lamia stared at the moon, growing silent in his contemplation of the night.

Leo cleared his throat, wishing to get this business done.

"We convinced these soldiers that they are angels. Do you believe this will work this time, Leo?" Michael turned to stare back at him with that annoying smirk.

"I see no wings or halos," Leo observed aloud.

"Unfortunately, we Lamia cannot fly," Michael stated.

Leo saw what appeared to be a brief moment of jealousy in Michael's eyes.

"But we are fleet of foot and we can jump. Do you think our innate inability to fly will hinder our new forces' belief that they are angels?" Michael queried.

"I do not know," Leo answered.

"But, you can convince them. After all, you are the Pope." Michael chuckled for a moment, but then the Lamia focused his eyes on Leo, once again. They glowed with a fierce fire.

"I will convince them," the Pope whispered.

"Good," his host answered. "I have no doubt. I believe your faithful are ready." He gestured towards the soldiers.

A chill moved down Leo's spine as he walked amongst the fallen bodies.

A few eyes turned towards him. Some appeared to recognize him, but no one stood to greet him.

He hoped he exuded serenity, as he continued walking to the middle of the group. Once he found the center, he pushed aside his cloak, revealing his vestments. "Rise my children," he called out, "I am your pope, and I have summoned you to do the Lord's work." He witnessed a few stand at attention. Leo spun slowly to see all the new Lamia. "My children," he repeated, "rise to the summons of your pope. The Lord God requires your service." Leo found great pleasure at seeing some begin to elbow sleepers and help the fallen to their feet. After a few moments, he saw that the wavering and tremulous had steadied themselves. Leo felt his own nervousness subside as all eyes transfixed on him. "You have all been chosen by God to be His angelic army on earth," he informed the soldiers. He heard scattered echoes of disbelief, surprise, and reverence move through his gathered flock.

"Each of you has been given Godly gifts," Leo continued. "These gifts can be used to fight those demons that menace us mere mortals. However, your gifts came with a great burden. You must not give in to the temptation to misuse your new skills. I know you must have many questions. God's servant, Michael," he said, motioning to the ancient immortal Lamia, "can teach you about your new gifts, as well as the consequences of misusing these tools. Follow Michael, and treat his word as the Word of God," he bade the new Lamia. Leo gulped upon feeling a gnawing sensation in the pit of his stomach, warning him against what he had just said, but he had to make sure these monsters would obey their leader. After concluding his speech, Leo heard General Gaius order the soldiers into ranks.

These Lamia move more quickly than I believed possible.

He stepped around them, hoping he would not be knocked over. Leo almost wished to join the others in formation. Instead, he wove his way back through the crowd. As he walked, Leo witnessed the general and his second dress down the soldiers, which seemed normal, until they began to talk of leaping to great heights and running at great speeds. Upon reaching Michael's side, Leo asked, "Was that acceptable?"

"Yes, you did quite well, Your Holiness." Michael beamed at him as if pleased with the performance. "By the way, my name is not Michael Tolomei."

"I thought not," Leo commented. "I am curious. Is your name mentioned in the secret documents and scrolls of the Church?"

The Lamia raised his brows, and his smile grew wider. It seemed that Leo had pleased his host. "One name that I go by, that most people call me, is Mandubratius."

Pope Leo closed his eyes and tried to remember history of the Roman Empire. "Your name rings with familiarity," he admitted.

"Yes. My family ruled part of the Anglo-Saxon kingdoms in the past," Mandubratius said.

"So, you are Anglo-Saxon? Why do you have a Roman name?" The Pope felt some confusion, since the history of the known world left him flummoxed, sometimes.

"No. Don't you remember? I'm a Briton. I told you before," the Lamia answered. "The people who lived in those lands before the Saxons and Rome invaded our homes. I have a Roman name, because very few Romans could pronounce my true name, which is Awvarwy."

Leo felt some embarrassment for forgetting. "I recall your saying something about being alive when Julius Caesar landed in Britannia. How old are you?" he whispered.

"I believe I'd seen well over thirty-five cycles of the seasons when I was sponsored," Mandubratius, or Awvarwy, answered. "That was over fifty years before your savior was born."

"How did you become Lamia?" Leo asked. He found himself full of questions about the past.

"You ask many personal questions of me, Leo. I do not mind answering these queries, but I must remind you of the old Roman phrase, 'quid pro quo'."

Leo's train of thought was interrupted, upon hearing General Gaius begin to instruct the Lamia on proper feeding techniques. Leo gagged.

"My apologies, Aw... Mandubratius, but I am not feeling well." The Pope found himself gasping for breath.

"Indeed. Many mortals find this distasteful." His host smiled again. "We can continue with your questions another time, Your Holiness." The Lamia lowered himself to his knees and took Leo's right hand to kiss the papal ring.

Leo could not ignore the insincere and insolent smirk on the Lamia's face, as he kissed the ring. He wished to yank his hand away, but he could not, out of his undeniable fear.

Mandubratius stood up and dusted his knees. "Good night, Leo." The Lamia then turned away and merged with the dark shadows of the barn and outlying forest.

Leo realized he'd felt the shadows move through his soul.

Will God ever forgive me? Please, sweet Jesus... don't let this be a mistake.

Leo walked away to join the driver at the carriage.

epilogue

~~The Journal of Julien, son of Emperor Charles, heir to the Imperial Throne~~
The Journal of just another bastard

y father, my true father... the man who seeded my mother, is Emperor Charles. Before now, I had not known this fact. All this time, I grew up believing that Burchard, Lord of Divio, was my father. So, for my entire life, I have been living a lie.

I have to ask myself: who knew the truth? Surely, my mother must have known, since it was through her spread legs that I was conceived... rather, that Lirienne and I were conceived. Did my sister know, or my brothers, or my half-brothers? I'm sure they suspected it, especially Reginald. He knew something, but how many at court knew? I'm starting to think that they all knew, at least the ones I interacted with, like Gundrada, the Emperor's late wives, and Louis, who has always disliked me.

Now I know why I advanced up the ranks... it was because my father manipulated circumstances, so I could get positions above my apparent station. How foolish could I have been to think that this was due to merit? After all, I was officially the third son of a lowly vassal. How should I feel about the position I find myself in? I am the son of an absent father, who tried to assist me in becoming more.

Were I still a mortal man, I would embrace this knowledge with gratitude that my father has always been here for me and that I would be welcomed into court with all knowing I was his heir and would be the next emperor. However, I'm not a mortal man. I'm Deargh Du. If I were not Deargh Du, I would be dead because of the Strigoi attack. As a Deargh Du, I can still thank my father for the upbringing he has given me, yet the gifts he wished to bestow upon me carry little value to someone who may see hundreds of winters. It pains me that I cannot be what my father wishes me to be.

I see the strife his other children brew in the empire. I see that without a strong heir to Emperor Charles, the empire will shatter upon his death. Without me, he has no strong heir that he can trust, and I know this because I've met them and even I find none of them trustworthy.

After turning down my father's offer to become his heir, I am now back to where I was, a fledgling Deargh Du with a lot to learn about the world. As a Deargh Du, the closest thing I have to a father is Marcus.

Since I cannot be what my father wishes for me to be, I will redirect my devotion to my grandfather-in-darkness. Still, I shall try to help my true father, even if he does not wish it.

continue the journey with...

Shards of Light
Morrigan's Brood Book V

2014

puBlished and future works

Title	Synopsis
Morrigan's Brood Morrigan's Brood Book I	Éire is invaded by a race of blood-drinkers seeking an artifact they believe will restore them to power. Yet the Deargh Du, the protectors of Éire, are not prepared to defend the island. Only with the help of a Roman general from an earlier time can they hope to rise up against the invaders.
Crone of War Morrigan's Brood Book II	The Lamia expeditionary force has gained a foothold in Éire and has formed an alliance with a powerful Irish chieftain and his malevolent mother. To reinforce them, a massive Lamia army, which is departing Rome, will soon give them enough power to conquer Éire and find their lost treasure. Will the Deargh Du and their new-found friends be able to protect Éire from the invaders, or will the Deargh Du's suspicion of other blood-drinkers allow their enemies to be victorious?
Madness & Reckoning Stories of the Morrigan's Brood Series	Following the events of 564 CE, madness strikes one of the Lamia's most important personages. Can the Lamia march on, or will this insanity cast them into civil war? Following the events of 564 CE, the Deargh Du must come to grips with change or see old strife resurface, which could tear the Deargh Du apart.
Dark Alliance Morrigan's Brood Book III	A new menace threatens the Balance within the Holy Roman Empire as vicious murders of both mortals and blood-drinkers spread throughout the empire like wildfire. Can a hastily formed alliance between archenemies thwart this new menace, or will festering hatred bring about the empire's doom?
Curse of Venus Morrigan's Brood Book IV	The Strigoi, the Cursed of Venus, have spread through the Holy Roman Empire and parts beyond like a plague. In response, Pope Leo III takes advantage of the scourge to settle an old score with the man he placed on the throne: Charlemagne. Will their bitter rivalry send the Empire further into chaos and destruction, or will their Deargh Du "angels" save them from themselves and from Venus' Cursed?
Shards of Light Morrigan's Brood Book V	Many sets of eyes peer through the mist, watching events unfold as the dark alliance seeks out an ancient device that they hope will uncorrupt the menace that has nearly brought the Holy Roman Empire to its knees. However, not everyone beyond the mist is content merely to watch.

Title	Synopsis
Dynasties of Night Morrigan's Brood Book VI	For centuries, two game masters, a brother and sister, have sat in front of the most intricate game imaginable and watched as the events they set in motion played out. At the forefront of this game are two dynasties of long-lived blood-drinkers: the Kyonshi of Japan, who, like their mortal brethren, strive for independence from China, and the Chiang-shih of China, who wish to maintain control of Japan and the Kyonshi. Will the masters continue to watch the game unfold, or will greed, jealousy, and vengeance bring about an end to this long-running game?
Odin's Chosen Morrigan's Brood Book VII	Odin hears the call of a proud king unable to feed his starving people and grants him an unusual gift: immortality. Fueled by the need for vengeance against those who murdered his warriors and condemned his people to starvation, Runolf, the new King of Odin's Chosen, leads his fledgling army of blood-drinkers in a war against Britain, Scotland, and Ireland. Little does he know that other races of blood-drinkers inhabit these lands... among them, the Deargh Du. How can Morrigan's Brood hope to maintain the balance when they are at the heart of Runolf's rampage?
Hera's Wrath Morrigan's Brood Book VIII	Many old, dark horrors lie imprisoned in realms unknown to mortal man. In one of these places outside of space and time sleeps a race of voracious eaters cast out of the world by the Tuatha dé Danann, the Gods and Goddesses of Éire. However, every prison has its keys, and Hera, Greek Goddess of Motherhood and Home possess most of them. Will Hera ransom the keys for a return to proper Greek family values, or will she unleash these dark horrors upon mortal man?

Other works include It's in the Cards (a novella that will appear within an anthology with other authors, in queue for publication) and A Year and a Day (novel, on hold).

about the authors

Heather Poinsett Dunbar

Born in Houston, Texas, Heather began writing her first book at age eight. While her grammatical structure left much to be desired, she continued to hone her writing and storytelling skills. During a college internship in London, England, her curiosity about ancient cultures and mythology intensified. She backpacked through Europe, fell in love with Scotland, cried at the retelling of part of the Ulster cycle, garnered ghost stories from the Beefeaters at the Tower, wandered the Roman ruins in Bath, and danced around the stones in Avebury.

After spending all her spare time studying these new interests in many libraries and on the road, she began working on her masters' in Library and Information Science at the University of North Texas. She now resides in the Houston area with her husband and three cats. She loves exploring the local culture as well as the many Celtic festivals and events in Texas. She also works as a librarian for a local college, and her favorite authors include Morgan Llewellyn, Neil Gaiman, Terry Pratchett, Evelyn Vaughn, Alison Weir, and Randy Lee Eickhoff.

Christopher Dunbar

Chris Dunbar was born in Greenport, Long Island, New York and then moved to Texas as soon as he could, at least that is the story he tells to native Texans, such as his wife. Chris keeps searching for ways to leave Houston, like moving to Auburn, Alabama, Dallas, and even San Antonio, but Houston just keeps reeling him back. Chris' day job is performing Business Continuity and Disaster Recovery, but his night job is coming up with creative ways to wound and maim the characters he and his wife Heather created. For fun, Chris enjoys the occasional novel and video game, but he also likes to delve into his Scottish ancestry and tool leather. When he can find the time, Chris pretends to play the Bodhran and the didgeridoo, much to the chagrin of his cats, Lucius, Ophelia, and Clyde, not to mention his wife Heather. Chris is also an avid wearer of the kilt.